Ruthlessly Royal

ROBYN DONALD
ANNIE WEST
FIONA HOOD-STEWART

MILLS &
BOON

Published in Great Britain 2014
by Mills & Boon, an imprint of Harlequin (UK) Limited,
Eton House, 18-24 Paradise Road, Richmond, Surrey, TW9 1SR

RUTHLESSLY ROYAL © 2014 Harlequin Books S.A.

Rich, Ruthless and Secretly Royal, Passion, Purity and the Prince and *The Royal Marriage* were first published in Great Britain by Harlequin (UK) Limited.

Rich, Ruthless and Secretly Royal © 2009 Robyn Donald
Passion, Purity and the Prince © 2010 Annie West
The Royal Marriage © 2006 Fiona Hood-Stewart

ISBN: 978 0 263 91171 8
eBook ISBN: 978 1 472 04466 2

05-0214

Harlequin (UK) Limited's policy is to use papers that are natural, renewable and recyclable products and made from wood grown in sustainable forests. The logging and manufacturing processes conform to the legal environmental regulations of the country of origin.

Printed and bound in Spain
by Blackprint CPI, Barcelona

RICH, RUTHLESS
AND SECRETLY ROYAL

BY
ROBYN DONALD

Robyn Donald says "I'm often asked what made me decide to be a writer of romances. Well, it wasn't so much a decision as an inevitable conclusion. Growing up in a family of readers helped; after anxious calls from neighbors driving our dusty country road, my mother tried to persuade me to wait until I got home before I started reading the current library book, but the lure of those pages was always too strong.

Shortly after I started school I began whispering stories in the dark to my two sisters. Although most of those tales bore a remarkable resemblance to whatever book I was immersed in, there were times when a new idea would pop into my brain—my first experience of the joy of creativity.

Growing up in New Zealand, in the subtropical north, gave me a taste for romantic landscapes and exotic gardens. But it wasn't until I was in my mid-twenties that I read a romance book and realized that the country I love came alive when populated by strong, tough men and spirited women.

By then I was married and a working mother, but into my busy life I crammed hours of writing; my family has always been hugely supportive, even the various dogs who have slept on my feet and demanded that I take them for walks at inconvenient times. I learned my craft in those busy years, and when I finally plucked up enough courage to send off a manuscript, it was accepted. The only thing I can compare that excitement to is the delight of bearing a child.

Since then it's been a roller-coaster ride of fun and hard work and wonderful letters from fans. I see my readers as intelligent women who insist on accurate backgrounds along with an intriguing love story, so I spend time researching as well as writing."

CHAPTER ONE

DRUMS pounded out into the sticky tropical night, their vigorous beat almost drowning out the guitars. Her smile tinged with strain, Hani Court surveyed the laughing, singing crowd from her vantage point at the other end of the ceremonial area.

The village people had thrown themselves into the celebrations with typical Polynesian gusto, the occasion their way of thanking the group of New Zealand engineering students who'd fixed and upgraded their derelict water system.

First there had been feasting, and now they were dancing. A teacher at the local school, Hani wasn't expected to join them.

Instead, watching the whirling, colourful patterns the dancers made, she resisted aching, nostalgic memories of Moraze, her distant homeland. There, beneath a tropical moon every bit as huge and silver as this one, men and women danced the *sanga*, an erotic expression of desire, without ever touching.

Here, half a world away on Tukuulu, the dancing was purely Polynesian but it shared the graceful hand movements and lithe sensuality of the *sanga*.

Six years ago Hani had accepted that she'd never dance the *sanga* again, never laugh with her brother Rafiq, never ride a horse across the wild, grassy plains of Moraze. Never hear her people cheer their ruler and his sister, the girl they'd called their little princess.

Never feel desire again…

Unfortunately acceptance didn't mean resignation. Pierced by longing for everything her stupidity had thrown away, she glanced around. She wasn't on duty, and no one would miss her if she sneaked back to her house in the teachers' compound.

A prickle of unease scudded down her spine. She drew in a breath, her stomach dropping into freefall when her eyes met a steel-blue scrutiny.

Transfixed, she blinked. He was taller than anyone else and the stranger's broad shoulders emphasised his height; hard, honed features provided a strong framework for a starkly handsome face. But what made him stand out in the exuberant crowd was his formidable confidence and the forceful authority that gave him an uncompromising air of command.

Every sense on full alert, Hani froze. Who was he? And why did he watch her so intently?

Quelling an instinctive urge to run, she felt her eyes widen as he walked towards her. Her tentative gaze clashed with a narrowed gleaming gaze, and a half-smile curved his hard, beautifully cut mouth. Colour swept up through her skin when she recognised the source of his interest.

Sexual appraisal.

OK, she could deal with that. But her relief was rapidly followed by shock at her body's tumultuous—and entirely unwelcome—response.

Never—not even the first time she'd met Felipe—had she experienced anything like the surge of molten sensation in every cell as the stranger came nearer, moving through the crowd with a silent, lethal grace. Her skin tightened, the tiny hairs lifting as though she expected an attack.

Warned by that secret clamour, she stiffened bones that showed a disconcerting tendency to soften and commanded her erratic heart to calm down.

Cool it! she told herself. He probably just wants a dance. Followed by a mild flirtation to while away the evening?

That thought produced an even faster pulse rate, pushing it up to fever pitch.

Perhaps he thought she was a local; although she was taller than most of the islanders her black hair and softly golden skin blended in well enough.

He stopped beside her. Bewildered and shocked, Hani felt his smile right down to her toes; it sizzled with a sexual charisma that emphasised the aura of controlled power emanating from him. With a jolt of foreboding she realised he was being eyed covertly or openly by most of the women within eyeshot.

Antagonism flared inside her. Here was a man who took his powerful masculine attraction for granted.

Just like Felipe.

But it was unfair to load him with Felipe's sins…

He said in a voice that made each word clear in spite of the background noise, 'How do you do? I'm Kelt Gillan.'

Struggling to dampen down her wildfire response, Hani smiled distantly, but she couldn't ignore the greeting or the fact that he obviously thought a handshake would be the next step.

Nor could she pretend not to feel the scorching along her cheekbones when she looked up and found his gaze on her mouth. Hot little shivers ran through her at that gaze—darkly intent, too perceptive.

'Hannah Court,' she said, hoping the aloof note in her voice would frighten him off.

Of course, he didn't scare easily. One black brow lifted.

Reluctantly she extended her hand, and his fingers closed around hers.

Hani flinched.

'Did I hurt you?' he demanded, frowning.

'No, no, not at all.' He had, in fact, judged to a nicety exactly how much strength to exert. Fumbling for a reason she could give him at her involuntary reaction, she hurried on, 'Just—I think someone walked over my grave.'

It took every shred of her fragile control not to snatch back her hand. His fingers were warm and strong—the hand of a person who worked hard.

But it wasn't his calluses that sent another bolt of sensation through her, so fiercely intense it numbed her brain and left her with nothing to say.

Rescue came from the band; abruptly, the drums and music fell silent. The dancers stopped and turned to the back of the dance floor.

The stranger looked over her head, his eyes narrowing as Hani found enough voice to warn, 'The elders have arrived. It's polite to be quiet.'

He didn't look like someone who'd care about the rituals of Polynesian society, but after a quick nod he watched the aristocratic council of men and women who ruled Tukuulu file past.

Hani dragged in a deep breath. The leaders would produce their best oratory to thank the group of students, and on Tukuulu it was an insult to leave while they spoke. So although she was stuck beside this man for some time, at least she wouldn't have to talk to him.

She'd have time to subdue the wild confusion attacking her. And then she'd think up some innocuous conversation. Not that she cared if he assumed she was a halfwit, she decided defiantly.

Willing herself to keep her gaze on the elders as they positioned themselves in front of the crowd, she wondered where he'd come from and what he was doing here. Although his height and those burnished eyes, the cold blue of the sheen on steel, hinted at a northern-European heritage, his olive skin spoke of the Mediterranean.

Perhaps he was Australian, or from New Zealand, although she couldn't recall an accent.

As for what he was doing here—well, right next door was the big nickel mine, Tukuulu's only industry, so possibly he had something to do with that.

If so, Hani thought trenchantly, she'd try to persuade him that the mine company needed to accept some responsibility for the school that educated its workforce.

About half an hour into the speeches, Hani blinked, then closed her eyes against the light from the flaring torches.

Not here, not now, she prayed fervently. *Please!*

Cautiously she lifted her lashes, only to blink again as the flames splintered into jagged shards that stabbed into her brain. Heat gathered across her temples, while a dragging ache weighted her bones.

The fever had returned.

Don't panic—just stay upright. Once they finish you can go.

For almost two months—ever since the last bout—she'd been so sure she'd finally managed to shake off this wretched bug. Fear hollowed her stomach; the last time she'd been ill with it the principal had told her that another bout would mean some months spent recuperating in a more temperate climate.

But she had nowhere to go, and no money…

Acutely aware of the silent woman at his side, Kelt Crysander-Gillan concentrated on the speeches. Although he couldn't follow all the allusions, the Tukuuluan dialect was close enough to Maori for him to appreciate the sentiments and the aptness of the songs that followed each speaker.

Pity the council hadn't waited another ten minutes or so to arrive. Then he'd have had time to introduce himself properly to the woman with the intriguing face and the aloof, reserved air.

Looking down, he realised that she was sneaking a glance at him from beneath her lashes. When their eyes clashed she firmed her luscious mouth and looked away, providing him with an excellent view of her profile.

Kelt switched his gaze back to the orator, but that fine line of brow and nose, the determined little chin and the sleek gloss of exquisite skin stayed firmly lodged in his mind.

An islander? No. Not if her eyes were as green as they seemed to be. And although her silky fall of hair gleamed like jet, a quick glance around the room confirmed that not a single Tukuuluan shared the red highlights that gleamed across the dark sheen. A staff member? Probably. When he'd come in she'd been talking to one of the teachers.

He'd already ascertained she wore no rings.

More than an hour after they'd arrived, the elders finally sat down, giving the signal for the celebrations to continue. Immediately the hall exploded in chatter, swiftly over-whelmed by the renewed staccato thump of the drums.

And the woman beside him turned without speaking and walked away.

An ironic smile pulled at the corners of Kelt's mouth as he watched her. So much for the notorious Gillan pulling power! He couldn't recollect any other woman flinching when he shook hands.

His gaze sharpened when she appeared to stumble. She recovered herself and stood with bowed head and slumping shoulders.

Without volition, Kelt took two steps towards her, stopping when she straightened up and set off into the hot, dark embrace of the night.

But something was definitely wrong. She wasn't so much walking as lurching down the avenue of coconut palms, and while he watched she staggered again, managed another few steps, and then collapsed heavily against the trunk of the nearest tree.

Kelt set off after her, long legs eating up the distance. Once within earshot he demanded, 'Are you all right?'

Hani tried to straighten up when she heard the deep, cool, aloof voice—very male. Even in her distress she was pretty sure she knew who was speaking.

Weakly she said, 'Yes, thank you,' humiliated to realise she sounded drunk, the words slurred and uneven. She probably looked drunk too, huddled against the palm trunk.

'Can I get you anything?' This time he sounded curt and impatient.

'No.' Just go away, she pleaded silently.

'Drink or drugs?'

She longed for her usual crisp, no-nonsense tone when she responded, 'Neither.'

Instead the word dragged, fading into an indeterminate mutter. Closing her eyes, she tried to ignore him and concentrate on staying more or less upright.

He made a disgusted sound. 'Why don't I believe that?' Without waiting for an answer he picked her up as though she were a child and demanded, 'Where were you going?'

Fighting the debilitating desire to surrender and just let him look after her, she struggled to answer, finally dredging the words from her confused brain. 'Ahead—in house.'

He set off silently and smoothly, but by the time they

reached her door Hani's entire energy was focused on holding herself together long enough to take her medication before the fever crashed her into nightmare territory.

'Where's your key?'

'B-bag.' Her lips felt thick and unwieldy, and she said it again, but this time it was an inarticulate mutter. Dimly Hani heard him say something else, but the words jumbled around in her head.

Chills racked her shaking body as she whispered, 'Cold... so cold...'

Unconsciously she curled into the man who held her, striving to steal some of his warmth. Kelt's unruly body stiffened in automatic recognition and, swearing silently, he took the bag from her limp fingers. His arms tightened around her and he said, 'It's all right, I'll get you inside.'

She didn't appear to hear him. 'B-bedside,' she said, slurring the word.

She was shivering so hard he thought he heard her teeth chattering, yet she was on fire—so hot he could feel it through his clothes.

Kelt set her on her feet, holding her upright when she crumpled. He inserted the key and twisted it, picking her up again as soon as he had the door open. Once inside the small, sparsely furnished living room he found the light switch and flicked it on.

The woman in his arms stiffened, turning her head away from the single bulb. Her mouth came to rest against his heart, and through the fine cotton of his shirt he could feel the pressure of her lips against his skin.

Grimly, he tried to ignore his body's consuming response to the accidental kiss.

Guessing that the open door in the far wall probably led to

a bedroom, he strode towards it. Through the opening, one comprehensive glance took in an ancient institutional bed. A rickety lamp on the chest of drawers beside it seemed to be the only illumination.

He eased her down onto the coverlet, then switched on the lamp. Hannah Court gave a soft, sobbing sigh.

His first instinct was to call a doctor, but she opened her eyes—great eyes, darkly lashed, and yes, they were green.

Even glazed and unseeing, they were alluring.

'Pills.' Her voice was high and thin, and she frowned, her eyes enormous in her hectically flushed face. 'T-top drawer…'

Kelt's expression lightened a fraction when he saw a bottle of tablets; although he didn't recognise the name of the drug, the dose was clearly set out, headed rather quaintly For the Fever.

He said harshly, 'I'll get you some water.'

When he came back her eyes were closed again beneath her pleated brows. She'd turned away from the light, rucking up her skirt around her hips to reveal long, elegant legs. Setting his jaw against a swift stab of desire, Kelt jerked the fabric down to cover her.

'Hannah.' Deliberately he made his tone hard and commanding.

Still lost in that region of pain and fever, she didn't answer, but her lashes flickered. Kelt sat down on the side of the bed, shook out the right number of pills, and repeated her name. This time there was no response at all.

He laid the back of his hand against her forehead. Her skin was burning. Perhaps he should call a doctor instead of trying to get the medication inside her.

Medication first, he decided, then he'd get a doctor. 'Open your mouth, Hannah,' he ordered.

After a few seconds she obeyed. He put the pills onto her

tongue and said in the same peremptory tone, 'Here's the water. Drink up.'

Her body moved reflexively, but she did as she was told, greedily gulping down the water and swallowing the pills without any problems.

She even managed to sigh, 'OK—soon…'

Kelt eased her back onto the pillow and slipped the sandals from her slender, high-arched feet. She wasn't wearing tights, and her dress was loose enough to be comfortable.

To his surprise she made a soft protesting noise. One hand came up and groped for him, then fell onto the sheet, the long, elegant fingers loosening as another bout of shivering shook her slim body with such rigour that Kelt turned away and headed for the door. She needed help, and she needed it right now.

He'd almost got to the outer door when he heard a sound from the room behind him. Turning in mid-stride, Kelt made it back in half the time.

Hannah Court had fallen out of the bed, her slim body twisting as guttural little moans escaped through her clenched teeth.

What sort of fever took hold so quickly?

When he picked her up she immediately turned into him, unconsciously seeking—what? Comfort?

'Hannah, it's all right, I'll get a doctor for you as soon as I can,' he told her, softening and lowering his voice as though she were a child.

'Hani,' she whispered, dragging out the syllables.

Honey? A play on Hannah, a pet name perhaps? She certainly had skin like honey—even feverish it glowed, delicate and satin-smooth.

His arms tightened around her yielding body and he sat on

the side of the bed, surprised when the close embrace seemed to soothe her restlessness. Slowly, almost imperceptibly, the intense, dramatic shivers began to ease.

But when he went to lie her down she clutched weakly at him. 'Stay,' she mumbled so thickly it was difficult to make out the words. 'Stay. Please…Raf…' The word died away into an indeterminate mumble.

Rafe? A lover? Surprised and irritated by a fierce twist of what couldn't possibly be jealousy, Kelt said, 'It's all right, I won't let you go.'

That seemed to soothe her. She lay quiescent, her breathing becoming more regular.

Kelt looked down at her lovely face. His brother Gerd would laugh if he could see him now. This small, stark room couldn't have been a bigger contrast to the pomp of the ceremony he'd just attended in Carathia, when their grandmother had presented Gerd, their next ruler, to the people of the small, mountainous country on the Adriatic.

His brother had always known that one day he'd rule the Carathians, and Kelt had always been devoutly thankful the fishbowl existence of monarchy wasn't his fate. His mouth tightened. His own title of Prince Kelt, Duke of Vamili, had been confirmed too. And that should put an end to the grumblings of discontent amongst some of the less educated country people.

Last year their grandmother, the Grand Duchess of Carathia, had come down with a bout of pneumonia. She'd recovered, but she'd called Gerd back to Carathia, intent on sealing the succession of the exceedingly wealthy little country. The ceremonies had gone off magnificently with the world's royalty and many of its leaders in attendance.

As well as a flock of princesses.

With a cynical movement of his hard mouth, Kelt
wondered if their grandmother would have any luck marrying
her heir off to one.

He suspected not. Gerd might be constrained by centuries
of tradition, but he'd choose his own wife.

And once that was done there would be children to seal the
succession again. He frowned, thinking of a Carathian tradition that had complicated the existence of Carathian rulers. It
had surfaced again—very inconveniently—just before the
ceremonies. Someone had resurrected the ancient tale of the
second child, the true chosen one, and in the mountains, where
the people clung to past beliefs, a groundswell of rebellion
was fomenting.

Fortunately he'd spent very little time in Carathia since his
childhood, so his presence was no direct threat to Gerd's rule.
But he didn't like what was coming in from his brother's in-
formants and his own.

Instead of a simple case of someone fomenting mischief,
the rumours were beginning to seem like the first step to a
carefully organised plan to produce disorder in Carathia, and
so gain control of over half of the world's most valuable
mineral, one used extensively in electronics.

The woman in his arms sighed, and snuggled even closer,
turning her face into his neck. Her skin no longer burned and
she'd stopped shivering.

He registered that the distant throb of the music had
stopped, and glanced at the clock on top of the chest of
drawers. He'd been holding her for just over an hour.
Whatever the medication was, it worked miraculously fast.

He responded with involuntary appreciation to her faint,
drifting scent—erotic, arousing—and the feel of her, lax and
quiescent against him as though after lovemaking. Cursing his

unruly body and its instant reaction, he moved her so that he could see her face.

Yes, she was certainly on the mend. The flush had faded, and she was breathing normally.

A moment later beads of perspiration broke out through her skin. Astoundingly fast, the fine cotton of her dress was soaked, the fabric clinging like a second skin, highlighting the elegant bowl of her hips, the gentle swell of her breasts, the vulnerable length of her throat and the long, sleek lines of her thighs.

Desire flamed through him, an urgent hunger that disgusted him.

He eased her off his lap and onto the bed. Once more she made a soft noise of protest, reaching out for him before her hand fell laxly onto the cover and she seemed to slip into a deeper sleep.

Frowning, he stood and surveyed her. He couldn't leave her like that—it would do her no good for her to sleep in saturated clothes.

So what the *hell* was he to do next?

The next morning, a little shaky but free from fever, Hani blessed modern medications and wondered who her rescuer— so very judgemental—had been. Kelt Gillan...

An unusual name for an unusual man. She could vaguely remember him picking her up, but after that was a blank, though with an odd little shiver she thought she'd never forget his voice, so cold and unsympathetic as he'd—what?

Ordered her to do something. Oh yes, of course. *Swallow the pills.* She gave a weak smile and lifted herself up on her elbow to check the time.

And realised she was in one of the loose cotton shifts she wore at night.

'How—?' she said aloud, a frown pleating her forehead. She sat up, and stared around the room. The dress she'd worn to the party was draped over the chair beside the wardrobe.

Colour burned her skin and she pressed her hands over her eyes. Her rescuer—whoever he was—must have not only stayed with her until the fever broke, but also changed her wet clothes.

Well, she was grateful, she decided sturdily. He'd done what was necessary, and although she cringed at the thought of him seeing and handling her almost naked body, it was obscurely comforting that he'd cared for her.

But for the rest of that day his angular, handsome face was never far from her mind, and with it came a reckless, potent thrill. Trying to reason it into submission didn't work. Instead of her wondering why she reacted so powerfully to the stranger when any other man's closeness repulsed her, the thought of his touch summoned treacherously tantalising thoughts.

Dim recollections of strong arms and a warmth that almost kept at bay the icy grip of the fever made her flush, a heat that faded when into her head popped another vagrant memory—the contempt in his tone when he'd asked her if she was drunk or drugged.

Although she'd never see him again, so she didn't care a bit what he thought of her...

CHAPTER TWO

THREE weeks later and several thousand kilometres further south, standing on a deck that overlooked a sweep of sand and a cooler Pacific Ocean than she was accustomed to, Hani scanned the faces of the five children in front of her. Though they ranged from a dark-haired, dark-eyed, copper-skinned beauty of about fourteen to a blond little boy slathered with so much sunscreen that his white skin glistened, their features showed they were closely related.

What would it be like to have a family—children of her own?

Her heart twisted and she repressed the thought. Not going to happen, ever.

It was the small blond boy who asked, 'What's your name?'

'Hannah,' she said automatically.

Her accent must have confused them, because the older girl said, 'Honey? That's a nice name.'

And the little boy nodded. 'Your skin's the same colour as honey. Is that why your mum called you that?'

In Tukuulu she'd been Hannah; she liked Honey better. Stifling the hard-won caution that told her it might also confuse anyone too curious, she said cheerfully, 'Actually, it's Hannah, but you can call me Honey if you want to. Now I've told you my name, you'd better tell me yours.'

They all blurted them out together, of course, but six years of teaching infants had instilled a few skills and she soon sorted them out. Hani asked the older girl, 'Kura, where do you live?'

'At Kiwinui,' she said importantly, clearly expecting everyone to know where Kiwinui was. When she realised it meant nothing to Hani, she added, 'It's in the next bay, but we're allowed to walk over the hill and come down here to play if we ask nicely. So we're asking.'

It would take a harder heart than Hani's to withstand the impact of five pairs of expectant eyes. 'I need to know first how good you are at swimming.'

'We're not going to swim because we have to have a grown-up with us when we do that,' Kura told her. 'Mum said so, and The Duke told us off when he caught us only paddling here, and the water only came up to our ankles.'

The *Duke*? Her tone invested the nickname with capitals and indicated that nobody messed with the man, whoever he was.

Curious, Hani asked, 'Who is the duke?'

They looked almost shocked. Kura explained, 'That's like being a prince or something. His nan wears a crown and when she dies his brother will be a duke too and he'll live in a big stone castle on a hill.' She turned and pointed to the headland behind them. 'He lives up there behind the pohutu-kawa trees.'

The Duke's brother, or The Duke? Hani repressed a smile. 'I'm happy for you to play here. Just come and tell me when you're going home again.'

With a whoop they set off, except for the small blond boy, whose name was Jamie. 'Why have you got green eyes?' he asked, staring at her.

'Because my mother had green eyes.' Hani repressed a familiar pang of pain. She and her brother had both inherited those eyes; every time she looked in the mirror she thought of Rafiq.

Surely she should be reconciled to never seeing him again by now!

Jamie nodded. 'They're nice. Why are you staying here?'

'I'm on holiday.' The day after her last attack of fever the principal had told her that if she didn't take up the offer to go to New Zealand—'long enough to get this fever out of your system'—the charity that ran the school couldn't accept responsibility for her welfare. Her air fares would be paid, and the beach house where she'd convalesce was rent-free.

Without exactly stating that they'd terminate her employment if she didn't go, he'd implied it so strongly she'd been persuaded to reluctantly leave the safety of Tukuulu.

Curiosity satisfied, Jamie said nonchalantly, 'See you later,' and scampered off to join the others.

Hani sat back down in the comfortable wicker chair on the deck. Airy and casually luxurious, the beach house was surprisingly big, with glass doors in every room opening out onto a wide wooden deck that overlooked the cove. Her landlord, an elderly man, had met her flight the previous night and driven her here to what he'd called a bach.

Remembering his very English accent, she smiled. No doubt those cut-glass vowels were why the children had decided he must be some sort of aristocrat.

After introducing himself very formally as Arthur Wellington, he'd said, 'The refrigerator and the pantry have been stocked with staples. If you need anything else, do ring the number on the calendar beside the telephone.'

Hani thanked him for that, but realised now that she'd missed telling him how much she appreciated being given the opportunity to stay here.

She'd do that when she paid him for the groceries he'd supplied.

On a long, soft sigh she took her gaze away from the children long enough to examine the cove. Sand like amber suede curved against the kingfisher expanse of water. Squinting against the bright sky, Hani eyed the headland where the landlord lived. Its steep slopes were hidden by more of the dark-leafed trees that lined the beach, their massive limbs swooping down over the sand.

A formal house to match her landlord's formal manner? She hoped not. It would look incongruous in this pristinely beautiful scene.

Loud shrieks from the beach dragged her attention back to the game taking place in front of the bach, one that involved much yelling, more laughter, and some frenzied racing around. For the first time in months she felt a stirring of energy.

Smiling, checking that little Jamie didn't get too close to the water, she failed to notice an intruder until he was almost at the cottage. The soft clink of harness alerting her, she swivelled around and saw a horse—a fine bay, strong enough to take its tall, powerfully built rider without effort.

Her startled gaze took in the rider. He sat easily on his mount—but that wasn't why her pulses revved into overdrive.

For a second—just long enough to terrify and delight her—he reminded her of her brother. Rafiq had the same coiled grace of strength and litheness, the same relaxed control of his mount.

The same air of authority.

Then she recalled when she'd seen this man before, and an odd, baseless panic froze the breath in her throat. In spite of the bout of fever she'd been suffering when she met him on Tukuulu, those hard-hewn features and hooded eyes were sharply etched into her memory.

As was the feel of his arms around her... And the knowledge that he'd stripped her saturated clothes from her and somehow managed to get her into the loose shift she wore at night.

What the *hell* was he doing here?

He swung down, looped the reins over a fencepost and opened the gate to come towards her. Subliminally intimidated by the arrogant angle of his head and the smooth, lethal grace of his stride, Hani forced herself to her feet, stiffening her spine and her knees.

Although tall for a woman, she couldn't match him. Her chin came up; unsmiling, breath locking in her throat, she watched him approach while a feverish awareness lifted the invisible hairs on the back of her neck.

He was—well, *gorgeous* was the only word she could come up with. Except that gorgeous made her think of male models, and this man looked like no male model she'd ever seen. That effortless, inborn air of command hardened his already bold features into an intimidating mask of force and power, emphasised by a cold steel-blue gaze and a thinning of his subtly sensuous mouth.

He was handsome enough to make any woman's heart shake—even one as frozen as hers—but something uncompromising and formidable about him set off alarms in every nerve.

He had to be The Duke. A swift stab of apprehension screwed her nerves even tighter. Felipe, the man she'd once thought she loved, had called himself a French count.

It was stupid of her, but the children's innocent misconception seemed somehow ominous.

Hani knew she should be relieved when he looked at her with a total lack of male interest. Scarily, she wasn't.

OK, so the last thing she wanted was a man to see her as

a sexual being, but… On Tukuulu he'd noticed her as a woman; now he looked at her with complete indifference.

And that stung.

Trying to keep this meeting on a sensible basis, she said warily, 'Hello. I didn't realise that you owned this place. Thank you so much for letting me stay here.'

'I hoped to see you looking a bit better,' he said curtly.

'I am much better.' Yes, her voice was fine—crisp, just as cool and impersonal as his, a far cry from her slurred tone that night at the ceremony. Meeting his merciless survey with an assumption of confidence, she hid her uncertainty with a shrug. 'Another thing I have to thank you for is your rescue of me.'

One black brow lifted. 'It was nothing; I happened to be the closest person around.'

Heat tinged her skin. Trying to sound professional and assured, she said crisply, 'It was very kind of you. I don't remember much—' only the sound of his voice, calm and re-assuring, and the wonderful comfort of his arms when he'd held her until the shivering stopped '—but I know I didn't change myself.'

His eyes narrowed slightly. 'Once the fever had broken I went back to the school dance floor, but everyone had gone by then. It didn't seem a good idea for you to sleep in wet clothes, so I removed your dress.' In a coldly formidable tone, he finished, 'I behaved as a brother might have.'

Colour burned into her skin. Hoping her words mingled the right blend of gratitude and distance, she said, 'Yes—well, I thought as much.' And then, changing the subject without finesse, 'Thanks again for being generous enough to let me stay in this lovely place.'

'You've thanked me enough,' he said a little curtly, adding with a faint smile, 'I went to school with your principal. When he asked if his teachers could use this bach I agreed. It's not used very often, and it seems a waste to have it sit here empty. You're the third teacher to come here, and I expect there will be others.'

So that was the connection. And he was making sure she didn't think she was special.

She said with cool assurance, 'I'm grateful. But to make things very clear, I was neither drunk nor drugged that night in Tukuulu.'

One straight black brow lifted. 'I wondered if you'd remember that. I'm sorry for jumping to conclusions—it didn't take me long to realise you were ill.'

For some reason she wasn't prepared to explore, she didn't want his apology. 'I sent you a letter thanking you for your help.'

'Yes, your principal passed it on.'

He hadn't answered. Well, for heaven's sake, she hadn't expected him to.

Without inflection, he said, 'I'm glad I was there when you needed someone. I'm Kelt Crysander-Gillan—although I don't use the first part of my surname—and I live just up the hill.'

Nothing about being some sort of aristocrat, she noted. Clearly The Duke was just a nickname, perhaps because of the double-barrelled name. They mightn't be common in New Zealand.

And he *looked* like a duke, someone of importance, his very presence a statement of authority. A very sexy duke, sexier than any other duke she'd ever met...

One who'd taken her clothes off and seen her naked...

Firmly she tamped down a sizzle of adrenalin. 'And of course you know that I'm Han-*Hannah* Court.'

Oh, he'd really unnerved her! For the first time in years

she'd almost given him her real name, catching it back only just in time. Startled, she automatically held out her hand.

'Welcome to New Zealand,' he said gravely, and his long, lean fingers closed around hers.

Her heart picked up speed. *Cool it*, she commanded her runaway pulse fiercely while he shook hands.

There was no reason for the swift sizzle of sensation that shocked her every nerve. Acting on pure blind instinct, Hani jerked her hand free.

Kelt Gillan's brows met for a taut second above his blade of a nose, but he turned when the children chose that moment to surge up from the beach, their shouted greetings a melee of sound.

He silenced them with a crisp, 'All right, calm down, you lot.'

She expected them to shuffle their feet, but although they obediently stayed silent their wide smiles told her he was popular with them.

Amazing, she thought, watching as he said something to each of them. And again she remembered Felipe, her first and only lover. He'd had no time for children; there was no profit to be made from them...

Kelt Gillan said, 'Miss Court has been ill and needs a lot of rest, so I want you to play on the homestead beach until she's better.'

Their attention swivelled back to her.

Into the silence Jamie said earnestly, 'I was sick too, Honey. I had mumps and my throat was sore and I couldn't eat anything 'cept ice cream and jelly and scrambled eggs.'

'And soup,' the lovely Kura reminded him officiously.

He pulled a face. 'And some soup.'

'I'm getting much better now,' Hani said, smiling at him. 'And I'm lucky—I can eat anything I like.'

'Honey?' Kelt said on an upward inflection, that taunting brow lifting again as his cool gaze inspected her face. 'I thought your name was Hannah?'

'I'll have to learn to talk like a New Zealander,' she said lightly, irritated by the colour that heated her cheekbones. In the last six years she'd worked hard to banish any vestige of the soft cadences of her birth country.

'Actually, it suits you,' he said, a sardonic note colouring his deep voice. He turned back to the children. 'All right, off you go.'

They turned obediently, all but Jamie. 'Where do you live?' he asked Hani.

Nowhere... 'On a hot little island called Tukuulu a long way over the sea from here.'

An older girl, Jamie's, sister—cousin?—turned. 'Come *on*, Jamie,' she commanded importantly, and the boy gave Hani a swift grin and scampered off.

'What charming children. Are they siblings?' she asked into the suddenly oppressive silence.

'Siblings and cousins. In New Zealand the term *whanau* is used to denote the extended family,' the man beside her said.

'You didn't need to warn them off,' she told him. 'I like children.'

Kelt Gillan said succinctly, 'Honey or Hannah or whoever you are, you're here to convalesce, and it's no part of that healing process to act as unpaid babysitter. Your principal asked me to make sure you didn't overexert yourself.'

His words set off a flicker of memory. The night he'd unhooked her from the coconut palm and carried her home he'd spoken in exactly that controlled, uncompromising tone. As though she were an idiot, she thought angrily.

She didn't care what Kelt thought, but it wasn't fair to

spoil the children's pleasure. 'Both you and he are very thoughtful, but I'm quite capable of making decisions like that for myself. Believe me, it didn't hurt me or tire me or worry me to sit in the sun and watch them. I enjoyed it.'

'Perhaps so,' he said inflexibly, 'but that's not the point. You're here to rest and regain your strength. I'll make sure their parents understand that they stay in Homestead Bay. Don't fret about curtailing their fun—they'll play quite happily there.'

Behind him his horse lifted its head from lipping the grass and took a step sideways, its powerful muscles fluid beneath satiny skin.

In Moraze, her homeland, herds of wild horses roamed the grassy plateau country that surrounded the central volcanic peaks. Descended from Arabian steeds, they'd been brought there by her ancestor, a renegade French aristocrat who'd settled the island with a rag-tag train of soldiers and a beautiful Arabian wife.

Hani's parents had given her one of those horses for her third birthday…

Long dead, her parents and that first gentle mount, and it was years since she'd ridden.

Hani was ambushed by a pang of homesickness, an aching sense of loss so fierce it must have shown in her face.

'Sit down!' Kelt said sharply, unable to stop himself from taking a step towards her.

One hand came up, warning him off. Apart from that abrupt gesture she didn't move, and the flash of something tight and almost desperate in her expression disappeared. Her black hair swirled around her shoulders in a cloud of fiery highlights as she angled her chin at him.

Looking him straight in the eye, she said in a gentle voice with a distinct edge to it, 'Mr Gillan, I'm neither an invalid nor a child. I make my own decisions and I'm perfectly capable of looking after myself.'

He examined her closely, but her lovely face was shut against him, that moment of despair—if that was what it had been—replaced by aloof self-assurance.

Kelt chose to live in New Zealand for his own good reasons, one of them being that Kiwinui had been in his grandfather's family for over a hundred years, and he felt a deep emotional link to the place. But as a scion of the royal family of Carathia he'd been born to command. Backed by their grandmother, the Grand Duchess, he and his brother had turned their backs on tradition and gone into business together as soon as he'd left university. Between them they'd built up a hugely successful enterprise, a leader in its field that had made them both billionaires.

Women had chased him mercilessly since he'd left school. Although none had touched his heart, he treated his mistresses with courtesy, and had somehow acquired a legendary status as a lover.

Women were an open book to him.

Until now. One part of him wanted to tell Hannah Court that while she was on Kiwinui she was under his protection; the other wanted to sweep that elegant body into his arms and kiss her perfect mouth into submission.

Instead, he said crisply, 'And I'll do what I consider to be best for the situation. If you need anything, there's a contact number by the telephone.'

Hani looked at him with cool, unreadable green eyes, the colour of New Zealand's most precious greenstone. 'Thank you; Mr Wellington told me about that.'

Kelt shrugged. 'Arthur works for me.'

Her head inclined almost regally. 'I see.'

'Tell me if another bout of fever hits you.'

'It's not necessary—I have medication to deal with it.' Another hint of soft apricot tinged her exotic cheekbones when she continued, 'As you found out, it works very quickly.'

Clearly, she had no intention of giving an inch. He wondered how old she was—mid-twenties, he guessed, but something in her bearing and the direct glance of those amazing eyes reminded him of his grandmother, the autocratic Grand Duchess who'd kept her small realm safe through wars and threats for over fifty years.

Dismissing such a ridiculous thought, he said, 'Do you drive?'

'Of course.' Again that hint of appraisal in her tone, in her gaze.

'Any idea of New Zealand's road rules?' he asked, making no attempt to hide the ironic note in his voice.

'I'm a quick learner. But how far is it to the nearest village? If it's close enough I can walk there when I need anything.'

'It's about five kilometres—too far for you to walk in the summer heat.'

Warily wondering if he'd given up any idea of looking after her—because he seemed like a man with an over-developed protective streak and a strong will—she pointed out, 'I'm used to heat.'

'If that were true, you wouldn't be convalescing here.' And while she was absorbing that dig, he went on, 'And somehow I doubt very much that you're accustomed to walking five kilometres while carrying groceries.'

Uneasily aware of the unsettling glint in his cold blue eyes, Hani shrugged. 'Don't worry about me, Mr Gillan. I won't be a bother to anyone.'

A single black brow climbed, but all he said was, 'Call me Kelt. Most New Zealanders are very informal.'

She most emphatically didn't want to call him anything! However, she'd already established her independence, so, hiding her reluctance, she returned courteously, 'Then you must call me Hannah.'

He lifted one black brow. 'You know, I think I prefer Honey. Hannah is—very Victorian. And you're not.'

The slight—very slight—pause before he said Victorian made her wonder if he'd been going to say virginal.

If so, he couldn't be more wrong.

Far from virginal, far from Victorian, she thought with an aching regret. 'I'd prefer Hannah, thank you.'

His smile was tinged by irony. 'Hannah it shall be. If you feel up to it, I'd like you to come to dinner tomorrow night.'

Caution warned her to prevaricate, fudge the truth a little and say she wasn't well enough to socialise, but she'd already cut off that avenue of escape when she'd made it clear she didn't need to be looked after by—well, by *anyone*, she thought sturdily.

Especially not this man, whose unyielding maleness affected her so strongly she could feel his impact on every cell. Even politely setting limits as she'd just done had energised her, set her senses tingling, and every time she looked into that hard, handsome face she felt a hot, swift tug of—of lust, she reminded herself bitterly.

And she knew—only too well—what that could lead to.

However, he was her landlord. She owed him for several things; his impersonal care on Tukuulu, the refrigerator full of groceries.

Changing her wet clothes...

Ignoring the deep-seated pulse of awareness, she said, 'That's very kind of you. What time would you like me to be there?'

'I'll pick you up at seven,' he told her with another keen glance. 'Until then, take things slowly.'

His long-legged strides across the lawn presented her with a disturbing view of broad shoulders and narrow hips above lean, heavily muscled thighs. He dressed well too—his trousers had been tailored for him, and she'd almost bet his shirt had too.

Very sexy, she thought frivolously, quelling the liquid heat that consumed her. Some lucky men were born with that *it* factor, a compelling masculinity that attracted every female eye.

And she'd bet the subject of her letting someone know if she had another attack of fever would come up again.

A few paces away he swivelled, catching her intent, fascinated look. A challenge flared in his narrowed eyes; he understood exactly what effect he was having on her.

Hot with shame, she wanted to turn away, but Kelt held her gaze for a second, his own enigmatic and opaque.

However, when he spoke his voice was crisp and aloof. 'If you need anything, let me know.'

It sounded like a classical *double entendre*; if he'd been Felipe it would have been.

It was time she stopped judging men by Felipe's standards. The years in Tukuulu had shown her that most men were not like him, and there was no reason to believe that Kelt Gillan wasn't a perfectly decent farmer with a face like one of the more arrogant gods, an overdeveloped protective instinct and more than his share of formidable male presence.

'Thank you—I will,' she said remotely.

And produced a smile she held until he'd swung up onto his horse and guided it away.

Her face felt frozen when she took refuge in the cottage and stood listening as the sound of hooves dwindled into the warm, sea-scented air. She shivered, crossing her arms and rubbing her hands over her prickling skin.

Again? she thought in mindless panic. The unbidden, unwanted surge of sensual appetite humiliated her. Why on earth was she attracted to dangerous men?

Not that she'd realised Felipe was dangerous when she first met him. And for some unfounded and quite illogical reason she couldn't believe Kelt would turn out to be like Felipe.

As well, the heady clamour Kelt Gillan summoned in her was different—more earthy and primal, nothing like the fascinated excitement she'd felt when Felipe had pursued her. He'd seemed such a glamorous, fascinating man, with his French title and his famous friends. At eighteen she'd been so green she'd run headlong into peril without a second thought.

Six years older, and much better able to look after herself, she sensed a different danger in Kelt Gillan—a more elemental attraction without the calculation that had marked Felipe's seduction.

Desperate to take her mind off her enigmatic landlord and his unnerving effect on her, she went across to the kitchen and put on the electric kettle.

'Displacement activity,' she said aloud, a mirthless smile curling her mouth as she spooned coffee into the plunger.

Wrapping her attraction to Felipe in a romantic haze had got her into deep trouble; this time she'd face her inconvenient response to Kelt Gillan squarely. Coffee mug in hand, she walked out onto the deck and stood looking out over the sea.

No emotions, no fooling herself that this was love, no silly claptrap about soulmates. She'd already been down that track and it had led to humiliation and heartbreak and terror. Felipe had played on her naivety, setting himself out to charm her into submission.

And succeeding utterly, so that she'd gradually been manipulated into an affair without fully realising where she was
heading. When she'd realised what sort of man he was she'd
tried to break away, only to have him bind her to him with the
cruellest, most degrading chains. To free herself she'd had to
sacrifice everything—self-respect, love for her brother, her
very future.

Closing her eyes against the dazzling shimmer of the sun
on the bay, she thought wearily that she hadn't planned for
her sacrifice to last the rest of her life.

In fact, she hadn't planned on any further life.

Well, a Mediterranean fisherman with smuggling as a
sideline had seen to it that she'd survived. She shivered, and
for a foolish few seconds wondered if Kelt Gillan had brought
on another attack of fever.

No, her chill was due to memories she wished she could
banish.

Only right now she needed them to remind her that no
person could ever see into the heart of another, especially
when they were blinded by lust.

Ruthlessly she dragged her mind back to the present, and concentrated on the problem at hand—her feelings for Kelt Gillan.

'Just think rationally,' she told herself.

What she felt when she looked at Kelt was a powerful
physical attraction for a man both formidable and enormously attractive—a primal arousal with a scientific basis.
Humans instinctively recognised the people they'd make
superb babies with.

Logic played no part in it, nor did common sense. But
both could be used as weapons against it, and if she'd learned
anything these past six years it was that any relationship
between lovers needed much more than desire to be a success.

And there would be no babies for her, ever.

So she'd have dinner with Kelt and then she'd stay well away from him.

Hani missed the children the next day, and not for the first time wondered what on earth she was going to do for three months. Too many empty weeks stretched before her, leaving her far too much time to think, to remember. Without the steady routine of school she faced more than simple boredom; she'd have to deal with emptiness.

At least the cottage had a set of bookshelves stuffed with books of all ages and quite a few magazines. After a brief walk along the beach that reminded her again how unfit she was, she sank into a chair on the deck with a cup of tea and a volume on New Zealand that looked interesting.

She flicked it open and saw a bookplate. Kelt Crysander-Gillan, it stated.

'Unusual,' she said aloud. There was an inscription too, but she turned the page on that, feeling as though she was prying.

With a name like that, and if Kelt's air of forceful authority had led to a nickname like The Duke, imaginative children could well come up with a crown-wearing grandmother somewhere in Europe.

At precisely seven o'clock he arrived to collect her as the sun was dipping behind the forest-covered mountains that ran down the central spine of Northland's long, narrow peninsula. He drove a large, luxurious four-wheel-drive, which gave Hani a moment of heart-sickness; her brother used to drive the same make…

Hani pushed the thought to the back of her mind. Rafiq thought she was dead, and that was the way she had to stay.

And then Kelt got out, lithe and long-legged, powerfully

magnetic and urbane in a short-sleeved shirt that echoed the steely colour of his eyes, and casually elegant trousers, and the bitter, heart-sick memories vanished, replaced by a reckless excitement.

When he opened the gate she went hastily out into the serene evening. The bach might be his, but she didn't want to sense his dominating presence whenever she walked into the living room.

She knew she looked good. For an hour that afternoon she'd pored over her scanty wardrobe, startled to find herself wistfully remembering her favourites amongst the designer clothes she'd worn in her old life.

In the end she'd chosen a modest dress she'd found in a shop in Tukuulu's small capital city. Although it was a little too loose on her, the clear salmon hue burnished the gold of her skin and the warm highlights in her dark hair.

Tempted to go without make-up, she decided after a critical survey of her reflection that a naked face might make her look conspicuous, and her security depended on blending in. So she compromised on lipstick a slightly deeper shade than her dress, and pinned her badly cut hair off her face with two frangipani clips made from the moonbeam shimmer of pearl shell.

Kelt waited for her beside the gate. Her shoulders held a little stiffly to hide an absurd self-consciousness, she walked towards him, sensing a darker, more elemental level beneath his coolly sophisticated exterior. Trying to ignore the smouldering need in the pit of her stomach, she saw him as a warrior, riding his big bay gelding into battle...

Not, she thought with an inner shiver, a man to cross swords with.

With a carefully neutral smile she met his gaze, and in a charged moment her wilful memory sabotaged the fragile veneer of her composure by supplying a repeat of how it had felt when he'd carried her—the powerful litheness of his gait, the subtle flexion of his body as he'd lifted her, his controlled strength...

CHAPTER THREE

KELT examined her face with the impersonal keenness of a doctor. 'How are you?' he asked, opening the door of the car.

Hani's smile faded. His persistent view of her as an invalid was—*demeaning*, she decided on a spurt of irritation that didn't quite mask a deeper, more dangerous emotion. After all, in the light of her unexpected attraction, it was far safer if he saw her as an invalid than as a woman.

A desirable woman.

With a hint of frost in her tone she answered, 'Fine, thank you.' And met his scrutiny with head held high and an immobile face that belied the unsteady rhythm of her heart.

'You still have dark circles under your eyes. Lack of sleep?'

Strangely enough, for the first time since she'd come to this side of the world all those years ago she'd slept deeply and dreamlessly, waking with an energy that seemed alien.

'No, not at all,' she told him evenly. Steering the conversation away from her illness, she asked, 'How far away is your house?'

'About a kilometre by road; half that distance if you walk across the paddocks—which I don't want you to do.' He set the car in motion.

'Why?'

He sent her a narrow glance. 'You could spook the cattle.' After a pause, he added, 'Or they might spook you.'

Hani examined some large, square animals, their coats glowing deep red-gold in the rays of the evening sun. 'They don't *look* excitable, but your point is well taken.'

Not that she planned to be going cross-country.

'And you?' he asked levelly, turning across a cattle grid.

She waited until the rattling died away before saying, 'I don't understand.'

'Are you excitable?'

Startled, she looked across at him, saw an enigmatic smile tuck in the corners of his hard mouth, and was shocked again by a fierce tug of arousal, sweet as honey, dangerous as dynamite.

Surely he wasn't *flirting* with her?

She felt winded and fascinated at the same time until a moment's reflection produced sanity. Of course he wasn't coming on to her. Not unless he was the sort of man who indulged in meaningless flirtations with any available woman.

Somehow she didn't want to believe he'd be so indiscriminate. A man with Kelt Gillan's effortless masculinity could have any woman he wanted, and he must know it. And unlike Felipe he had nothing to gain from seducing her.

In her most sedate tone she said, 'Not in the least. Teachers can't afford to be volatile. It's *very* bad for discipline.'

That should tell him she wasn't in the market for a holiday affair. To clinch it, she said, 'Don't worry, I won't walk in your fields or excite your cattle.'

'Paddocks,' he said laconically, explaining, 'New Zealanders call anything with animals in it a paddock. *Fields* are what we play sport on, and as far as we're concerned meadows don't exist.' He nodded at the setting sun. 'And that range of hills to the west is covered in native bush, not forest or woods.'

Intrigued, she said, 'I do know about bush. One of the Australian teachers at the school explained it to me. It's fascinating how countries colonised by the same power could develop such different words to describe things. In South Africa—'

She stopped suddenly, her mind freezing in dismay, then hastily tried to cover the slip by asking the first question that came to mind. 'What are those trees, the ones that grow in groups in nearly all your f—paddocks?'

'They're totara trees.'

'Oh. Do they flower?'

'Not noticeably—they're conifers. As for terminology—well, the world would be a boring place if we were all the same. Settlers in different countries adjusted to different conditions.' He paused a beat before adding casually, 'You're not South African, are you?'

'No,' she said, dry-throated.

'But clearly you've been there.'

Trying to banish any reluctance from her voice, she admitted, 'I spent a holiday there when I was young.'

He accepted that without comment. 'So what made a young Englishwoman decide to spend years teaching in a village school in a place like Tukuulu? The lure of tropical islands I can understand, but once you'd got to Tukuulu and realised it's really nothing but a volcano with a huge mine on it—beaches of dead coral, only one fleapit of a hotel, no night life—what kept you there?'

A little shudder tightened her skin, but she kept her gaze fixed steadily ahead. Let him probe as much as he liked; she had her story down pat.

'I wanted to help. And they were desperate for teachers. It's really hard for them to keep staff. But the principal is your friend so you must know that.'

After a moment's pause he said, 'How long do you plan to live there?'

'For several years yet,' she evaded.

'I imagine it's unusual for anyone to stay for long in a Pacific backwater like Tukuulu.' Let alone a young Englishwoman, his tone implied.

'You're a sophisticated man but you don't seem to mind living on a remote cattle station in a Pacific backwater like New Zealand,' she retorted sweetly.

He gave her swift, ironic smile. 'Don't let any New Zealander hear you call the place a backwater. We're a proud people with plenty to be proud of.'

'The Tukuuluans are proud too, and doing their best to move into the modern world without losing the special things that make their culture so distinctive.'

'I suspect that's an impossible task,' he said cynically.

'I hope not. And I like to think I'm helping them in a small way.'

They crossed another cattle grid and drove through a grove of the big trees she'd noticed before, their great branches almost touching the ground.

'Oh,' she exclaimed in involuntary pleasure, 'the leaves are silver underneath! From a distance the trees look so sombre—yet how pretty they must be when there's any wind.'

'Very, and when they flower in a month or so they'll be great torches of scarlet and crimson and maroon. I'll take you over the top of the hill so you can look over Kiwinui and get some idea of the lie of the land.'

Kelt slowed the vehicle to a stop, switching off the engine so that the silence flowed in around them, bringing with it the sweet scent of damp grass and the ever-present salt of the sea.

Gaze fixed in front of her, Hani said on an indrawn breath, 'This is glorious.'

'Yes.'

That was all, but his controlled voice couldn't hide the pride of ownership as he gazed out at his vast domain.

At the foot of the hill a sweeping bay fronted a large, almost flat, grassed area with what appeared to be a small settlement to one side. More huge trees fringed the beach and a long jetty stitched its way out into the water towards a sleek black yacht and a large motorboat.

'The working part of Kiwinui,' Kelt told her. He leaned slightly towards her so he could point. 'Cattle yards, the woolshed, implement sheds and the workers' cottages.'

Hani's breath stopped in her throat. He was too close, so near she could see the fine grain of his tanned skin, so close her nostrils were teased by a faint, wholly male scent. Hot little shivers snaked down her spine, and some locked, previously untouched part of her splintered into shards.

Desperate to overcome the clamour of her response, she scrambled from the car and took a couple of steps away. When Kelt joined her she didn't dare look at him.

Several measured breaths helped calm her racing heartbeats, and as soon as she could trust her voice she waved a hand at the nearest hill. 'What's that mown strip over there?'

'An airstrip. Kiwinui is too big to fertilise except from the air.' His words held a lick of amusement, as though he had sensed her stormy reaction to him and found it entertaining.

Mortified and bewildered, Hani wondered if the forced intimacy of their first meeting had somehow forged this—this wild physical reaction.

Yes, that had to be it. Relief eased her shame; her response was not some weird aberration or a frightening return to the servitude of her affair with Felipe. Kelt had held her closely, given her comfort while she fought the fever—changed her clothes—so naturally her body and mind responded to his presence.

Well, they could stop it right now. Discipline was what was needed here. She didn't want to feel like this every time she saw him, completely unable to control herself!

Trying to block out his presence, she concentrated on the view. To the north a series of ranges scalloped the coast, the lower-slopes pasture, the gullies and heights covered by forests—no, *native bush*—that reminded her of the jungles of Moraze. Between them she glimpsed a coast of sandy beaches and more green paddocks.

Stretching to the eastern horizon was the restless sea, its kingfisher-coloured expanse broken by a large, high island that formed an offshore barrier.

And, to cap it all, she heard the high, exquisite trill of a bird, joy rendered into song that soared into the golden light of the setting sun. Pierced by sudden delight, Hani dragged in a long breath.

And even as she thrilled to it, she knew that the man beside her somehow intensified her mood, her appreciation, as though his presence had the power to magnify her responses.

Felipe had never done that.

Hani swallowed. 'It's so beautiful,' she managed. 'What's the bird that's singing?'

He gave her a sharp look. 'It's a thrush,' he said. 'They were introduced here by the early settlers. He'll be perched on top of one of the pohutukawa trees.'

Bother, she thought on a surge of irrational panic, oh, bother and double-bother! Too late she remembered a poem she'd learned at school; if she were as English as her accent she'd probably recognise a thrush's song...

On the other hand, why should Kelt be suspicious? And even if he was, he wouldn't be able to find out who she was. Once she'd escaped Felipe she'd covered her tracks so well that even he, with all his resources in brutal men and tainted money, hadn't been able to hunt her down.

Kelt told her, 'The original homestead was down on the flat, quite close to the workers' cottages you can see, but when it burned down early in the twentieth century the new one was built up here.'

Hani filed away the fact that in New Zealand—at least in the countryside—substantial houses were called cottages. 'What's the difference between a cottage and a homestead and a bach?'

'A bach is a holiday cottage, always casual, very beachy. They used to be small and primitive, but nowadays that isn't necessarily so.'

'No indeed,' she said, thinking of the bach she was staying in.

He gave her an ironic smile. 'My grandmother made quite a few renovations to it. She enjoyed the simple life for a short time, but had no intention of giving up any comfort.'

His grandmother had clearly been a sophisticate. Well, Kiwinui was a big farm, and Hani didn't need to know the size of his bank balance to accept that Kelt was a wealthy man.

Kelt said, 'As for workers' cottages, the term's a hangover from the days when they were fairly basic. Nowadays no worker would be happy with basic housing, and even if he was his wife certainly wouldn't be, so they're usually good-sized family homes.'

'And a homestead is where the owner of the farm lives?' she guessed.

'Either the owner or manager's house on a farm or station.'

Hani nodded. 'Is this estate—Kiwinui—a farm or a station? What's the difference?'

'Basically a station is a larger farm—usually settled early in New Zealand's history. The first Gillan arrived here about a hundred and forty years ago. And yes, Kiwinui is a station.'

Hani looked down at the bay, frowning at the abrupt change of colour in the water. 'It looks as though it gets deep very quickly there,' she observed. 'Surely my cove—' colouring, she hastily corrected herself '—I mean, the one with the bach, would be safer for the children? I truly don't mind them coming, and I'd be happy to supervise their swimming. And young Kura seems very capable.'

'We'll see how things go.' His tone was non-committal. 'When those dark circles disappear then perhaps the children can pay you visits.'

Hani sent him a sharp look. 'The darkness under my eyes will go in its own good time. And I enjoy children's company.'

'You'll enjoy it more when you're stronger.'

His tone left no room for negotiation. Fuming, Hani decided that autocratic wasn't emphatic enough to describe him. Clearly he was accustomed to giving orders and seeing them obeyed.

And yet—she didn't feel suffocated as she had when she'd fancied herself in love with Felipe.

But then, after the first few times she'd never argued with Felipe. Unpleasant things happened to those who crossed him.

Chilled, she turned to get back into the car.

Kelt retraced their path, turning off over a cattle grid when they reached the drive to the homestead. More great trees shaded them, deciduous ones with fresh green foliage. Amongst them she recognised a flame tree, and a pang of homesickness tore through her, so painful she bit her lip and turned her head away. On Moraze the flame trees bloomed like a cloak of fire across the island…

You'll never see Moraze again, she reminded herself starkly.

Kelt's fingers tightened on the wheel. The sheen of moisture in her great green eyes struck at something fundamental in him. Just what the hell was going on inside that black head with its gleaming fiery highlights?

Probably nothing more than a lack of control due to her prolonged illness.

Yet behind Hannah Court's cool, serene facade he sensed something stronger, more deeply emotional than a physical weakness, and had to repress an urgent desire to tell her that whatever her problems, he'd probably be able to help.

This fierce urge to protect was something new, and he distrusted it. Because he avoided breaking hearts, he'd always made sure his lovers had been capable of looking after themselves.

Damn it, he didn't want to lust after a woman who was here to recuperate from a severe bout of tropical fever. So it was infuriating that he couldn't prise the image of Hannah, sleek and desirable in the hot, tropical night, from his mind. He felt like some lecherous voyeur.

Abruptly he asked, 'How long have you been driving?'

Her brows lifted, but she answered mildly enough. 'Since I was sixteen.'

For some reason—one he wasn't prepared to examine— her dismissive tone exasperated Kelt. 'And do you have an international licence?'

'Yes.'

He braked as they came up to the portico of his home. 'I'll lend you a vehicle, but you'd better read New Zealand's road rules before you take it out.'

She gave him a startled glance. 'That's very kind of you, but—'

'That way you'll be independent,' he said coolly.

Hani chided herself for feeling deflated. Naturally he wouldn't want a total stranger relying on him for transport. Yet her pride baulked at accepting the use of a car.

'Are you sure? I mean—you don't know anything about me. And lending me a car isn't necessary—'

'I've lent the same car to every other teacher who's stayed at the bach, and so far it hasn't had a scratch.' His tone was amused yet definite. 'If I thought you'd break the mould I wouldn't be offering.'

'I—well, thank you very much.' It didn't seem enough, but all she could think of was to repeat lamely, 'It's very kind of you.'

The vehicle stopped. The warm light of the westering sun emphasised the classical framework of his face as he turned to her. In a voice that gave nothing away, he said, 'Welcome to my home,' before opening the door and getting out.

Awkwardly she unclipped herself and scrambled free, wondering why she'd been so affected by the unsmiling look that accompanied his conventional words.

Cool it, she commanded herself; stop seeing things that don't exist. As with the offer of a car, he wasn't being *personal*. No doubt he said exactly the same words to everyone who came to his house for the first time. She had to stop foolishly seeking hidden meanings in every steel-blue glance, every alteration of tone in the deep voice.

Farming, she decided with a slight shock while she absorbed the full extent of the house, must have been exceedingly profitable during the first quarter of the twentieth century when this was built. The big wooden building had been designed in an Arts and Crafts style that fitted seamlessly into the ageless, almost primeval land and seascape.

Kelt showed no sign of pride when he escorted her to the door and opened it. Did he take it for granted—as she, in her self-centred youth, had viewed the *castello*, her family home in Moraze?

Trying not to stare around like a tourist, she said, 'This is very beautiful.'

'Thank you,' he responded gravely.

Feeling foolish and gushing, she asked, 'Have you lived here all your life?'

He didn't look at her. 'No.' After a pause so slight she barely noticed he went on, 'My mother wasn't a New Zealander, and I spent quite a lot of time in her country. However, this is my home.'

Another door opened further down, and a middle-aged man came through—her driver from the airport, carrying a large fish in a flax basket. He stopped abruptly.

Absurdly cheered by a familiar face, Hani smiled at him, and said, 'Hello, Mr Wellington. How nice to see you again.'

'Nice to see you again too, Miss Court,' he responded courteously, adding, 'And my name is Arthur.'

Kelt said, 'Hannah thought you owned Kiwinui.'

The older man looked a little taken aback. 'There's only one master here, Miss Court.' His tone indicated she just might have committed sacrilege. He indicated the basket and said, 'I hope you like fish.'

Trying to ease the tension that knotted her nerves, she told him, 'I love it.'

'Good.' He beamed at her. 'This is snapper, freshly caught with my own fair hands today. But when you come next time I'll make sure we have beef—I know it can be difficult to get good beef in some of the smaller islands in the Pacific Ocean.'

'It is, and I'll enjoy it enormously.' Not that she planned to come again...

He nodded and disappeared through another door, presumably into the kitchen.

Kelt indicated a door further down the hall. 'This way.'

The room he took her into opened out onto a terrace; the sun had almost sunk beneath the ranges and the clouds were edged with gold and vivid raspberry and ruby highlights. Hani looked around her, insensibly relaxing in the gracious room, one wall a bank of French windows that opened out onto a terrace. Wide stone steps led down to a lawn surrounded by shrub and flower borders that blended into taller trees.

'Oh, your garden is magnificent.' She gazed across the expanse of stone flagging and took a deep breath, relishing the fresh, summery scent of new-mown grass. Nothing could have been a greater contrast to the school, set in a landscape scarred by its huge mine.

Kelt must have picked up on her thoughts. 'A little different from Tukuulu.'

'A lot different.' This was just an ordinary social occasion, so behave like a normal person, she told herself.

Her appreciative smile faded a little when she met his hooded gaze, but she kept it pinned to her lips. 'Unfortunately the mine is Tukuulu's only source of income.'

'It doesn't look as though its owners care much about their neighbours,' he said austerely.

'I suppose you can't blame them, but—well, most of the mine-workers' children go to the school. You'd think they'd give it some support. That's the problem with big conglomerates owned by people from overseas who have no personal interest in the people they're employing.'

She'd spoken a little heatedly, and he sent her another keen look. Curiosity drove her to ask, 'Was it the first time you'd been to Tukuulu?'

'Yes. Your principal's been suggesting a visit to me for years but it's never been convenient before.'

Hani found it hard to imagine what Kelt had in common with the slightly older man who'd devoted his life to the school he ran on a shoestring.

He went on, 'He needs help, of course, and he'll probably get it. He's an expert at arm-twisting.'

That might be so, but Kelt didn't seem a man who'd yield to persuasion if he didn't want to. 'It's just as well he is,' she said crisply. 'The Tukuuluan government is pushed for money, so the school doesn't get much from them.'

Nodding, Kelt asked, 'Can I get you a drink? Wine? Something a little stronger? Or without alcohol?'

'Wine, thank you, if you have a light white.'

The wine he poured for her had a faint golden tinge, and the flavour was intense—a sensation-burst of freshness that almost persuaded her she was drinking champagne.

In spite of—or perhaps *because* of, she thought mordantly—being so acutely aware of him, she enjoyed Kelt's company. It was stimulating to match his incisive conversation, and a little to her surprise she discovered was he had a sense of humour. The half-hour or so before the meal went quickly.

Yet she had the feeling she was being tested, that for him the innocuous conversation was motivated by something more than social politeness. His hard eyes were always hooded, and she found herself weighing her words before she spoke.

That was worrying; she'd spent the past six years polishing a rather shallow, cheerful teacher persona that seemed to convince everyone she'd met.

Except this man. This man she was fiercely, *mindlessly* attracted to.

So, what was new? She'd felt lust before, and it had taken her into degradation and a never-ending fear that still kept her a prisoner in hiding.

And although there seemed to be a vast difference between her response to Felipe and her host for the evening, it was still lust. Better by far to ignore it—to pretend that she wasn't affected a bit by Kelt, that she didn't notice every tiny thing about him from the boldly arrogant lines of his profile to the easy grace of his movements. Even the sight of his lean, tanned hands on the white tablecloth over dinner sent shuddery little stabs of excitement through her.

Forget that night in Tukuulu. A cold shiver tightened her skin when she thought of what Felipe would do in the same situation. He'd take full advantage of her helplessness and vulnerability.

Kelt hadn't. And she had to respect him for that.

Dinner was served in a conservatory. Intoxicating perfume from the clusters of soft, creamy-pink flowers on a potted frangipani drifted through the room; Hani had always loved the fragrance, but here it seemed imbued with sensuous overtones she'd never noticed before.

But then, everything seemed suddenly more…more *more*, she thought, half-terrified at such foolishness. Colours seemed more luxurious, the food tasted sublime, and light gleamed off the glass and silverware with greater intensity. Just the sound of Kelt's voice produced a blooming of inner heat, a kind of nervous anticipation mixed with an excitement.

'Are you cold?' he asked.

'Not at all.'

Leaning back in his chair, he surveyed her through slightly narrowed eyes. 'You shivered.'

He saw too much. She said stiffly, 'It's nothing. Just someone walking over my grave.'

To her astonishment he leaned forward and covered her hand. His was large and warm and relentless; when shock jerked her backwards his fingers closed around hers, holding her still.

'You *are* cold,' he said, those eyes narrowing further so that he was watching her through a screen of long black lashes.

Apprehension froze her into stillness. But he wasn't like Felipe, and his touch didn't repel her…

She swallowed and said in a constricted voice, 'I'm warm enough, thank you. Let me go.'

Although he released his grip his hard gaze didn't leave her face. 'I'll turn on some heat.'

Her eyes widened. However, one glance at his face told her there was no double meaning to his words.

'I don't need it. I'm perfectly comfortable,' she said curtly, her brows drawing together as she sent him a level glance that should have convinced him.

His brows drew together and he got to his feet. 'I'll be back in a moment.'

Before she could voice an objection he left the room.

Hani swallowed again. He was the most infuriatingly autocratic man—and she didn't want him watching her so closely that he noticed something as inconspicuous as the shiver that had started this. Some men were predators, hunters by nature, and although Kelt didn't show any signs of that, neither had Felipe at first.

Thrusting the vile memories back into the dark cupboard in her brain where she hid them, Hani waited tensely for Kelt to come back.

CHAPTER FOUR

THE wrap Kelt brought into the conservatory matched the intense blue of lapis lazuli, and when he dropped it around Hani's shoulders it settled like a warm, light cloud. 'My cousin left it behind the last time she was here,' he said without moving. 'She won't mind you wearing it—she's the most generous person I know.'

Horrified by something that felt treacherously like a spark of jealousy, Hani said, 'I'll write her a note to thank her for the use of it.' Hairs lifted on the back of her neck, and she had to fight back an instinct to turn around and look up into his face.

'No need,' he said casually, walking away to sit down again. 'I'll tell her you were duly appreciative.'

Hani picked up her knife and fork and applied herself to the food on her plate, exasperated to find that the warmth of the pashmina was very welcome.

'Does Arthur cook all your meals?' she asked into the silence.

'He deals with dinner,' Kelt told her. 'I forage for myself when it comes to lunch and breakfast. As well as supervising the housekeeping and cooking, he likes to garden, and—as you discovered—he's a great fisherman.'

'He's a brilliant cook. This meal is superb.'

'Good. You need feeding up.'

Startled, she said forthrightly, 'That's hardly tactful.'

His answering smile was a masterpiece of irony. 'I'm not noted for my tact. And clearly you've lost weight while you've been ill.'

'I'm feeling much better,' she said defensively.

'You're still looking fragile. When I agreed that you could stay at the bach I was told the chances of you having another attack were pretty remote. However, you still have that delicate look. I'd prefer you to stay here rather than at the bach.'

He spoke as though he had the right to demand her agreement.

Hani's head came up and she stared incredulously at him. Fortunately her days of obeying men were over.

Fighting back a bewildering mixture of emotions—outrage at his high-handedness mingled with an odd warmth because he seemed to care about her welfare—she said evenly, 'That won't be necessary. I carry my medication with me all the time now, so any attack will be stopped before it has time to start.'

Although his expression didn't alter, she sensed a hardening in his attitude. 'Do you intend to stay inside the bach all the time?'

'Of course not, but I won't stray too far from it either.'

He said bluntly, 'No further than a hundred metres? Because that's about how far you were from the party when I found you, and by then you were incapable of moving. If no one had come along you'd have collapsed under the coconut palm you were clinging to.'

Her colour flared, but her eyes stayed steady when they met his. 'The circumstances were unusual.'

'In what way?' Clearly he didn't believe her.

'I knew during the speeches that I was getting an attack, but I stayed because in Tukuulu leaving while someone is making a speech is a huge insult.'

'Your cultural awareness does you credit.' The sardonic inflection in his tone flicked her on the raw. 'You must have realised you were letting yourself in for an attack of fever.'

'It's important to the Tukuuluans,' she retorted.

'Why didn't you get someone to help you to your cottage and make sure you got some medication into you?'

Lamely she admitted, 'I wasn't thinking straight by then. It won't happen again. Normally I just take medication and go to bed. When I wake up I'm fine.'

Heat burned across her cheekbones at the memory of waking and realising he'd changed her clothes. She didn't dare look at him in case he realised what she was thinking—and suspect that occasionally she fantasised guiltily about his hands on her skin, his gaze on her body...

He asked, 'What happens if you delay taking the medication?'

'I collapse, but the fever eventually passes,' she told him reluctantly.

'How long does that take?'

She parried his critical gaze with a level one of her own. Sorely tempted to gloss over the truth, she admitted, 'Quite some time.'

'You're being evasive.'

Her indignant glance made no impression on him. Meeting the burnished sheen of his gaze, she said belligerently, 'The first time I was in bed for almost a week.'

'How soon after the first symptoms do you need to take the drug?'

'The sooner the better.'

'How long, Hannah?'

Hani suspected that he'd continue interrogating her until she told him everything out of sheer exhaustion.

'Oh, about ten, fifteen minutes,' she flashed. 'But you needn't worry. I'm not going to collapse on the beach because—as I told you a few seconds ago—I take my medication with me all the time.'

He frowned. 'It's not good enough. You'd be much better off here where someone can keep an eye on you.'

For years Hani had managed to contain her naturally quick temper, but Kelt's ultimatum set a fuse to it. 'Have you any idea how arrogant you sound?' she demanded before she could bite the words back. 'You have no right—no right at all—to impose conditions on me. I can look after myself.'

'I might believe that if I hadn't *seen* the way you look after yourself,' he countered, startled by a swift stir of sensual appetite.

That serene façade she presented to the world was a sham, a mask to hide a much more animated personality. Her face was made for emotion—for laughter, for anger that came and went like summer lightning…for tenderness.

How would she look in the throes of passion?

His body responded with the now familiar need, hungry and reckless as wildfire. With lethal determination he reined it in, watching with half-closed eyes while she regained enough control to impose a rigid restraint over those mobile features. It was like watching a light being extinguished.

'All right,' she said shortly, 'I actually started to go, but the elders came in before I could. But I do not need cosseting or constant watching or checking. Think about it—*you'd* hate it. Why should I be any different?'

He lifted his brows, but said bluntly, 'I accept that, but I'd be a lot happier if you'd check in each day—say, in the evening.'

Would she recognise the classical negotiation gambit—make an outrageous demand, then offer a compromise? Kelt watched her face, almost sombre as she hesitated. What was she thinking?

Looking up with open challenge in those sultry eyes she said, 'And if I won't?'

He surveyed the lovely face opposite him, her sensuous mouth tightly controlled, and a rounded little chin held at an obstinate angle.

And she called *him* arrogant, he thought with hard amusement. Who exactly was she, and why was her crystalline English accent occasionally gentled by a soft slurring that somehow managed to sound piercingly erotic?

A woman of mystery in many ways—and obviously a fiercely independent one. He'd asked the principal about her background, and been surprised at how little his friend knew. She'd simply appeared one day at the school, offering to help in any way she could.

'Usually people who wash up in Tukuulu are on the run from something,' his friend had told him. 'Alcohol or drugs or the law or the media, or a romantic break-up that's convinced them their life is ruined. They think they can leave it all behind them and make a new start in the tropics, not realising that until they've faced it, everyone carries their past like a burden. People like that are no use to us.'

'But Hannah Court is.'

'Yes, we were lucky. She's great with the children. When we realised she had a talent for teaching she took every extramural course she could, and now she's a fully qualified infant teacher. Better still, she's got a small income from somewhere, so she can manage on the pittance we pay.'

'What nationality is she?'

His friend had looked a little self-conscious. 'I shouldn't be discussing her with you, but I assume she's English.'

'And you know nothing of her past or her circumstances?'

'She never speaks of them.'

'So she's a fugitive too.'

That was greeted by a shrug. 'Possibly. But she's not encumbered by any obvious baggage. And she's kept a low profile—no love affairs, no breakdowns, no binges. What matters to us is that she fits really well into the island culture and she's turned into a good, conscientious teacher.'

Naturally that was all that mattered to the principal of a struggling school in the tropics, Kelt thought dryly now. But it seemed a wicked waste for any woman as young and vibrant as Hannah Court to hide away from the world. No love affairs didn't, of course, mean she wasn't running from one that had gone wrong. But after six years surely she'd have got over such an experience.

That leashed awareness in Kelt stirred into life again.

He frowned, wondering why she intrigued him so much. Partly it was masculine interest—even with the pallor of illness she was lovely, her too slender body alluringly curved, and from the way she'd curled into him he suspected she was no inexperienced virgin. And although he'd learned to control his urges he had a normal man's needs and hunger.

But this wasn't purely sexual.

From the first, even when he'd been sure she was either drunk or stoned, he'd felt intensely protective towards her. What the hell was she hiding from?

She'd blocked his every probe, either changing the subject or simply ignoring his questions, so she was hiding *something*—and that something had to be pretty shattering.

Perhaps he should just let it go, but when he looked at her he sensed a life wasted, a sorrow so deep she couldn't bear to face it.

In Kelt's experience, the best thing to do with pain was meet it head-on, accept it and deal with it, and then move on.

Kelt made up his mind. He'd use kidnapping as a last resort if she refused to compromise. 'If you won't agree to check in, I'll contact your principal.'

Her lovely face set into lines of mutiny. Common sense—and a strong sense of self-preservation—warned him that Hannah Court's past wasn't his business, and that he'd be foolish to tangle himself in her affairs. But he wasn't going to let her retreat to the bach without that promise.

Before she could say anything, he went on, 'And I want your word that you'll let me or Arthur know if you feel another attack coming on.'

Head held high, she met his steady gaze with cold composure. 'If it makes you feel happier I'll let someone know. And I'll ring the homestead every evening.' She added sweetly, 'Anything to please the man who is letting me live in his bach rent-free.'

Hani knew she sounded ungracious, but being backed into a corner made her feel wildly resentful. She'd feared Felipe's brutal domination, but at that age she'd been so sheltered she'd had no way of dealing with it. And then he'd made sure she couldn't escape it.

To be faced now with another dictatorial man angered her more than it frightened her—and that, she conceded reluctantly, was a relief.

'That's not an issue,' Kelt said shortly. 'Certainly not a personal one.'

'You can't actually stop me being grateful,' she snapped, 'but I won't bore you with it.'

'I don't want your damned gratitude!'

She opened her mouth to hurl an injudicious reply, then abruptly closed it before her intemperate words could burst forth. 'How did you do that? I never lose my temper!'

He stared at her, then gave a slow, wicked smile that sizzled through her defences, reducing her to silence.

But his tone was ironic when he said, 'Neither do I. As for how I managed to make you lose yours—according to my brother, a cousin and my grandmother,' he drawled, 'I suffer from a power complex.'

'They know you well.' She didn't try to hide the caustic note in her voice.

Kelt's raised eyebrow signified his understanding of her reluctance, but he appeared to take her surrender at face value, saying coolly, 'Thank you. I'll warn Arthur. He has a first-aid certificate and so do I.'

Irritated again, she blurted, 'I won't *need* first aid—well, not unless I fall off a cliff. I'm perfectly capable of looking after myself.'

There was a moment's silence until he said with silky clarity, 'I hope you don't intend to renege. I really don't like people who lie.'

Then he'd *hate* her—her whole life was built on lies. She said unevenly, 'You're just going to have to trust me.'

He held her gaze, then nodded and stretched out his hand. 'So shake on it.'

She should be getting accustomed to the way his touch burned through her, but it seemed to be getting more and more potent.

Fighting a sensuous weakness as they shook hands, she managed to produce something that resembled a smile. 'I'm sorry, I'm being dull company, but I have to confess to getting tired very early in the evening.'

As she knew he would, he examined her face with that analytical gaze before getting to his feet. 'Far from dull. In fact, the more I know of you the more interesting I find you,' he said ambiguously, 'but I'll take you home.'

His instant agreement should have pleased her. Instead it made her feel as though she'd been rejected. *Idiot*, she scolded herself fiercely and went to put down the pretty shawl.

Kelt said, 'Keep it on. It will be cool outside now, and you'll need it.'

Arthur saw them out, his face crinkling with restrained pleasure when she said, 'That was a superb meal, thank you.'

'My pleasure, miss,' he said with a half-bow.

Kelt was right; the air was much crisper than it had been before sunset, and Hani had to bite her lips to stop them trembling. Snuggling into the shawl in Kelt's big Range Rover, she realised that if she wanted to be comfortable for the next three months she'd have to buy new clothes.

She fought back a twinge of panic. Her trust fund—a secret between them, her godmother had told her with a wink when she revealed its existence on her seventeenth birthday, because every woman needed money she didn't have to account for— provided her with a small income, but it wasn't enough to stretch to clothes she'd never wear again.

Perhaps there was a secondhand shop in a nearby town.

'What's the matter?' Kelt asked as they went over the cattle grid onto the road that led to the bach.

He must be able to read her like a book. Forcing her brows back into their normal place, she said airily, 'I was just thinking I need new clothes. I know it's summer, but I'm used to tropical heat.'

'There are a couple of quite good boutiques in Kaitake, our service centre,' he told her. 'Unless you need the clothes urgently I'll take you there the day after tomorrow. I'm going there on business, and you can have a look around.'

Boutiques she didn't need—too expensive. 'I could walk—'

'No, it's not the local village—that's Waituna, and it's about five kilometres north, but it's just a small general store and a petrol station. Kaitake is on the coast about twenty minutes' drive away.'

'I see.' After a moment's hesitation she said formally, 'Thank you, that's very kind of you.'

He shrugged. 'You'll find the copy of the road code I promised you in the glove pocket.'

Back at the homestead, Kelt strolled into the kitchen and got himself a glass of water, looking up as Arthur came in through the door that led to his own quarters.

'Tell me, Arthur, what part of the UK does Miss Court come from?'

'She's not English,' Arthur said promptly and decisively.

Kelt lifted an enquiring eyebrow. 'She sounds very English.'

'Not to me. She speaks it superbly, but I'd wager quite a lot of money that English is not her first language.' He frowned and said slowly, 'In fact, I think I detect hints of a Creole heritage.'

'Caribbean?' Interest quickened through Kelt. He set the glass down on the bench.

'Could be,' Arthur said slowly, frowning, 'but I doubt it. I just don't know—but I'm certain she's not English.'

During the night Hani woke from a deep, deep sleep and heard rain quietly falling onto the roof, and in the morning everything outside glittered in the sunlight as though dusted with diamonds.

The water in the bay was a little discoloured, and when she went for a walk after breakfast she discovered one side of the small stream had fallen in, the clay damming the stream so that it backed up and was already oozing up to the farm road.

Back at the bach she rang through to the homestead. And was *not*, she told herself stoutly, disappointed when Arthur answered.

'Right, I'll make sure the farm manager hears about it,' he said. 'Thank you very much for reporting it, Miss Court.'

Later in the day she walked back along the road and came upon someone clearing the stream. One of the huge trees hung over the water there, its leaves sifting the sunlight so that it fell in dapples of golden light across the man in the water.

Kelt, she thought, her heart soaring exultantly.

He'd taken off his shirt, and the sun played across the powerful muscles of his bronze shoulders and back. An urgent heat flamed in the pit of her stomach as her eyes lingered on each powerful thrust of his arms as when he dug through the temporary dam with fluid strength, tossing shovelfuls of clay back up the bank.

Her response shocked her—a wild rush of adrenalin, of heady anticipation, a swift, unspoken recognition in the very deepest levels of her heart and mind.

As if her passionate claiming had somehow sent out subliminal signals, Kelt looked up. His tanned face showed a flash of white as he smiled, but his gaze was coolly assessing.

Without altering the steady, smooth rhythm of his shovelling, he said, 'Good morning.'

'Good morning,' Hani replied sedately, hoping her voice sounded as impersonal as his. Triumphantly she fished in her pocket and held out a container of pill capsules.

His smile reappeared. 'Good girl.'

Reaching up to a low branch, he used it to swing himself up onto the bank. With a smile that turned her sizzling appreciation into a flame, pure and keen and intense, he said, 'And thanks for being a good citizen and reporting the blockage in the creek.'

'It looked as though it might wash out the road.' Hani felt shy and foolish, the urgent instructions of her mind at war with the eager pleading of her body.

'It could have.' He turned and surveyed his handiwork. He'd opened enough of a breach for the discoloured water to start flowing sluggishly out onto the beach. 'Once I took over Kiwinui I started a programme of fencing the gullies and riversides off from stock and planting them up with native plants. This land erodes badly if it's not cared for, and the farm manager who ran it when I was under age cared more for production than for conservation.' He shrugged. 'He was a man of his time.'

Hani nodded. After her father's death Rafiq had introduced a variety of conservation measures to Moraze, somewhat to the astonishment and dismay of many of his subjects. 'How do you stop the bank from eroding?'

He indicated a tray of small plants on the tray of a small truck. 'We run a nursery where we grow seeds from the native plants on the station. Our native flax loves wet feet, and is extremely good at holding up banks. As well, this summer the road to the bach is being moved further up the hill so that it's not running across a natural wetlands area.'

'Are you going to plant those little seedlings?' she asked.

'Once I've finished clearing this away, yes.'

Impetuously Hani said, 'I'll help.'

His brows shot up. 'You'll get dirty.'

She shrugged. 'So? I've been dirty before, and as far as I know it all washed off.'

'You haven't got gumboots.'

'I can go barefoot,' she told him, exasperated by his obvious image of her as a useless creature. She sat down and slid her feet out of her elderly sneakers, aware that Kelt stood and watched her.

When she stood up again he said, 'Do you know how to plant things?'

'I'm not an expert,' she said, sending him a look that held more challenge than was probably wise, 'but if you tell me what you want me to do and where the plants should go, I'm sure I can cope.'

Still with that infuriating air of amusement he did, digging holes for the plants, then going back to clean up the sides of the stream while she planted, patting the earth around each little flax bush with care.

They didn't talk much, although she learned that in this part of New Zealand there were no streams, only creeks. And although she was still acutely, heatedly aware of him, she found the silence and the work oddly companionable, even soothing.

Well, soothing if she kept her eyes on the plants and didn't let them stray to Kelt, she thought mordantly, lowering her lashes after a peek at the smooth sheen of his skin when he threw another shovelful of clay up onto the bank.

'There,' she said when she'd finished.

Two long strides brought him up beside her. 'Well done.' He paused, and into the silence fell a sweet, echoing peal of birdsong. 'A tui,' he told her laconically, pointing out a black bird, sheened with green and bronze and with a bobble of white feathers at the throat. 'They visit the flax flowers to get nectar.'

She eyed the tall, candelabra-like stalks that held wine-coloured flowers. The bird sank its beak into the throat of another one, then climbed to the top of the stalk and, as if in thanks, lifted its head and sang again, its notes pealing out like the chime of small silver bells into the warm, sea-scented air.

Sheer delight prompted Hani to murmur, 'It's just—so beautiful here.'

There was another silence before he said, 'Indeed it is.'

Something in his tone made her glance up.

He was looking at her, not at the tui, and deep inside her desire burned away the warnings of her mind so that they crumbled into ashes. Hani forgot she had muddy hands and feet; she'd wiped sweat off her face and there was probably mud there too.

Under his hooded scrutiny her lips and throat went dry. Tension arced between them like lightning.

Get out of here, she thought frantically, *before you do something stupid, like tilt your head towards him*. She fought back an imperative desire to do just that and find out once and for all what Kelt's kiss would feel like.

As though he sensed her desperate effort to keep calm, she saw him impose control, his eyes darken, and the dangerous moment passed.

Yet he'd wanted her…

Nothing, she thought with a flash of pure rapture, could ever take that away. But far more wondrous was that *she* wanted *him*. After six years of being sure Felipe had killed that part of her, she felt passion and desire again.

Kelt said, 'And it will be even more beautiful when these plants grow. Thank you. Kiwinui will always have some part of you here.'

Unexpectedly touched by the thought, she said, 'I enjoyed doing it.'

'I just hope it doesn't make you feel worse. Remember, any shiver, anything that worries you, ring the homestead.' He glanced at his watch. 'I'm afraid I have to go—I'm expecting a call from overseas.'

Back at the bach she told herself she should be grateful to that unknown person who was calling him long-distance.

Falling in lust with Kelt was one thing, but her headstrong desire to know him far more intimately was a much more dangerous development.

CHAPTER FIVE

WHEN she rang that night, Arthur answered again. He enquired after her health, said Kelt had told him she'd helped plant the flax and hoped her hard work hadn't made her condition worse.

'No, I'm very well, thank you,' she replied politely. After she'd rung off she thought sombrely that Kelt was probably out with some local beauty.

Trying to laugh herself out of that foolish mood didn't work, so she went to bed and dreamed of him, only to wake cross and crumpled in the big bed the next morning.

'Enough,' she told her reflection severely as she applied moisturiser. 'OK, so you think he's gorgeous. No, let's be embarrassingly honest here—you want to go to bed with him. Very, very much.'

And even more since she'd seen him clearing the stream—*creek*, she amended hurriedly—shirtless, his bronzed torso exposed in lethal power and forceful energy.

Her breath caught in her throat. Hurriedly she finished the rest of her morning regime, telling herself sternly, 'But even if he feels the same way, there's absolutely no future for this. In three months' time you're going back to Tukuulu, where you're safe.'

And she'd never be able to forge any sort of future with him—or any man, not so long as Felipe was alive.

But Felipe hadn't found her, she thought, stopping and staring sightlessly into the mirror. And here, in New Zealand, she felt just as safe as she had in Tukuulu.

Perhaps there was a chance...

'Forget it!' she said curtly. 'It's not going to happen, not now, not ever.'

So Kelt had moments when he wanted her. Big deal; for most men that meant very little. If she allowed herself to surrender to the erotic charge between them, he'd probably enjoy an affair, then wave her goodbye at that tiny airport without anything more than mild regret.

Or—even more cringe-making—perhaps he hadn't liked what he'd seen when he'd taken off her wet dress and slipped the shift over her head...

Whatever, an affair was out! So when he arrived in a few minutes she'd be cool and dismissive and completely ignore the chemistry between them.

Dead on time he drove down the track. He was already out of the vehicle when Hani walked out to meet him, her heartbeat racing into an erratic tattoo. Lean and lithe and very big, he surveyed her with an intimidating scrutiny for several seconds before his smile not only melted her bones but also set her wayward pulse off into the stratosphere.

Dizzily she said, 'Good morning,' in her most guarded voice.

Until he'd smiled at her she'd been very aware that this day was considerably cooler than the previous one. Now however, she felt almost feverish.

His gaze hardened. 'You're looking a bit tired.'

'I'm fine,' she said quickly, dismissively.

A glance at the sedan he'd driven made her fight back a

gurgle of laughter. He so did *not* look like that four-cylinder, family-style vehicle! No, he should be driving something wickedly male and dangerous…

So what did it mean that he thought this sedate vehicle suitable for her?

Nothing, she reminded herself staunchly; don't go reading symbolism into everything he does. He was extremely kind to offer what was probably his only spare vehicle; that it happened to be a reliable, boring car was all to the good!

Now, if only she could satisfy him that the past few hours spent devouring the contents of the road code had turned her into a fit driver for New Zealand roads.

'Hop behind the wheel,' Kelt said, making it sound rather too much of an order.

With a touch of asperity Hani said, 'Thank you,' and climbed into the car. Once there, she spent time familiarising herself with the instrument panel.

Kelt got in beside her, immediately sucking all of the air out of the interior.

'Ah, an automatic,' she said, memories of being taught to drive flooding her. 'My brother used to say…'

Appalled, she bit back the rest of the comment, hoping desperately that he hadn't heard her.

Not a chance.

'Your brother used to say—?'

Bending forward, she hid her face by groping for the lever that moved the seat. 'That they're for old ladies of both sexes.'

'I wonder if he'd feel the same once he'd driven on some of Northland's roads,' Kelt said dryly.

'Perhaps not.' Her shaking fingers closed on the lever, but

she was so tense she misjudged the effort needed, and the seat jerked forward. However, the several moments spent adjusting it to her liking gave her precious time to compose herself.

Straightening, she said in her most cheerful tone, 'That's better—I can reach the pedals now. Not everybody has such long legs as you.'

'I wouldn't call yours short.'

An equivocal note beneath the amused words brought colour to her cheeks, but at least she'd diverted the conversation away from Rafiq. 'They certainly aren't in the same league as yours,' she said brightly, and put the car into gear.

On Tukuulu she'd sometimes driven the school's elderly four-wheel-drive, wrestling with gears that stuck, barely functioning brakes and an engine that had to be coaxed, so this well-maintained car was no problem. Nevertheless she drove cautiously, keeping the speed down; the farm road might also be well-maintained, but it wasn't sealed, and the gravel surface was a challenge.

Showing an unexpected understanding, Kelt stayed silent while she found her own way around the instruments and got the feel of the vehicle. By the time she'd taken them past the cluster of workers' cottages and big sheds, she was feeling quite at home behind the wheel, but at the junction with the sealed road she braked, and looked sideways at Kelt.

Eyes half-hidden by thick lashes, he said coolly, 'You're an excellent driver, as I'm sure you know. Your brother taught you well.'

Hoping he didn't notice the sudden whiteness of her knuckles, she loosened her grip on the wheel. 'Do you want to take over now?'

'No. There's not another car in sight. The speed limit's a hundred kilometres an hour.'

'Not on this road, surely,' she muttered, loosening her hold on the wheel to steer out.

'Officially yes, but you're right—most of the time it's safer to stick to eighty. Some of the corners aren't well-cambered.'

Oddly enough, his presence beside her lent Hani confidence. There wasn't much traffic, although she found the frequent huge trucks intimidating.

'It's the main highway north,' he said when she voiced her surprise at the number. 'The railway doesn't come this far, so everything is transported by truck.'

One day, she thought, she'd like to be a passenger and really check out the countryside. She'd seen nothing on that night drive from the airport with Arthur, and her occasional sideways glance revealed a landscape of dramatically bold hills and lush valleys.

'Take the left turn at the next intersection,' Kelt instructed after a few minutes.

It delivered them to a small town situated on an estuary. Shaded by palms and bright with flowers and subtropical vegetation, it looked prosperous and charming. Not even the mangroves that clogged the riverbank could give it a sinister air.

'Kaitake,' Kelt told her. 'Turn right here and then a left into the car park.'

He waited until she'd switched off the engine before saying, 'I'll meet you here at twelve-thirty. That should give you time to have a good look at several of the boutiques before I buy you lunch.'

'You don't have to buy me lunch,' she protested, firmly squelching a forbidden spurt of pleasure and anticipation.

'You drove me here,' he said, not giving an inch. 'One good turn deserves another.'

He stopped any further objection by removing himself

from the car and coming around to open her door. Baulked, Hani grabbed her bag and got out, taking a deep breath.

'That's not so. I'd like to buy you lunch,' she said crisply, looking up into his hard, handsome face.

Bad move; once more her pulses ratcheted up and that odd weakness softened her bones. She had to suck in a rapid breath and steady her voice before she could go on. 'You're lending me the car and, although lunch seems a pretty poor recompense for your kindness, it's the least I can do.'

'The car would be idle if you weren't using it. Are you always so fiercely independent?'

Independence kept her safe. She shrugged, her mouth tightening. 'Yes,' she said in a deliberately offhanded voice.

That disbelieving brow lifted. 'Very well, you can buy me lunch. By now you must know I have a hearty appetite.'

And possibly not just for food... The sexy little thought popped into her head as she forced herself to say airily, 'That's no problem.'

Of course he ate well—he was a big man—but he also exuded a prowling sensuality that probably meant he was an extremely good lover as well.

And no doubt there were plenty of women who responded to that magnetic, masculine charisma. Plenty of women had wanted to go to bed with Felipe—a situation he used with cynical disregard for them. Would Kelt?

She tried to relax her tight muscles. Forget Felipe; it had been sheer bad luck—and her own trusting foolishness—that the first man she'd fallen for had been a career criminal who'd seen her as a means to an end.

'Is something the matter?'

Kelt's voice, forceful and uncompromising, jolted her back to the present.

'I—no, no, of course not,' she said quickly and, hoping to deflect his attention, she went on with a brightness she hoped didn't sound too brittle, 'Nothing could possibly be wrong— I'm about to buy some clothes!'

His unyielding blue gaze held hers a second longer before his mouth curved into a smile that sent a sizzle of excitement through her, one that burned away all her sensible decisions and left her open and exposed to this wildfire hunger, this sensuous craving that was trying to take her over.

He startled her by taking her elbow. At the touch of his hand—strong and purposeful—Hani tensed. Dry-mouthed, she sent him an anxious glance, only relaxing when she saw his calm expression. Swallowing, she concentrated on putting her feet down precisely, every cell in her body taut and alert.

Yet in spite of his closeness and that light grip on her elbow, no panic kicked beneath her ribs; in fact, she thought worriedly, she felt oddly protected and safe.

And that was really, really dangerous.

Talk! she commanded herself.

Aloud she said brightly, 'I didn't expect to see verandas out over the streets in New Zealand. It gives the place a very tropical look.'

'Our sun's not as hot as it is in the tropics, but we live beneath a hole in the ozone layer,' Kelt told her, 'and it can rain just as heavily here as it does there.'

'It's so…fresh.'

'If you're comparing it to Tukuulu, industrial areas aren't noted for their beauty and freshness,' he observed on a dry note.

Several passers-by greeted him, their gazes coming inevitably to rest on her. She felt too conspicuous, their interest setting her nerves on edge. Kelt's compelling combination of raw male charisma and formidable authority would always attract attention, she thought with a hint of panic. So she wouldn't come here again with him.

Uncannily detecting her unease, he glanced down at her. 'What is it?'

Hani said the first thing that came into her mind. 'You promised me boutiques. I can't see any here.'

'There's one about a hundred metres from here, and another just around the corner.' That far too perceptive gaze swept her face. 'You're sure you're all right?'

'I'm fine,' she said, and tried out her best smile, sweetly persuasive.

It failed entirely; if anything, his eyes hardened and his voice turned caustic. 'Stop playing games with me.'

'I will when you stop being so—so mother-hennish,' she retorted, chagrined because he'd seen through her so easily. 'If it helps you to stop fussing, I'll agree that the doctor at Tukuulu was right; I did need a holiday in a cooler place. Since I've been here I've been sleeping like a log, and my appetite's come back. And I feel more energetic. I don't need to be watched and monitored and scrutinised as though I'm going to faint any minute.'

His survey didn't soften, but his mouth quirked. 'Is that what I was doing?'

'That's what it felt like,' she said, startled to realise that, as much as his concern irked her, it satisfied something she'd been unaware of—a debilitating need to be cared for. Her colleagues were kind and helpful and friendly, but they had their own lives, their own affairs to worry about. The friendships she'd formed at the school were genuine, but she'd deliberately kept them superficial.

A voice from behind cooed Kelt's name. Hani's heart clamped when she saw the woman who'd caught them up.

Hardly more than a girl, the newcomer was stunning. Hair an artful shade of auburn, her eyes huge and golden-brown in a beautiful, cleverly made-up face, she looked like sunshine and laughter and innocence, her curvy little body emphasised by clothes that hadn't been bought in any small town.

Her radiance made Hani feel old and tired and depraved, her past cutting her off from such exuberant, joyous youthfulness.

'Kelt, you're the tallest man around. I saw you from the other end of the street,' the newcomer said, beaming at him. She turned to Hani, and her smile widened. 'Hello, you must be the new guest in the bach. How are you liking it?'

'Very much, thank you,' Hani said politely.

In a neutral voice Kelt said, 'Hannah, this is my cousin, Rosemary Matthews.'

'Rosie,' Kelt's cousin said with an admonitory gaze at him. She shook hands with vigour, and added cheerfully, 'No one ever calls me Rosemary. And just between you and me, our relationship is more *whanau* than cousin—so distant it doesn't count.' Her smile turned wicked. 'Consider me one of the aspirants for Kelt's hand.'

Hani's social smile turned into a startled laugh. She glanced up at Kelt, who was studying his cousin with a mixture of austerity and amusement, and asked involuntarily, 'One of the aspirants? How many are there?'

'Dozens,' Rosie told her without any sign of embarrassment, 'if not *hundreds*—they come full of hope, and they go away broken-hearted. I spend quite a lot of time patting shoulders and supplying tissues to weeping women who've realised they don't have a chance.' She heaved a theatrical sigh. 'My heart bleeds for them, but I have to be strong so I can plead my own case.'

'Stop teasing,' Kelt said indulgently. 'Hannah might just take you seriously.'

'She seems far too sensible to do that,' Rosie returned, eyes sparkling with impudence. But when she transferred her gaze back to Hani some of the laughter went from her face. 'Have we met before? I seem to know you—and yet I don't think we've been introduced, have we?'

Of all the people to induce that frantic kick of panic beneath Hani's ribs, this sunshiny girl was the last she'd have imagined. She shook her head and steadied her voice to say, 'This is my first visit to New Zealand.'

Kelt said briefly, 'Hannah lives in Tukuulu—in the islands. She's been ill and needs to recuperate in a cooler climate. What are you doing here? I thought you were going to Auckland with your mother.'

She shrugged. 'I decided not to go—she's off to the opera with the new boyfriend, and you know, tubby little tenors angsting in high Cs at shrieking ladies with huge bosoms are *so* not my thing.' She looked from one to the other. 'Are you going to lunch, because if you are can I come too?'

Amused, Hani glanced at Kelt, who was scanning that vivid little face with a certain grimness.

'No,' he said calmly. 'Hannah needs rest, and you are not restful.'

Hani blinked. He sent her a silent, don't-get-mixed-up-in-this warning.

Mournfully Rosie responded, 'I'll take that as a compliment. Of course, I could just keep quiet and enjoy the ambience.'

'Quiet? You?' Kelt asked, his dry tone not quite hiding his affection. 'Go on—catch up with the friend I can see waiting for you outside the café.'

Rosie gave a wounded sigh, rapidly followed by another of those infectious smiles. 'I try so hard to outwit him,' she confided to Hani, 'but he sees through me every time. It's been nice talking to you—we must get together when you feel up to being stimulated! Although quite frankly, I think Kelt is more than enough excitement for any woman, let alone one who's convalescing!'

With a saucy glance at her cousin, she set off down the street, hips swaying seductively, the sun burnishing her superbly cut hair to copper.

Kelt said dryly, 'She's nowhere near so ingenuous as she seems, but there's no harm in her.'

'She's very forthright,' Hani ventured cautiously, adding because her words seemed like criticism, 'but I imagine she's great fun.'

'She has an interesting sense of humour,' he conceded, checking his watch. 'All right, I'll see you back at the car park. Have fun shopping.'

Hani nodded and walked sedately towards the boutique he'd mentioned, wondering whether his cousin would be lying in wait somewhere. However, there wasn't a sign of her anywhere in the busy street. And one glance at the boutique window told her she couldn't afford anything it sold, but in case Kelt was still able to see her she went inside.

She'd been right. The racks were full of clothes she'd love to buy, but not at those prices. Possibly Rosie had bought some of her outfit here after all.

The quick interplay between the cousins and their obvious affection for each other made her sadly envious. Or enviously sad… Rafiq had been her adored big brother, but he was quite a bit older and their relationship had become less close after their parents had died and he'd had to rule Moraze.

Oh, she'd always known he loved her, but there wasn't the easy camaraderie she'd seen between Kelt and Rosie. And those few minutes in their company had shown her another side of the man she found so dangerously interesting; they convinced her that her instinctive trust of him was justified.

After a quick, regretful smile at the saleswoman she left, resigned to the same experience in the next shop. That wasn't so upmarket, but still too expensive.

Finally she tracked down a secondhand shop in one of the back streets, between a pet shop and an internet café.

Ignoring the delectable puppies tumbling around in the window, she hurried inside the charity shop, and to her relief found exactly what she wanted—several light tops, a pair of sleek black trousers in a very fine woollen fabric, a pair of jeans and two merino-wool jerseys, all good chain-store quality.

'Are you going off on holiday to the northern hemisphere?' the woman behind the counter asked as Hani examined herself in the one big mirror in the shop.

Hani said, 'That would be lovely, but no, I've been living in a warmer climate.'

'They could have been made for you,' the woman said, in-specting the well-cut trousers and a feather-soft merino jersey in a soft peach that lent a golden gleam to Hani's skin. 'Look, if you're cold, why don't you wear them away? They've all been washed and dry-cleaned. I'll pack your own clothes in with the other ones you've bought.'

New Zealanders—well, the ones she'd met, Hani thought wryly as she walked out—were a helpful lot. On the street she checked her watch, allowing herself another wistful glance at the puppies before she hurried to the car park.

Kelt was waiting, not impatiently but as though no one had ever been late for him. He turned as she came towards him, and once more she saw that gleam in his eyes, a hooded glitter of appreciation.

Something strange and dramatic happened to her heart;

it seemed to soar within her, and she was filled by breath-less anticipation, as though the world was full of wonderful possibilities.

After a swift scrutiny Kelt said, 'You look stunning.'

'I— Thank you.' Too breathless to go on, she groped for the keys she'd dropped into her bag. 'I'll just put my purchases in the car.'

'Do you want to drive again?'

Keys in hand, she looked up at him, his tanned face angular, his expression controlled. 'Aren't we eating here?'

'There's a very good restaurant in a vineyard not far away.'

Too late now to hope it wasn't expensive. She'd thought they'd eat at a café. Abandoning caution, she said, 'I might as well get as much experience as I can while you're here to ride shotgun. I still haven't quite got my bearings.'

'You don't need anyone to oversee your driving.'

'Thank you,' she said, the warmth of his comment lasting until they reached the vineyard in the hills a few kilometres from town.

'It could almost be some part of Tuscany,' she observed when they were seated on the wide terrace beneath a canopy of hot-pink bougainvillea flowers. It overlooked a small valley filled by a body of water too big to be called a pond, too small for a lake.

Kelt asked idly, 'Have you been there?'

She'd spent a holiday with a school friend in a magnificent villa in the heart of Tuscany. 'I've seen a lot of photographs,' she returned, hating the fact that she'd fudged. Still, she might be implying something that wasn't true, but at least she hadn't come out with a direct lie.

Perhaps something in her tone alerted him, because he sub-jected her to another of those coolly judicial looks. She was prickly with embarrassment when he said, 'A glass of wine?'

'No, thanks.' She gave a rueful little smile. 'I tend to drift off to sleep if I drink in the daytime. Not a good look over the lunch table, or behind the wheel.'

'Not a good look in most places.' A note of reservation in his voice made her wonder whether he was remembering the night she'd collapsed in his arms.

They'd felt so good…

Heat touched her cheeks; she bent her head and applied herself to the menu.

Which, she noted with a sinking heart, had no prices. In her experience that meant the food was astronomically expensive. Well, she'd insisted on paying; no matter how much it cost she'd manage. Thrift was something she'd learned over the past years.

Clearly Kelt was well-known; the woman who'd shown them to their table had greeted him with a warm smile and by his first name. She was too professional to make her curiosity about Hani obvious.

Kelt ordered a beer for himself and freshly squeezed lime juice with soda for her, before saying, 'It looks as though you had a satisfactory morning shopping for clothes.'

'Thank you,' she said politely, adding, 'Is Rosie the cousin who owns that shawl?'

'Yes.' A strand of golden sunlight probed through the leafy canopy over the terrace, summoning a lick of fire from his hair.

A fierce, sweet sensation burst through her, startling her with its intensity. After her treatment by Felipe she'd never thought to experience desire again—in fact, she'd welcomed her total lack of interest in the opposite sex because it kept her safe.

But this was desire as she'd never known it—a cell-deep hunger that pierced her with helpless delight. And with fear. She didn't dare fall in love again.

But she could perhaps exorcise Felipe's malign influence over her life by—

By what? An affair…

Shocked yet fascinated by this outrageous thought, she said in her most sedate tone, 'Then I must write her that note to thank her.'

'Oh, you'll see her again. She's as curious as a cat. In a few days she'll be down at the bach trying to lure you out of your solitude.'

Rosie was a nice, neutral topic. Relieved, Hani seized on it. 'What does she do? Is she at university?'

'Gap year,' he said succinctly. 'Her mother decided she was too immature to be let loose on an unsuspecting world, so she's staying at home.'

Something in his voice made her say, 'You don't approve.'

'I think she should be doing something, not just swanning around having fun,' he said uncompromisingly. 'She's got a damned good brain beneath that red hair, and she needs to exercise it instead of wasting time flitting from party to party.'

'Perhaps she needs a year of enjoying herself. High school is hard work.'

'She's never had to work hard for anything.' He dismissed the subject of his cousin. 'So tell me what you're planning to do while you're here.'

A mischievous impulse persuaded her to say, 'I haven't decided yet. Perhaps I'll do some running around too.'

He cocked that brow at her. 'It shouldn't do you any harm, although you're still looking a bit fine-drawn.'

His tone was impersonal, but a note in it fanned the forbidden, smouldering flame inside her. Ignoring it she said steadily, 'Actually, I'm not the flitting type.'

'Are you going to be able to go back to the tropics?'

Startled, she said, 'Of course. This is the twenty-first century, not the nineteenth.' She lifted her glass of lime juice. 'Here's to the miracles of modern medicine.'

'I'll drink to that,' he said, and did so.

As he set his glass down Hani looked out across the valley and said, 'The vines look like braids across the hillside. They must be stunning in the autumn when the leaves change colour.'

'We don't get intense autumn colours this far north,' Kelt told her. 'For those you need to go to the South Island.'

He'd moved slightly so that his back was presented to a group just being seated, and she wondered if he was ashamed of being seen with her. These women seemed overdressed for a casual vineyard lunch, but their clothes—like Rosie's—bore the discreet indications of skilful design and obvious expense.

Kelt might be a snob—she hadn't seen him with other people enough to know otherwise—but his enviable aura of self-assurance surely meant any embarrassment was unlikely.

He'd certainly shrugged off his *distant* cousin's open claim to him—not to mention her statement that women wept when they realised he wasn't interested in them. And without so much as a tinge of colour along those sweeping, stark cheekbones. Perhaps it was a joke between them?

A comment from Kelt broke into her anxious thoughts. 'That's an interesting expression.'

Hani was saved from answering by the arrival of the first course—iced soup for her, a considerably more substantial dish for him.

As she tackled the soup she thought ironically that she hadn't eaten with a man for over six years, and here she was, for the second time in two days, sharing a meal with the most interesting man she'd ever met.

And one of the best-looking. Apart from Rafiq, she thought loyally, but of course her brother didn't affect her like—

Her thoughts came to a jarring halt.

Well, OK, she *was* affected by Kelt.

But only physically. She was safe from the shattering emotional betrayal she'd suffered at Felipe's hands.

Kelt had shown her he wasn't at all like Felipe—that lick of contempt in his voice when he'd asked if she was drunk or drugged, his affection for his cousin, the children's innocent, open respect and liking…

Any woman who took him for a lover wouldn't end up with splintered self-esteem and a death wish.

And she'd learned a lot in six years, grown up, become a different woman from the child-adult who'd fallen headlong for Felipe's false charm. Even then, it hadn't taken her too long to realise she'd fallen in love with a carefully constructed image, a mirage.

A trap.

And if she wanted to free herself from the lingering after-effects of her experience with Felipe, prove that she was able to handle a mature relationship, then Kelt would be the ideal lover. Miraculously he'd woken the long-dead part of her that was able to respond.

And he wanted her…

Common sense did its best to squelch the secret thrill of excitement, warning Hani not to allow herself the forbidden luxury of impossible dreams. Nothing had really changed; as long as Felipe was alive she'd never be safe, and neither was anyone else she knew.

CHAPTER SIX

KELT'S voice—aloof, rather cool—broke into Hani's tumbled thoughts. 'Don't you like that soup? I can order something else for you if you'd rather.'

'No, it's delicious, thank you.' Startled, she drank some more without tasting it. She was not going to let herself fantasise about an affair with him—it was altogether too dangerous. Reining in her too vivid imagination, she said sedately, 'They have a great chef.'

'She's an American woman with a Brazilian background who met her New Zealand husband in London. When he decided to come back here and grow grapes she set up the restaurant. It's becoming rather famous.'

'I can understand why,' she said, suddenly longing for the potent chilli dishes of her homeland.

A large dog of indeterminate breed wandered around the corner, accompanied by an entourage of ducks. They parted ways, the ducks heading downhill to the pond, the dog stopping to survey the diners. After a few seconds of sniffing, it headed for Hani.

'Shall I send him away?' Kelt said. 'He's well-behaved and very much a part of the restaurant, but if you're wary of dogs he can look intimidating.'

'I like dogs.' Quelling a bitter memory, she held out her hand, back upwards, so that the dog could scent her. It obliged delicately, and with excellent manners refrained from actually landing the automatic lick on her skin.

'Yes, you're a handsome creature,' Hani said softly. 'What's your name?'

Kelt waved away a waiter who'd started towards them. 'Rogue. And he's not allowed to beg.'

'He's not begging, are you, Rogue?'

A woman called from behind a screen, and obediently Rogue bounded off.

'I can see you know how to deal with dogs,' Kelt remarked.

'I grew up with them,' she said simply.

Felipe had bought her a puppy. She'd learned to love it— and then, a month or so later, they'd quarrelled.

She'd gone out, and when she'd got home the puppy was dead. He'd got one of his servants to drown it. To teach her a lesson, he'd said and, when she'd wept, told her negligently that because she'd learned that lesson he'd buy her another one.

That was when Hani had realised that to him she was every bit as expendable as the puppy—something he'd bought, something he could order to be killed just to make a point…

Her throat closed; she swallowed and smiled and said much more brightly, 'I wonder what interesting mix of bloodlines led to Rogue's conformation.'

'German Shepherd, certainly, and perhaps a hint of bull terrier—with border collie? Apart from that, who knows?'

The shutters had come down again, barring him from her thoughts. Kelt's eyes narrowed as he surveyed her calm, emotionless face. Hannah Court's stubborn refusal to give him any information about herself was getting to him.

She was nothing like the women he usually wanted. After

an experience when he was young and callow enough to break a woman's heart he'd been careful to choose lovers as sophisticated as he was. He'd given up expecting to fall in love—and he had no intention of falling in love with Hannah Court either.

But she was an intriguing mystery, one he wanted to solve. He hadn't missed the moment of stiffness when Rosie had suggested she might have seen her before. She wore that disciplined composure like armour, yet flashes of tension broke through it—when he touched her, when she'd inadvertently revealed she had a brother.

He doubted that she'd been involved in anything criminal, but possibly her six years in the mining wasteland of Tukuulu was self-punishment. Was she expiating some sin?

Or was she afraid?

She hadn't pulled away when he'd touched her—she'd actually flinched, as though expecting pain. A violent surge of outrage took him completely by surprise; he had to stop his hand from clenching into a fist beside his plate.

Hani looked up at him, those dark eyes green and unreadable even though she was smiling. 'Probably a couple of other breeds too,' she said. 'I'm glad Rogue's well looked after. People shouldn't have dogs if they aren't prepared to love them.'

Kelt heard the momentary hesitation, the flicker of grief in her voice, and watched with narrowed eyes as she scrambled to her feet and said, 'If you'll just excuse me...'

Without waiting for a response she headed across the terrace and into the restaurant.

What the hell had precipitated that? Bitter memories, or another attack of fever? If she wasn't back in five minutes he'd get the waitress to go in after her. Or go in himself.

He didn't have to wait that long, just long enough to call the waiter over and arrange to pay half of the bill.

'I don't want my guest to know about it,' he said.

The waiter nodded, and left, casting a curious glance at Hannah as she came back.

Leaning back in his chair, Kelt watched her walk towards him, and something tightened in his gut. Unconsciously seductive, the exotic contours of her face were enhanced by the smile that curved her lips. Her hair gleamed in the sunlight like burnished silk, its dense darkness shot with elusive sparks of red. And the graceful sway of her hips had caught the eye of every man on the terrace.

Kelt got to his feet on a fierce rush of adrenalin, an arrogant male need to proclaim to the world that she was with him. Without thinking, he took her hand.

'All right?' he asked abruptly.

She gave him a veiled look. 'I'm fine, thank you,' she said in a tone that had an edge to it.

But her fingers trembled in his, and he could see the pulse beating in the vulnerable hollow of her throat. Fear?

No. Her colour came and went, and her eyes clung to his. A dangerous triumph burning through him, Kelt released her as the waiter came towards them.

Something had happened, Hani realised as they sat down again. Her nerves were jumping in delicious anticipation because she both wanted and feared that *something*.

But she wanted it much more than she feared it. Fortunately she had to deal with the waiter, who was trying to persuade her to order what he described as a sinfully decadent chocolate mousse.

'I'm already full, but you have some,' she urged Kelt, refusing to think of the cost.

He said, 'Not for me, but if you're having coffee I'll have some of that too.'

Still sizzling with a kind of delicious inner buzz, she surrendered to the urge to say yes, to prolong the moment. 'Coffee sounds great.'

After it had been ordered Kelt leaned back in his chair and surveyed her lazily. 'What do you plan to do while you recuperate?'

'I might write a book.'

One black brow hitched upwards. 'Do you write?'

'Not yet,' she admitted, playing with the idea. 'But everyone has to start.'

'Would you make use of your experiences in Tukuulu?'

'No, it would seem like exploiting the school and the pupils.' Another thought struck her. 'Or I could learn to paint. I've always wanted to do that.'

'The local high school has night classes, and I think there's a group that offers lessons as well,' he commented, those dispassionate eyes intent on her face. 'Anything else you can think of?'

'No,' she said quietly, some of her lovely anticipation draining away at the thought of the three long months ahead.

'You could study something that would help you with your career. There's a tertiary institute in Kaitake. Are you a New Zealand citizen?'

Through his lashes he watched her keenly, not surprised when the drawbridge came up again.

'No,' she said crisply. 'And I don't have residency either, which makes study difficult.' And prohibitively expensive.

He frowned. 'So where did you gain your qualifications?'

After a moment's hesitation she said, 'From an Auckland tertiary institute. The principal organised everything.' And the charity had paid the fees.

Uneasily she wondered whether the governing body would

want repayment if she couldn't go back to Tukuulu. Brusquely she dismissed the thought; already she felt so much better. The fever had to be on the run.

Kelt said, 'If you want to study, I'd contact the same institute again. But you should make sure you're up to whatever you feel like doing.'

Years of forced independence had made such concern unusual.

And perilously sweet.

Picking up the spoon that came with the coffee, she played with it for a moment before saying with a bite to her tone, 'I certainly don't think I'm likely to collapse in public again. Apart from anything else, it might give people the wrong impression.'

His brows lifted at the allusion. 'I've apologised for my misconception,' he said with formidable detachment.

He had, so why had she reminded him of it again? Because she was reverting back to the terrified woman who'd avoided any sort of emotional connection for the past six years.

She drew in her breath to apologise in her turn, but he forestalled her by holding out his hand.

'Shake on it, and we'll forget it happened,' he said, knowing he wouldn't be able to.

From beneath lowered lids he watched her, noting the subtle signs of unease, the momentary hesitation before she held out her hand.

Why the hell was he trying to help her? If his suspicions were correct she was damaged in some way that needed professional help, possibly several years of therapy. Normally he'd stay well out of it—after making sure she got that help.

So what was different?

Hannah was different, he realised with a shock of anger and

frustration. And so was he. He was already deeper in this than he wanted to be, which meant it was time to bail out.

And even as the words scrolled through his mind, he knew he wasn't going to. This, for example—her initial involuntary flinch at his touch had eased to a certain tension.

He'd like her to welcome the feel of his hands on her skin, not be afraid of it. As she extended her hand he forced himself to be gentle, letting her control the quick handshake.

She gave him a fleeting apologetic smile when she picked up the teaspoon again, glancing away so that she accidentally met the eyes of a woman a few tables away. Skilfully made-up, with superbly cut blonde hair, clothes that made the most of some very sleek physical assets, a very opulent diamond on one elegantly manicured finger—she gave Hani a long, openly speculative stare.

Hani blinked, gave a stiff little nod and turned back to Kelt. He had noticed, of course.

'She's the soon-to-be ex-wife of one of the more notorious property developers. He's just dumped her for a woman ten years younger,' he said dismissively. 'He bought a farm further north—on the coast—and built a large and elaborate holiday house and is trying to deny the locals access to his beaches.'

As though his words had summoned her, the woman at the other table got to her feet and came across.

'Hello, Kelt.' Her smile was as fulsome as her tone, and her eyes flicked from Kelt to Hani, and back again, devouring him with a bold, open appreciation that set Hani's teeth on edge.

'Tess,' he said formally, getting to his feet.

Hani realised they were under intense covert scrutiny from the people at the other table, and wondered what was going on.

Kelt introduced Hani without giving any more information than her supposed name, and their conversation was short and apparently friendly enough, but Hani suspected that not only did Kelt disapprove of the woman, but he also disliked her.

Not that you could tell from his attitude, she thought, wondering whether she was being foolish and presumptuous. After all, she didn't *know* Kelt.

Tension knotted beneath her ribs as Tess Whoever left after one more fawning smile, and walked back to her table.

'She seems pleasant enough,' she said foolishly to fill in the charged silence when Kelt sat down again.

'I suspect I've just been put on a list of possible replacements.' He glanced at her empty coffee cup. 'Are you ready to go?'

'Yes.'

Hani half expected him to insist on paying but he made no attempt to, and to her intense relief the bill was about the amount she'd have expected to pay in a good café.

They had almost reached the turn-off to Kiwinui when she braked and drew into the side of the road.

Kelt asked, 'Something wrong?'

'I just want to look at the view,' she told him.

He nodded and got out with her, standing beside her as they looked out over a wide valley with an immense, slab-sided rocky outcrop almost in the middle.

'That's the remnant of an ancient volcanic plug,' Kelt told her. 'There are burial caves there, and—' He stopped abruptly, turning to frown at a clump of straggly trees on the side of the hill.

'What is it?' Hani asked anxiously.

Over his shoulder he said, 'I heard a noise. Listen!'

Obediently she strained to hear, but heard nothing except the soft sound of the wind in the trees. In a voice pitched barely above a whisper, she asked, 'What sort of noise?'

'A whimper, like something in pain.'

He strode towards the trees, but when Hani caught him up he stopped her with a hand on her arm, and ordered, 'Stay here.'

'Why?' The hair lifted on the back of her neck. Acutely conscious of the latent strength in the fingers curled above her elbow, she looked up into a face set in rigid lines of command.

Blue eyes hard and intent, he said, 'I don't know what it is,' he said. 'I'll go and check it out. I want you to stay here until I call you.'

'Surely you don't think—'

'I don't *know*,' he emphasised. 'And if I yell, run back to the car, lock yourself in and call emergency on the cell-phone you'll find in the glove pocket.'

When she didn't answer he said, 'Perhaps you should do that now.'

'I'll wait by the car,' she said flatly. 'But I think you're overreacting.'

He gave her a thin smile. 'Of course I am. Humour me,' he said, and watched as she walked across to stand by the vehicle.

'Be careful!' she mouthed silently as he walked into the head-high scrub.

Tensely she waited, every nerve on edge, relaxing a few minutes later when he emerged carrying a small black and white animal.

'What is it?' she asked as she ran across to him. 'Oh, it's a puppy!'

Under his breath he said something she was rather glad she couldn't hear, adding distinctly, 'And it's terrified.'

So distressed she had to swallow to control her voice, she said, 'Give it to me!' and held out her hands.

Kelt shook his head and carefully, gently manipulated each fragile limb. The puppy settled down immediately, lifting its sharp little face to him and neither flinching nor whimpering when he ran his lean, competent fingers over it.

'Get into the car and I'll drive us to the vet,' Kelt said austerely. 'It doesn't seem to be in any pain but it needs to be checked in case it's sick, or too young to be separated from its mother. In which case it will have to be put down.'

Hani quelled her instinctive outcry. She knew enough about dogs to realise that he was right.

He looked down at her and the grimness faded. 'I suppose you want to carry it?'

'Of course.'

Kelt put the squirming pup into her eager hands.

'There, there, you're all right,' she murmured, her voice low as she cuddled the little animal to her breast. Immediately it relaxed, staring earnestly up into her face.

Cradling the pup, Hani climbed into the passenger seat. 'She doesn't look sick at all,' she said when Kelt came in beside her.

'She?'

'Yes, she's a female, and she looks really healthy—fat and glossy. Her eyes are clear and bright, and she's alert. She can't have been thrown out of a car. Perhaps whoever did this wanted her to be found.'

Kelt switched on the engine and said harshly, 'If they had they wouldn't have tied her up in a sack and hidden her behind a patch of manuka scrub.'

Wishing he hadn't pointed out that inconvenient fact, she remained silent.

He must have guessed, because he sent her a swift, sideways glance. 'It's always better to face the truth,' he said. Once they were on the road he gave a humourless smile. 'Did I sound sententious and smug?'

'Yes, you did,' she told him spiritedly, stroking the puppy's downy little head. 'Unfortunately that doesn't make what you said any less true.'

'In my experience almost as much havoc is wrought by people who stubbornly make excuses for inexcusable behaviour as by the people who indulge in that behaviour.'

'Oh, dear, as well as sententious and smug you sound very old and jaded,' she teased.

To her surprise his mouth twitched at the corners, but he didn't answer, and her gaze drifted to his hands on the wheel—sure, competent, controlled...

He'd handled the pup so carefully, his long fingers gentle as he'd manipulated the tiny limbs. Into her head there sneaked an image of those hands on her skin, their lean, tanned strength a potent contrast to her pale gold.

That secret warmth blazed into life, sending a wave of hot excitement through her. Stunned, she banished the seductive fantasy and sat upright, concentrating on the animal now asleep in her lap.

But before long she stole a glance at the man beside her, unconsciously measuring the arrogant profile—all angles and straight lines except for the sexy curve of his lips.

'OK?' he asked without looking at her.

How did he know she'd been watching him? Confused by her reaction, she swallowed and said, 'Yes, she's asleep, poor little scrap. How *could* anyone be so cruel as to abandon her like that to a lingering and painful death? It's—just horrible.'

'They probably couldn't bring themselves to kill her, so they stuffed her into the sack like rubbish and dumped her— out of sight, out of mind.' Kelt's tone was coldly disgusted.

Chilled, because Felipe always had someone else do his dirty work for him, she said thinly, 'That's appalling—horrifying.'

'Indeed.'

The vet, a middle-aged woman with an expression that told them she'd seen worse things than this, said, 'She's in excellent condition. I'd say she was the only pup in the litter and that she's just been taken from her mother. She's about two months old—part border collie with something like a corgi.' She looked at Kelt, her eyes amused. 'She'll probably make a good cattle dog, Kelt.'

He smiled at that, looking at the puppy protectively cradled in Hani's arms.

'What do you want done with her?' the vet asked.

Hani said, 'I'll look after her.'

She felt the impact of Kelt's frown without seeing it, but his tone was neutral and dispassionate when he said, 'Are you sure? Puppies are a bit like babies—they need fairly constant attention and that often means getting up at night to take them outside.'

'I know.'

'You'll be sorry when you have to leave her behind.'

'Surely someone—perhaps on the station—will adopt her once I've got her housetrained and taught her some simple commands?'

'Every child on Kiwinui will want her,' Kelt said dryly, then shrugged. 'Your decision,' he said, and turned to the vet. 'Thanks for looking at her. We'd better buy some necessities before we go.'

The vet said, 'Well, let me sponsor her for that, anyway. Quite frankly, I'm glad you're not leaving me with the problem of what to do with her.'

Kelt said ironically, 'I'll stand godfather and buy her first lot of food.'

'It's all right—' When he lifted that quizzical brow Hani

stopped, realising she couldn't accept the vet's professional services then refuse Kelt's offer.

Lamely she said, 'Thank you very much, both of you.'

Halfway home Kelt asked, 'What will you call her?'

'I don't know.' She laughed. 'My brother always said dogs choose their own names if you just give them a bit of time.'

And stopped, her heart banging uncomfortably in her chest. For years she'd never spoken of Rafiq—tried not to even think of him because it hurt so much—yet somehow this man had got through her guard enough for her to mention her brother twice in as many days. She'd have to be much more careful.

He said casually, 'Your brother is probably right. You could call her Annie.'

For a horrified second she thought he'd said Hani. The puppy squirmed in her lap as though sensing the panic that kicked beneath her ribs. Then she realised what he'd actually said. Relief cracked her voice when she replied, 'Annie?'

'Little Orphan Annie, alone and friendless in the world.'

The allusion clicked into place. She kept her eyes fixed on the pup, asleep again. 'Well, she's probably not an orphan, and she's certainly not alone or friendless now—thanks to you.'

She sensed rather than saw his broad shoulders lift. 'You're the one who made the decision. I just hope you're not too shattered when you have to leave her behind.'

Hani bit her lip, then was struck by a thought. '*If* I have to leave her behind. I might be able to take her with me. I can't see why not.'

For the first time since she'd fled Felipe she was ready to risk loving again. An emotion unfurled inside her, softly and without limit, a sense of freedom and relief.

She'd believed Felipe had killed an essential part of her—

that part willing to give trust and love—when he'd ordered the death of her puppy.

But he hadn't.

It had just gone into hiding.

So she'd allow herself to love this helpless, abandoned little thing, and she'd fight to take her back to Tukuulu. After all, she'd saved the pup's life, and saving something meant it was up to you to look after it to the best of your ability.

Feeling slightly winded, as though she'd taken a huge step into the unknown, she stroked the puppy again.

'The vet said she'll grow into a working dog,' Kelt reminded her.

'So?'

'That means she'll need constant stimulation—work to occupy her mind—or she'll become frustrated and neurotic.'

Hani digested that silently before saying, 'I'll see how things go.' She sent him a quick, defiant look. 'But whatever happens, I'll always be glad we stopped to look over the valley.'

He nodded. 'Me too.'

CHAPTER SEVEN

THE PUPPY SETTLED DOWN well in her new basket, but in the middle of the night Hani woke with a headache and the telltale signs of a bout of fever. Glumly she gulped down her medication, then remembered her promise to Kelt; aching and reluctant, she forced herself out to the telephone, squinted at the number she'd been given, and fumbled to press the buttons.

When she finally got the combination right Kelt answered. 'I'll be right down,' he said tersely. 'Get back to bed.'

By the time he arrived she was shivering under the covers, and the low hum of his approaching vehicle was probably the most wonderful sound she'd ever heard.

Learning to rely on Kelt would be almost more dangerous than falling in love with him, but at that moment she was utterly grateful he had an overdeveloped sense of responsibility.

Although she strained to hear, she didn't realise he was in the house until he opened the bedroom door and the puppy, secure in her basket in the corner of the room, woke, made a funny squeak and scrabbled at the side of her basket.

'Go back to sleep,' he said, and of course the little thing settled down again.

He came silently across to the bed and scrutinised Hani, and in spite of her heart's warning she relaxed and closed her eyes, allowing herself to yield to the effortless authority emanating from him.

'You've taken your medication?'

He frowned, because her smile was a pale imitation of the real thing. 'Yes, sir.' The words were slurred and unsteady, and she spoke with difficulty, but she added, 'I'm glad you're here.'

Kelt took her hand, surprised at the way her fingers curled around his. 'Try to relax. I'll get you a drink. Hot or cold?'

The narrow brows pleated as though she didn't understand, and a minuscule nod was followed by another shiver that racked her slender body.

'Hot,' she whispered.

He made tea and brought it in, scooping her against his chest and holding the cup to her lips as she took tiny sips of the warm liquid. He didn't know if adding sugar would help, but on the chance it might he'd sweetened it. Although her brows drew together again, she drank most of it.

To his critical eye this attack was nowhere as severe as the first one he'd witnessed, but it was bad enough. She was on fire and in pain, and there was nothing he could do but hold her and wait for the fever to subside.

He looked down at the even features, the flushed, honey-coloured skin like silk satin. She might pretend to be English, but with her superb eyes closed a heritage of more exotic bloodlines was obvious. Those eyes were set on a slight upwards tilt, their long lashes flickering and her sensuous mouth tightening as the fever burned mercilessly through her.

The thought of her enduring this alone and uncared for roused a fierce, powerful compassion in Kelt, fuelling his helpless anger at knowing the only thing he could give her was the comfort of his arms.

Eventually the fever broke dramatically, and once again she

was drenched. Relieved, he glanced at his watch. This bout was over in half the time of the previous one.

Meanwhile, what to do about her soaked clothes? She'd hate it, but she was just going to have to deal with the fact that once again he'd got her out of the wet garments and into something dry.

At the thought his body quickened, protectiveness replaced by a rush of forbidden desire. He gritted his teeth and set her back onto the bed.

Her lashes flickered again, then lifted, forced up by sheer will.

Hani stared at the dark, stony face above her, familiar yet strangely alien. Slowly her sluggish brain processed enough information for her to recall what had happened. Although exhaustion softened her bones and loosened her muscles, she shuddered at the feel of her wet hair against her throat and the clammy embrace of her clothes.

After a couple of tries she managed to say, 'Th-thank you.'

The steely blue gaze that held her prisoner didn't change. 'Do you think you can shower by yourself?'

Shying away from the only alternative, she muttered, 'Yes.'

When she tried to pull herself up he said curtly, 'Stay where you are. I'll turn the shower on and carry you in.'

But when he came back she was sitting on the side of the bed, brows knotted and panting slightly.

'I said I'd carry you in,' he said, but his tone was resigned rather than irritated.

'I can manage,' she said, defiance plain in her tone.

To her surprise he didn't object. 'OK, give it a try.'

Hani eased her feet onto the floor and grabbed the headboard, exerting the very last of her strength to stand up. Her legs shook so much that she might as well be shivering, she thought miserably.

Kelt didn't say anything; he just picked her up as effort-lessly as though she were a child and carried her across the room. As the door closed behind them she saw the puppy's eyes on them.

'I'm glad you can smile,' he said, easing her onto the chair he'd put in the shower.

'The puppy thinks we're crazy,' she managed to say, her voice wobbling.

Eyes revealing grim amusement, he examined her through a haze of steam. 'She's almost certainly right,' he told her. 'If you think you can cope, I'll leave you to it. If you can't, I'm afraid you're just going to have to grit your teeth and bear my ministrations.'

Again—only this time she was conscious. Colour prickled up from her breasts. 'I can do it,' she said quickly.

He gave her another hard stare and nodded. 'Yell if you need help,' he said succinctly, and left her.

Gathering strength, she sat for some moments just relish-ing the clean warmth of the water on her sweat-soaked body, but when she tried to get out of her clothes that same water made her clothes clinging and uncooperative. Gritting her teeth, she was able to wriggle free of her briefs, but the top resisted her every attempt.

She was shaking with useless frustration when there was a knock on the door. 'J-just a moment,' she called desper-ately, tugging at the recalcitrant shift as it refused to come over her arms.

Humiliatingly exposed, she looked around for her towel, then grabbed the one he'd put outside and wrapped it around herself. Where, of course, it immediately got wet. Hot, furious tears welled up in her eyes and ached in her throat so she couldn't produce a word.

He said, 'Hannah?'

Her silence brought him straight inside; he took in the situation immediately and said, 'It's all right.'

She flinched away as he opened the door into the shower. Face rigid, he paused for a second to strip off his shirt, then reached in and turned off the shower.

Hani could have died with embarrassment, but to her amazed bewilderment she wasn't afraid. Efficiently and without changing expression he removed her top and, while she blushed from her waist to the top of her head, he got his shirt and cocooned her in it, hiding everything down to her thighs.

'Let that wet towel drop now,' he said.

Her hands were shaking so much she couldn't even untie the one she'd knotted around her waist. Embarrassing tears filled her eyes. In a goaded voice she said, 'I f-feel so useless...'

'Nobody is at their best after a bout of tropical fever,' he said in a cool, level voice, and undid the towel for her, letting it drop.

His hands against her were—wildly exciting. They set her skin on fire.

No, they set her whole body alight. Dumbly, she stared at him, and started to shake again—delicious, fiercely erotic tremors of sensation that filled her with a tempting strength. Hani forced herself to lift her eyes from his torso—a powerful incitement in itself, strong and lean and bronze, the muscles flexing slightly as though he stayed still only with a great effort.

She met his eyes, recklessly responding to the glitter of hunger in their blue depths.

For—how long? Measured by heartbeats, an eternity. His fingers tightened around her waist, almost easing her closer, and she held her breath, everything in her focused on the warmth of his hands on her skin, the faint, primal body scent that was his alone, emphasised by the shirt she wore.

Somehow the fever had sensitised her whole body so that it longed for his touch. More than anything in the whole world she wanted him to take that final step, wanted to let her head rest on his broad shoulder, let him…

His eyes went cold, and he set her away from him, his hands closing on her shoulders to propel her out of the shower and into the bathroom.

'You need to sleep,' he said, his voice totally lacking inflection. 'Have you got a hairdryer?'

'Yes.' Every bit of passion drained away, leaving her cold and so utterly humiliated it took all her energy to produce the word.

She wanted to insist he let her walk into the bedroom, but he gave her no choice; he simply picked her up and carried her through, depositing her on the side of the bed. In spite of her bitter embarrassment Hani thought she'd never felt so safe in all her life…

'The puppy wants to go outside,' he said, and left the room.

As she shed the bath towel and struggled into a gaily-patterned wrap he'd found, she heard him talking to the puppy. The outside door rasped open, closing again a few moments later.

From the bedroom door he asked, 'Are you OK?'

'Yes.'

He came in with a dry towel, which he used to dry off her hair. He was so gentle, she thought dreamily, by now so tired she couldn't produce a coherent thought. Tomorrow she'd wake and remember what he looked like—strong and lithe, the light burnishing his tanned, powerful shoulders.

Then he turned on the hairdryer, saying grimly, 'I should have called Rosie for this part.'

Hani gave a prodigious yawn. 'You're—it's fine,' she murmured. Her half-closed gaze lingered on the scroll of dark hair across his chest.

His detachment should have reassured her. Shamefully, she was undermined by another, more searing emotion—a fierce resentment that he could be so unaffected when she felt like melting like a puddle at his feet.

Eventually he said, 'It's dry now.'

She fell onto the sheets, eyes closing as she felt the covers being pulled over her. Dimly she realised that he'd changed the bedlinen, and then exhaustion devoured her.

Kelt looked down at her. Hannah—Honey suited her much better, he thought sardonically—lay on her side, a cheek cupped in one hand, her breath coming evenly between her lips and her colour normal.

He glanced at his watch again. If she followed the previous pattern she'd sleep like that until morning, and wake up in remarkably good shape.

So he could go home to his very comfortable bed in his own room.

He picked up his shirt and pulled it on again, stopping as the faintest fragrance whispered up to him from the cloth. Jaw set, he went into the living room and opened a door onto the deck. Little waves flirted onto the sand. The tide was going out, he noticed automatically, and looked along the beach.

Mind made up, he came back in and lowered himself onto the sofa.

Hani woke to a plaintive little snuffle from the puppy, and cautiously stretched. She felt—*good*, she decided, and eased herself out of the bed.

'Yes, all right,' she said softly. 'Just give me time to find my feet...'

The medication had worked its magic; she was still a bit

wobbly, but that would go once she got some food and a cup of good coffee inside her.

Heat swept up from her throat at all-too-vivid memories of Kelt's impersonal, almost indifferent ministering to her—until the moment when his hands had released the towel around her waist.

And then, in spite of his cool self-possession, for taut, charged moments he hadn't been able to hide his desire.

For her...

Hani's breath came swiftly through her lips as she relived her own emotions—a hungry passion backed by intense confidence, as though this mutual desire was *right*, the one thing that could bring some peace and harmony to her.

OK, so he'd controlled his own reaction immediately. She wished he hadn't.

More colour flooded her skin when she remembered her dreams—tangled, happy, erotic fantasies without the shame and fear that usually dogged her night visions. Last night they'd been a fairy tale of love and passion and peace, and she'd woken with a smile.

As she scooped up the puppy and carried its wriggling body across to the door, she reminded herself that dreams were all she dared to savour as long as Felipe Gastano was alive.

She pushed the door open and stopped abruptly, eyes fixed on the man asleep on the sofa.

He'd stayed? Warmth suffused her, and a kind of wonder that he should feel so responsible for someone he didn't really know. He looked raffish, the arrogance of those strong features neither blurred nor gentled by the dark stubble of his beard.

The puppy wriggled, and she looked down at the little creature, realising that she had on only the thin cotton wrap. Torn, she half turned to get her dressing gown, but it appeared that things were getting desperate for the puppy, so she tiptoed across the room, holding her breath as she eased the door onto the lawn open.

Once placed on the grass the puppy obliged, and Hani smiled, remembering other occasions like this. Although the *castello* had been run efficiently by a team of servants, her parents had always insisted she look after her own pets.

Now, damp grass prickling the soles of her feet, she shielded her eyes against the sheen the rising sun cast on the sea, and the edge of shimmering gold outlining the big island that sheltered this coastline. Her lungs expanded, taking in great breaths of salt-scented air. She had never been in a place so beautiful, so free.

She could live here very happily, she thought wistfully. Perhaps she was attuned to living on an island in the middle of a vast sea...

Moraze was smaller than New Zealand, Tukuulu even smaller, a mere dot in the ocean, but all were thousands of miles from the nearest country, and perhaps such places bred a different kind of people.

Whatever, she could learn to love New Zealand. This part of it anyway.

The puppy sniffed its way back to her and licked her bare toes. 'Hello, little thing,' she said softly, and stooped to pick it up. 'I hope you find your name soon, because I can't go on calling you puppy, or little thing. It's demeaning. What do you think, hmm?'

The puppy swiped her chin with a pink tongue, then yawned, showing sharp white teeth in excellent condition.

On a quiet laugh Hani turned and walked back to the bach, hoping fervently that Kelt was still asleep. It seemed stupid and missish that after last night she should be so embarrassed—the wrap covered her from neck to ankle—but she couldn't help it.

Any more than she could help that *frisson* of excitement that ran down her spine whenever she met his eyes, or the suspicious heat that smouldered into life at his lightest, least erotic touch.

Again she held her breath, keeping a wary eye on the sprawled figure dwarfing the sofa. Her breath came noiselessly between her lips as she passed the sofa, only to have that relief vanish when his rough, early-morning voice stopped her in her tracks.

'How are you feeling?'

'Good,' she blurted, turning to face him with the puppy clutched to her breast like a squirming shield. Guiltily she loosened her hold and added brightly, 'It was very kind of you to come down.'

He lifted his brows, and ran a hand across the stubble. 'There's no need to thank me.' His tone changed from the gravelly drawl to a clipped note that barely concealed anger. 'Have you had to suffer all your other attacks by yourself?'

'I managed,' she said defensively.

'Why wasn't someone with you? Once you start to shiver you have no idea what you're doing.'

Heat burned along her cheekbones. What *had* she done? Only shown him that she wanted him.

Defensively she said, 'I'm getting much better.'

'And you'd rather suffer in silence than ask for help,' he said curtly. 'But your colleagues must have known you needed help, even if you refused to ask for it.'

'I asked for it last night,' she pointed out, chin lifting.

He showed his teeth. 'You didn't, you simply told me you were coming down with another bout, and you only did that because I extracted a very reluctant promise from you.'

Her silence must have told him that he was dead on the mark. The puppy wriggled in Hani's hands again and his frown disappeared. 'Put her down. She probably wants to explore the place.'

Sure enough the little thing started to sniff the sofa leg. Hani said, 'She should know it well enough by now—she spent most of yesterday afternoon either sleeping or smelling around.'

'It will take her more than a few turns around the room to get used to being here.'

A single lithe movement brought him to his feet. Automatically Hani took a step backwards. He was so tall he loomed over her, and he had a rare ability to reduce her to a state of shaming breathlessness.

His eyes hardened. 'Why are you afraid of me?' he asked in a level voice that was more intimidating than a shout would have been.

Not that she could imagine him shouting. He'd lose his temper coldly, she thought with an inward shiver, in an icy rage that would freeze anyone to immobility.

'I'm not.' It sounded like something a schoolchild might blurt.

His brows climbed. 'If you're not afraid of me, why did you jump backwards just then, as though you think I might pounce on you?' His steel-blue eyes surveyed her mercilessly.

Very quietly, she said, 'You take up a lot of room.'

He frowned. 'What does that mean? Yes, I'm a big man, but that doesn't make me violent.'

'I know that.' She was making a total hash of this, and she owed it to him to explain that he was reaping the heritage of another man who hadn't been violent either—not in action. Felipe had never hit her. His speciality had been mental torture, a feline, dangerous malice that had irreparably scarred her.

But the words wouldn't come. After a deep breath, she continued, 'I suppose the... I feel embarrassed by being such a weakling.'

'You're not weak,' he said impatiently, 'you're ill. There's a difference.'

Rattled, she floundered for a few seconds. 'I mean, I'm grateful—'

He cut in, 'I've done no more for you or with you than your brother or father would have done. There's no need for gratitude, and certainly no need for the kind of fear you seem to feel.'

'I know,' she said quickly. 'You've been amazingly kind to me, and you don't...I don't...' She took another jagged breath. 'Look, can we just leave it?'

He said abruptly, 'Sit down.'

And when she continued to hover, he continued, 'It seems to me that you're either a virgin—'

Her abrupt headshake stopped him. The thought of Hani helpless and brutalised fanned a deadly anger inside him that demanded action. Unfortunately he had no way of finding out what had happened without forcing her to relive the experience.

Keeping his voice level and uninflected, he went on, 'Or you've had a bad experience.'

At her involuntary flinch, he said in a silky voice that sent shudders down her spine, 'So that's it.'

Hani bit her lip. 'No, actually, it's not what you're thinking.'

'Care to talk about it?'

The thought made her stomach lurch sickeningly. 'No.'

After several charged moments he said in a level, objective tone, 'You need help—therapy, probably.'

'I'm fine,' she returned, automatically defensive.

'That's your attitude to everything—just leave me alone, I'm fine,' he observed with a sardonic inflection. 'Unfortunately it doesn't seem to be working.'

Pride lifted her head. 'Sorry, I don't feel like being psychoanalysed.' His narrowing eyes made her add tautly, 'Neither your kindness nor my gratitude gives you any right to interfere with my life.'

'The fact that you're staying in my house on my property means I've accepted some responsibility for your well-being.'

'I'm a grown woman. I'm responsible for myself—and apart from these bouts of fever I'm perfectly capable of looking after myself.'

He looked at her with an irony that was reflected in his words. 'Really? You could have fooled me.'

'That is ridiculous,' she retorted hotly. 'In fact, this whole conversation is ridiculous!'

'It's a conversation that should have taken place years ago between you and a therapist,' he said evenly. 'Before you decided that the only way to expiate the sin of being brutalised was to devote your life to doing good works.'

She went white. 'You don't know what you're talking about.'

'You flinch whenever a man comes near you. Nothing and no one has the right to do that to you.'

'I do not!'

Eyes half-concealed by those dark lashes, he covered the two paces that separated them and took her by the upper arms, holding her with a gentleness that didn't fool her—if she struggled those hands would pin her effortlessly.

Fierce heat beat up through Hani, an arousal that softened her bones and rocketed her heartbeat into panicky, eager anticipation that undermined her anger and outrage.

'You're not shaking—yet,' he said calmly. 'But if I kissed

you you'd faint. You're clenching your teeth now to stop them chattering.'

'You're an arrogant lout,' she flung at him. Desperate to banish from her treacherous mind the image of his mouth on hers, she surged on, 'Why are you doing this?'

'By *this*, do you mean holding you close?' His eyes gleamed with the burnished steel of a sword blade, but his voice was level and uninflected. 'See, you can't relax, even though you must know I won't force myself on an unwilling—or unconscious—woman.'

Neither had Felipe. He'd been able to make her want him—until she'd understood the true depths of his character, and fear and loathing had overwhelmed that first innocent, ardent attraction. And by then it was too late to run…

Still in that same neutral tone Kelt said, 'If you're afraid, Hannah, all you have to do is pull away.' He loosened his already relaxed grip.

Something—a wild spark of defiance—kept her still. A basic female instinct, honed by her past experiences, told her she had nothing to fear from Kelt—he didn't possess Felipe's cruelty, nor the lust for power that had ruled him.

And Kelt's taunt about devoting her life to good works stung. Running away had eased her visceral, primal terror for her own safety, but she'd chosen to teach because she'd wanted to help.

Staring up into the hard, handsome face of the man who held her, she realised that Kelt had somehow changed her—forcing her to face that what she was really hiding from was her own shame, her knowledge that she had let her brother down so badly.

It was as though a switch clicked on in her brain, bringing light into something she'd never dared examine. Before she could change her mind she said quietly, 'I'm not afraid of you.'

Kelt's expression altered fractionally; the glittering steel-blue of his gaze raked her face.

Hani held her breath when his mouth curved in a tight, humourless smile. 'Good.'

And she closed her eyes as he bent his head.

CHAPTER EIGHT

HANI had no idea what to expect; eyes clamped shut, she waited, her heart thudding so noisily she couldn't hear anything else.

'Open your eyes,' Kelt ordered softly, his voice deep and sure and almost amused.

'Why?' she muttered.

His laughter was warm against her skin, erotically charging her already overwhelmed senses, but a thread of iron in his next words made her stiffen.

'So you know exactly who you're kissing,' he said.

'I do know,' she whispered. 'The man who looked after me last night.'

Impatiently, every nerve strained and eager, she waited for the touch of his lips. When nothing happened she opened her eyes a fraction and peered at him through her lashes.

In spite of the smile that curved his mouth his face was oddly stern. 'The man who wants you,' he corrected.

Colour burned her cheeks. When she realised he was waiting for an answer she mumbled, 'It's mutual.'

He gave her another intent look, one that heated until her knees wobbled. And then he bent his head the last few inches and at last she felt his mouth on hers, gentle and without passion as though he was testing her.

Into that fleeting, almost butterfly kiss she said fiercely, 'I'm *not* scared of you.'

'You can't imagine how very glad I am to hear that,' he said, his voice deep and very sure, and he gathered her closer to his lean, hardening body and kissed her again.

Hani felt something she'd never experienced before—a sensation of being overtaken by destiny, of finding her heart's one true fate.

The warnings buzzing through her brain disappeared in a flood of arousal. Kelt tasted of sinful pleasure, of erotic excitement, of smouldering sexuality focused completely on her and the kiss they were exchanging, a kiss she'd never forget.

She was surrounded by his strength and she wasn't afraid, didn't feel like a stupid child who'd fallen into a situation she didn't understand and couldn't control...

It shocked her when he lifted his head a fraction and said something. 'Hannah?'

No, my name's Hani! But of course she couldn't say that. Hani de Courteville no longer existed; she'd drowned six years ago. This kiss was for Hannah Court, not the pampered darling of an island nation who'd failed everyone so badly.

Opening dazed eyes, she tried to regain command of her thoughts. 'Yes?' she asked in a die-away voice.

'All right?'

From somewhere inside her she found the courage to say with a smoky little smile, 'Right now I don't think I've ever felt better. Kiss me again.'

He laughed, and she raised a hand and traced his mouth, the beautifully outlined upper lip, the sensuous lower one that supported it. Something hot and feverish coiled through her. Felipe had never wanted her caresses—forget about

Felipe, she commanded wildly. He'd never made her feel like this, either—so deliciously wanton, confident in her own sexuality.

Kelt's lips closed around her finger and he bit the tip delicately, sending more erotic shivers through her.

His breath was warm against her skin when he said, 'I will, once you stop playing with my mouth.'

Greatly daring, she cupped his jaw with her two hands, relishing the opportunity as her fingertips tingled. He let her explore, and when at last she dropped her hands he caught them and pressed the palm of each to his mouth before pulling her back into his arms and kissing her again.

No butterfly touch this time, but one that frankly sought a response from her, a response she gave eagerly, losing herself in the restrained carnality of their kiss.

Until Kelt lifted his head to say on a note of laughter, 'I think your small protégé needs another run outside.'

'Oh!' She pulled away, hiding her disappointment by bending to pick up the puppy, which was making plaintive noises at her feet.

'I'll take her,' he said crisply.

She handed the puppy over and while he took it through the door into the sunlight she dashed into the bathroom and combed her tumbled hair into some sort of order.

More of those sexy little chills ran through her as she remembered him holding her head still while he'd kissed her, doing with his mouth what her fingers had done to the jut of his chin and the clean, unyielding line of his jaw.

She'd been completely lost in passion, so far gone that nothing but Kelt's kiss had been real to her. She hadn't even heard the puppy.

But Kelt had.

'Oh, dear God,' she whispered, pressing a cold cloth to her hot cheeks and tender mouth.

Was she doomed to be attracted to inherently cold men totally in control of their emotions, their passions?

After she'd realised that Felipe's interest in her had been only because she was Rafiq de Courteville's sister, she'd vowed never to lose her head over a man again.

But Kelt had been so kind, some pathetic part of her pleaded. Felipe had teased and amused her, flattered and caressed her, but she could never remember him being kind…

OK, so Kelt wasn't like Felipe, but he was still dominant, accustomed to being in charge.

So was Rafiq.

Tormented, she stared at her reflection—big dark eyes still slumberous in her flushed face, her trembling mouth full and well-kissed. She simply didn't know Kelt well enough to even guess what sort of man he really was.

Quite probably he'd kissed her on a whim—or because he'd rather liked what he'd seen when he'd helped her out of the shower.

He certainly couldn't feel anything more for her than a physical desire.

But that's what you want, she reminded herself. This is just sexual passion, nothing more. You're not in love with him. You don't want him to love you.

Yes, I do.

With a horrified inward groan, she turned away and grabbed a towel, hiding her face in it for a second before turning to face her reflection.

All right, she silently told the wanton woman in the mirror, falling in love with Kelt Gillan is simply not an option. So you'll call a halt right now. Yes, it's going to make you feel like an idiot, but you've been behaving like one, so it serves you right.

She dried her face, applied a light film of gloss to her mouth, then turned away, squaring her shoulders, and walked out into the sitting room just as Kelt, this time with the puppy gambolling at his heel, walked through the French door into the room.

Her gaze skipped from broad shoulders to the width of his chest and the narrow, masculine hips. One of those sensuous little shivers scudded down her backbone.

Abruptly, before she could change her mind, she blurted, 'I hope you don't think that this…ah, those…what we did…'

'Those kisses?' he supplied smoothly.

His cool, confident tone gave her the strength to say stolidly, 'Yes. I hope you don't think they meant anything.'

'Beyond that you want me?' This time his voice was cynically amused.

'Exactly,' she said, almost cringing at the undercurrent of embarrassment in the word. However, having handed him the opportunity to mock her, she just had to wear it with as much grace as she could.

Quailing inside, she called on every scrap of courage she possessed to meet his coolly measuring survey with a pretence of confidence.

'I assume you're trying to tell me that, just because you kissed me with enthusiasm and a charming lack of pretence, it doesn't mean you're going to sleep with me,' he said blandly.

Shaken by his bluntness, Hani bought a moment by stopping to pick up the puppy, who licked her chin lavishly and promptly dozed off.

'That's exactly what I mean.' She prayed she could bring this awkward and humiliating conversation to an end without seeming any more foolish than she already did.

He said with cutting emphasis, 'A few kisses, however hungry and sweet, don't constitute an invitation to sex, so you can relax. Don't ever judge me again by whatever bastard made you so afraid of men. When I feel the urge to take you to bed, I'll make sure you know well ahead of time, and I'll let you make the decision.'

Hani said in a goaded voice, 'I'm sorry—'

'Like your gratitude, an apology isn't necessary,' he cut in without emphasis. He looked down at the sleeping puppy. 'Has she decided on a name for herself yet?'

Hani forced herself to respond. 'I don't think Sniffer would be a nice name for a puppy,' she said, hoping he didn't notice her brittle tone. 'I'll wait a few days, and if she doesn't come up with something more suitable I'll have to choose a name myself.'

Kelt nodded. 'In spite of what your brother said. Where is he, by the way?'

Hating the lie, Hani said shortly, 'He's dead,' and turned away. 'I'll just put her in her basket.'

He stopped her with one hand. 'I'll go back to the homestead,' he said, blue eyes hooded and unreadable as he scanned her face. 'But just for your information—although I find you very attractive, you're quite safe with me. And if you're thinking that naturally I'd say that—'

Wishing she could deal with this with a light hand and not make blunder after blunder, she broke in, 'Look, it's not important. Truly. I suppose I overreacted—just like you did when you heard her whimpering.' Colour high, she met his opaque gaze with desperate candour. 'Of c-course I find you attractive too, but I'm not—I don't want to embark on an affair that will have to stop when I go back to Tukuulu.'

Kelt's arrogant black brows drew together. 'You must

realise by now that this latest bout of fever reduces your chances of going back to Tukuulu.'

She stared at him. 'What do you mean?'

His frown deepened. 'If you go back to the tropics the fever could well recur.'

'That's not much of a problem; the medication works every time. You've seen how well I respond to it.'

He said harshly, 'Constant use produces a raft of quite nasty side-effects.'

Her eyes widened, then went blank. 'The attacks are getting further and further apart.'

'Because you're in New Zealand,' he told her with brutal honesty. 'People can become permanent invalids from this, Hannah. Some still die. If you go back to Tukuulu that's a possibility the school has to take into account.'

Grabbing for composure, she babbled, 'No, that won't happen. The medication works really well.'

'How well are *you* going to work if you keep having attacks? How much use will you be to the school?' He switched subjects. 'As for the side-effects—do you have a computer?'

She shook her head.

'Then come up to the homestead and I'll show you the information I found in a search that took me five minutes.'

Torn, she hesitated, but this was important. 'I have to get dressed—'

Ten minutes later, clad in trousers and one of her new jerseys, she found herself inside his Range Rover, the puppy in her lap. While Kelt drove silently towards his house she stared out through the window, worrying away at his statement.

Stop it, she told herself sturdily. He might be wrong.

But he wasn't a man who made mistakes.

Though hadn't she read somewhere that only the naïve trusted everything they'd read on the internet?

It wasn't until she sat in front of his sophisticated computer set-up in his scarily modern office that panic closed in on her, producing something terrifyingly close to nausea.

'How do I know this is accurate?' she asked thinly, staring at the words that danced on the screen. She blinked several times and they settled down, spelling out a frightening message.

'Because it comes from a respected medical journal.' He waited, noticing the absolute rigidity of her spine, as though if she relaxed something might shatter. Frowning, he said, 'Finish it.'

Dark head bowed, she read silently and swiftly. Once she finished she didn't turn to look at him, but dropped her gaze to the keyboard.

And when at last she spoke her voice was flat and completely without emotion. 'I wish they'd told me.'

'Your doctor should have,' he said, coldly angry because nobody seemed to care much about her.

'He's old, and…' She couldn't go on.

'It's not the end of the world,' he said calmly. 'A couple of years in a temperate climate will almost certainly make sure you recover.' Without giving her time to digest that he went on, 'Do you want me to get in touch with the expert in tropical medicine they quote?'

She couldn't afford some expensive expert. And if she couldn't get back to Tukuulu… Panic kicked Hani beneath the ribs, temporarily robbing her of rationality.

She had nowhere else to go, nothing else she could do. Her homeland was forever banned to her. Rafiq would never forgive her for putting him through the agony of losing a sister who'd not only figured in a sleazy scandal, but had also tried to take the easy way out by committing suicide.

Besides, he was married now, and a father. She'd picked up an elderly magazine in the hospital in Tukuulu, and seen a photograph of the ruling family of Moraze—a wife who'd looked like someone Hani could love, and two handsome sons. Rafiq had other people to love, closer to him than a sister could ever be.

She'd felt she was doing something worthwhile in her job on Tukuulu, but if she couldn't go back…

Her godmother's inheritance wouldn't support her, and she suspected that her qualifications wouldn't help her find a job in New Zealand unless she actually emigrated. And she didn't want to do that; it would mean too much enquiry into her past.

Kelt said crisply, 'I'll make an appointment with the specialist.'

'No,' she said thinly. She turned and met his eyes, shivering a little at the burnished sheen that made them unreadable.

'Why not? If you're worried about money—'

'No,' she repeated more briskly this time, and got to her feet, taking in a deep breath as he put out a hand to help her.

Hani ignored it, but in spite of the scared thoughts churning in her brain, his closeness triggered a swift, uncontrollable excitement. His kisses had sensitised her to him, linking them in some intangible way so that her body ached with forbidden longing.

What was he thinking?

She tried to smile. 'If that's true, then it looks as though my time on this side of the world could soon be over,' she said, struggling to project a voice that sounded light and casual.

So much for thinking she could learn to love this place!

'You'll go back to the UK?' Kelt asked neutrally.

'Where else?' she said, trying to avoid a direct lie. She hated the falsehoods her foolish decisions forced on her; they made her feel cheap and dirty, a woman tarnished by her many mistakes.

Kelt's scrutiny hardened, and this time the shiver down her spine had little to do with the erotic physical excitement he conjured in her. Apprehension was a much colder, more threatening sensation.

'If you don't want to go back to England you could always stay here.' His tone and expression gave nothing away.

In spite of that, her foolish heart leapt in her breast. Hastily she said, 'Emigrate? I doubt very much that I have any skills New Zealand requires.'

'We always need good teachers. You'd probably have to do some more teacher training, but I'm sure you could manage that.'

She didn't dare. If anyone ever suspected that Hannah Court was the supposedly dead sister of Rafiq de Courteville, ruler of the island of Moraze, the news would be splashed across the world media, just as her death had been! In Tukuulu she'd arrived as a tourist, her passport barely glanced at. Once she'd been asked to stay on at the school she'd been accepted with no further enquiries.

Coming into New Zealand on leave had been simple enough, but emigration was a whole different affair. She struggled to control her fear, reminding herself that her passport was perfectly legitimate. Her mother had been the daughter of the ruler of a small Middle Eastern state, and her children held dual citizenship.

But emigration officials might probe deeper than that. She didn't dare take the chance.

Shrugging, she said lightly, 'Well, I'll wait until I know for certain whether I can go back to Tukuulu.' She gave the computer a quick glance. 'But thanks for finding that information for me. Just in case, I'll do some serious thinking about the future while I'm here.'

'Get better first,' he advised, still in that coolly objective tone. He indicated the puppy, snoozing on a rug. 'And find a name for that dog.'

Pretending an amusement she didn't feel, she said wryly, 'Right now, I think Sleepy would be perfect.'

A knock turned his head. 'Yes?'

Arthur peered around the door. After a quick smile at Hani he said succinctly, 'Your cousin's here.'

'Thanks,' Kelt said, his voice giving nothing away.

'I'll walk back,' Hani said immediately. Right then she didn't feel like dealing with the ebullient and rather too frank Rosie Matthews.

'Nonsense,' Kelt said, black brows meeting for a second as he looked down at her.

Rosie appeared in the doorway, looking theatrically stunned. 'Good heavens—you've let her into the inner sanctum!' she exclaimed. 'What an honour! He must be in love with you, Hannah! Nobody ever gets into Kelt's office—it's *verboten*!' She stared around as though she'd never seen it before.

Although Kelt's mouth curved, he said evenly, 'Knock it off, Rosie. All those exclamations will frighten the puppy.'

'*Puppy?*' Her mobile features softened when her gaze fell on the small animal curled up on the mat. 'Oh, what a charmer,' she crooned, and glided gracefully into the room. 'But not your style, Kelt—it looks a definite bitser. You like brilliantly pedigreed Labs.'

Briefly he explained the circumstances of the puppy's arrival.

Rosie looked at Hani with interest. 'What are you going to call her?'

'I suggested Annie,' Kelt told her.

'As in Little Orphan?' When he nodded, she said indignantly. 'No, that's horrible. Besides, she isn't an orphan any longer.'

Hani said, 'She'll find her own name soon enough.'

Rosie looked up at her cousin and fluttered her lashes. She had, Hani noticed with a hint of chagrin, very long, very curly lashes.

'Actually, Kelt,' she said in a syrupy voice that made Hani's mouth curve, 'I came to ask a favour.'

One black brow lifted. 'Ask away.'

She sighed. 'I don't know how just lifting one eyebrow is so intimidating, but it works every time,' she complained.

'Stop stalling.'

Hani said, 'Perhaps Rosie would prefer to talk to you alone.'

'She would not,' Rosie said immediately. She took a swift breath and said, 'I thought you might like to give a party.'

Kelt asked, 'Why can't your mother do it?'

'Because she's in Borneo.'

This time both brows rose. 'Your mother?' Kelt asked with an edge to his voice. 'In Borneo? I thought she was going to Auckland to the opera.'

Rosie shrugged elaborately. 'Well, this new man in her life has a thing about orang-utans, and there's this place where they introduce baby ones back into the wild. She thought she'd rather do that than see *Carmen* again, especially as she doesn't like the tenor—'

'Spare me,' Kelt cut in dryly. 'So why can't you ask your father to give you this party?'

Rosie sent him a look. 'You know very well he's writing another book.' Her tone indicated that this was answer enough.

'I'll remind him he has a daughter,' Kelt said grimly.

Kelt's open protectiveness for his cousin reminded Hani of

her brother; he too had been protective—possibly too much so. If she'd had half of Rosie's sophistication she might not have fallen for Felipe.

'No, don't do that,' Rosie said swiftly.

Kelt frowned, but didn't press the issue. 'Who do you want to invite?'

'Oh, just the usual crowd.' Rosie looked vague.

Relentlessly Kelt asked, 'Who in particular?'

Flushing, his cousin admitted, 'There's this man—he's staying with the O'Hallorans at their bach. I thought it would be a neighbourly thing to have a party for them.'

'What's his name?'

With an exasperated glower Rosie said, 'Alonso de Porto, but he's got a stack of other names to go with that. He's from Spain. He's been doing a grand tour of New Zealand.'

Hani froze, her skin leached of all colour, and beads of sweat burst out at her temples. Desperately she stooped and picked up the puppy, hoping the abrupt movement would hide her shock.

CHAPTER NINE

YAWNING sleepily, the pup snuggled into the cup of Hani's hands. She kept her eyes on it for as long as she could, forcing her mind into action.

The Alonso de Porto she'd known was a handsome boy who'd hung about on the fringes of Felipe's circle for a few weeks until his parents whisked him out of harm's way.

It couldn't be the same man. New Zealand was as far from the jet-setting sophistication of Europe as he could get.

Or be sent.

After all, if his parents had sensibly removed him from Felipe's influence once, possibly they'd had to do it again. But to New Zealand?

Entirely too much of a coincidence, she thought frantically, all her illusions of safety shattered.

Could Felipe have found her and sent Alonso…?

She took a deep breath. Why would Felipe use a Spanish grandee to track her down when he had professionals to do that sort of thing?

But if it *was* the Alonso she remembered, would he remember her?

She tried to calm her racing heart and dispel the coldness

spreading beneath her ribs. When they'd met she'd been at university, struggling to fulfil her study obligations in spite of Felipe's obstruction, so she hadn't seen a lot of young de Porto.

And then relief washed through her as she realised she'd been so busy panicking she hadn't thought of the most obvious way of avoiding discovery. All she had to do was stay safely hidden at the bach!

Forcing herself to relax, she let her lashes drift cautiously up. Her stomach clamped when she met Kelt's cool, hard scrutiny. *He knows,* she thought for a taut second, feeling the familiar chill of shame.

But of course he couldn't.

Easing her grip on the squirming puppy, she parried Kelt's gaze with all the composure she could produce, forcing her brows upwards in a questioning look.

'I think I've met him,' Kelt said neutrally. 'A nice enough kid, and surprisingly unspoiled for the scion of a Spanish family with a pedigree that goes back a thousand years or so, and a fortune to match.'

Oh, God, that sounded like the Alonso she knew...

She steadied her breath, willing her heartbeat to settle down and her legs to stop shaking.

Rosie glared at Kelt, then laughed. 'Of course, you know everyone who's anyone, don't you? Although it's a bit daunting to hear the best-looking man I've ever seen described as *"a nice enough kid"*. Kid? He can only be four or five years younger than you!'

Kelt eyed her with amusement. 'All right, you can have this party, but you'll organise it yourself. Arthur will have enough to do with the cooking.'

'Super.' Rosie hurled herself into his arms, kissed his cheek with fervour, then tore free.

Hani felt a pang of—jealousy? Surely not, she thought, horrified.

That horror was intensified by Rosie's next enthusiastic words. 'I thought a nice *casual* party, a beach-and-barbecue sort of thing, starting around seven because it's such a super time in summer. One for Hannah—to introduce her to everyone.'

'So it could,' Kelt said, his keen gaze on Hani's face.

Stricken, she said as lightly as she could, 'Oh, no, you mustn't. A summer party doesn't need a reason beyond the season, surely?'

'But this would be perfect!' Rosie swept on. 'After all, if you're going to be here for three months you might as well meet all the usual suspects. And their visitors,' she added with a brilliant smile.

'Just remember Hannah's here to convalesce,' Kelt said. He gave his cousin a direct, intimidating look. 'I don't want her roped into helping you.'

'Cross my heart,' Rosie said after a speculative glance at Hani.

'I'm getting better, not dying,' Hani said briskly, earning herself another thoughtful look from the younger woman.

'Cool. We must get together some time and have lunch,' Rosie said, then blew an airy kiss to Kelt and whirled out of the room, leaving Hani breathless.

So much for hiding…

Still, she had the perfect excuse—her illness.

To the sound of his cousin's teasing voice in the hall and Arthur's indulgent replies, Kelt said ironically, 'Don't let her bulldoze you into doing anything you don't want to.'

'That's very thoughtful of you,' Hani said, 'but I wish you hadn't given her the impression that you had any right to monitor my behaviour.'

'I doubt if she's at all surprised. She frequently tells me I'm arrogant and overbearing, not to mention inflexible and old-fashioned.'

'She knows you well,' Hani said on a false, sweet note.

Kelt's answering smile sent excitement curling through her. His kisses were thrilling, but his smile had the power to reduce her to abject surrender. Not that it softened the hard lines of his face, but there was genuine humour behind it, and an appreciation of her tart irritation with him.

'I'm the big brother she never had,' he said. 'Or possibly the father. Her own is so wrapped up in his work he can only see her as an interruption.'

Hani's face must have shown what she thought of this, because he said, 'Oh, he loves her, but more when she's at a distance. That's why she lives with her mother.'

'Poor Rosie,' she said involuntarily. 'What sort of books does her father write?'

'He's a historian.' He gave her a sardonic look as though expecting her to be bored. 'At the moment he's writing a tome on Chinese exploration in the Indian Ocean; he's planning to head off to Moraze, an island a thousand miles or so off the coast of Africa, to research some ruins there. He's convinced they're Chinese.'

Hani froze. She knew those ruins.

It seemed everything—from Alonso de Porto to Rosie's father's sphere of interest—was leading back to her old life.

Oppressed by a feeling of bleak inevitability, she said brightly, 'How interesting. And don't worry about me—I won't overdo things.' Grateful for the excuse he'd given her, she said, 'I doubt if I'll get to Rosie's party so I'll make sure she doesn't use me as the reason for it.'

'Leave Rosie to me,' he said briefly. 'You look as though you could do with a cup of tea. Or coffee, perhaps.'

Right then she just wanted to get away and hide. The unexpected links between her old life and her new had shattered her precarious composure. She produced a smile, hoping he'd put its perfunctory nature down to tiredness. 'Thank you, but actually I'd rather go back to the bach.'

And met his keen survey with as limpid and innocent a look as she could manage.

His brows drew together but he said evenly, 'Of course. Rosie tends to have that effect on people. If we could harness her energy we'd probably earn megabucks from selling it to the national grid.'

Hani's gurgle of laughter brought an answering smile to his mouth, but the hard eyes were still uncomfortably intent.

So she said brightly, 'I can walk back. I could do with some fresh air.'

'I'll take you back.'

And that was that. He left her at the bach with an injunction to rest, and a feeling of being safe and protected by his concern.

You don't need care and concern, some tough inner part of her warned.

After all, she'd been independent for six years, forging her own way. And in the process she'd discovered things about herself: that she was good with children, that she could teach, that she liked the satisfaction of working hard and making a difference. Life at Tukuulu had shown her that she could cope without the protective influence of her older brother.

Her mind skittered away from the memory of Kelt's kisses. One lesson she'd learned thoroughly before she washed up on Tukuulu was that men didn't necessarily feel anything for the women they made love to. Felipe had seen her as a tool he could use, deliberately wooing and seducing her with no more emotion than lust and a desire for power.

Oh, he'd enjoyed their lovemaking; with a shudder she thought he'd found some vile satisfaction in debauching innocence.

Driven by restlessness, she got to her feet. 'How about a walk on the beach, little one?' she said to the puppy.

Once breathing in the clean, salt-scented air, the sun warm on her head and the sand firm and cool beneath her bare feet, with the puppy snuffling happily around a piece of dried seaweed, she thought that at least there had been no undercurrent of exploitation in Kelt's kisses; he'd treated her as an adult fully aware of what she was doing. And she'd been gripped by a far more primal, intense chemistry than when she'd been so sure she was in love with Felipe.

A sweet, potent warmth washed through her. She didn't dare let things go any further, but she'd always treasure the memory of Kelt's kisses.

And not just his kisses. Somehow, just by being his masterful, enigmatic, uncompromising self, by looking after her, even because of the way he dealt with Rosie, he'd restored her faith in men.

But was it wise to trust her instincts?

'Probably not,' she said to the puppy, who startled them both with a high-pitched yap.

The little animal sat back on its haunches and stared at Hani as though suspecting that the noise had come from her.

'Hey, you can talk!' She bent to stroke her, and received a lick on the wrist and another little yap.

'OK, that clinches it,' Hani said, chuckling. 'You've found your name. How do you do, Gabby?'

Gabby cocked her head, then yapped again and scratched

herself with vigour, sending a spray of sand a few centimetres into the air.

Hani felt tears burn her eyes. It had been so long since she'd dared to love; the puppy had broken through her protective armour, opening her to emotions she'd shunned for six dark years.

Actually, no—meeting Kelt had cracked that shell she'd constructed around herself with such determination.

She stooped to pick up a bleached piece of driftwood and drew a pattern in the sand. Just because she'd met a man who made her feel like a woman with heated passions and deep-seated needs didn't mean she could allow Kelt to become important to her in any way. Caution warned her that this new-found capacity to feel could hurt her all over again.

The puppy came up to investigate this new activity, pounced on the stick and promptly fell over.

'Oh, poor baby!' Hani said, then watched, intrigued, as Gabby got up and sank her tiny needle-teeth into the wood, growling fiercely.

'You've probably got it right, Gabby,' she said aloud. 'Fall over, pick yourself up and start over again. And again if necessary. Perhaps that's what I should have done instead of running away.'

Except that she'd had bigger issues to deal with than a dose of heartbreak—staying alive and out of Felipe's clutches being the most important.

Resolutely pushing the grim memories to the back of her mind, she walked up to the bach, stopping halfway to rescue the exhausted Gabby, who drank lavishly once they got back then sprawled out in the sunlight on the floor and went to sleep.

Smiling, Hani made herself a snack and sat down to eat it,

but pushed it away as the memories intruded. Could Alonso still be part of Felipe's circle?

If he was, and he recognised her and mentioned it to Felipe, she'd be in danger. Before she'd 'died' she'd told Felipe she was leaving him.

He'd been quite calm about his response, wielding his power with consummate artistry. 'Of course you may go if you no longer want to stay with me. But if you do, you will be signing your brother's death warrant as well as your own.' He'd watched the colour drain from her skin and smiled. 'And neither his death nor yours will be quick,' he'd said calmly.

Desperately she got to her feet and walked the length of the terrace, her haunted eyes ignoring the beauty before her.

That was what had pushed her into informing Rafiq that Moraze was threatened, and her despairing decision to kill herself. Although she hadn't managed to achieve that, she'd managed to convince the world she was dead, buying six years in a peaceful limbo.

If those years had taught her anything, it was that losing your head only made things worse.

First of all, she needed to know if this Alonso de Porto was the same one she'd known back then, and if he still made up part of Felipe's circle.

If only she had a computer she could go onto the internet and search for Felipe's name. He'd be easy enough to track down—presumably he still figured in the social pages of various glossy magazines.

If Alonso was still part of his circle she'd have to leave Kiwinui.

Running again, around and around like a rat in a cage…

Although she'd occasionally used the one school computer

she'd never dared look for Felipe, or even for Rafiq and Moraze. Tracking software enabled the teachers to check on the sites the students visited.

Into her mind there sprang the image of the superb set-up in Kelt's office. No doubt he needed to keep up-to-date with farming matters, but a smile hovered on her lips because it seemed the impregnable farmer was a techno-freak.

He had no children to guard, so there'd be no need for him to have tracking software.

She could ask…something…and if he offered her the use of his computer…

Appalled, she pushed the idea away.

But during the rest of the afternoon it came back to her again and again, and that night it vied with other, more tender images of Kelt's kisses, until in the end she woke sobbing from a nightmare in which Kelt had morphed into Felipe.

Shaking, she made herself a cup of tea and sat out on the deck watching the sea wash gently in and out on the beach, the moon catching the white tips of the waves as they broke into lacy patterns on the sand.

She'd been passive for too long. Now she needed to take charge of her life. And she could only do that if she had information.

And then she remembered seeing an internet café close to the pet shop.

'Oh, for heaven's sake!' she whispered.

So much for taking charge of her life! Why on earth hadn't she thought of that hours ago? No need to ask Kelt—no need to do anything more frightening than pay for half an hour of internet access. 'Tomorrow,' she promised herself, half-terrified, half-eager.

The next morning Kelt rang. 'I'm going into town

shortly,' he said, 'and I wondered if you need anything or if you'd like to come.'

Hani's first instinct was to say no, and drive into town later when he was safely home again. But she thought of passing his house, or just possibly seeing him on the farm…

So she said, 'Well, yes, as it happens I do.'

'I'll pick you up in half an hour.' He rang off.

The day was warm, so she chose a pair of loose-fitting cotton trousers the same green as her eyes, and topped them with a neat cap-sleeved T-shirt that matched her skin colour. All she needed to complete the theme, she thought with wry humour as she applied lip gloss, were black shoes that gleamed red in the sun like her hair. Failing those, she made do with a pair of tan sandals.

'I won't be too long,' she promised Gabby, who blinked at her and went straight back to sleep.

Her heart jumped when the car came down the hill, and jumped again when Kelt got out. What he did to her nerve cells, she thought with an involuntary shiver, was positively sinful…

He subjected her to a long, considering look, then smiled. 'You've obviously been sleeping very well.'

'I have,' she replied, hoping her sedate tone didn't tell him that it was his presence that gave her cheeks colour and lightened her step.

Kelt closed the door behind her and slid behind the wheel. 'And how is the puppy?'

'Her name is Gabby.' Hani grinned at his cocked eyebrow. 'She's just discovered that she can yap, and she's been practising often. But she only woke me once last night.'

All morning she'd been fighting a faint nausea at the prospect of seeing even a photograph of Felipe again, but Kelt's arrival had put paid to that. In his company everything seemed at once infinitely more complex, yet straightforward; colours were brighter, scents more seductive. His presence sharpened her appreciation of the blue of the sky and the brilliant green of the fields—*paddocks*, she corrected herself with a half-smile—and the stark loveliness of the countryside.

It wasn't exactly comfort—let alone comfortable—but she was buoyed by a sense of exhilaration, a feeling that life could be filled with richness and delight if she allowed herself to deserve it.

That newly awakened confidence faded fast once she walked into the internet café. Heart pounding and the nausea returning in full force, she sat down and keyed in the search engine, then glanced around. There were only two other people there—tourists—and they couldn't have been less interested in her.

Twenty minutes later she paid her money and sat down limply at one of the tables, waiting for the strong black coffee she'd ordered.

Felipe was dead. The words echoed in her head. He'd died on Moraze four years ago in a shoot-out with the military. The news items had been brief and carried very little information. Clearly Rafiq had clamped a lid on Press speculation.

Hani waited for relief, for joy, for anything but this vast emptiness. Nothing came.

She could go back home.

No, she could never go back. Rafiq wouldn't welcome her—how could he, when she'd caused him so much grief and pain?

She had chosen to die, and it would be far better for those she'd left behind if she stayed as dead as they thought her. She glanced around the shop, the customers drinking tea and coffee, the people walking the streets outside, the sights and smells of normality…

Here she could build a new life. The thought lingered. No one knew her here. She could start afresh…

Her mind returned to those moments she'd spent in Kelt's arms, his mouth on hers producing such ecstatic excitement that she could feel it now in every cell of her body, like a delicious electric current that revived joy and brought a kind of feverish hope.

'Hannah?'

Kelt's hard voice broke in on her scattered thoughts, making her jump. Thank God, she thought in a spill of relief, she'd finished at the computer before he came in.

The concern in his tone warmed her. 'Oh—hi. I'm waiting for my coffee.' Surprisingly, her voice was level. She indicated the chair opposite her. 'Why don't you join me?'

The coffee arrived then, and he ordered for himself, then settled back in his chair and said, 'You looked—a bit disconnected.'

She shrugged. 'Just daydreaming.'

'About what?'

'Nothing,' she said instantly, flushing under his sardonic gaze.

His beautiful mouth tightened. 'It didn't seem a pleasant daydream.'

'Daydreams are pleasant by definition, surely?' She drank some of her coffee. The excitement he roused in her returned, bringing with it the feeling that everything could work out, that the world was a better place when she was in Kelt's company. She set the cup down on its saucer and finished, 'Anything else would be a daymare, and I don't think there is such a thing.'

CHAPTER TEN

HANI said lightly, 'The thing about daydreams is that we control them, so they're always wish-fulfilment. Therefore they're always pleasant.'

Kelt eased his big body back into the chair. 'So tell me, what's your favourite daydream?'

She stared at him, saw his mouth curve, and said demurely, 'When I was five it was to be a bareback rider in a circus. I wanted to wear a short, frilly skirt with sequins all over it, and have long, golden hair that floated behind me while I rode a huge white stallion around the ring. What was yours?'

'When I was five?'

He accepted the coffee from the waitress, a woman who'd given Hani only a perfunctory smile. Her interest in Kelt was obvious, her smile broader and tinged with awareness, her eyes lingering on his hard, handsome face.

Hani squelched the same unwelcome prickle of jealousy she'd felt when Rosie had kissed him. Darn it, she thought in frustration, she was behaving like an idiot, so caught up in his male physical magic that she'd lost all sense of proportion.

OK, so he'd kissed her, and she'd kissed him back, lost in some rapturous wonderland she'd never experienced before. But honing a natural talent to his present expertise probably meant he'd kissed a lot of women. It was just plain stupid to feel that his care for her when she'd been feverish had somehow impressed her body so much it craved his touch.

'When you were five,' she reminded him once the waitress had reluctantly taken herself off.

Broad shoulders lifted in a slight shrug. 'A very boring ambition, nothing as romantic as yours; I wanted to be an astronaut, the first man to stand on Mars. Then I decided that an explorer—Indiana Jones-style—would be even more interesting. We had an old bullocky—a bullock driver—living on Kiwinui then, and he showed me how to use a whip. The first time I got it to crack I thought I'd reached the pinnacle of life's achievements.'

When she laughed delightedly, he smiled. 'That was just before my pirate period, when I roared around the Caribbean on my ship with a loyal crew of desperadoes and gathered vast amounts of treasure.'

Hani had a sudden glimpse of him as he must have been— always a leader, even as a child, his innate authority bred in him.

She opened her mouth to tell him that Moraze had an interesting history of fighting against and sometimes in alliance with the corsairs who'd once infested the Indian Ocean. Just in time, she called back the words, but he'd noticed.

He always noticed, she thought, confused by mixed emotions.

'You were going to say?' he prompted.

She summoned a smile. 'Just that we've both proved my point—it's impossible to have unpleasant daydreams because we always star in them.'

'You have an interesting habit of appearing to be about to speak, only to check yourself and come out with a platitude.'

His voice was conversational, but when she glanced up at him his eyes were uncomfortably keen.

She parried, 'Learnt from experience; teachers who blurt out comments or statements without thinking first can get themselves into trouble.'

Although he gave her abraded nerves a chance to settle down by steering the conversation into neutral channels, she suspected that every slip of her tongue was filed away in his mind.

But on the way home he asked, 'What are your plans if you aren't able to return to Tukuulu?'

Tension tightened her skin. 'I'll leave making plans for when I'm sure I can't go back—*if* that happens.'

'So you're determined to return if you can?' At her nod he said with cool detachment, 'You're a very dedicated teacher.'

'It's what I do.'

Again she endured that penetrating survey. 'No daydreams of children of your own, a husband, of falling in love?'

Her chin came up. 'I could ask you the same question,' she evaded. 'After all, you're quite a bit older than I am.'

'I'm thirty.'

'Well, why—at six years older than I am—are you still single?'

He looked amused. 'I haven't met anyone I'd like to marry.'

'Same with me.' And that, she thought with a quiver of pain, was yet another lie to add to her list.

He undercut her momentary triumph by saying, 'So we're both unattached.'

His tone hadn't altered but something—an edge to his words that hadn't been there before—set her senses onto full alert. 'I am,' she said, holding on to her reserve with determination.

'I am also. Completely.'

Hani had no idea how to reply to this, or what to do. Was

this how he wooed a possible lover, or was he warning her off? Excitement roiled through her in a series of sparks, setting fire to her imagination and her body.

Why not? Why not follow this wildfire attraction and see where it led?

Kelt wasn't like Felipe. She knew that in her innermost heart.

No, it was impossible. She realised they were passing the stream where she'd seen him digging out the blockage. Felipe would have considered such work degrading.

Just *stop* this, she told herself. Stop comparing Kelt to Felipe.

She said, 'So none of the women Rosie has comforted meant anything to you?'

His expression was amused. 'Rosie is a born exaggerator,' he said dryly, 'and you realised that five minutes after meeting her, so don't use her to back up your decision.'

A decision? As the car approached the bach, she gathered the courage to say carefully, 'I'm not sure what's going on here.'

He didn't reply until he'd stopped the car and switched off the engine. His silence was too intimidating, she thought, and scrambled out, turning to face him with her chin held high as he came around the car to stand in front of her.

His expression unreadable, he asked, 'How old were you when you went to Tukuulu?'

After a moment's hesitation she answered, 'Eighteen.'

'Barely more than a child,' he said, frowning. 'What the hell were your family thinking?'

'I have no family,' she said, hating the lie.

'And since then you've had no relationships?'

'That's none of your business,' she said coldly, aware that heat was emphasising her cheekbones.

'In other words you haven't.'

Reduced to frustrated silence by his blunt statement, she gave him a haughty glare and started off down the path towards the bach.

From behind he said deliberately, 'I'm trying to tell you that I find you very interesting—and very desirable. Did you enjoy being kissed?'

Keeping her head down, she groped in her bag for the key and said the first thing that came into her head. 'If I hadn't I'd have slapped your face.'

Oh, how banal! Hastily, her skin by now scorching, she found the key and unlocked the door. Without turning her head, she said, 'But I'm not in the market for a casual affair.'

'It wouldn't be casual,' he said mildly enough, and when she lifted her astonished face towards him she saw something like amusement glitter in his eyes.

Only it wasn't; her heart quivered in her breast as he smiled down at her with a narrowed intensity.

Why not? she thought again, unbearably tempted by a passionate longing that urged her to fling away common sense and accept what he was offering.

Even feverish and barely able to see him, she'd been aware of his potent masculine impact, her body responding instinctively and instantly.

The breath stopped in her throat when she realised that this was already more than simple sexual hunger. Oh, she'd be physically safe, but if she surrendered to this overwhelming need, she'd face a far greater risk—that of losing her heart irretrievably and forever.

The sudden flash of understanding gave her the strength to pull back. Quietly, steadily, she said, 'I don't—I don't think I'm ready for any sort of relationship right now, Kelt.'

It was the first time she'd said his name except in her mind.

He looked at her for too long, his gaze so piercing she had to stop herself from closing her eyes against it, and then he nodded. 'Perhaps it's for the best,' he said with a cool smile. 'And don't let Rosie talk you into any of her mad schemes.'

Aching as though she'd been beaten, Hani went inside while he walked down the path. Later that afternoon, Arthur Wellington drove the car down.

'Before he left, Kelt said to tell you it's fully insured and that you're to use it as much as you like,' he said.

'That's very kind of him.' She didn't have any right to ask where Kelt had gone.

He gave her a thoughtful look. 'He can certainly be kind,' he agreed.

Although the sun shone from a brilliant sky she felt cold and bereft, as though she'd thrown away something of great value.

But she'd have ended up paying a bitter, lifelong price for passion, she thought, trying to fortify her resolve. Because Kelt had offered her nothing beyond that.

Even if he had, she'd have been forced to refuse; it was bitterly ironic that Felipe's death resolved nothing except the fear that had been an ever-present shadow. She couldn't, with honour, return to Moraze or resume her old life.

The thought of media attention filled her with horror. Far better to stay dead.

The next afternoon she drove into town to buy groceries and check Alonso on the internet; although he and his family were easy to find, in all the references and photographs there was nothing that could connect him to Felipe's circle.

But even so, she didn't dare run the risk of him recognising her and remembering her supposed death.

As Gabby played with leaves and spindrift, and made her first forays into the sea, her mistress tried to map out a future.

Without success; her thoughts kept finding their way to Kelt. Unconsciously she'd grown to rely on seeing him, and it was painful to discover just how empty and barren life without him could be.

Her heart felt like a stone in her breast, and her dreams became forlorn affairs of pain and loss and frantic searching, as though some essential part of her was missing.

So when Rosie arrived just after lunch one day she greeted her with real pleasure until she started to discuss her plans for the beach party—plans that involved Hani as guest of honour.

'No,' Hani said firmly.

After her attempts at persuasion had failed, Rosie pulled a face. 'You're just as stubborn as Kelt! He said I wasn't to bother you, and threatened to call the whole thing off if I asked you to do *anything*. All I said was that this beach would be wonderful for the party—it's so pretty and sheltered, and it's great for swimming—but he vetoed that too. And now Alonso's gone back home!'

'Kelt's got this thing about my illness,' Hani offered, so relieved by this that she felt giddy for a moment. At least she wouldn't have to skulk around the bach for three months!

'How are you?' Rosie examined her. 'You look fine— much better than you did the first time I met you, actually.'

'I feel great.' Hani smiled. 'Gabby's seeing to it that I get a fair amount of exercise, and it's so beautiful here. I expected the water to be too cold for me, but I love its briskness.'

'Oh—hasn't Kelt forbidden you to swim alone?' Rosie sounded surprised.

'No.' Paddling was as far as she'd got; she hadn't swum for six years. 'And I doubt if I'd take much notice of him if he did. Why would he do that?'

'His mother drowned while she was swimming on her own off Homestead Bay. He found her body.'

'Oh, how awful,' Hani said involuntarily, repressing memories she tried to keep in the darkest recess of her mind. 'Poor Kelt.'

'Yes. She was a darling.'

The next day, shopping for groceries, Hani realised that the school holidays must have started. The car parks were full and there were children everywhere, fizzing with a palpable air of enjoyment beside their harried parents.

Summer holidays, she thought reminiscently, eyeing a small tot in a frilly sundress with an old-fashioned sun bonnet protecting her freckled face—apparently the latest fashion for under-twos here.

Kelt's words came to her: '—a husband, children...'

By cutting herself off she'd given up any hope of such a future. In fact, she thought now, she'd simply given up hope. Her attempt to kill herself had failed, but in a way she'd committed emotional suicide.

For the first time she appreciated the full impact of the decision she'd made at eighteen. As she was convinced that not only had she failed to live up to her brother's standards, but also that she was a definite threat to him and to the islanders her family had ruled for hundreds of years, the decision had been understandable.

Now she realised that her shamed self-absorption had prolonged Felipe Gastano's power over her. And in a way, her refusal to accept Kelt's delicately worded proposition had been a continuation of that mortification.

But Felipe was dead. Did she dare emerge from her exile and take what she could from life?

Even if it couldn't lead to anything permanent?

Back at the bach she unpacked her purchases and put them away, then took Gabby for a short run, before curling up on a lounger in the sun, the puppy a sleepy little bundle against her bare legs.

'No, no playing,' she said, stroking the soft little ears. 'I have to sort out my thoughts.'

Her gaze drifted to the top of the tree-clad ridge between her little cove and Homestead Bay. Only a few weeks ago her actions had seemed perfectly logical and sensible—until Kelt woke something inside her, a yearning that had turned her life upside down.

'So instead of just reacting,' she told Gabby, 'I need to think this through carefully.'

Except that it was so easy to let her mind drift off into wonderful daydreams. Ruthlessly banishing them, she began to make mental lists.

Surely it would be safe to settle in New Zealand? After all, her qualifications were New Zealand ones; that would help her case. And the charity that ran the school on Tukuulu was based here—maybe they'd organise her a job.

She might even be able to marry…

No, that was just another daydream, a fantasy like her dreams of being a circus rider. Marriage would involve trusting someone with her secrets.

'Stop right there!' she said out loud, astonished by her wayward thoughts.

Gabby woke with a start, and after a lavish yawn that revealed every one of her needle-teeth indicated that she wanted to get down. Once on the ground, she staggered across to drink heartily from her water bowl, then arranged herself in the sun for another nap.

Not marriage—not that. Not ever. Marriage would mean

living a lie, because she couldn't tell Kelt—any prospective husband—about that sordid episode in her past, and her cowardice.

But an affair was a different matter. Excitement beat through Hani—sweet, intense, potent. Softly, her eyes on the little dog, she said aloud, 'I want to know what desire—what passion—is like when there's no hidden agenda, when the emotions are open and honest and not confused with love.'

No marriage, no commitment—just a straightforward, uncomplicated relationship between two people who wanted each other and had no reason not to act on that erotic attraction.

'A thoroughly modern affair,' she said into the heavy air, scented by sun and sea and greenery.

Her breath came faster between her lips, but her voice trailed away. So how did a woman go about indicating to a man—whom she'd already rebuffed—that she wasn't averse to changing her mind?

She had no idea.

But nothing ventured, nothing won.

A large motorboat swung around the headland and roared into the bay, its huge wake creaming the water before crashing into the rocks at the base of each headland.

Gabby woke with a start and let off a couple of startled yaps. 'It's all right,' Hani soothed her, picking her up and holding her in her lap. 'They'll go as soon as they've had a look around.'

But they didn't. A few metres off the beach the engine cut and the anchor rattled down. The silence was broken by loud yells as the people on board—all men, she noted—dived over the side.

With a shock she realised they were naked and the hair on the back of her neck lifted in a primitive intimation of danger.

She bit her lip. No, she was being foolish. Clearly they thought they were alone in the bay, and on such a glorious day, why not swim naked?

She took Gabby inside and tried to read, but while the sun eased down the sky her apprehension grew stronger as she listened to the new arrivals' increasingly raucous yells and laughter.

She'd made up her mind to ring Arthur when she saw a car heading down the drive. With a sigh of relief she went out to the gate.

Her relief turned to joy when she realised that the driver was Kelt. One hand clutching the gatepost, she watched him get out of the big farm vehicle, and her heart expanded within her and soared.

Yes, she thought, giddy with elation, yes, this is what I want. This is right for me now.

The future could look after itself. She might grieve when this was over, but she'd never regret it.

After one searching scrutiny he demanded, 'Have they come ashore?'

'No. No, I'm fine, but I was getting a bit worried.'

He said austerely, 'I've only just got home. Otherwise I'd have been down sooner.'

'They're not actually doing anything I could object to, just making a noise,' she said, adding, 'But I was about to ring. How did you know they were here?'

'I checked the bay when I drove in. I know the owner of the boat; his son and some of his friends—all at university— have been on a cruise around the Bay of Islands, and this is their last night. They're good enough kids, but clearly they've been drinking.' As if it was an afterthought, he went on, 'A lot of deaths at sea are linked to alcohol.'

Of course, his mother had drowned. Quietly Hani asked, 'What can you do?'

'Hail them from the beach, then take them back to the marina.'

Unthinkingly she said, 'How will you get home? Arthur?'

He gave her another keen glance, something kindling in the depths of his eyes that set her pulse dancing. 'Arthur's planning to go out tonight. Why don't you drive to Kaitake and pick me up from there?'

Hani realised that she'd been offered her chance to countermand her rejection. A wild, sweet excitement charged her body with delight. 'Yes, of course.' Before she could say anything else a particularly noisy yell made her glance anxiously over her shoulder. 'But will you be safe? They sound violent.'

'They're just horsing around,' he said with such rock-solid confidence that she almost stopped worrying. 'To be fair, they probably don't know there's someone in residence here.'

Apprehension warred with acceptance. One of the reasons she'd learned to trust Kelt was that sense of responsibility; he wouldn't have been Kelt if he hadn't decided to take them back.

But when he turned to go she grabbed his sleeve. 'Kelt—wait. I don't think—'

He looked down at her. 'Don't worry,' he said calmly. 'I'm not stupid. If I didn't know them I'd get back-up, but they're not bad. Just a bit wild and, at the moment, more than a bit drunk.'

Hani stared at him, then reached up and kissed his mouth. He went rigid, and she was just about to pull back in sick humiliation when he snatched her into his arms and returned the kiss with an uncompromising passion that sent hunger rocketing through her.

Eyes gleaming, he put her away from him and surveyed her with narrowed, glittering eyes. 'You shouldn't do that sort of thing if you don't want to arouse false hopes.'

'I do,' she said, flushing hotly.

'Do what?'

That fierce kiss had unsealed something inside her, let loose a need that ached through her like a sweet fever.

'Do want to arouse,' she repeated, holding his gaze as more colour scorched across her face. 'And the hopes wouldn't be false.'

CHAPTER ELEVEN

EYES narrowed and intent, Kelt looked down at her. Hani gave him a tremulous, shy smile. He made as if to step towards her, then stopped. His hands clenched at his sides, and he said between his teeth, 'I'll hold you to that.'

Hani's heart pounded, almost blocking out the sound of the waves on the sand. *What had she done?* But it was right; some primal womanly instinct told Hani that if she didn't surrender to this moment, this man, she'd regret it for the rest of her life.

Trying to look cool and sophisticated, she said, 'I'll see you at the marina.'

'It will take the cruiser about half an hour to get there.' He paused another charged moment, then turned and strode off towards the beach without looking back.

Tensely, anxiously, Hani watched him come to a stop just above the tidemark. He didn't have to hail the boat; the men on the cruiser saw him, and after a short shouted exchange of words a small rubber dinghy came hurtling recklessly towards the shore, grounding on the sand with a jerk that almost hurled the driver overboard.

Kelt said something that set the driver laughing as he collected himself. With one strong, sure movement Kelt heaved the dinghy into deeper water, then swung lithely into the craft and took the controls.

Hani relaxed, thinking with a trace of irony that her anxiety had been entirely wasted. But she stayed there, fingers knotted together, her straining gaze fixed on his tall, athletic figure until he climbed into the cruiser. The other men crowded around him, clearly welcoming his arrival. Ten minutes later the anchor rattled up, and the big boat swung smoothly around, a faint wake feathering the water as it made its way out between the tree-clad headlands.

Almost half an hour later to the minute, Hani watched the big cruiser ease into a mooring at the marina. The disembarked sailors were less noisy by now, and became noticeably more subdued when they were met by a man—presumably the owner of the boat. Kelt spoke to him, and the two men shook hands before Kelt started towards her.

Her heart picked up speed again, and her eyes turned hungry. He looked...wonderful. Tall and lithe and—hers. For tonight, anyway.

Oh, she hoped so.

'Everything's OK,' he said briefly as he got into the passenger seat.

Feeling oddly pleased that he trusted her to drive him home, she put the car in gear and concentrated on backing out. 'Obviously you didn't have any trouble with them.'

He looked a trifle surprised. 'Not after I pointed out that by letting me take them back they might—*just*—be trusted to take the cruiser out again, whereas they wouldn't have a show if I had to ring the owner and ask him to come and deal with the situation.'

Her laugh took him by surprise. Low and huskily seductive, it rippled through the car like music. 'You should do that more often,' he said without thinking.

'What? Reverse?'

'Laugh. I don't think I've heard it before.'

What the hell had happened to her? Something so traumatic that it had killed her laughter.

Her sideways glance reminded him of a hunted animal, but her voice was level and cool. 'I'm sure you must have—or am I that glum?'

'I wouldn't describe you as glum.' Look at the road, he told himself. If he kept his eyes off her perhaps he could restrain his reckless hunger, so heady it threatened to unleash the control he'd always kept over himself.

He'd never had any worry about restraint before, but tonight, with Hannah, he'd need to temper his carnal craving. She'd had at least one bad experience; he didn't want to terrify her, or hurt her.

He wanted to make it perfect for her.

She startled him by saying, 'If I haven't laughed in the time you've known me I must be lousy company.'

'Fishing?' he asked laconically, because talking nonsense might help. 'You must realise that I find your company extremely—stimulating. Your laughter was worth the wait.'

More than anything—even more than satisfying the carnal hunger that prowled through him—he wanted to hear her laugh again.

Fiercely Hani concentrated on driving. His words twisted her heart, adding something vital to the purely physical charge between them.

If she kept on this way, she thought in a sudden panic, she might end up loving him, a willing prisoner of desire.

She didn't dare.

She just didn't have the courage to open her heart again, to accept the possibility—no, she admitted starkly, the *inevitability*—of pain.

About to tell him she couldn't go through with it, she clamped her lips together. Don't dress this up as love, she advised herself trenchantly. You did that once before, and look where it got you…

Think of making love to Kelt as medicine you have to take to get well again.

Nice medicine…

And could have laughed at the banality of her thoughts. Making love to Kelt would be a sensuous, mind-blowing delight, nothing like medicine.

And she was going to do it because she'd let Felipe's brutality crush her instincts for far too long. But more—oh, so much more, some hidden part of her jeered—because she *wanted* Kelt. Wanted him so much she could actually taste the longing on her tongue; she ached with it, afire with the hunger that now seemed so normal, so natural. Anticipation ran hotly through her, melting her racing, tumbled thoughts, her inhibitions in a flood of hungry desire.

She said, 'I'll see to it that I laugh more, then.'

'I'll look forward to it,' he told her with a narrow smile that made her concentrate on keeping her breath steady.

The rest of the trip home was conducted in almost complete silence.

Home? she thought in bewilderment, shocked at the mental slip. Moraze had always been her one true home, but somehow this beautiful, peaceful place had become precious.

Slowing down as they approached the turn-off to his house, she said, 'Oh, I forgot. Your car is at the bach.' She flashed him a glance. 'Would you like to stay to dinner?'

She didn't dare look at him again during the short silence before he said, 'Thank you, yes. I need a shower, so drop me off here and I'll walk down.'

Obediently she did that, saying just as he got out, 'I've already made chilli, but I like it hot. If you don't I can make something else, although it won't be meat.'

'Don't worry, I like it hot too,' he said, his cool tone very much at variance with the dark gleam in his eyes.

Hani drove off, wondering what on earth had pushed her into that invitation. A weak effort to give their lovemaking some context, a feeble pretence that it meant more than a soulless connection of bodies?

Probably, she thought, but at least this time she knew what she was doing.

Gabby greeted her with joy from amidst a newspaper in shreds over the sitting-room floor. Laughing, Hani cleared it up, took the pup for a short walk outside, then hurried through the shower and into a sunfrock with a pretty little bolero to cover her upper arms as the sun went down.

As she took the chilli from the fridge she wondered whether she should try to reduce its bite. Well, she had a large pot of New Zealand's superb yoghurt and some coriander. If Kelt burnt his mouth he could ease it with that.

With it she'd serve rice and a large green salad, followed by strawberries and the yoghurt. A bubble of anticipation expanded in her stomach.

But she had no wine. After a moment she shrugged. It wasn't necessary, and besides, wine and chilli didn't always go well together. Anyway, she didn't need alcohol; she was half-intoxicated already, as though the very best French champagne were circulating through her veins.

When Kelt came in through the door the feeling of delirious

lightness morphed into something darker, more potent. Deep inside her a smouldering erotic hunger blazed into desperate life at the hard-honed angles of his handsome face, the air of power and command that controlled his compelling masculinity.

In a raw voice he said, 'I brought some champagne, but I don't need it. Just looking at you is enough to make me drunk.'

Hani had no idea what to say. Unevenly she finally managed, 'Put it in the fridge.'

She'd imagined them sitting outside as the sun sank over the hills, talking a little, but suddenly she felt she couldn't wait. Trying to hide the heady clamour of desire, she stirred the chilli, but when the silence stretched too far she had to glance up.

He was still watching her, his eyes narrowed and intent, his mouth a hard, straight line.

Hunger tore at her. Smiling tremulously, she put the spoon down.

He took a step towards her before stopping to say in a thick, driven voice, 'I'm not going to touch you. Not yet.'

Something splintered into shards of sensation inside her. In a tone she didn't recognise she said, 'In that case, do you mind if I touch you?'

'Hannah,' he said, and then with a tight, humourless laugh, 'No, you should be Honey. It suits you much better. Warm and golden and sweet—you've been tormenting me ever since I saw you. Once you touch me I doubt very much if I'll be responsible for anything that happens.'

Dazzled by the thought of affecting him so strongly, she came slowly towards him, eyes darkening as she took in the control he was exerting, the clenched hands, his waiting, predatory stillness.

She should be afraid, she thought exultantly, but she wasn't scared of Kelt.

Hands behind her back, she stood on tiptoe and kissed the tanned hollow of his throat. He made a muffled sound and his arms came around her, pulling her against him so hard she could feel every rigid muscle, the powerful male strength he was keeping in check, the rapid uneven pounding of his heart—and the hunger that met and matched hers.

And then he lifted her, and she remembered how amazingly safe she'd always felt in his arms. Hers tightened around his neck as he shouldered through the door into the bedroom and across to the big bed, sitting her down on the side with a gentleness that reassured every drifting, hardly recognised fear.

He dropped a swift, famished kiss on her throat, then straightened, looking down at her with a glitter in his eyes that set her pulses racing so fast she thought she might faint with anticipation.

'I don't even dare undress you,' he said with a taut smile. 'I might tear this pretty thing, and that would be a shame.'

He was talking, she realised, to ease the tension that gripped them both. A swift relief swept over her at his understanding. In a soft, low voice she said, 'Then perhaps we should undress ourselves.'

'An excellent idea.' He stepped back and his hands went to the opening of his shirt.

Fascinated, she watched his lean fingers flick open the buttons to reveal the broad chest beneath, his powerful muscles emphasised by a scroll of hair across the sleek, tanned skin. Excitement clamoured through Hani, a fierce demand she'd never known before.

When he'd shrugged out of his shirt she said on a sharp, indrawn breath, 'You are—magnificent.'

'Thank you.' One black brow rose when she continued drinking him in.

Flushing, she pulled off her tiny bolero, revealing her bare shoulders. Heat kindled in the cold blue flames of his eyes, but he made no move towards her as she eased the sundress over her head.

Too shy to let it drop to the floor, she let it hang loosely in front of her. Dry-throated, she said, 'I think it must be your turn.'

He removed his shoes and socks, then let his trousers drop to the floor.

Hani dragged a startled breath into empty lungs. Long legs, strongly muscled from riding, narrow hips, and he was— big, she thought, her eyes darting from the sole part of his anatomy that still clothed.

'May I?'

Closing her eyes for a second, she nodded, opening them only when he'd taken her dress from her nerveless fingers and put it on the chair beside the bed.

Clad only in one small scrap of cotton, she had never felt so naked.

Harshly he said, 'You are utterly beautiful.'

And for him she felt beautiful. With a trembling smile she held out her arms, and he came down beside her with a rush, tumbling her backwards so that her breasts were exposed and open to his eager mouth.

But first he kissed her lips—tender, quick kisses that stoked the fires between her loins unbearably. Then he possessed himself of her mouth, plunging deep in an imitation of the most intimate embrace of all. Almost immediately she shuddered with hunger, her straining body afire against the hard, potent length of his, her breath coming in short, hoarse pants, her eyes wild as she stared up into his face.

Hani expected him to take her there and then, but instead he kissed her breasts, made himself master of her body, caressing with his hands and his tongue so that her every cell recognised and responded to his touch.

And he gave her the freedom to do the same to him until she learned intimately the swell of muscle and line of sinew, the fine matte texture of his skin, the contrast with the scrolls of hair across his chest, the way his body tensed beneath her seeking hands...

Frantic, driven by a voluptuous desire, a longing so desperate all her fears disappeared, she pulled at him, her hands tightening across the sleek skin of his back, her voice urgent and importunate.

Until at last he moved over her and with one smooth, easy thrust took her.

Every muscle in Hani's body contracted, welcoming him, clinging to him, beginning an involuntary, automatic rhythm that soared higher and higher into a place she'd never known, so when at last the climax overwhelmed her in delight and ecstasy she cried out and surrendered completely.

Only to be hurled further into that unknown rapture when he joined her there, his big body tense and bowed, his head flung back. Locked in erotic union, they reached that place together, and eventually came down together, slick bodies relaxing, their hearts slowing into a normal rhythm until Kelt turned to catch her in his arms again and pull her against him.

He kissed her wordless murmur into silence, and said against her lips, 'Tired?'

'Mmm,' she said, and he laughed, and held her while she slid into sleep unlike anything she'd ever known before.

It was dark when she woke, and she knew instantly that he was awake. She was sprawled across him, her head pillowed on one shoulder, her hair streaming across his chest.

He must have sensed her wakening, because he said, 'It's almost midnight.'

'Oh, lord,' she said, suffused with guilt, 'and I haven't fed you! How long have you been awake?'

'Long enough.' He dropped a kiss on the top of her head. 'Long enough for what?'

The silence was so short she thought it hadn't happened until he drawled wickedly, 'To work up an appetite.'

She spluttered into laughter, and hurtled off the bed. 'Then we'd better eat that dinner—if it's still edible,' she said, climbing into her dressing gown.

Smiling, he got up, and together they ate, took Gabby out, and drank a little champagne, only to leave it unfinished when desire overpowered them once more.

Hani slept again, but woke to tears aching behind her eyes, tears that spilled across Kelt's chest. Grateful that he stayed asleep, she surrendered to bitter-sweet joy. In his arms she'd found true fulfilment, and now she knew that when this interlude was over she'd spend the rest of her life longing for him.

But she had never been so happy. Making love with Kelt had been—amazing and wonderful and glorious and sensuous and…just plain *magnificent*.

Just as amazing was that she hadn't thought of Felipe once.

For the first time she felt well and truly loved in every respect.

Except the emotional, she realised as days and nights passed in a voluptuous feast for all her senses—a dazzling, mind-blowing parade of sensuousness in which Kelt taught her just how wonderful making love could be.

Each day she fell deeper and deeper into love—and knew with a hopeless hunger that Kelt didn't love her. Although he showed her he could be tender and generous as well as passionate and demanding, she sensed an unbridged distance between them.

She didn't ask for anything more; she even tried to convince herself that she was well content. But as the summer lazed on, she found herself wondering if perhaps—just perhaps—they might some time cross the invisible, unspoken boundaries they'd set on their affair.

Daydreaming again…

One evening, coming back into the bay after a picnic on a tiny offshore island, he asked, 'It's over six weeks since you had that bout of fever.'

Hani trailed her hand in the water and frowned as she counted the days. 'So it is.' She watched him rowing the old wooden dinghy, letting her eyes drift meaningfully over his shoulders, the muscles bunching with each smooth flick of the oars. 'I've been occupied with other things,' she said sweetly, and flicked some water his way.

He grinned. 'Mind over matter?'

'Or the placebo effect.'

He laughed, his eyes gleaming. 'Perhaps there's something to it. We could get all scientific about this; I have to go away in three days' time, so we could see whether you keep count of the time while I'm away.'

Lost in the wonder of being his lover, Hani had to bite her tongue to stop herself from asking him where he was going.

'I'll be away about ten days,' he said calmly. 'I'd ask you to come with me—'

Before he could come up with whatever excuse, she shook her head and interrupted. 'No.' Her heart twisted. Not ever. She hurried on, 'As for the fever, I think it's gone. I feel—strong, somehow. Good.'

The dinghy grounded on the sand and things went on

exactly the same—at least, that was what Hani told herself. But for the three days she found herself tensing whenever he came, almost as though she had to extract every ounce of pleasure, commit to memory every tiny alteration in his deep voice, the way his smile melted her bones—even the exact shade of his eyes, so close to the border between blue and steel-grey that it was impossible to state categorically what colour they were...

And that, she thought robustly, was stupid. He'd only be away for a week and a half.

The days dragged. Oh, she had the delicious memories of the night before he'd left when he'd made love to her as though—as though he wasn't coming back, she thought, trying to laugh at herself.

But memories weren't enough. She wanted Kelt. No, worse than that—she *needed* him.

The night before he was due back restlessness and an oppressive cloud of foreboding drove her to seek refuge from her own thoughts and longings, and she sat with Gabby in her lap—a bigger and more sturdy puppy now, showing every sign of developing a strong character. The soft, warm weight comforted her a little, but she longed to see Kelt again, to tell him...what?

I love you? 'Not likely,' she said forlornly, and got up and turned off the television.

Later, she heard the low sound of a car come down the hill. She began to shake, then got to her feet and walked carefully to the door, opening it as Kelt raised his hand to knock.

His face was drawn, but he was smiling. Every cell in her body recognised him with joyous outcry. Holding out her hands, she drew him in with her and lifted her face in mute invitation.

He kissed her with a famished intensity that banished every

last inhibition. When at last he lifted his head, she said, 'You were away nine days, eleven hours and forty-three minutes.'

'I know.' His eyes gleamed with sensuous amusement. 'And every one of them dragged.'

'I know.' She laughed softly, huskily, and kissed his throat. 'Food first?'

Or do you want to go straight to bed?

Her unspoken question astonished her. How had she summoned the courage to be so—so brazen?

A darting look up from beneath her lashes revealed the strong framework of his face, as though the tanned skin had tightened over it.

And his voice was raw when he said, 'If you keep that up we won't make it to the bed.'

Boldly she lifted her head and kissed his chiselled mouth, then outlined it with the tip of her tongue. His heart thudded against her, strong and fast. Heat bloomed her skin, and she could have breathed in the faint, elusive male scent of him, tangy and arousing, for the rest of her life.

'That would probably shock Gabby,' she murmured. And added, because she had to, 'You guessed I'd had a bad experience. It's—finished with, Kelt. I'm not afraid any more.'

He looked down at her, eyes narrowed into blazing slits, so piercing she could hardly meet his gaze. 'You're sure?'

'Completely sure.' And to seal it she initiated another kiss, one that was frankly voracious, showing him just how much she wanted him.

This time he returned it—with interest—before sweeping her up in his arms and carrying her once more into the bedroom.

This time—oh, this time there was none of the practised gentleness she'd come to expect. Kelt made love to her as though he'd spent just as many lonely night hours longing for her as she had for him, as though they were lovers separated by years that had only whetted their desire, once more together.

Glorying in his ardour, she allowed her needs and desires free rein, responding to each kindling caress, each sensuously tormenting kiss, with everything she was, everything she felt.

And although their lovemaking was fast and fierce, when that moment of release came again it threw her even higher as wave after wave of pleasure surged through her, sending her to that rapturous place where desire and satisfaction melded into mutual bliss.

Much later, safe in his arms, she accepted that she loved him. And that it didn't matter. The sheer grandeur of her feelings for him outweighed the knowledge of pain to come, when she left him.

She murmured, 'You were away too long.'

'I won't need to go back to Carathia for a while,' he said calmly.

'Carathia?' She yawned. 'Isn't that a little country on the edge of the Adriatic? What were you doing there?'

'I was there on business, but in the end I helped my brother put down a rebellion,' he said dryly.

Love-dazed, her tired mind barely registered the words, but when they sank in she sat up and stared down at him, her heart shaking inside her at the sight of him, long and lean and tanned against the white sheets.

He was smiling, without humour, and his eyes were sombre.

'What? *What* did you say?' she spluttered.

'My brother is the ruler of Carathia.' His expression hardened. 'I went there because there was a spot of bother, and he needed me.' He smiled and pulled her down again, kissing the swell of her breast. 'Mmm,' he murmured against her skin, 'you smell delicious. I sometimes think it's what I miss most about you.'

Little tremors of sensation raced through her, urgently and pleading. Ignoring them, she whispered, 'What do you mean— the ruler?'

The children on the beach had called Kelt the Duke, and talked of a grandmother who wore a crown. Oh, God, why hadn't she listened? Why hadn't she asked?

Kelt turned her face up so that he could see it, and a frown drew his black brows together. 'My brother, Gerd, is the new Grand Duke of Carathia.'

Dreams Hani hadn't even recognised crashed around her. Unbeknown to herself she must have been fantasising— *hoping?*—that somehow, she might be able to forge some sort of connection with Kelt. That with him she'd be able to make a life here in this enchanted place.

That perhaps there might be a future for them if she could trust him enough to be able to tell him about herself and her past.

'I didn't know,' she said in a stunned voice. 'No one told me.' No one but the children...

'Most people around here are aware of it; my grandparents used to come and stay here on occasion, and my brother and I spent all our holidays here.' He finished coolly, 'It's no big deal.'

Hani turned to hide her head in his chest. His casual words had killed every inchoate, wordless hope. She didn't dare have any sort of relationship with a man whose wealth and good looks and ancient heritage made him food for gossip mills. Even as his mistress she'd shame him—she cringed, thinking of the way the tabloids would treat her reappearance.

Kelt asked, 'What is it? Tell me.'

'I didn't know,' she said faintly. And because she couldn't

tell him what that knowledge had done to her, she asked, 'But why do you live here—in New Zealand?'

He shrugged, and his arms tightened around her. She lay with her face against his heart, listening to the slowing beat, inhaling his beloved scent, and felt her world crumble around her again, her splintered hopes painfully stabbing her.

'It's no big deal,' he said again casually. 'Our grandparents met while my grandmother was fighting a nasty little rebellion amongst the mountain people, one fomented by her sister. Our grandfather was a New Zealander, and he saved her life in an ambush. Kiwinui was his heritage, just as it's been mine. They were married, and had one son. Our mother was a Greek princess. We spent quite a lot of time here as children. My brother has always known he'd be Grand Duke one day. I've always preferred New Zealand.'

Hani sensed that he wasn't telling her everything, but she didn't dare speak. Instead she nodded, letting loose a swathe of black hair across his skin. Their hips met, moved together with sensuous languor, and she felt him stir against her.

Tomorrow, she thought weakly. She would steal one more night of paradise in his arms, and tomorrow she'd tell him that it was over.

CHAPTER TWELVE

HANI woke, to find Kelt, fully clothed, bending over her. She smiled and he bent and kissed her.

Against his lips she murmured, 'What…?'

'I am expecting a call from Gerd,' he told her. Then he smiled, and said in a warmer voice, 'Go back to sleep.'

But by then she'd remembered, and her eyes were agonised when he turned and walked out of the door into the half-light of dawn.

When the sound of his vehicle had died away she got up and put Gabby outside. A sliver of golden light against the horizon heralded another summer day, but in her heart it would always be winter.

Dragging her footsteps like an old woman, she walked into the bedroom, Gabby gambolling at her heels. She had to get out of here, before he came back. She'd take the car into Kaitake and catch a bus to—to anywhere. No, to Auckland, because it was big enough to get lost in. She'd leave Gabby with plenty of water and food and ring tonight to make sure they knew she was there. She wasn't worried about getting Kelt; Arthur answered the phone at the homestead.

She'd leave Kelt a note. Feverishly she started composing it in her mind: *It's been great, but I have to go—thank you so much for all you've done for me. Please look after Gabby for me...*

He'd never know just how much he had done for her. Making love with him had wiped the tainted memories of the past, leaving her whole again and stronger than she'd ever been.

'No,' she said out loud, startling herself. 'No, he deserves better than a stupid note.'

Last time she'd run without telling anyone it had been for her life. This time it would be sheer cowardice. She wouldn't leave Kelt without an explanation of why she had to go. Although it would be savagely painful and embarrassing to tell him that she suspected she was falling in love with him, she could at least salvage some sort of honour.

By lunchtime her suitcase was packed and she'd rung for the bus timetable, and was taking the coach that came through later in the afternoon.

A knock on the door froze her into place. She didn't need Gabby's happy little greeting to tell her who it was. I'm not ready, she thought, panic-stricken, knowing she'd never be ready.

Dragging a deep breath into her compressed lungs, she came out of the bedroom and closed the door behind her.

Gabby was prancing around the door, her tail wagging. White-faced, Hani opened the door to Kelt, who took one look at her and demanded, 'What the hell is the matter?'

Before she had time to think, she blurted, 'I have something to tell you.'

His eyes hardened, but he came in and closed the door behind him. 'Are you sure? It's early days yet, but don't worry. We'll get married.'

Hani's heart gave a great leap, then settled like a lead weight in her chest. Retreating a few paces, she said, 'I'm not pregnant.' Pain stabbed her, sharp and brutal.

His brows drew together and she saw the warrior, angular and relentless. 'All right, what is it?'

'I'll be leaving soon,' she said quietly. 'I just wanted you to know that you've made me very happy and I'll always remember you.'

His eyes narrowed. In a silky voice he said, 'If that's so, why are you going? And before you say anything, I know you love me, so it has to be something else.'

Hani stared at him. 'How arrogant you are,' she said, but the spark had gone from her voice and she had to force herself to meet that merciless gaze. 'We made love, that's all. There's a difference.'

A cold kick of fear silenced her as she watched his hands clench into fists by his sides. 'Is that all it was?' he asked in a voice like molten metal. He smiled, and came towards her, and for the first time ever she felt truly afraid of him.

Yet she didn't flinch when he raised his hands and his fingers settled gently around the golden column of her throat. He was so close she could see the pulse beating in his jaw, smell the hot, primal scent that was his alone; if she lifted the hand that itched to move of its own accord, she'd feel the heat of his fine-grained skin against her fingertips.

And she'd melt in abject surrender.

He said softly, 'How could it be so unimportant when it made you cry? That first night—you thought I was asleep, but I heard you, felt the hot tears soak into my skin, and I knew then that whatever you felt for me wasn't something you'd ever forget.'

Do it now. Make it clear. Head held high, she met his narrowed gaze and said coolly, 'I had issues from the past. You showed me how unimportant they were. I'll always be grateful to you for that.'

'I don't believe you,' he said between his teeth. 'Tell me the truth, Hannah.'

If she did he'd despise her. Dumbly she stared up into icy eyes.

His fingers smoothed over the rapidly beating pulse at the base of her throat, then he dropped his hands and stepped back, smiling without humour. 'So you've had your *past issues*—' he said the words with caustic emphasis '—resolved by extremely good sex, and now you're leaving, no bones broken, no hearts cracked.'

Instantly Hani felt cold, abandoned. She owed him the truth. In a low, shamed voice, she said, 'Why didn't you tell me you weren't what I thought you were, an ordinary New Zealand farmer—?'

'I *am* a New Zealand farmer—'

'You're much more than that. Your grandmother is a grand duchess, and you are not only rich, you're also hugely powerful. You must have known I didn't know.'

'Oddly enough,' he said in a caustic voice, 'I found your attitude interesting, and very refreshing. But what difference does any of that make?'

She braced herself. 'A lot. You really don't know anything about me. I'm afraid I've lied to you again and again.' It took all of her courage to go on, but she had to make him understand. 'Starting with my name. It's neither Hannah nor Honey. Until six years ago I was Hani de Courteville, and my brother was Rafiq de Courteville, the ruler of Moraze.'

'Moraze?' She watched as his keen mind processed the information and slotted it into place. His lashes drooped. 'Go on.'

Everything about him—tone, stance, the formidable intensity of his gaze—was intimidating, but he didn't seem shocked. In fact, she thought wonderingly, her revelation seemed to have confirmed something he'd already suspected.

A small warmth of hope gave her the impetus to continue.

'I spent my childhood there, and went to boarding-school in England, and then to a French university. I was eighteen, and too young—too stupid—to be let loose.' She took another agonising breath. 'My brother organised a chaperone-cum-companion for me, who introduced me to a man called Felipe Gastano. He said he was a French count; later I found out that it was his half-brother who had been born to the title. Unfortunately the brother died conveniently from a drug overdose not long before I met Gastano.'

'Keep going,' Kelt ordered, his gaze never wavering.

She looked down at her hands. The knuckles were white and she was holding herself so stiffly her spine ached. 'He was enormous fun and possessed great charm. I won't bore you with details of our affair; it began with me convinced I had found the man I wanted to marry, and ended when I tried to commit suicide, and only failed by good luck. Or bad luck, as I thought it at the time.'

He said something in a lethal voice, then in a totally different tone, 'My poor girl.' And then his voice changed. 'So why do you plan to leave?'

She could have held out against his anger; that flash of tenderness struck home like an arrow.

In a thin thread of a voice Hani said, 'Felipe introduced me to drugs. I know now that he did it quite deliberately. By the time I decided to commit suicide I was an addict and in desperate trouble.' She didn't dare look at him. 'Felipe intended to take over Moraze and use it as a depot to ship drugs to Europe.'

'How?' Kelt demanded forcefully. 'Your brother would never have allowed that.'

'I was the lever, the hold Felipe would have had over Rafiq. And he—Rafiq—was the lever Felipe used on me.'

A flash of fury in the steel-blue eyes was swiftly extinguished, but she felt it emanating from him, fiercely controlled but violent. Before he could speak she hurried on, 'I told him I was leaving him, but he threatened to have Rafiq killed if I did.'

'Go on,' Kelt said evenly.

She could read nothing—neither condemnation nor sympathy in his expression. Chilled, she forced herself to continue, 'I knew then that the only thing I could do was die. But not before I'd written to Rafiq, telling him what Felipe planned to do. Then I went to a small Mediterranean island where Rafiq and I had holidayed once. I just walked into the water, and it was such a relief when I finally gave up swimming and surrendered to the sea.'

She could see the rigid control he was exerting, and some part of her was warmed by it.

'So how did you survive?'

'I don't know,' she said simply. 'I lost consciousness, but before I could drown a fisherman found me.'

Kelt said through his teeth, 'You should have told your brother what had happened to you—he wouldn't have blamed you.'

She gave a bleak, cynical smile. 'Perhaps I should have, but I was an addict. They don't make sensible decisions.' And she'd been so bitterly ashamed. She still was.

'So why did the fisherman not turn you over to the authorities?'

'He was a smuggler, but he was a kind man. He dragged me into his boat and took me to his family. I pleaded with them not to tell anyone where I was.'

'So you could have another go at killing yourself?' he demanded harshly.

'At first,' she admitted, pale and cold under his implacable gaze. 'His wife and mother nursed me through the aftermath of drug addiction, and they all kept quiet about the fact that I'd survived. I owe my life and my sanity to them, and although I was sure I'd never, ever be happy again, they made me promise not to try to kill myself. They said I owed them that, as they'd saved me.' She gave a pale smile. 'The grand-mother told me I had to live so that I could make amends for what I'd done.'

In a voice she'd never heard him use before Kelt said, 'I'd like to meet that family. But I would like even more to meet this Gastano.'

'You can't—he's dead; I searched for him on the internet that day in Kaitake. It's horrible—wicked—to be glad a man is dead, but I am.' At least Kelt and Rafiq were safe now. 'Felipe didn't kill people himself—he ordered others to do it, and it would have been done.' She shivered. 'Even a puppy he bought for me—once he asked me to do something—' She stopped, unable to go on.

'What exactly did he want from you?' Kelt's voice lifted every tiny hair on her body in a reflex old as time.

She'd started this; she had to finish it. 'I'd agreed to go out to lunch with a friend from school. Felipe didn't want me to go, but I made a feeble attempt at asserting my independence and went anyway. He got his chauffeur to kill the puppy while I was away.'

'What happened to him?' Kelt's voice was corrosive.

'Felipe must have tried to use Moraze anyway, because he was killed there in a shoot-out with the military. I suppose he thought that even without me to use as a hostage he could force Rafiq to obey him.' She said in a shaking voice, 'He didn't know Rafiq, of course.'

'When you found out this Gastano was dead, why didn't you let your brother know you were alive?'

'I am ashamed,' she said in a low, shaking voice. 'There are people who know what I was reduced to—who know about me. Young Alonso de Porto, for one.'

'You were targeted and preyed upon,' he said between his teeth. 'Who cares about them?'

'If only you were an ordinary New Zealand farmer it wouldn't really matter,' she said passionately, dark eyes begging him to understand, her voice completely flat, without hope. 'But you're not—you are rich, you have royal links and if we…if we continue our affair, it would soon turn up in the tabloids and then—I'd be found again!'

'Why is that a problem?' he asked relentlessly.

Hani was wringing her hands. Forcing them into stillness, she took several deep breaths and looked him straight in the eye. 'You deserve better than to be embroiled in such a scandal.'

It was impossible to read his face when he demanded, 'Do you love me?'

Don't do this, her heart whispered. She hesitated, huge, imploring eyes fixed on his face. 'I—' She swallowed, unable to say the words. Why wasn't he satisfied with what she'd already told him? Did he want her heart on a plate?

Ruthlessly he said, 'I didn't think you were a coward. Do you love me, Hani?'

Hani flinched. The sound of her real name was inexpressibly sweet on his tongue. 'Think of the uproar if it ever got out that I am alive and was your mistress! Like Rafiq and his family—his wife and two little boys—you'd be shamed in the eyes of the world.'

Willing him to understand, she gazed at him pleadingly, but his expression was controlled, all violence leashed. 'Answer my question.'

Something in his tone alerted Gabby, who stretched elaborately and climbed out of her basket, fussily pacing across to sit on Hani's feet, where she indulged in a good scratch.

Hani hesitated again, her breath knotting in her throat.

'One simple word,' Kelt said inflexibly. 'Either yes or no.'

'I'm afraid,' she whispered.

'I know. But you have to say it.'

She licked her lips. 'I—oh, you know the answer!'

'Tell me.'

Tears magnified her eyes. He didn't come near her, but she could feel him willing her to answer. And from somewhere she found the courage. Unable to bear looking at him, she said in a muffled voice, 'Yes. Yes, of course I love you. I would die for you. But I couldn't bear it if you were humiliated or hurt or made a laughing stock because I was stupidly naïve and—'

'Very young,' he said, and at last came across and took her into his strong embrace.

'But once people know who I am, the whole sordid story will be in every tabloid, and people will sneer at you.' She stared up into his dark, beloved face, then grabbed his arms in desperation and tried to shake some sense into him. It was like trying to move a rock. 'Have you thought of that?'

He asked, 'Have you ever been tempted to use drugs again?'

'Oh, no.' Near to breaking, she shuddered. 'No, not ever again. That was why I came down with such a bad case of fever—I don't like taking anything in case I become addicted.'

'Then you can chalk the whole hideous experience up to youthful folly.'

Unevenly she said, 'Kelt, it's not so simple. What will your brother think?'

He gave her a little shake and said, 'Look at me.'

Slowly, not daring to hope, she lifted her eyes.

Speaking firmly, he said, 'I don't care what Gerd or anyone

else thinks. I'm not going to let you spend the rest of your life expiating sins you didn't commit. You were young, and you were deliberately targeted by an evil man.'

She had to make him see sense. 'Rafiq,' she said urgently. 'My brother—'

Frowning, he interrupted, 'If it had been your brother this had happened to, would you turn away from him?'

More tears ached behind her eyes. 'Of course not,' she said quickly, 'but—'

'I understand why you had to escape, but that reason no longer applies,' Kelt said, his calm tone somehow reinforcing his words. He paused and let her go, taking a step backwards and leaving her alone and cold and aching with love.

When she said nothing, he went on, 'It comes down to one thing only; either you join me in my life and trust me to look after you and our children—stop shaking your head, of course we'll have children!—or I will simply have to kidnap you and keep you here, chained to my side.'

Colour came and went in her skin, and a wild, romantic hope warred with fear. She stared at him, saw uncompromising resolve in his expression, in the straight line of his beautiful mouth, and although her heart quailed joy fountained up through her.

'You're a hard man,' she said, her voice shaking. 'And I love you. But I can't, Kelt. I don't—I just don't have the courage.'

'You had the courage to tell your brother what was going on, to try to sacrifice yourself for him and your country, to hide to keep them safe. You have the courage to do this.'

Her breath caught in her throat. 'You make me out to be more than I am.'

'You are much more than that, my valiant warrior, and I look forward to a long life together so I can convince you of that. I don't blame you for not wanting your story blazed across the media, but it can be managed. I can protect you, and together we'll stare the world down.' Then he smiled, and her heart melted. 'So, can you take that last step and tell me where you'd like to live?'

Hani drew in a sobbing breath and surrendered. He hadn't said anything yet about loving her, but she didn't care. As long as he wanted her she would treasure each day she spent with him.

'I'll live wherever you are,' she told him quietly, her gaze never leaving his beloved face. 'Because if I don't, I won't really be living at all—just existing, as I have been for years. But—could it be here? I love this place.'

This time the loving was different. She expected—longed for—a wild triumph from him, but he was all tenderness, a gentle lovemaking that was strangely more erotic than anything they'd shared before, spun out so long that she lost her composure completely and gave him everything he wanted, demanded everything from him.

And when it was over he cradled her into his lean body and said against her forehead, 'I love you. I want you to marry me as soon as you can organise a wedding.'

Astounded, Hani stared up at him. 'All right,' she whispered, then wept into his shoulder.

'I didn't know,' she finally muttered when he'd mopped her up.

'That I love you?' His voice was harsh, raw with an emotion she had to accept. 'Of course I love you. I've loved you ever since I saw you. Never doubt me.' He paused, his face hardening, and said, 'But before we marry, you need to get in touch with your brother.'

'I—' She froze. 'Oh, God,' she whispered, her throat closing.

'You know you must,' he said quietly. 'I intend to show the world that, whatever happened in the past, I'm not ashamed of loving you. I want to flaunt this precious gift I've been given, and I can't do that if you insist on hiding away like a criminal. You can do it. You're no longer the terrified girl who tried to kill herself and then had to run, and I'll be with you.'

She dragged in a shivering breath. Like this, skin to skin, the sound of his heart in her ears, his body lithe and powerful against her, here in his arms, she could be brave.

And his words had made her think; she would never have turned away from her brother.

'How can Rafiq forgive me for everything I did?' she asked in a muffled voice. 'Most of all for my cowardly silence, allowing him to think I was dead, after the suicide attempt.'

'You'd forgive him.'

'Rafiq would never be so weak—so stupid. He is strong.'

'So are you,' Kelt said, his voice very tender. 'And you're no longer the green girl he once knew—you've grown and matured and gained self-command.'

She looked up into his beloved face. 'And if I don't do this I'll be letting Felipe win.'

He nodded, holding her eyes with his. If Rafiq rejected her she'd be devastated, but she wouldn't be alone. Not any more.

Capitulating, she dragged in another shuddering breath. 'Then I'll go to Moraze.'

'I'll come with you.'

Thirty-six hours later she was walking down the steps of the private jet Kelt had chartered, her knees shaking so badly she didn't dare look around the international airport at Moraze. Kelt slung an arm around her shoulders.

'Relax,' he said calmly. 'Everything will be all right.'

'I know.'

An hour previously she'd rung Rafiq's personal number, and the memory of that conversation was seared in her brain. He had organised for them to land in the military area and a helicopter was standing by to take them to the *castello*.

Sitting tensely in the chopper as it approached the grey castle that once kept watch over the approach to Moraze's harbour, she clutched Kelt's hand.

'It will be all right,' he repeated calmly, sliding his arm around her.

'I c-can't—he *cried*, Kelt. He *cried* when I convinced him that I am alive.'

He kissed her into quietness. 'Of course,' he said. 'If I had a dearly loved sister returned to me from the dead I'd weep too.'

Fortified by her love and Kelt's unfailing support, she no longer automatically assumed every man was like Felipe Gastano, but this startled her into silence.

'I should have met you six years ago,' she said forlornly, then added, 'No, I was too young. Tukuulu taught me things I'll never forget—that I can survive on my own, that I can do work that is worthwhile, that there are people infinitely worse off than I could ever be, and that people are basically the same the world over. I grew up there.'

She wore sunglasses, keeping them on even when the servant—someone she didn't know—ushered them through the *castello*. Kelt's steady hand at her elbow gave her comfort and resolve.

The servant opened the door into Rafiq's study. Her brother was standing by the window, but he turned to look across the room as she took off her sunglasses and produced a wobbly smile for him.

'I'm so sorry,' she said uncertainly. 'So sorry I let you down, and so very sorry I let you believe I was dead.'

He still said nothing, and she went on in a muted voice, 'You see, I thought then it—it was best.'

He came towards her then, his handsome face set in lines that showed her how much control he was exerting. In their shared language he said quietly, 'I have always blamed myself for letting you go without a proper person to look after you.' He held out his arms.

With a choked little cry she ran into them, and for long moments he held her, gently rocking her as she wept on his shoulder.

At last, when she was more composed, he held her away from him and said in English, 'You were always beautiful, but you are radiant now.' His green eyes flicked from her face to that of the man watching them. 'So, having had you restored to me, I understand I am to lose you again? Introduce your man to me.'

Much later, when she and Kelt were alone on the terrace in the shade of the starflower tree, with the moon shining kindly down onto a silver lagoon, he asked, 'All demons slain now?'

'Yes, thank God,' she said soberly, so happy that it hurt. 'When Rafiq told me that everyone in Felipe's organisation was either dead or in prison, I felt a weight roll off my back.'

'I can't help but wish I'd had some hand in Gastano's death,' Kelt said evenly.

She shivered. 'He was an evil man, and nobody will be sorry he's dead.'

'Those who live by death and treachery, die that way,' Kelt said, his tone ruthless.

She was silent for a few moments, then turned and looked up into his face. Kelt could be hard and she suspected that he could be even more dangerous than Felipe had ever been, yet he'd shown her tenderness unsurpassed, and understanding and love.

Stumbling, her words low and intense, she tried to tell him what he meant to her. 'You have stripped his memory of power. You have shown me that there is nothing more potent than love. I'll never be able to thank you enough—'

'Thanks aren't necessary or wanted,' he broke in, his voice rough. 'Will you be happy with the life we'll lead? It will be mainly in New Zealand, because I can't live in Carathia.'

Something in his tone alerted her. 'Why not?' she asked anxiously.

'In the country districts there is a legend that the country will only ever be at peace when the second child in the royal family rules. The rebellion my grandmother fought off was an attempt by her younger sister to take the throne from her. I am the second child.'

She stared at him. 'And this is a problem for your brother?'

'At the moment, yes. The legend has resurfaced, and with it stirrings of rebellion, only my security men have discovered that it's being fomented by a cartel that want to take over the mines.'

'Like Felipe with Moraze,' she said in a low, horrified voice.

'Indeed.' His tone was layered with irony.

Slowly, wondering at the coincidence, she said, 'So you understand.'

'I do indeed. Except that for me there has never been any sense of exile. I have no desire to rule Carathia, and since I was young I've always considered myself more of a New Zealander than a Carathian. I can run our enterprise as easily from New Zealand as Carathia, although there will always be occasions when I have to travel.'

'I'll come with you,' she said quickly. 'But is everything all right for your brother now?'

'Yes, the rebellion has been well and truly squashed.'

'How? Were you—was there fighting?'

'No,' he said calmly. 'I toured the area and told the people that I would never rule Carathia, that I was planning to marry and live for the rest of my life in New Zealand. It seems to have done the trick; once they realised I was in earnest, the agents who were stirring the trouble were greeted with curses.'

She said fiercely, 'It must have been dangerous. Don't you ever dare to do anything like that again.'

He drew her to him, his expression softening. 'You and our children will always come first with me.'

The kiss that followed was intensely sweet. When at last he lifted his head she clung, so filled with joy she couldn't even stammer a word.

He said, 'And once we've said goodbye to Rafiq and Lexie you have my family to meet. You'll like my brother—and he'll like you. Hell, you'll probably even like Rosie's mother, who's as flaky as they come!'

'I can deal with flake,' she told him exuberantly, eyes mischievous in the glamorous witchery of moonlight. 'I'm so happy I can deal with anything. I can't wait to marry you and live with you in your house on the hill overlooking our bay.'

He laughed, drew her into the warm circle of his arms, and kissed her again. Home at last, Hani knew that from now on she would always be safe in Kelt's love.

* * * * *

PASSION, PURITY AND
THE PRINCE

BY
ANNIE WEST

Annie West spent her childhood with her nose between the covers of a book—a habit she retains. After years preparing government reports and official correspondence she decided to write something she *really* enjoys. And there's nothing she loves more than a great romance. Despite her office-bound past, she has managed a few interesting moments—including a marriage offer with the promise of a herd of camels to sweeten the contract. She is happily married to her ever-patient husband (who has never owned a dromedary). They live with their two children amongst the tall eucalypts at beautiful Lake Macquarie, on Australia's east coast. You can e-mail Annie at www.annie-west.com, or write to her at PO Box 1041, Warners Bay, NSW 2282, Australia.

CHAPTER ONE

'HIS HIGHNESS will be here soon. Please remain in this room and *do not wander*. There are strict security controls and alarms in this part of the castle.'

The prince's aide spoke in clipped English and gave Tamsin a stern look. As if after finally passing the barriers of royal protocol and officious secretaries she'd run amok now she was within the royal sanctum.

As if, after weeks working in the Ruvingian royal archives and living in her suite on the far side of the castle courtyard, proximity to flesh and blood royalty might be too much for her! She'd never seen the prince. He never deigned to cross the courtyard to the functional archive room.

She stifled an impatient sigh.

Did she look the sort of woman to be overcome by pomp and wealth? Or be impressed by a man whose reputation as a womaniser and adventurer rivalled even that of his infamous robber baron ancestors?

Tamsin had more important things on her mind.

Secret excitement rippled through her and it had nothing to do with meeting a playboy prince.

This was her chance to rebuild her reputation. After Patrick's brutal betrayal she could finally prove herself to her colleagues and herself. Her confidence had shattered after the way he'd used her. He'd damaged her professionally but far worse, he'd hurt her so badly she'd wanted only to crawl away and lick her wounds.

She'd never trust again.

Some scars wouldn't heal. Yet here, now, she could at least kick start her career again. This was a once in a lifetime opportunity and she was ready for the challenge.

For ten days Prince Alaric had been too busy to meet her. His schedule had been too full to fit her in. Clearly an expert on old books didn't rank in his priorities.

The notion ignited a shimmer of anger inside her. She was tired of being used, dismissed and overlooked.

Had he hoped to fob her off by seeing her so late in the evening? Tamsin straightened her spine, clasping her hands in her lap, ankles crossed demurely under the massive chair.

'Of course I won't leave. I'll be content here until His Highness arrives.'

The aide's dubious expression made it clear he thought she was waiting her moment to sneak off and gape at the VIPs in the ballroom. Or maybe steal the silverware.

Impatient at the way he hovered, she slipped a hand into her briefcase and pulled out a wad of papers. She gave the aide a perfunctory smile and started reading.

'Very well.' His voice interrupted and she looked up. 'It's possible the prince may be…delayed. If you need anything, ring the bell.'

He gestured to a switch on the wall, camouflaged by the exquisite wood carving surrounding the huge fireplace. 'Refreshments will be brought if you need them.'

'Thank you.' Tamsin nodded and watched him bustle away.

Was 'delay' code? Was the prince busy seducing a glamorous beauty from the ball? If gossip was right Prince Alaric of Ruvingia, in line to the crown of Maritz, was a playboy *par excellence*. Pursuing women would be higher on his priorities than meeting a book curator.

Tamsin ignored a fizz of indignation.

Her gaze strayed to the ceiling height bookshelves. The inevitable spark of interest quickened her blood. Old books. She smelled the familiar scent of aged paper and leather.

If he was going to be late…

Not allowing herself second thoughts, Tamsin walked to the nearest bookcase. It was too much to hope it would yield anything as exciting as what she'd unearthed in the archives, but why sit reading documents she knew by heart?

Her reluctant host was probably hours away.

* * *

'You must excuse me, Katarina. I have business to attend to.'
Alaric disengaged himself from the countess's clinging grasp.

'So late? Surely there are better ways to spend the night?' Her
ruby lips parted and her silvery eyes flashed a familiar message.
Sexual promise, excitement and just a touch of greed. She swayed
forward, her barely covered breasts straining against her ball
gown, her emerald-strewn cleavage designed to draw the eye.

Acquiring lovers had always been easy for Alaric but he was
tired of being targeted by women like Katarina.

His rules were simple. First, no long term commitment. Ever.
Emotional intimacy, what others called love, was a mirage he
knew to be dangerous and false. Second, he did the chasing.

He needed diversion but on *his* terms.

Katarina, despite her genuine sexual desire, was another who'd
set her sights on marriage. Permanency. Royal prestige. Wealth.
Right now he had more significant concerns than satisfying the
ambitions of a grasping socialite.

'Sadly it's a meeting I can't avoid.' Over her head he caught
the eye of the steward hovering at the entrance. 'Your car is
here.' He lifted her hand, barely brushing it with his lips, before
leading her to the door.

'I'll call you,' she whispered, her voice sultry.

Alaric smiled easily, secure in the knowledge she wouldn't
get past his staff.

Five minutes later, with the last guests gone, he dismissed his
personal staff and strode down the corridor, his mind returning
to the recent conversation with Raul.

If anyone else had asked him to stay here, cooped up through
winter, Alaric would have ignored them. The need to be out and
doing something, keeping busy, was a turbulent tide rising in his
blood. The idea of six more months tied to his alpine principality
gave him cabin fever.

It might be home, but he felt hemmed in. Constricted. Prey
to the darkness clawing from within.

Only constant action and diversion kept him from succumbing.
Kept him sane.

Alaric forked a hand through his hair, impatiently flicking his cape off one shoulder. That was another thing to thank his distant cousin and soon-to-be monarch for. An evening wearing the outmoded uniform of two centuries ago.

Yet he'd given his word. He must help Raul.

After decades of peace, the recent death of the old king, Raul's father, had reignited unrest. Alaric's principality of Ruvingia was stable but elsewhere tensions that had almost led to civil war a generation ago had reopened. With careful management danger would be averted, but they couldn't take chances.

He and Raul had to ensure stability. In their nation of Maritz, clinging to monarchical traditions, that meant a calm, united front in the lead up to his cousin's coronation and the reopening of parliament.

So here Alaric was, cutting ribbons and hosting balls!

He swung into another corridor, itching for action. But this wasn't as simple as leading a commando squad to disarm combatants. There was no violence. Yet.

Alaric's belly twisted as the ghosts of the past stirred, a reminder of how suddenly tragedy could strike.

With an effort he shoved aside the lingering pain and glanced at his watch. He was miles late for his last obligation of the day. As soon as it was over he'd escape for a few hours. Take the Aston Martin over the mountain pass and try out its paces on the hairpin bends.

Alaric quickened his step at the beckoning sense of freedom, however temporary.

Another twist in the ancient passage and there was the library door. Automatically he slowed, acknowledging but not yielding to the frisson of discomfort feathering his spine.

This would never be his study, no matter what the staff expected. It was his father's room, his brother's. Alaric preferred the mobility of a laptop he could use elsewhere. Preferred not to be reminded he walked in dead men's shoes.

Too many dead men.

Fragmented images rose. At the forefront was Felix, his talented, capable, older brother.

The one who should be here instead of Alaric.

Who'd died because of Alaric.

The frisson of awareness froze into a gut-stabbing shaft of ice. Familiar guilt engulfed him. Pain tore his chest and throat with each breath.

He accepted it as inevitable. *His punishment.* The weight he would always bear.

Eventually he forced his breathing to slow and his legs to move.

The room was empty. Logs burned in the fireplace, lamps glowed but no expert waited to harangue him about the state of the archives. If the matter was so urgent surely she'd have stayed.

All the better. He could be on the open road in ten minutes.

He was turning away when a stack of papers caught his attention. A battered briefcase sagged on the floor. Immediately he was alert, his gaze narrowing.

Then he heard it, an almost imperceptible swish from above. Instincts honed on the edge of survival sharpened. He flexed his fingers. An instant later, hand on the hilt of his ceremonial sword, he faced the intruder.

For long moments he stared, then his hand fell away.

The room had been invaded by a...mushroom.

On top of the ladder fixed to the bookshelves perched a shapeless muddle of grey-brown. A long granny cardigan the colour of dust caught his eye and beneath, spread across the ladder top that now served as a seat, a voluminous grey skirt. It was a woman, though her clothes looked like something that had sprouted on a damp forest floor.

A wall sconce shone on dark hair, scraped back, and a glint of glasses above a massive book. White-gloved hands held the volume up, obscuring her face. And beneath...his gaze riveted on the rhythmic swing of a leg, bare to just above the knee.

One seriously sexy leg.

Alaric paced closer, his attention gratefully diverted from sombre remembrances.

Skin like moonlight. A shapely calf, trim ankle and neat foot. Toes that wriggled enticingly with each swing.

Masculine appreciation stirred as his gaze slid back up her leg. Even her knee looked good! Too good to be teasing a man who was restless and in desperate need of distraction.

He crossed to the base of the ladder and picked up a discarded shoe. Flat soled, plain brown, narrow and neat. Appallingly dowdy.

He raised his brows. Those legs deserved something better, assuming the one tucked beneath that horror of a skirt matched the elegant limb on show. They demanded heels. Stiletto sharp and high, to emphasise the luscious curve of her calf. Ankle straps. Ribbons, sexy enough to tease a man till he took them off and moved on to other pleasures.

Alaric shook his head. He'd bet all the jewels in the basement vault the owner of this shoe would be horrified at the extravagance of footwear designed to seduce a man.

A tingle of something dangerously like anticipation feathered his neck as he watched her leg swing and her foot arch seductively. This time the little wriggle of her toes seemed deliciously abandoned as if the drab clothes camouflaged a secret sybarite.

Alaric's mood lightened for the first time in weeks.

'Cinderella, I presume?'

The voice was deep and mellow, jolting Tamsin out of her reverie. Warily she lowered the volume enough to peer over it.

She froze, eyes widening as she took in the man gazing up at her.

He'd stepped out of a fantasy.

He couldn't be real. No flesh and blood man looked like that. So mouth-wateringly wonderful.

Numb with shock, she shook her head in automatic disbelief. He could have been Prince Charming, standing there in his elaborate hussar's uniform, her discarded shoe in one large, capable hand. A bigger, tougher Prince Charming than she remembered from her childhood reading. His dark eyebrows slashed across a tanned face that wasn't so much handsome as magnetic, charismatic, potently sexy.

Like Prince Charming's far more experienced and infinitely more dangerous older brother.

Eyes, dark and gleaming, transfixed her. They were… aware.

Meeting his unblinking regard she had the crazy notion that for the first time ever a man looked and really saw *her*. Not her reputation, not her misfit status but the real flesh and blood Tamsin Connors, the impulsive woman she'd tried so hard to stifle.

She felt vulnerable, yet thrilled.

A lazy smile lifted one corner of his mouth and a deep groove creased his cheek.

Stunned, she felt a squiggle of response deep in her abdomen. Tiny rivers of fire quivered under her skin. Her lungs squeezed her breath out in a whoosh of…of…

The book she held shut with a snap that made her jump. Instantly the other volumes in her lap slid and she grabbed for them. But they were cumbersome and she didn't dare let go of the precious herbal in her hands.

In dry mouthed horror she watched a book tumble out of her grasp. It fell in slow motion, turning over as it went. Even knowing it was too late to save the volume she scrabbled for it, barely keeping her precarious perch.

'Don't move!' The authority in his voice stopped her in mid lunge.

He strode forward a step, stretched out his hand and the book fell into his grasp as if it belonged there.

Dizzy with relief, Tamsin shut her eyes. She'd never have forgiven herself if it had been damaged.

How had he done that? The volume was no paperback. It weighed a ton. Yet he'd caught it one-handed from a fall of twelve feet as if it were feather light.

Tamsin snapped her eyes open and saw him turn to place the book on the desk. The indigo material of his tunic clung to his broad shoulder and muscled arm.

That formidable figure wasn't the result of tailored padding.

She swallowed hard, her gaze dropping to long powerful thighs encased in dark trousers. The crimson stripe down the side drew attention to the strength of those limbs.

No pretend soldier. The straight set of his shoulders and the contained power of each precise movement proclaimed him the real thing.

Abruptly he turned, as if sensing her scrutiny. His gaze pierced her and she shivered, overwhelmingly aware of him as *male*.

She worked with men all the time, but she'd never met one so undeniably masculine. As if testosterone radiated off him in waves. It made her heart race.

'Now to get you safely down.' Was that a glint of humour in his eyes?

'I'm OK.' She clutched the books like a lifeline. 'I'll put these back and—'

'No.' The single syllable stopped her. 'I'll take them.'

'I promise you I'm not usually so clumsy.' She sat straighter, annoyed at her stupidity in examining the books here instead of taking them to the desk. Normally she was methodical, logical and careful. It was no excuse that excitement had overridden her caution.

'Nevertheless, it's not worth the risk.' He walked to the foot of the ladder and looked up, his face unreadable. 'I'll relieve you of your burden first.'

Tamsin bit her lip. She couldn't blame him. She'd almost damaged a unique volume. What sort of expert took such risks? What she'd done was unforgivable.

'I'm sorry, I—'

Her words cut out as the ladder moved beneath her, a rhythmic sway as he nimbly closed the distance between them.

Tamsin became excruciatingly self-aware as his ascent slowed. Warm breath feathered her bare ankle then shivered against her calf and to her horror she couldn't repress a delicious little shudder.

A moment later a dark head appeared in the V between her splayed knees. Something hard and hot plunged down through her abdomen as she met his gaze.

From metres away this man was stunning. Up close, where she could see the twinkle lurking in midnight-blue eyes and the sensuous curve of his full lower lip, he stole her breath. Tiny lines beside his mouth and eyes spoke of experience and a grim endurance at odds with his easy humour. Yet they only accentuated his attractiveness.

Her heart beat a rapid tattoo that pulsed adrenaline through her body and robbed her of coherent thought.

'Allow me.' Large hands reached out and scooped the book from her lap, barely ruffling her skirt. Yet his heat seared through her clothing and suddenly she felt dizzy. She clutched the herbal to her breast.

Then he was gone, swarming down the ladder with an ease that spoke of supreme fitness and agility.

Tamsin drew a deep breath into constricted lungs, searching for composure. She'd never been distracted by male beauty before. She dismissed as irrelevant the knowledge that she'd never seen anyone so magnificent.

She shook her head. He's just a man, just—

'This one, too.' There he was again. She'd been so caught up in her thoughts she hadn't noticed his rapid ascent. He reached for the book in her arms.

'It's all right. I can carry it.' For suddenly, close enough to inhale his subtle spice and forest and man scent, she didn't want to relinquish the barrier between them. She clung to it like a talisman.

'We don't want to risk another accident,' he drawled in his easy, perfect English. 'Do we, Cinderella?'

'I'm not…' She stopped herself. Despite his mock serious expression there was amusement in his eyes.

Anger welled. Self-consciousness tightened her stomach. Patrick laughed at her too. All her life she'd been a misfit, a figure of speculation and amusement. She'd learned to pretend not to notice but still it hurt.

Yet this was her fault. She'd put herself in this ridiculous position because she'd been too curious to sit meekly waiting. She'd never be taken seriously now. Just when it was vital she win confidence and trust.

Had she single-handedly wrecked her chance of success?

Summoning the scraps of her dignity she unclamped stiff fingers and lowered the volume into his waiting hands.

Calloused fingers brushed hers through the thin gloves she'd donned to protect the books. An electric shock shot up her arm and across her breasts. She jerked her hands away.

Tamsin bit the inside of her cheek and looked away from his knowing gaze, her emotions too raw for comfort.

He stood still. She felt his stare, tangible as a trailing touch, move across her face to her throat then back up again. Her breathing shallowed.

She told herself she was used to being a curiosity, out of step with her peers. Stubbornly she ignored the hurt lancing her chest.

An instant later he clattered back down the ladder and she let out her breath in a sigh.

Time to climb down and face the music. She unfolded the leg tucked beneath her. Pins and needles prickled, proof she'd sat here longer than she'd realised. Gingerly she wriggled, pulling the bunched hem of her skirt down where it had rucked up. Grasping the ladder she rose, ready to turn.

His appearance before her prevented her moving.

'I need space to turn around.' Her voice was betrayingly uneven.

Instead of descending, he rose, his hands grasping the top of the ladder so his broad shoulders and powerful arms surrounded her.

Something fluttered in Tamsin's chest at the sensation of being caught within his embrace, though he didn't touch her. The force field of his presence engulfed her. It made her feel small and vulnerable and edgy.

Her breath hissed in.

His head was at breast height now. She leaned back towards the shelving, trying to put space between them.

'Whoa. Easy now.' His deep voice lowered to a soothing pitch, as if steadying a fractious animal.

'I can climb down alone.' Her words were sharper than she'd intended, betraying her embarrassment at the storm of inexplicable reactions bombarding her.

'Of course you can.' His lips pursed ruminatively, drawing her eyes. Heat washed her neck and cheeks as she stared. In a less rugged face that perfect mouth would look almost feminine. But on him those lips simply looked sensuous and dangerously inviting.

Like the deeply hooded eyes that steadily surveyed her.

Tamsin swallowed and felt her blush burn hotter. Could he read her thoughts? He must be accustomed to women gaping. The realisation didn't ease her embarrassment.

'But accidents happen and I wouldn't want you losing your footing.'

'I won't lose my footing,' she said in a horribly breathless voice.

He shrugged those wide, straight shoulders, mesmerising her with the movement. 'We hope not. But we won't take chances. Think of the insurance claim if you're injured.'

'I wouldn't—'

'Of course you wouldn't.' He rose further and she backed so her shoulders touched the bookshelf and there was nowhere else to go. 'But your permanent employer might sue for damages if you're injured due to our negligence.'

'It's not your negligence. I climbed up here.'

He shook his head. 'Anyone with an ounce of understanding would realise what temptation this ladder is to a woman who loves books. It's asking for trouble.'

Something flickered in his eyes. She was sure he was laughing but his sympathetic expression couldn't be faulted. 'It was irresponsible to leave it here, just begging to be climbed.'

He conveniently ignored the fact that the ladder was fixed top and bottom to the rails placed around the walls.

'You're talking nonsense.'

His eyebrows arched and a flash of something that might have been approval lit his eyes.

'Very probably,' he murmured. 'The tension must be getting to me. Heights can affect people like that, you know.' His lips curved up in another one of those half-smiles that melted something vital inside her. 'Take pity on my nerves and let me get you down from here.'

Tamsin opened her mouth to end his games. She refused to be the butt of his jokes. But before she could speak large hands pulled her towards him, warming her through several layers of clothing and jamming the words in her throat. For a moment panic threatened as she plunged forward, but an instant later she was draped over one solid shoulder. He clamped her close with his arm and then he was moving, descending the ladder with her firmly in his hold.

'Put me down! Let me go, *right now!*' She couldn't believe he'd grabbed her.

'Of course. In just a moment.'

To her horror Tamsin *felt* his deep voice rumble through his torso and hers.

Tamsin shut her eyes rather than look at the distant floor, or, more disturbingly, the intriguing sight of muscles bunching in the taut backside inches from her face.

But closing her eyes heightened other senses. She felt him against the length of her body, his strength undeniably exciting as ripples of movement teased her breasts and thighs. Disturbing warmth swirled languidly in the pit of her stomach.

She shouldn't be enjoying this. She should be outraged. Or at least impervious. She should...

'There.' He lowered her into a chair and stepped back. 'Safe and sound.'

His eyes weren't laughing now. They were sober as he stared down at her. His mouth was a firm line, his brows tipped into a slight frown as if the joke had turned sour. His jaw clamped hard and she had the fleeting impression he was annoyed rather than amused.

Tamsin wanted desperately to conjure a witty quip. To redeem herself as clever and insouciant, taking the situation in her stride.

Instead she gazed helplessly, enmeshed in a web of unfamiliar reactions. Her breasts tingled from contact with him, her nipples puckering shamelessly. Her thighs were warm from his touch. Her gaze caught on his black hair, now slightly rumpled. Heat sizzled inside like a firecracker about to explode.

It wasn't the sexy cavalry uniform that made him look so good, despite the gilt braiding that moulded his tapering torso, the cut of clothes that made him look every inch the fairy tale hero. What unnerved her was the flesh and blood man whose shadowed eyes glowed like an invitation to sin.

She tried to tell herself he was vain enough to have a uniform designed to enhance the incredible colour of his eyes. But the gravity of his expression when he wasn't smiling told her he didn't give a toss for his looks.

Tamsin's breath sawed as he dropped to one knee and took her bare foot in his hand. Tremors rippled up her leg and she felt again that strange molten sensation pooling low in her belly.

She squirmed but he didn't release her. Instead he fished something out of his pocket and slid it onto her foot. Soft, worn familiar leather. Her discarded shoe.

'So, Cinderella. Why did you want to see me?'

Tamsin's pulse faltered. For the last ten minutes she'd pretended he was a guest, even a member of staff. Yet deep inside she'd known who he was.

Prince Alaric. The man who held her career and her reputation in his hands.

Already she amused him. How he'd laugh if he knew that in ten minutes, without trying, he'd seduced one of Britain's last dyed in the wool virgins to mindless longing.

Tamsin swallowed convulsively. She shot to her feet and stepped away, busying herself by stripping off her gloves and stuffing them in a pocket.

'It's about the archives I'm cataloguing and assessing for conservation.' A cache of documents recently discovered when a castle cellar had been remodelled.

She turned. He stood by the chair, frowning in abstraction. Tamsin lifted her chin, breathing deep.

'They include some unique and valuable papers.'

'I'm sure they do.' He nodded, his expression blandly polite. Obviously he had no interest in her efforts.

'I have a copy of one with me.' She reached for her briefcase, grateful for an excuse to look away from his hooded gaze.

'Why don't you just tell me about it?'

Cut to the chase, in other words.

He'd had plenty of time to dally, amusing himself at her expense, but none to spare for her work.

Disappointment curled through her, and annoyance.

'One of the documents caught my attention. It's a record of your family and Prince Raul's.' She paused, excitement at her find bubbling up despite her vexation.

'There's still work to be done on it.' Tamsin paused, keeping her voice carefully even. 'I've been translating from the Latin and, if it's proved correct…'

'Yes? If it's proved correct?'

Tamsin hesitated, but there was no easy way to say it. Besides, he'd surely welcome the news.

'If it's genuine you're not only Prince of Ruvingia, you're also the next legitimate ruler of Maritz. Of the whole country. Not Prince Raul.' She paused, watching his expression freeze.

'It's you who should be crowned king.'

CHAPTER TWO

ALARIC'S body stiffened as her words sank in with terrible, nightmare clarity.

Him as ruler of Maritz!

The idea was appalling.

Raul was the crown prince. The one brought up from birth to rule. The one trained and ready to dedicate his life to his country.

Maritz needed him.

Or a man like Alaric's brother, Felix.

Alaric wasn't in the same mould. Even now he heard his father's cool, clipped voice expressing endless displeasure and disappointment with his reckless second son.

Alaric's lips twisted. How right the old man had been. Alaric couldn't take responsibility for the country. Bad enough he'd stepped into Felix's shoes as leader of a principality. Entrusting the wellbeing of the whole nation to his keeping would be disaster.

He, whose conscience was heavy with the weight of others' lives! Who'd failed them so abysmally.

Horror crawled up his spine to clamp his shoulders. Ice froze his blood. Familiar faces swam in his vision, faces distorted with pain. The faces of those he'd failed. The face of his brother, eyes feverish as he berated Alaric for betraying him.

He couldn't be king. It was unthinkable.

'Is this a joke?' The words shot out, harsh in the silence.

'Of course not!'

No. One look at her frown and her stunned eyes made that clear. Tamsin Connors wasn't kidding.

He'd never seen a more serious, buttoned-up woman. From her tense lips to her heavy-framed glasses and scraped-back hair, she was the image of no-nonsense spinsterhood.

Except for that body.

Hard to believe she'd felt so warm and lithely curved. Or that holding her he'd known a curious desire to strip away that fashion crime of an outfit and explore her scented femininity. A desire completely dormant in the face of so many blatant sexual invitations from tonight's beauties!

Beneath her bag lady clothes Tamsin Connors was only in her mid-twenties. When she forgot to prim them her lips were surprisingly luscious. He looked into her frowning face and knew he was avoiding the issue. The impossible issue of him being king!

'What exactly is in these papers?' His voice sounded rusty, as if his vocal cords had seized up.

'They're old records by a cleric called Tomas. He detailed royal history, especially births, deaths and marriages.' She shifted, leaning imperceptibly closer.

Did he imagine her fresh sunshine scent, warm in a room chilled with the remembrance of death?

With an effort he dragged his focus back to her.

'Take a seat, please, and explain.' He gestured to one of the armchairs by the fire then took one for himself.

'According to Tomas there was intermarriage between your family and Prince Raul's.'

Alaric nodded. 'That was common practice.' Power was guarded through alliances with other aristocratic families.

'At one stage there was a gap in the direct line to the Maritzian throne. The crown couldn't pass from father to son as the king's son had died.'

Her words flayed a raw spot deep inside him. A familiar glacial chill burned Alaric's gut. The knowledge he was a usurper in a better man's shoes.

That he was responsible for his brother's death.

'There were two contenders for the throne. One from Prince Raul's family and…' Her words slowed as she registered his expression. Some of her enthusiasm faded.

'And one from mine?'

She shifted as if uncomfortable, but continued.

Two rival princes from different branches of intertwined families. A will from the old king designating one, the eldest by some weeks, as his successor. A tragic 'accident' leading to the accession of the alternate heir and a desperate decision by the dead prince's widow to send her newborn son to safety far away. The suppression of the old king's will and a rewriting of birth dates to shore up the new monarch's claim to the throne.

It was a tale of treachery and the ruthless pursuit of power. But in his country's turbulent history, definitely possible.

How was it possible she'd found such a contentious document?

The likelihood was staggeringly remote. For centuries historians had plotted the family trees of the royal families in each of the neighbouring principalities.

Yet her earnestness, her straight-backed confidence caught his attention.

Obviously she'd found something. This woman was no one's fool, despite her up-tight demeanour. He remembered reading her CV when she had been recommended for the job of assessing and preserving the archives. Multiple qualifications. Glowing references. Her first degree in her teens and a formidable amount of experience since then.

It was tempting to believe this was a mistake, that she'd jumped to the wrong conclusion. Yet she didn't strike him as a woman prone to taking risks.

'You're not pleased?' she ventured, her brows puckering. 'I know it's a shock but—'

'But you thought I'd be thrilled to become king?' His words were clipped as he strove to suppress a surge of unfamiliar panic. He had to fight the rising nausea that clogged his throat.

He shook his head. 'I'm loyal to my cousin, Dr Connors. He will make the sort of king our country needs.'

Alaric succeeding in his place would be a nightmare made real.

Hell! The timing couldn't be worse. The country needed stability. If this was true…

'Who else have you told?' Alaric found himself on his feet, towering above her with his hands clamped on her chair arms. She shrank back as he leaned close.

In the flickering firelight she looked suddenly vulnerable and very young.

The pounding thud of his heartbeat slowed and he straightened, giving her space.

No need to intimidate the woman. Yet.

'I haven't told anyone.' Wide eyes stared at him from behind those ugly glasses and a twist of something like awareness coiled in his belly. 'I had to tell you first.'

The tension banding his chest eased and he breathed deep. 'Good. You did the right thing.'

Tentatively she smiled and he felt a tremor of guilt at having scared her. Even now one hand pressed to her breast as if her heart raced. He followed the rapid rise and fall of her chest. An unexpected trickle of fire threaded his belly as he recalled her feminine softness against him.

'When I get the test results back we'll know if the papers are what they seem to be.'

'Results?' He stilled. 'What tests are these?'

'There are several,' she said slowly, her expression wary. Alaric thrust his hand through his hair, fighting the impulse to demand she explain instantly.

Instead he took another deliberate step away from her and laid his forearm along the mantelpiece. Immediately the tension in her slim frame eased.

'Would you care to enlighten me?'

She blinked and blushed and for a moment Alaric was sidetracked by the softening of her lips as they formed an O of surprise. She looked charmingly female and innocently flustered in a way that threatened to distract him.

An instant later she was brisk and businesslike. 'I've sent pages for testing. We need to know if the parchment is as old as it appears. That it's not a modern forgery.'

She'd sent papers away? Who had them now? This got worse and worse.

'Plus the style of the text is unusual. I've sent copies of some pages to a colleague for verification.'

'Who gave you permission to do this?' His voice was calm, low, but with the razor edge honed on emergency decisions made under fire.

She jerked her head up, her body stiffening.

'I was told when I started that, so long as the usual precautions were taken, testing of documents found in the archives was allowed.'

'If you're right these aren't just any documents!' His hands fisted. Had she no notion of the powder keg she may have uncovered?

'That's why I was particularly careful.' She shot to her feet, hands clasped before her; chin lifted as she met his gaze. 'None of the pages I sent for testing were, by themselves, sensitive.' She paused then continued with slow emphasis. 'I realise this information must be kept confidential until it's confirmed. I followed the protocols set out when I took on the job.'

Alaric let out a slow breath. 'And if someone put those pages together?'

'No.' She shook her head then paused, frowning. 'It's not possible.' Yet she didn't look so certain.

Alaric determined to get his hands on the pages as soon as possible.

'It would have been better to keep this in house.' Even if it turned out this was a mistake, rumour could destabilise a delicate situation.

Fine eyebrows arched high on her pale forehead.

'Ruvingia doesn't have the capacity "in house" to run such tests.' She paused and he watched her drag in quick breaths, obviously battling strong emotion.

'I apologise if I've overstepped the mark.' Her tone said he was being unreasonable. 'I would have checked with you earlier but it's been hard getting an appointment.'

Touché. Meeting to discuss the royal archives hadn't been on his priorities.

'How long before you get the results?'

She launched into detail of how the document would be authenticated, her face growing animated. All the while he was busy reckoning the risks posed by this discovery. The need to verify her findings and keep the situation under wraps.

Yet he found himself watching her closely as she shed that shell of spiky reserve. There was a fire in her that had been lacking before. Or had it been hidden behind her starchy demeanour?

Despite the gravity of the situation, something in Alaric that was all male, functioning at the most primitive level, stirred.

Behind her dowdy appearance he sensed heat and passion in this woman.

He'd always been attracted by passion.

Alaric wrenched his mind back to the problem at hand.

'A short wait, then, before the results come through. In the meantime, who has access to this chronicle?'

'Only me. The assistant from your national museum is working on other material.'

'Good. We'll keep it that way.' Alaric would personally arrange for it to be kept under lock and key.

'I'm also keeping my eyes open for other papers that might confirm or disprove what I've found. There's still a lot to investigate.'

There could be more? Even if this document conveniently disappeared there might be others?

Damn. A simple solution had been tempting. An accident to destroy the evidence and remove the problem. Yet it would only make precautions around the remaining documents tighter and subsequent accidents more suspicious.

Self-knowledge warred with duty. The former told him the country would be better off in his cousin Raul's hands. The latter urged Alaric to face his responsibility no matter how unpalatable.

He speared a hand through his hair and paced, his belly churning. In thirty years he'd never shirked his duty, no matter how painful.

He'd warn Raul. They'd develop a contingency plan and make a discreet enquiry of the royal genealogist, a historian known for his expertise and discretion. Alaric needed to know if this far-fetched story was even possible.

Genuine or not, the papers were dynamite. If spare copies existed, and if Tamsin Connors was the innocent, earnest professional she appeared, he needed her onside.

If she was what she appeared.

Was it possible forged papers had been planted for her to find and disrupt Raul's coronation? Unlikely. Yet how convenient she'd found them after just a couple of weeks.

Too convenient?

He narrowed his gaze, taking in her heavy-framed glasses and appalling clothes. The way her gaze continually slipped away from his.

His gut tightened at the idea she was hiding something. A link to those stirring discontent? It was preposterous, but so was this situation.

He'd get to the bottom of it soon.

Meanwhile Tamsin Connors had his undivided attention.

'Of course, I understand,' Tamsin murmured into the phone.

She should be disappointed by the news she'd received. She *was* disappointed, but she was distracted by the man prowling the confines of the workroom. His long stride gave an impression of controlled impatience, at odds with his meticulous interest in every detail.

Intently she watched every move, miserably aware Prince Alaric didn't need a splendid uniform to show off his physique. In dark trousers, plain T-shirt and a jacket, he was compelling in the afternoon light.

Until last night she hadn't known she had a weakness for tall broad-shouldered men who looked like they could take on the world. For men whose eyes laughed one minute and clouded with grim emotion the next as if he saw things no man should.

She'd thought she preferred men driven by academic pursuits, preferably fresh faced and blond, like Patrick. Not sizzling with barely suppressed physical energy.

How wrong she'd been.

Her skin drew tight, every nerve end buzzing, as he paced.

'Thank you for calling. I appreciate it.' Carefully she put the phone down.

'A problem?' He approached, eyes watchful.

Tamsin dragged in a breath and placed her hands on the desk. She'd prayed her reaction last night had been an aberration. But seeing him in the flesh again scotched every hope that she'd imagined her response to his potent masculinity. His vitality, that sense of power and capability, were as fascinating as his stunning looks.

With his black hair, midnight-blue eyes, high-cut cheekbones and strong nose, he looked every inch the powerful aristocrat. Yet his mouth was that of a seducer: warm, provocative and sensual.

Tamsin blinked. Where had that come from?

'Dr Connors?'

'Sorry. I was…thinking.' Frantically she tried to focus. 'I've just heard the date test will be delayed.'

He frowned and she hurried on. 'I'd hoped for an early result on the age of the parchment but it will take longer than I'd hoped.'

The reasons she'd just been given were plausible. But the embarrassed way Patrick's assistant repeated herself made Tamsin suspicious.

Wasn't it enough Patrick had stolen the job that was by rights Tamsin's? He'd been the first man to show any interest in her, cruelly using her naïve crush to string her along. All those extra hours she'd put in helping him and he'd passed her work off as his own. He'd been promoted on the basis of it then dumped her unceremoniously. Pride had stopped her revealing his duplicity and her own lack of judgement. Instead she'd withdrawn even further into herself, nursing a bruised heart and vowing never to risk it again so readily.

Was he low enough to stymie this project, too?

Once it would never have occurred to her. Now she wondered if the whisper she'd heard was right and he saw her as a professional threat.

Would he really let ego get in the way of scientific research? The idea sickened her. How had she not seen his true character?

'They're returning the papers?' The prince's eyes sparked indigo fire and she watched, fascinated.

'Not yet. Hopefully it won't be a long delay.'

Tamsin watched his mouth compress. He was impatient. Despite what he'd said last night, he must be excited at the possibility of becoming king. Who wouldn't be?

'These are the rest of the newly found documents?' He gestured to the storage down one side of the long room.

'A lot of them. Some of the less fragile ones we've left until we can assess them properly.'

'Yet there may be more sensitive papers among them?'

'Possibly. But not many people would be able to read them. Even with my expertise, some of the texts are hard to decipher. It's time consuming and difficult.'

'That doesn't matter. We need secure storage for them all.' He strode restlessly down the room, assessing the set-up. Despite her intentions she followed every step, drinking in the sight of his powerful body. 'I want you to calculate exactly what you need and tell me today. They'll be locked with access only on my approval.'

Tamsin shook her head. 'It's not just a matter of space, it's about a properly regulated environment and—'

'I understand. Just let me know and it will be done.'

'It will be expensive.'

The prince waved a dismissive hand. He was notoriously wealthy. Money was no object now his self-interest was engaged.

Tamsin strove to stifle a pang of disappointment, recalling how her work had been virtually ignored earlier. She supposed his proprietorial attitude was justified. After all they were talking about proof of kingship. And if it meant proper care for the archives, all the better.

She stood. 'In the meantime, could I have the text to work on? I'll translate some more this evening.'

Late last night, after hearing her news, the prince had insisted on accompanying her here to see the original document. Then, without warning, and despite her protest, he'd taken it away. It worried her that he didn't fully appreciate how fragile it was.

'Certainly.' He glanced at his watch, obviously eager to be elsewhere. 'But not today—it's late.'

'But—'

He crossed the room to stand close, too close. She felt his heat, inhaled the spicy clean scent of his skin and wished she were still sitting.

'But nothing. I gather you've done little except work since you arrived. By your own admission this is taxing work.' He looked down at her with eyes that sparkled and a tremor rippled down her legs. Desperately she locked her knees, standing straighter.

'I'm not a slave driver and I don't want you making yourself ill working all hours.'

'But I want to!' What else did she have to do with her evenings?

He shook his head. 'Not tonight.' He turned and headed for the door, pausing on the threshold. 'If you could send me those storage requirements…'

'I'll see to it straight away.'

He inclined his head and left. Tamsin stood, swaying slightly and staring at the place where he'd been.

She'd hoped to spark his interest with her discovery. She hadn't thought to be sidelined in the process.

Sternly she told herself that wasn't what he'd done. She was allowing her experiences with one deceitful, good looking man to colour her judgement.

It was good of Prince Alaric to be concerned for her welfare. It was sensible that he took an interest in storing the documents properly.

So why did it feel like she was being outmanoeuvred?

Mid-evening Alaric headed for the gym on the far side of the castle compound. He needed to work off this pent up energy. His sleep patterns were shot anyway, but last night Tamsin Connors had obliterated any chance of rest.

The genealogist had warned today that proving or disproving a claim to the throne took time. Alaric wanted it sorted, and preferably disproved, *now*. It went against the grain to wait, dependent on forces beyond his control.

Plus, infuriatingly, his investigators had turned up little on the Englishwoman.

Surely no one had such a straightforward past? They'd reported on her academic achievements, her reputation for hard work and a little on her quiet childhood with elderly parents. But nothing about boyfriends. Any friends for that matter. Only an unconfirmed hint of some affair with a colleague.

In other circumstances he'd take her at face value: a quiet, dedicated professional. But he couldn't take chances. Not till he knew she was what she seemed.

She *seemed* too innocent to be believed.

He slowed as he passed the viewing level for the squash court. Lights were on and he paused to see which of the staff were playing.

There was only one. A woman, lithe and agile as she smashed the ball around the court in robust practice.

Alaric frowned, momentarily unable to place her. She lunged, twisting, to chase a low ball and for a moment her breasts strained against her oversized T-shirt. An instant later she pivoted on long legs with an agility he couldn't help but applaud.

His eyes lingered on the shapely length of those legs below baggy shorts. A sizzle of lazy heat ignited inside and he smiled appreciatively.

There was an age old remedy for insomnia, one he used regularly. A pretty woman and—

She spun round and a spike of heat drove through Alaric's torso, shearing off his breath.

He tensed instantaneously, hormones in overdrive.

It was Tamsin Connors. Yet not.

He should have guessed it was her, in those ill-fitting outfits. Yet she looked so different.

His mouth dried as he registered the amount of bare skin on view. Skin flushed pink and enticing from exertion. She really did have the most delicious legs. When that shirt twisted he realised her breasts were fuller than he'd guessed in her granny clothes. Her hair was soft around her face, escaping a glossy ponytail that swung like a sexy invitation to touch every time she moved. She breathed hard through her mouth, her lips not primmed any more, but surprisingly lush. Her eyes glittered—

Her eyes! No glasses.

Suspicion flared as he saw her face unmarred by ugly glasses. Maybe she wore contact lenses? But why hide the rest of the time behind disfiguring frames?

Had she tried to disguise herself? She'd done a remarkable job, concealing the desirable woman beneath a drab exterior and prickly professionalism.

Why? What had she to hide?

It was as if she deliberately tried to look like an absent-minded academic, absorbed in books rather than the world around her. She seemed too honest and serious to deceive. Yet instinct niggled, convincing him this was deliberate camouflage.

Alaric catapulted down the nearby stairs. On a bench beside the door to the court were an ugly cardigan and a case for glasses.

He flipped the latter open and held the glasses up to his face. Realisation corkscrewed through him and he swore under his breath. They gave only minuscule magnification.

Why did she wear them?

This time suspicion was a sharp, insistent jab. She was a stranger, in disguise. What a coincidence that she'd uncovered papers that could shatter the peace of the nation.

Tamsin Connors wasn't what she seemed. Was she part of a plot? An innocent dupe?

He'd just put the glasses down when she emerged.

Her thickly lashed eyes widened to bright dazzling amber, snaring his breath despite his anger. Amazing what those glasses had obscured. Her lips rounded in a soft pout of surprise and instantly fire exploded in his belly.

Slowly she approached.

Conflicting messages bombarded his brain. Caution. Distrust. Curiosity. Lust. *Definitely lust.*

His jaw hardened as he reined in that surge of hunger. This was no time to let his libido override his brain.

One thing was for certain. He wasn't going to let Tamsin Connors out of his sight till he got to the bottom of this. Already a plan formed in his head.

He smiled slowly in anticipation.

He and Dr Connors were about to become much more intimately acquainted.

CHAPTER THREE

TAMSIN'S steps faltered.

This man had invaded her thoughts, even haunted her dreams last night. Yet she'd forgotten how overwhelming he was in person.

So big. So vibrant. So powerfully *male*.

The air seemed to swirl and tickle her sensitised flesh as he subjected her to a short, all-encompassing survey. Heat blazed in her stomach and her skin tightened.

His eyes glittered and his mouth curved in welcome and her heart danced faster than it had on the squash court.

Would he look so welcoming if he knew she'd exhausted herself trying desperately to banish him from her thoughts? That she felt *excited* by his presence?

No. He paid her salary while she worked on loan here. He was her employer, an aristocrat living a glamorous, privileged life. A man with no interest in her or her work except that it made him eligible for the crown.

He'd be horrified by her reaction to him.

Even now her befuddled brain told her his smile wasn't a simple welcome. That it signified a deeper level of pleasure, a hint of danger. The sort of danger a sensible woman would ignore.

See? Her instincts were awry. She couldn't trust them.

Quickly she looked away, scared he'd read her thoughts. Patrick had read her longings like a book. She couldn't bear to reveal her weakness to this man, too.

The fact that she felt any weakness at all after the events of the last six months astounded her.

'Dr Connors.' His deep voice rippled like ruched velvet across her skin. She shivered, unable to suppress voluptuous pleasure at the sound.

Seeking distraction she reached for her cardigan and glasses, holding them close to her heaving chest.

'I hope you don't mind me using the court,' she murmured. 'Your steward said I could but I hadn't realised you might…'

'Of course I don't mind. It's good to see it in use. If I'd known you played I'd have invited you to a match.'

Startled, Tamsin looked up, straight into clear indigo depths that seemed warm and inviting.

He looked serious!

Her gaze strayed across muscled shoulders, down to the deep curve of a solid chest outlined against a black cotton T-shirt. She swallowed, her mouth drying at the latent power of him. His arms, tanned and strong, reminded her of the way he'd hoisted her over his shoulder as if she weighed nothing. Of how, despite her outrage, she'd revelled in his effortless he-man act.

He looked mouth-wateringly good in gym gear. As good as in uniform! It wasn't fair.

She stepped back, her eyes flicking away nervously.

'I don't think I'd be in your league.' Fervently she hoped he'd put her breathlessness down to her workout.

'I watched you play. You're quick and agile and know how to use your body.' His smile changed, became almost intimate, sending tendrils of heat winding around her internal organs. 'I'm sure we'd be very well matched.'

Tamsin's mind filled with an image of them matched in another way altogether. Tanned skin against pale. Hard masculine muscle against female softness.

Heat exploded, scalding her throat and face at the lurid, unfamiliar picture. Horrified, she ducked her head to fumble with her glasses case.

He couldn't know what she was thinking.

That didn't stop her embarrassment.

'It's kind of you to say so,' she mumbled. 'But we both know it would be an uneven match.'

She cast a furtive glance at his muscled arms and wished he'd cover himself up. It was hard not to stare.

'You underestimate yourself, Dr Connors.' His words sliced through her thoughts. 'Why is that? You struck me as a very confident woman when we discussed your work.'

Confident? She'd talked too much last night as they'd visited the archives. Nerves and guilt about the risks she'd taken with his books in the library had made her overcompensate. Anxiety had made her garrulous.

'That's different.' Reluctantly she lifted her chin and met his gaze. Even braced for the impact, the connection sent shock waves of pleasure racing through her. 'I've worked hard to develop my expertise. My work is what I'm good at. What I love.'

Tamsin had buried herself in work for years. At first because immersing herself in books had been an escape in her lonely childhood. Then from habit, especially as a student, when her age had set her apart from older colleagues. More recently it had been easier to be a workaholic than cultivate a personal life. She shivered. Her one foray into romance had been disastrous.

She waved a hand at the court. 'I lead a sedentary life. This is just a way to keep fit.' And a welcome outlet for troubled emotions.

He tilted his head, his gaze shrewd. 'Yet your focus was impressive. And your speed. You'd be a formidable opponent.'

The lazy approval was gone from his face, replaced by a seriousness that made her still.

Like last night Tamsin again had the suspicion he saw *her*: not just her academic reputation, but *whole*, talents and doubts, confidence and uncertainties. Saw the real person.

The notion thrilled yet made her feel oddly vulnerable.

She shoved an arm into her cardigan, pulled it round and slid her other arm in. Its familiarity steadied her, a reminder of her everyday world, devoid of handsome princes with dark chocolate voices.

She opened the case in her hands to take out her glasses. She felt naked meeting his scrutiny without them. But the sudden intensity of his stare arrested her. She closed the case with a snap.

'Hardly formidable, Your Highness. But thank you for the compliment.'

She made to turn away then stopped. This might be her only chance to talk to him. After today he'd probably be as elusive as before.

Steadfastly Tamsin ignored a sudden pang of disappointment. They had nothing in common. What did it matter if she never saw him again?

'Tomorrow, could I work on the text again? I'm eager to make more progress.'

'I'm sure you are.' Yet there was no answering enthusiasm in his face. If he was excited about the possibility of becoming monarch he hid it. His expression was flinty.

Had she said something wrong?

Finally he nodded. 'It will be brought to you tomorrow so you can pursue your…investigations.'

Tamsin sat absorbed, one bare foot tucked beneath her.

The more she delved into this manuscript, the more it fascinated. The choice of words, the phrasing, it was unique, even without the bombshell revelation that generations ago the wrong heir had become king. The intricate detail about life at court was incredible.

Take this word. She tilted her lamp to better view the idiosyncratic spelling. It should mean…

She paused, frowning as her thoughts strayed.

There was no sound, no movement on the periphery of her vision. Yet suddenly her focus was shot. The hairs on her arms prickled in atavistic awareness. Did she imagine a change in the atmosphere?

Tamsin focused again, trying to fathom the meaning of a convoluted sentence. Yet the more she tried to concentrate the more aware she became of…something else.

Finally in exasperation she looked up. And saw him.

The overhead lights were on against the fading afternoon. He stood under one, his black hair glossy in the spill of light. He was motionless, feet apart and hands in pockets in a masculine stance that reinforced the air of tough capability she'd noticed from the first.

Her heart throbbed an agitated tattoo. How long had he silently watched her? Why did he look so grim?

More than that, she wondered, as she sat back in her seat, what was he doing here?

'You've been working since seven-thirty this morning and you barely paused for lunch.' He dragged his hands from his pockets and approached. 'It's time you stopped.'

Tamsin frowned. 'You're keeping tabs on me?' She didn't feel indignant. She was too busy grappling with surprise.

He shrugged those superb shoulders and she stifled rising awareness. 'My staff have upped security given the importance of your find. I asked them to keep me informed.'

Informed of her meal breaks? Surely he had more on his mind than that? She opened her mouth to question him.

'You're translating?' He leaned over, one broad hand on the desk just inches from the manuscript.

Unaccountably heat washed her as she stared at his long fingers splayed close to hers. His masculine scent made her draw a deep, appreciative breath.

'Yes.' She sat straighter. 'It's a fascinating document, even apart from the succession issue.' She looked at the closely written text but all her attention was on the man who'd casually invaded her space.

'And now you've finished for the day.'

For a long moment Tamsin debated. It wasn't a question. She could contradict him and stay, working on the translation. Normally she worked much later. Yet her concentration had shattered. She found herself stretching, cramped muscles easing as she moved.

'Yes. I've finished.' She shoved her chair back and stood, busying herself packing up. By rights she should feel less overawed by him now she was on her feet. Instead, she inhaled his fresh scent as he leaned close and became aware of the way his body hemmed her in. It made her edgy.

'Good. You're free to come out.'

'Out?' Her brow knitted.

'How long since you left the castle?'

'I…' There had been her walk down to the river a few days ago. Or had it been a week? She'd been too busy to count days. 'I've been occupied lately.'

'As I thought.' He nodded. 'Come on. Pack that up.'

'I'm perfectly capable of getting fresh air myself.'

Eyes of dark sapphire held hers as he leaned across the desk. 'I'm sure you are. You're a most capable woman, Dr Connors.'

His mouth kicked up in a smile that lit his face and made her suck in her breath. The way he spoke her name, using her formal title as if it were an endearment, made her ridiculously flushed.

A warning bell clanged crazily in her head.

'Why are you here?' She braced her hands on the desk rather than lean towards that stunning smile. 'What do you want?'

She was no bedazzled fool, no matter how her pulse pattered out of control and illicit excitement shimmied along her backbone. Men like Prince Alaric didn't waste time on women like her. Women who weren't glamorous or sexy. She'd learned the hard way where she stood with the opposite sex and she wasn't making that mistake again.

'You don't pull your punches. I like your bluntness.'

Did he have any idea how gorgeous he looked, with laughter lines crinkling from his eyes and that conspiratorial grin turning rakishly handsome into devastatingly irresistible?

No wonder he had a reputation as a rogue. He'd only have to ask to get anything he wanted from a woman. The knowledge shored up her sagging defences.

She turned away to slip her notebook into a drawer.

'I do want something. I have a proposition for you.' She looked up, startled, and he raised a hand before she could inter-

rupt. 'But not here. It's late. You need a break and I need to eat.
I'll show you some of our Ruvingian hospitality and we can
discuss it after we've eaten.'

Instinct warned her something was amiss. There was no reason
for a prince to take an employee to dine. Yet the sparkle in his
eyes invited her to forget her misgivings and take a chance.

Curiosity gnawed. What sort of proposition? Something to
do with the archives?

'If you'd like someone to vouch for me…' he began.

Her lips twitched. 'Thank you, but no.'

Despite his easy charm there was a tension about his jaw that
hinted at serious intent. Maybe what he had to say was important
after all, not just a whim.

'Some fresh air would be welcome. And some food.' Suddenly
she realised how hungry she was.

'Excellent.' He stepped back and the fragile sense of intimacy
splintered. 'Wear warm clothes and comfortable shoes. I'll meet
you by the garages in twenty minutes.'

'I'll see to this.' But as she reached for the text he pulled
cotton gloves from his pocket and picked it up.

'I'll take care of that. You go and get ready.'

He didn't trust her to keep the chronicle safe. Last night he'd
taken it away, saying he wanted it locked up. Disappointment
was a plunging sensation inside her.

If he didn't trust her with that, how could he trust her to do
her job? And why would he have a proposition?

Tamsin felt completely out of place in the luxurious, low-slung
car as it purred out of the cobbled courtyard and over the bridge
that connected the castle with the steep mountain spur. A last
glimpse of the castle, a floodlit fantasy with its beautiful, soaring
towers, reinforced her sense of unreality. She slid her fingers over
the soft leather upholstery, eyes wide as she took in the state of
the art controls. She'd never been in a car like this.

Or spent time alone with a man like Prince Alaric.

In the confines of the vehicle he was impossible to ignore. So
big and vital. Electricity charged the air so it buzzed and snapped.
It was hard to breathe.

She told herself lack of food made her light-headed. She should have eaten lunch instead of skimping on an apple.

He nosed the car down a series of swooping bends and she risked a sideways look. A smile played around his mouth as if an icy road after dusk was just what he loved. His powerful hands moved easily on the wheel, with a fluid sureness that hinted he enjoyed tactile pleasures.

Tamsin shivered as an unfamiliar yearning hit her.

'You're cold?' He didn't take his eyes off the road. How had he sensed the trawling chill that raked her spine?

'No, I'm warm as toast.'

'So it's the road that bothers you.' Before she could answer he eased his foot onto the brake.

It was on the tip of her tongue to protest. He hadn't been speeding. She'd enjoyed the thrill of the descent, instinctively sensing she was safe with such a capable driver. Disappointment rose as they took the next bend at a decorous pace but she didn't contradict him. She didn't want to try explaining the curious feelings that bombarded her when she was with him.

'What's this proposition you have for me?'

He shook his head, not looking away from the road as it curved one final time then disappeared like a dark ribbon into the forest at the foot of the mountain. 'Not yet. Not till we've eaten.'

Tamsin tamped down her impatience, realising her companion had no intention of being swayed. For all his light-hearted charm she sensed he could be as immoveable as the rock on which his castle perched.

'Tell me why you took this position. Being cooped up here in the dead of winter hasn't got much to recommend it.'

Was he kidding? Tamsin slanted another glance his way and saw nothing but curiosity in his expression.

'The place is beautiful. Its heritage listed for outstanding scenic and cultural significance.'

'But you've barely been out of the castle.'

Tamsin stiffened. Had his staff been reporting her movements? Why? The unsettling discovery didn't sit well with the sense of freedom she'd enjoyed.

'I'd planned to explore. But once I got engrossed in my work and found Tomas's chronicle, I never found time.'

'You came to Ruvingia for the views?' Disbelief edged his tone.

'Hardly.' Though the picturesque setting was a bonus. 'It was the work that fascinated me.'

'You don't mind spending an alpine winter so far from family and friends?'

Tamsin looked away, to the dark forest crowding close. She was grateful for the heating which dispelled any chill. 'My parents were the first to urge me to apply. They know how important my work is to me.'

They didn't care about her not being home for the festive season. As far as her father, a single-minded academic, was concerned the holidays were simply a nuisance that closed the university libraries. Her mother, wrapped up in her art, found it easier catering for two than three. Theirs was a distant kind of caring. They were dedicated to their work and Tamsin, an unexpected child after years of marriage, had fitted between the demands of their real interests. She'd grown self-sufficient early, a dreamer losing herself in a world of books.

'What about your friends? Surely you'd rather be with them at this time of year?' He probed the sore point, making her want to shrink inside herself.

Tamsin had friends, but none were particularly close.

Except Patrick. She'd expected to see a lot of him over the holidays. Had expected their relationship to blossom into something wonderful.

Before she'd discovered what a gullible idiot she'd been.

She turned to find Prince Alaric watching her closely. In the dim interior light she sensed an intensity to his stare that surprised her. Why did this interest him so?

'You don't understand how exciting this job is.' With an effort she pinned on a bright smile. 'A previously unknown hoard of documents. The opportunity to be of real value, preserving what might otherwise be lost. Not to mention the excitement of discovery. The chance to...' She hesitated, unwilling to reveal how important this job was at a more personal level.

This had been an escape route she'd gratefully seized. She couldn't bear Patrick gloating over his success and sneering at her naivety. Plus there'd been her colleagues' pitying looks.

It was also an opportunity to shore up her battered self-esteem. To prove that despite her appalling lapse of judgement with Patrick, she was good at what she did. Even, she admitted now, to show those who'd doubted her abilities they'd made a mistake promoting Patrick instead of her. His work was inferior but he had the charm to make the most of every opportunity. They'd soon realise their mistake but Tamsin wouldn't be human if she didn't want to banish her growing self-doubts with a coup of her own.

'The chance to...?'

Tamsin dragged herself back to the conversation. What had she been saying? 'The chance to be part of this exciting discovery. It's a once in a lifetime opportunity.'

'But you can't have known that when you applied for the job.' His riposte was lightning fast. He speared her with a penetrating look before turning back to the road.

'No, but I...'

She couldn't tell him how desperately she'd needed to escape. Escape Patrick lording his new position over her; Patrick with his old girlfriend on his arm again. Her forlorn heart had shredded whenever she'd seen them.

'I wanted a change. This sounded too good to miss.' She sounded stilted, falsely bright, but she wasn't about to bare her soul.

'Too good to be true, in fact.' His voice deepened on a curiously rough note. In the streetlights of the town they'd entered he looked stern.

Had he grown bored? He was probably used to more scintillating conversation. Tamsin was more than happy to change the subject.

'Where are we going?' They were in the old town, where roads narrowed and cobblestones glistened. Lights were strung between lampposts, giving the streets a festive air as pedestrians strolled, looking at decorated shop windows.

Tamsin wished she could be one of them. Away from prying questions. Away from memories that taunted her.

'The winter market is on,' he said. 'We'll eat and you can see some of the sights.'

Tamsin felt a flicker of excitement. The town looked quaintly romantic with half-timbered houses, brightly painted shutters and steep, snow-capped roofs.

But with a prince by her side relaxation was impossible. Instead she fretted over his mysterious proposition and the growing sense of something wrong. Why this interest in her?

A couple strolled hand in hand across the street, catching her eye. They were barely aware of anyone else, completely absorbed in each other. She felt a small pang of envy. Once she'd hoped she and Patrick…

Tamsin had never been close to anyone like that. Never experienced all-encompassing love, even from her parents. Never even fitted in, finishing school before her age peers and being so much younger than her university colleagues.

She turned away, setting her mouth firmly. She refused to pine for what she'd never had. One perilous venture into romance had proved what she'd always suspected. Love wasn't for her. She just didn't inspire that sort of affection.

But she had her work. That was compensation enough.

Alaric viewed the woman beside him with frustration. Two hours in her company and she was still an enigma.

On one level she was easy to read. Her peal of laughter at the antics of children on the outdoor ice-skating rink. Her enthusiasm for markets filled with local handcrafts and produce. She was pleased by simple delights: watching a woodcarver create a nutcracker dragon, or a lace-maker at work, asking questions all the time.

Most women he knew would complain of the rustic entertainment!

It was tempting to believe her innocent of deception.

But she'd prevaricated in the car and he'd sensed there was more to her reasons for coming here. Her tension when he pushed for answers, and the way she avoided his gaze made him suspicious.

She was back in disguise, hiding behind thick-rimmed glasses and a scrunched up bun, with an anorak the wrong colour for her complexion and a pair of shapeless trousers.

Was she trying to banish any memory of her in shorts?

His mouth twisted grimly. That particular image was emblazoned on his brain.

With rapt attention she watched a stallholder cook pancakes and fill them with dark cherries, walnuts and chocolate. It was pure pleasure watching her. Her face was blissful as she bit into the concoction, oblivious to the sauce glistening on her bottom lip or Alaric's testosterone-induced reaction as it dripped to her chin.

She swiped her lips with a pink tongue. To his horror his groin tightened and throbbed as if she'd stripped her ugly clothes away and offered him her soft body.

Right here. Right now...

What was going on? She was nothing like his usual women. He wasn't even sure he could trust her.

Yet her combination of quick mind, buttoned up formality, prickly challenge and hidden curves was absurdly, potently provocative.

She was like a special treat waiting to be unwrapped. The perfect diversion for a man jaded by too many easy conquests. Too many women seeking to trap him with practised seduction and false protestations of love.

Someone bustled past, bumping her close and branding her body against his. His mouth dried. He had to force himself to let go after he'd steadied her.

'Come,' he said abruptly. 'Let's find somewhere quiet.'

Tamsin looked up at his brusque tone, pleasure waning as she read his stony expression. Clearly he'd had enough.

She couldn't blame him. He'd gone out of his way to show her sights that must, for him, be unremarkable. Plus all evening he'd been approached by citizens eager to talk. He'd had no respite.

To her dismay her hackles had risen at the number of women who'd approached him, simpering and laughing when he turned his blue eyes in their direction. What did that say about her? Hastily she shoved away her petty annoyance at them.

She'd watched fascinated as he handled requests with good humour and practicality. He made his royal obligations look simple. She noticed he didn't have any obvious minders with him but mixed easily with the crowd. Perhaps his security staff blended in.

'Of course,' she murmured. 'Somewhere quiet would be—'

A crack of sound reverberated, then a shout. Her breath caught as a young boy raced in front of her, skidding on the cobbles and catapulting towards a vat of simmering spiced wine. She cried out, instinctively reaching for him.

A large figure plunged forward as the cauldron teetered. It overturned just as Alaric hauled the youngster away. There was a crash, a sizzle of hot liquid and a cry of distress, then a cloud of steam as the boy was thrust into her hands.

In the uproar that followed Tamsin lost sight of the prince as the crowd surged forward. Then, out of the confusion he appeared, pocketing his wallet and nodding to the smiling stallholder. He accepted thanks from the boy's parents but didn't linger. Moments later he propelled Tamsin across the square and into an old hotel.

Only when they were ushered into a private dining room did Tamsin see his face clearly. It was white, the skin stretched taut across sculpted bones, his lips bloodless.

'Are you all right?'

It was clear he wasn't. Rapidly she scanned him, looking for injury. That's when she noticed the large splash staining his hand and her stomach turned over.

Tamsin propelled him to the bench seat lining one wall. He subsided and she slid in beside him, moistening a linen napkin from a water carafe and pressing it to his hand.

He sat silent and unmoving, staring ahead.

Tamsin washed the wine away, revealing a burn to the back of his hand. She pressed the wet cloth to it again.

'Is it just your hand? Where else does it hurt?'

Slowly he turned his head, looking blankly at her. His eyes were almost black, pupils dilated.

'Your Highness? Are you burned elsewhere?' She cupped his hand, reassured by the warmth of his skin against hers, though the chill distance in his eyes worried her. Frantically she patted his trousers with her other hand, testing for more sticky wine.

Finally he looked down.

Her hand stilled, splayed across the solid muscle of his thigh. Suddenly her eagerness to help seemed foolish.

'I'm fine. No other burns.' He threw the wet cloth onto the table, drawing a deep breath as colour seeped along his cheekbones. His free hand covered hers, sandwiching it against living muscle that shifted beneath her palm.

Fire licked Tamsin's skin. Something curled tight inside her at the intimacy of that touch.

Ink blue eyes surveyed her steadily and long fingers threaded through hers, holding her hand prisoner. Tingles of awareness shimmied up her arm to spread through her body.

'In the circumstances you can forget the title.' His voice was as smooth and seductive as the cherry chocolate sauce she still tasted on her lips. 'Call me Alaric.'

His mouth lifted in a tiny smile that made Tamsin's insides liquefy. A smile that hinted at dangerous intimacies, to match that voice of midnight pleasures.

Abruptly she leaned back, realising she'd swayed unthinkingly towards him.

'You're sure you're not hurt?' Her voice was scratchy, as if it were she who'd lunged in to save the boy, not him. The blankness had gone from his face as if it had never been, yet she couldn't help wondering what secrets lurked behind his apparently easy smile.

'Positive. As for this...' he flexed his burned hand '...it's fine. Though thank you for your concern.' He leaned forward, eyes dancing. Had she imagined those moments of rigid shock? It had seemed so profound. So real.

'Now we're alone, we can talk about my proposition.' He was so close his breath feathered her hair and cheek. Tamsin had to fight not to shiver in response.

'Yes, Your...yes, Alaric.' She strove for composure, despite the wayward excitement that welled, being so close to him. 'What did you have in mind?'

His fingers flexed around hers. His strength surrounded her. It was strangely comforting despite the way her nerves jangled at the look in his eyes.

His smile broadened and her breath snared.

'I want you to be my companion.'

CHAPTER FOUR

'YOUR...companion?' Tamsin snapped her mouth shut before she could say any more.

He *couldn't* mean what she thought.

Companion could have all sorts of interpretations. It was shaming proof of the way he turned her brain to mush that she'd immediately thought he meant *lover*.

Her heartbeat ratcheted up a notch and her breathing shallowed as, unbidden, another graphic picture filled her brain. The two of them, stretched naked on the carpet before the fire in his library. Limbs entwined. Lips locked. His hard, capable hands shaping her body.

Was that answering heat in his eyes? He watched her so closely. Could he guess her thoughts?

Tamsin forced her breathing to slow and sat straighter. She reminded herself she was known for her analytical mind. Not flights of fantasy.

He kept her hand anchored against him. Foolishly she couldn't bring herself to pull it away.

'That's right.' He nodded.

Companion to Prince Alaric of Ruvingia. Women would kill for time with Europe's most notorious bachelor. For the chance to persuade him into marriage or just to experience his vaunted expertise as a lover.

Desperately Tamsin told herself she wasn't one of them.

'You've mistaken me for someone else.' She lifted her chin, bracing for the moment he told her this was a joke.

Instead he shook his head.

'No mistake, Dr Connors.' He paused, his lips pursing ruminatively. To her horror, Tamsin couldn't take her eyes off his mouth. 'Perhaps I'd better call you Tamsin.'

A delicious little shudder tickled every nerve ending as he said her name like that.

As if it pleased him.

As if he looked forward to saying it again.

Reality crashed down in a moment of blinding insight. *He was playing with her.* A man like him would never view a woman like her in that light.

'Feel free.' She forced her voice not to wobble. 'What is it you're proposing?'

One straight brow lifted, giving him a faintly superior air. 'Exactly what it sounds. I need a companion and you'd be perfect. There'd be benefits for you too.'

Tamsin resisted the impulse to shake her head to clear her hearing. She'd watched him speak. She knew what he'd said. The excited patter of her pulse was testament to that.

No man had described her as *perfect* before.

'My invitation this evening wasn't totally altruistic,' he continued.

Did he realise he'd begun absent-mindedly stroking the back of her hand with his thumb as he clamped it to his leg? 'I wanted to see if we're compatible.'

'Compatible?'

His lips stretched in a brilliant smile that made something flip over inside. Only the hooded intelligence in his bright stare hinted this wasn't as simple as it seemed.

Sternly Tamsin told herself to be sensible. Logical. All the things she didn't feel when he touched her, smiled at her like that.

'I need a companion who won't bore me in the first half-hour.'

'I take it I passed muster?' Anger ignited at the notion of being assessed. Had it occurred to him she might have better things to do with her time?

She was sure she'd think of them in a minute.

She tugged her hand but he didn't release it.

His expression sobered. 'I needed to be sure you'd handle it, too. It's not necessarily fun keeping me company while I play prince-in-residence for all comers.'

Tamsin stared, curious at the bitterness in his voice as he spoke of his princely role. Was it real or feigned?

'I wasn't bothered.' She'd felt privileged to be with him and to see the able way he'd dealt with requests from the light-hearted to the serious. He had an easy manner with people. She envied that. 'But I still don't understand.' She took a deep breath and willed herself to concentrate. 'Why do you need a companion? And why me?'

'Ah, I knew you'd go to the crux of things.'

Alaric watched her troubled face and realised he'd have to do better. He'd only aroused her suspicions.

He supposed it was the shock of rescuing the boy that had done it. The initial explosion of sound: probably a firecracker but for an instant so like the report of a firearm. The need for urgent action combined with the feel of those small, bony shoulders beneath his hands, the distress on the kid's face. The huge, fearful dark eyes that for a moment had looked so hauntingly familiar. Together they'd triggered memories Alaric usually submerged beneath the everyday demands on his time.

It had only taken seconds, but that was enough to tip the balance and slide him into a nightmare world of guilt and pain. In an instant he'd been back in another time, another place. To another life he'd been unable to save.

Only the touch of Tamsin's hands, the concern in her voice and her insistence had dragged him out of a state he'd prefer not to think about. It was a condition he usually managed alone, never sharing with others.

That was the way it would stay.

'Commitments mean I'm staying in Ruvingia for a while.'

She nodded, wariness in every line of her face.

'And…' He paused, wondering how best to phrase this. How to appeal to this woman he couldn't read? 'While I'm here I need a companion.'

Amber eyes regarded him unblinkingly through the lenses of her glasses.

'Why? You can't be lonely.'

Couldn't he?

No matter how frenetically he'd pursued pleasure through Europe's glittering capitals, no matter how many lovers warmed his bed, Alaric remained profoundly alone. And when he was alone the memories came. Hence his constant need for action, for diversion.

She didn't need to know any of that.

'Not lonely, precisely.' He favoured her with a smile that had won him countless women.

She appeared unmoved, staring back with a slight frown as if she couldn't quite place him in a catalogue. Irritation surfaced. Why couldn't she be like the rest and fall in with his wishes? Why did she have to question everything?

Yet there was something about her seriousness, about the fact that she held herself aloof, that appealed.

'It would make my life easier if I were seen out and about with the same woman. A woman who didn't expect that to lead to a more permanent arrangement.'

As he said it, Alaric realised how weary he'd become of socialites and trophy mistresses. It would be a relief to be with someone who didn't fit the conventional mould of glossy beauty and vacuous conversation.

She tilted her head to one side, her mouth flattening primly. 'You want a decoy? Because you're tired of being chased by women out to snare you?'

'You could say that.' He shrugged and watched her gaze flicker away. 'There's something about a royal title that attracts women eager to marry.'

'I'd have thought you could cope with that.' Her words were tart. 'You've got a reputation for enjoying yourself in short term relationships. Surely you don't need to hide behind any woman.'

He read the stiffness in her body and realised he'd have to offer more. There was no sympathy there. If anything she looked disapproving.

'These are delicate times, Tamsin.' He lingered on her name, liking the sound of it. 'Power blocs are jockeying for position and they include some aristocratic families who'd love to cement their status by linking to royalty.'

'Marriage to you, you mean?'

He nodded. 'I've had aristocratic ladies paraded before me for months and it's getting harder to avoid them.'

'You're an adult. You just have to say you're not interested!' She tried to withdraw her hand but he refused to relinquish it. This wasn't going as he'd anticipated.

'It's not so simple. Even a rumour that one contender is favoured over another could change the perceived balance of power. My cousin Raul is under the same pressure.'

Alaric leaned forward, using his most cajoling tone. 'All I'm asking is some help to keep them at a distance. Is that unreasonable?'

Her lips thinned and she surveyed him coolly.

Impatience spiked. He was tempted to cut through her questions and demand acquiescence the easy way.

He'd drag her glasses away, cup her head in his hand and kiss her till her mouth grew soft and accommodating and she surrendered to his wishes. Till she blushed a delicate pink all over as she had on the squash court, this time with pleasure and anticipation.

Till she capitulated and said she'd do whatever he wanted. *Anything* he wanted.

Heat poured through him as he remembered her parted lips, ripe with cherries. The swipe of her tongue licking up sauce in a move so innocently sexy it had tugged him towards arousal. The feel of her breasts against him as he carried her down the library ladder.

Alaric's pulse quickened, his hold on her hand tightening.

'I can see it might be useful to have someone to keep other women away.' Her tone told him her sympathy was limited. 'But what's that got to do with me?'

'You're already here living at the castle. You're not impressed by my position.' Despite the importance of persuading her, Alaric's lips twitched as he saw her flush. Few women could have made it clearer his title and money meant nothing. She had no notion how refreshing that was. To be viewed as just a man. 'You won't get ideas about companionship turning to something more.'

He raised her hand to his lips and kissed it, inhaling the summery fragrance of her satin skin, enjoying the little shiver of
awareness she couldn't hide. Tamsin was different from other
women. He couldn't remember any of them intriguing him so.
Protecting his country had never coincided so well with personal
inclination.

They said you should keep your friends close and your enemies closer. Alaric wasn't sure yet if she was an enemy or an
innocent, but he'd enjoy keeping Tamsin Connors close. Very
close.

Tamsin's heart faltered and seemed to stop as his lips caressed her
hand in a courtly gesture. The trouble was, to her overwrought
senses it felt provocative, not courtly, evoking reactions out of
proportion with the circumstances.

There was no mistaking the amusement in his eyes. He was
laughing at her. Did he take her for a fool?

She yanked her hand away, anger and hurt bubbling in a bitter
brew that stung the back of her throat.

'No one would believe it.'

'Why not? People will believe their eyes.'

She shook her head, wishing he'd stop this game.

'Tamsin?' He frowned and she realised she was blinking eyes
that felt hot and scratchy. Hurriedly she looked away at the old
mural of convivial wine makers on the far wall.

'I'm not the sort of woman to be companion to a prince.' Even
if it was make-believe.

'I know my record with women is abysmal but surely you
could make an exception in the circumstances.'

'Oh!' She shot to her feet. 'Just stop it!' Tamsin paced the
room then whirled to face him. 'No one would ever believe you'd
really taken up with someone like…' The words choked as her
throat constricted. 'Like me.'

He rose, eyes fixed on hers. 'Nonsense.'

Tamsin felt like stamping her foot. Or shouting.

Or curling up in a ball and crying her eyes out.

All the weak, emotional things she'd wanted to do when
Patrick had revealed he'd only spent time with *a woman like*

her because she was useful to his ambitions. All the things she hadn't let herself do because she'd been busy pretending it didn't matter.

'Look at me.' She gestured comprehensively to her practical, unglamorous clothes. 'I'm not...' But she couldn't go on. She knew she wasn't attractive, that she didn't inspire thoughts of romance or even plain old lust. But she refused to say it out loud. She had some pride.

'I see a woman who's intelligent and passionate and intriguing.' His words snapped her head up in disbelief.

When had he moved so close?

He loomed over her, making the room shrink so it seemed there was only her and him in a tiny, charged space.

Tamsin's throat worked as anger roiled. 'I refuse to be the butt of your joke.' She swung away but he caught her elbow, turning her implacably to face him.

'It's no joke, Tamsin. I was never more serious.'

She angled her chin higher. 'I don't think my clothes would pass muster for consorting with royalty, do you?' Easier to focus on that than the shortcomings of the woman who wore them.

'I don't give a damn about your clothes,' he growled, a frown settling on his brow. 'If they bother you replace them. Or let me do it if you don't have the cash.'

'Oh, don't be absurd!' As if it was just the clothes. Tamsin knew how men viewed her. No one would believe she was a sexpot who'd snared the interest of a playboy prince!

'Absurd?' The single word slid, lethally quiet into the vibrating silence, raising the hairs on her nape.

His eyes sparked fire. Suddenly the danger she'd once sensed in him was there, staring down at her.

A frisson of panic crept through her.

She backed a step. He followed.

'You don't believe me?'

Silently she shook her head. Of course she didn't believe him. She had no illusions. She—

In one stride he closed the gap between them. His hands cupped her face, fingers sliding into her hair, dislodging pins. The sensation of him tunnelling through her hair, massaging her scalp was surprisingly sensual.

Tamsin stared up into eyes darkening to midnight-blue, so close she could barely focus. She told herself to move away but found her will sapped by the look in his eyes. The floor seemed to drop away beneath her feet as she read his expression, his fierce intent.

That look bewildered her. She'd never seen it before.

'I—'

Her words stopped as his lips crushed hers. She gasped, inhaling his scent and the spicy taste of his skin. Her thoughts unravelled.

Taking advantage of her open mouth Alaric devoured her. He was determined, skilful, dominant. He overwhelmed every sense, blotted out the world. Stole her away to a place of dark ecstasy unlike any she'd known.

He held her so firmly she couldn't move. His body was hard, awakening unfamiliar sensations that rippled and spread, a trickle turning into a torrent of excitement.

Dimly Tamsin realised she didn't want to move. That in fact her hands had crept up around his neck, linked there to stop herself falling. Neither did she mind the sense of him surrounding her, legs planted wide to anchor them both. Her eyes closed as her thoughts scrambled.

Bliss beckoned.

This was nothing like Patrick's lukewarm attentions. Or the hesitant clumsiness she'd felt in his embrace.

For the first time Tamsin felt passion burst into scorching life. All she could do was acquiesce. And enjoy.

His kiss was fervent, almost angry, yet Tamsin had never known such delight. He ravished her mouth so fiercely she trembled with the force of it, bowed backwards as he surged forward, seemingly unable to slake his need.

And she welcomed him.

Despite his sudden aggressive ardour she wasn't afraid. Instead it made her feel…powerful.

Vaguely she wondered at that, but her mind refused to compute the implications. She simply knew that with Alaric she was safe. Even if it was like stepping off a skyscraper into nothingness. His strong arms hauled her close and she gave herself to delight.

She kissed him back, revelling in the warm sensuality of their mouths melding. He licked her tongue and she moaned, her knees quaking at the impact of this sensual onslaught.

The kiss altered. He didn't bend her back quite so ferociously, though he still strained against her. His hungry ardour eased into something more gentle but no less satisfying.

She breathed deep as he planted kisses along her jaw. Sensation bloomed with each caress. Her skin tingled and her breasts grew heavy. She thrust herself against him, needing his hardness just there. Her breath came in desperate gasps as she struggled to fill air-starved lungs. She clung tight, wanting more.

He moved to kiss her on the mouth again and bumped her glasses askew.

Instantly he froze. As if that simple action reminded him who he was kissing. Not a svelte sophisticate but plain Tamsin Connors.

He stilled, lips at the sensitive corner of her mouth. Tamsin held her breath, desperate for him to kiss her again. Craving more of his magic.

His steely embrace loosened and firm hands clasped her shoulders, steadying her as if he knew her legs felt like stretched elastic. He pulled back and she swayed, bereft of his heat and strength.

A protest hovered on her swollen lips but she swallowed it. She would not beg for more. Not now she saw the dawning horror on his face. The unmistakeable regret in the way his gaze slid to her mouth then away.

'Are you OK?' His voice was gruff, his expression stern. He was embarrassed, she realised.

Pity had provoked the kiss, but the reminder of who it was he embraced had stopped him in his tracks.

The lovely, lush taste of him turned to ashes on her tongue. The thrill that had hummed through her with every caress died.

There was no magic. It had been a kindness gone wrong. *An act of charity from a man who felt sorry for her.*

Anger and regret chased each other in a sickening tumble of emotions. At least, she told herself, he hadn't deliberately set out to dupe her, like Patrick.

She'd duped *herself* into believing that kiss was real.

Now she had to pick up the pieces. Pretend it didn't matter that he'd unthinkingly awoken heart-pounding desire in a woman who'd never known its like before.

Tamsin wanted to howl her despair.

But she had the torn remnants of her dignity. She might only be suitable as a decoy, not wanted for herself, but he needn't know he'd shredded her self-respect.

Deliberately she lifted a hand to set her glasses straight on her face. It was a gesture of habit, but never had it held such significance.

'I'm fine, thank you, Alaric. How are you?'

Alaric stared at the cool-eyed woman before him and struggled with his vocal cords. They'd shut down, just like his brain when he'd hauled her into his arms and slammed his mouth against hers.

Even now he was barely in control of himself! One moment of madness had turned into something more. Something that threatened the boundaries he used to keep from feeling, from engaging fully in the world around him.

He'd kissed countless women but not one had made him *feel*. Not like this.

Who the hell was she? What had she done to him? Passion was a pleasure, a release, an escape. Never had it overwhelmed him like that.

'You're sure?' He sounded strangled, like an untried teen, hot and bothered by his first taste of desire.

'Of course.' Her brows rose in splendid indifference. As if being accosted by lust-ridden strangers was an inconsequential distraction.

Alaric scrubbed a hand over his face, annoyed to note the slight tremor in his fingers.

Tamsin Connors might dress like someone's ancient maiden aunt but she kissed with all the generous ardour any man could want. The feel of her lush body melting against his, her mouth hot and welcoming, had driven away the last shred of his sanity. Their passion had been volcanic.

Hard now to believe her apparent hurt and self-doubt had appalled and angered him. It had provoked him into doing what he'd wanted for so long now: kiss the woman silent. When he'd dislodged her glasses he'd come to his senses and been horrified at the idea he'd taken advantage of her. Possibly scared her.

Had her earlier pain been real? Or had she played on his sympathies?

It infuriated him that he was no closer to understanding her. She was a bundle of contradictions. Fiery yet reserved. Confident in professional matters yet still vulnerable. Thrilled by a rustic fair but unimpressed by his title. A siren who shattered his control like no other.

He wanted to rip away the façade she presented the world and uncover the real Tamsin Connors.

He wanted to run from what she made him feel.

But mostly he wanted her back in his arms.

He drew a deep breath. One thing he knew for certain. *She was the most dangerous woman he knew.*

'I apologise,' he said stiffly. 'I shouldn't have done that.'

'No, you shouldn't.' She glared at him and it was all he could do not to reach for her again. With her eyes snapping gold fire, her hair in tumbled waves around her shoulders and her lips reddened and full she was too alluring. Even the glasses couldn't hide that now.

How had he ever thought her ordinary?

'As I said, Tamsin,' he lingered appreciatively over her name, 'clothes are immaterial.' He watched colour flush her cheeks and felt savage pleasure that she wasn't as unmoved as she pretended. 'I look for more than fashion in a woman.'

'I'm not *anyone's* woman.' Her chin angled up.

'Just as well,' he murmured, as something primitively possessive surfaced. 'We wouldn't want the complication of a jealous boyfriend, would we?'

'No fear of that.'

She looked away. Her expression didn't change but suddenly he regretted baiting her to salve his pride. Whatever had happened, whoever she really was, Tamsin had been caught like him in the conflagration erupting between them. At least he hoped so. The alternative was unthinkable.

'You're surely not still serious about this?'

'Never more so.' He watched her turn. She drew a slow breath as if gathering herself.

'You said if I spent time with you there'd be a benefit in it for me.' Her voice was crisp, her demeanour completely business-like. 'What did you mean?'

Disappointment reared at her about-face; her obvious self-interest. Alaric told himself it was easier to deal with her now than when she was warm and willing in his arms. A pity he didn't believe it.

'I've been thinking about the job we've contracted you to do. It would be easier if you had more staff.'

The light in her eyes told him he'd finally snared her interest. He squashed a spark of annoyance that he came second in her priorities to a pile of mouldering books.

'Not easier, but there's a chance of further damage in the time it takes us to assess what we've got.' She chewed her lower lip. Heat scorched Alaric's lower body as he focused on its softened contours. In repose Tamsin's mouth was a perfect Cupid's bow of invitation.

'The offer only applies if I become your *companion*?' The twist of her lips and her chilly look told him how little she liked the prospect. 'That sounds like blackmail.'

Alaric shrugged. His gaze drifted to her mouth and he remembered her moan of delight as they'd kissed. She only feigned disinterest.

'If you agree it will mean some time away from your work. Putting extra resources into the archives will compensate. Two qualified full time staff.' He watched excitement light her face.

'And you may want to come with me when I open a new wing of the national museum. There's a collection behind the

scenes that may interest you. Illuminated gospels that I believe
are noteworthy.' Those treasures had never been outside the
country. Neither had foreign experts viewed them.

Her eyes widened eagerly. In other women it was the sort of
look reserved for a gift of emeralds or rubies.

Tamsin Connors was unique. In far too many ways.

'This…arrangement would only interrupt my work occasionally?'

Alaric gritted his teeth. Women vied for his attention. He'd
never needed to bribe one to be with him!

'That's right.'

Still she hesitated. She clasped her hands before her in a gesture he'd come to realise signalled vulnerability.

'We're not talking about anything more than spending time
together? Being seen in public?'

He nodded curtly.

'Then…' She paused and licked her lip as if her mouth had
dried. Alaric's groin tightened as he remembered her lush sweetness. 'Then I accept. On one condition.'

'Yes?' He hauled his gaze from her mouth.

The glacial expression he found in her eyes would have frozen
a lesser man.

'No more kisses. Nothing…intimate.'

Alaric bowed stiffly, all dignity and insulted pride.

'You have my word that I won't take advantage. Nothing
intimate except at your express request.'

She pretended to abhor his touch?

She'd soon be on her knees begging for his kisses.

CHAPTER FIVE

'I'M SORRY, ma'am. You can't go this way.'

Tamsin looked at the burly man blocking the path and drew her jacket close. His wide stance and implacable stare made the crisp morning feel chillier. Or was it that he automatically spoke in heavily accented English? As if he knew who she was and had been waiting for her?

'Why not?' This was the path to the village and she needed a walk to clear her head. After days working long hours she was no closer to finding the peace she'd always taken for granted in her job.

That peace had been missing since *he'd* taken her out four days ago. Since he'd kissed her till her head swam and her senses reeled and she'd forgotten she was plain Tamsin Connors. Since he'd proposed a fake relationship then promptly disappeared, leaving her wondering if she'd conjured the idea as a wish-fulfilling fantasy.

Each day she'd waited, nerves on edge, for him to summon her. Only to learn today he was away in the capital.

It rankled that he'd left without telling her. As if he had to report his movements! Yet after what he'd said she'd expected to see more of him.

Not that she was disappointed.

It was just that she wanted to work on the chronicle. She couldn't access it in his absence. *That's* what frustrated her.

'A landslip has taken part of the path.'

The stranger didn't move his eyes off her, neither did he smile. Tamsin's gaze strayed to his walkie-talkie. He didn't look like a groundsman, more like heavy duty security.

'How far along? Maybe I could take a detour.'

'Sorry, ma'am, but the surface is unstable. I couldn't allow it.' Steel threaded his voice for all his deference.

'I see.' She scanned the wooded hillside. There must be other tracks.

'If I might suggest, ma'am?'

'Yes?'

'There's an easy circuit walk above the castle.'

Tamsin repressed a sigh. She needed more than a tame stroll. This restlessness demanded a better outlet. She'd avoided the squash court in case she met the prince again. Perhaps she should try to work off her excess energy there.

'Thanks. I'll think about it.' She smiled, acknowledging his nod, and turned uphill.

The track curved and she looked back. He was still there, watching, as he spoke into his walkie-talkie.

She shivered. It was nonsense to think he was reporting her movements. Yet the claustrophobic feeling that dogged her intensified. In the archives the new staff meant she was never alone and whenever she left her rooms she seemed to run into staff.

Tamsin paused as the castle came into full view. A thrill sped through her as she took in the circular towers, crenellated battlements and banners fluttering black, blue and gold against the bright sky.

Just the place for tales of romance and derring do. For princes on white chargers rescuing damsels in distress.

Cradled by snow-capped peaks, its grey stone rose sheer from the mountain, high above the dark forest. It had an eagle's eye view down the valley to lands its owners had ruled for generations.

A nineteenth-century fad for gothic architecture had turned the once-grim stronghold into a fairy tale showpiece.

Yet below were grim dungeons where enemies had languished. The prince's word had always been law here and the ruthlessness of Ruvingian princes was legendary. They always got what they wanted.

Shadows moved beneath the portcullis. Tamsin's pulse danced and her breathing shallowed as she recognised the man in the lead: tall, powerfully proportioned and aristocratic with his confident stride and strong features. He matched his home perfectly.

Then it was too late to stand gawking. He'd seen her. He turned and dismissed his staff.

And all she could think of was how it had felt cradled tight in his arms. The intensity of his kiss. The passion that had ravaged her senses and left her craving more.

Every night she'd tossed in her bed, remembering. Imagining things that left her feverish and unsettled. Furiously she tried to repress the blush staining her cheeks, hoping he'd put it down to the chill wind.

'Tamsin.' He stopped a few paces away.

Despite her embarrassment her lips curved in response when he smiled, a dimple grooving his cheek.

She could almost believe he was pleased to see her, though she told herself he didn't really care. She tried to dredge up anger. He'd kissed her out of pity.

'Alaric.' She liked saying his name. Too much. 'How are you? I thought you were away?' Too late she realised she sounded far too interested in his activities.

'Business kept me away until today.' Was that a cloud moving over the sun or had his bright gaze shadowed?

'We need to talk about my work.' She drew herself up straight, reminding herself that was all that mattered. Not her shocking weakness for indigo eyes. 'I haven't been able to access the chronicle to continue my translation. Your staff claim not to know where it is.' Indignation rose that he didn't trust her with her own find!

'My priority is ensuring absolute secrecy till we confirm it's genuine.' His expression grew stern.

Tamsin opened her mouth to protest that it shouldn't stop her work. 'However, arrangements will be made to enable you access while maintaining security.'

'Thank you.' Her indignation fizzled, leaving her feeling wrong-footed.

'Now, would you like to come out with me tonight?'

He sounded like a polite host, entertaining a guest. Except he'd bought her cooperation, bribed her with staff for her project.

The knowledge stopped her pleasure in his smile. The staff had turned up days ago and now it was time to deliver on her part of the bargain.

'Where are we going?' She might as well be gracious about it.

His smile broadened and her lungs squeezed. He really was the most stunning man.

'To a ski resort.' He named a town famous for exclusive luxury that drew the world's most prestigious VIPs. 'There's an event I must take part in then we'll stay for dinner.' No mention of her role as decoy. The man was a diplomat when he wanted to be.

'Fine.' She stepped forward and he turned, shortening his stride to match hers.

'Watch the icy path.' He clasped her elbow and she tensed. Heat rayed from his touch, countering the wintry air.

He held her arm even when they reached safer ground. Tamsin didn't fuss by telling him to release her. He'd think she read too much into the gesture. Hurriedly she searched for something to say.

'What should I wear?'

He slanted her a piercing glance and the air sizzled between them. He was remembering, too.

I don't give a damn about your clothes, he'd said.

And then he'd kissed her.

Tamsin's pulse accelerated painfully as she watched his impassive face. Or had their kiss meant so little he'd forgotten it?

'Some will be in ski gear and the rest dressed for an evening out. Take your pick.' Heat shimmied through her as their gazes collided and she felt again that sensation like chocolate melting, deep inside.

Spending time with Alaric had to be the biggest mistake of her life! Yet despite her doubts, Tamsin couldn't resist the invitation in his smile and the intriguing mystery of his cool, blue eyes.

Even when he annoyed her, Alaric made her feel alive; brimming with an effervescence she'd never known.

* * *

Tamsin stood on the terrace of an exclusive resort hotel, huddled into the soft luxury of the full length faux-fur coat that had been delivered just before she left.

She'd been about to object, uncomfortable with accepting clothes Alaric had bought when she'd seen his note.

To keep you warm tonight. This was my mother's. I'm sure she'd approve its loan.

He'd lent her something of his mother's? Ridiculous to feel such pleasure that he'd trust her with the gorgeous garment. Yet she couldn't dispel delight that he'd thought of her comfort. Without being obvious, he'd also ensured she wouldn't look too out of place in this A-list crowd.

Tamsin glanced at the glamorous, beautiful people surrounding her, some of the faces familiar from press reports. They quaffed vintage champagne as if it were water. And the jewels—even by lamplight some of the women almost blinded her with their casually worn gems.

She stroked the soft coat. For now it didn't matter that beneath its elegant lines she wore a chain store dress and a pair of plain court shoes, her best, which she'd bet none of the sophisticated women here would be seen dead in.

'Here they come!' Excitement rippled through the gathering and Tamsin turned to look up at the blackness of the mountain looming above.

Butterflies danced in her stomach. It was hunger, not excitement at the idea of Alaric joining her.

'There they are.'

Now Tamsin saw it. A flicker of colour high on the mountain. As she watched the flicker became a glow then a tiny jewel-like thread of colour trailing down the slope.

The moon emerged from behind clouds to illuminate the imposing outline of one of Europe's most famous peaks. Its cool brightness intensified the scene's magical quality.

She couldn't take her eyes from the ribbon of rainbow colours descending in swooping curves through the silver gilt night. She'd never seen anything like it. Excited murmurs in a dozen languages buzzed in her ears and she found herself grinning, rapt in the spectacle.

Her spine tingled as a clear chorus of voices rose. A cluster of people, many in traditional Ruvingian costume, waited on a flat area beside the hotel.

The singing stopped and in the silence Tamsin heard the whoosh of skis. The stream of colour descended to the clearing, resolving into dozens of skiers, each holding a coloured lantern in one hand and a basket in the other.

'They skied that slope with no hands?' The mountain was notoriously dangerous.

'It's tradition,' said a woman in cherry red ski clothes and scintillating diamonds. 'Didn't you know?'

Tamsin shook her head, her gaze on the lead skier. Alaric. Her knees gave a little wobble as she took in his proud, hand-some face and his easy grace as he slid to a flourishing halt. He handed the basket to a blonde who curtseyed and blushed. Each skier delivered a basket and was rewarded with a goblet.

'Mulled wine,' said the woman beside her.

There was a bustle as Alaric stepped out of his skis and headed purposefully through the crowd. It parted before him and Tamsin wondered what it would be like to have that effect on people.

His progress wasn't entirely easy. Others moved towards him, all women, she noted, frowning.

No wonder he had a reputation as a ladies' man. He didn't even have to search them out!

Some smiled, others greeted him and still others reached out to touch. A twist of something sharp coiled through Tamsin's stom-ach as she watched a beautiful redhead kiss him on the cheek.

Tamsin's sense of not belonging rushed back full force. Why was she here? Companion indeed! This was a farce.

'Your Highness.' The woman beside her bobbed a curtsey then Tamsin forgot her as she looked up into eyes like midnight. Black hair flopped roguishly on his brow and his lips curved in an inti-mate smile that sent shivers of longing scudding through her.

'Tamsin.' He lifted the silver goblet in his hand. She had a moment to notice its intricate design, then the scent of spiced wine filled her nostrils and its sweet pungency was in her mouth.

Heat exploded within, surging through her blood. An instant later it exploded again as she watched Alaric lift the goblet to his lips, turning it deliberately to drink from the same place she had. His eyes held hers as he tilted it and drank. Not a sip like hers but a full bodied swallow.

Fire sparked across Tamsin's skin at the blatant sexual message in his eyes. She told herself it was an act.

Yet a crazy part of her wished the message she read in his stare was real. She must be losing her mind!

Seated at a quiet table by a window overlooking the resort, Tamsin tried to relax. It was impossible with Alaric, like a sleek, dark predator, on the other side of the table.

The taste of spiced wine was on her tongue but it was the taste of *him* she remembered. Why couldn't she get that kiss from her mind? Heat flooded her cheeks as she sought for something to say, convinced his brooding eyes read too much of her inner turmoil.

'Tell me about the night ski. Is it an old tradition?'

Alaric settled back in his chair and stretched his legs. Tamsin shifted as they brushed hers.

'Since the seventeenth century. The locals have re-enacted it ever since.'

'Re-enacted what?' Maybe if she focused on this she wouldn't react to his lazy sensuality.

'It was the worst winter on record. Avalanches cut the valley off and crop failure meant the villagers were starving. In desperation some young men set off through near blizzard conditions to get supplies, though everyone believed the trek doomed.' Alaric's voice was as dark and alluring as the rest of him. Tamsin felt it curl around her like the caress of fur on bare skin.

'Fortunately one of the avalanches also brought down rock and opened a new route out of the valley. Weeks later they returned with supplies. Ever since the locals have commemorated the feat, and the salvation of the village.'

'And the wine?' She couldn't shake the idea there'd been hidden significance in the way he'd shared that goblet.

'Just to warm the skiers.' His eyes gleamed.

'That's all?'

He leaned forward, his gaze pinioning her till her only movement was the pulse thudding at her throat.

'You think I've deviously tied you to me in some arcane tradition? That we're betrothed, perhaps?'

Her cheeks grew fiery. 'Of course not!'

His brows arched disbelievingly but she refused to admit how the simple act of sharing his wine had taken on such ridiculous significance in her mind. If only he hadn't looked so sinfully sexy and dangerous as he'd deliberately drunk from her side of the cup.

'Don't fret,' he purred, reaching out to cover her hand in a blatantly possessive gesture. 'Our companionship has a purpose and my actions were designed to achieve that purpose. They succeeded, don't you think?'

'Admirably! Everyone got the message.' She tugged her hand free and placed it in her lap, conscious of the interest emanating from the rest of the restaurant. There were celebrities aplenty here but Alaric was the man drawing every eye.

He raised a glass of delicious local wine in a toast. 'To more success.'

Reluctantly she lifted her glass. 'And a speedy resolution.'

Alaric smiled as he watched her sip the wine. Not the usual practised smile that he'd learned to put on like a shield from an early age. But a smile of genuine pleasure. Tamsin Connors pleased him, and not just because she was refreshing after so many grasping, eager women.

He enjoyed her company, even when she was prickly. And tonight the glow in her cheeks gave her a softness at odds with the strict hairstyle and unimaginative dress.

His silence unnerved her. He saw it in the way she shifted in her seat. Yet he didn't try to ease her tension. If she was on edge she was more likely to reveal her true self. He needed to understand her, find out how far he could trust her.

'You know,' she mused, her eyes not quite meeting his, 'there's a way out of your problem. Fall in love with a nice, suitable princess and marry. Women won't bother you then.'

Instantly Alaric's sense of satisfaction vanished. He stiffened, fingers tightening around the stem of his glass. 'I'm in no hurry to marry. Besides,' he drawled, aiming to cut off this line of conversation, 'the princes of Ruvingia never marry for love.'

For an instant he allowed himself to remember his brother, the only person with whom he'd been close. Love had barely featured in their lives and when it had it had been destructive. Felix had been ecstatic in his delusion that he'd found the love of his life. He'd been doomed to disappointment.

Ruthlessly, Alaric clamped a lid on the acrid memories.

'What about the princesses?'

'Pardon?' Alaric looked up to find Tamsin, far from being abashed by his offhand response, was intrigued.

'Do princesses of Ruvingia ever marry for love?'

'Not if they know what's good for them,' he growled.

The hint of a smile curving her lips died and she sat back, her expression rigid and her eyes wide.

Damn. He felt like he'd kicked a kitten when she looked like that. He speared a hand through his hair and searched for a response that would ease the hurt from her eyes.

'Royal marriages are arranged. It's always been that way.' Until Felix had made the mistake of thinking himself in love.

Love was an illusion that only led to pain.

'Even your parents?' she said wistfully. 'That wasn't a love match?'

Clearly Tamsin Connors had a romantic streak. She'd probably grown up reading about princes rescuing maidens, falling in love and living happily ever after. Obviously she had no idea how far from the truth her fantasy was.

'My parents married because their families arranged a suitable match.'

'I see.' She looked so disappointed he relented.

'I was too young to remember but I'm told my mother was besotted with my father, though it was an arranged match.'

'She died when you were little? I'm sorry.'

Alaric shrugged. You didn't miss what you'd never known. Maternal love was something he'd never experienced.

'It must have been hard for your father, left alone to bring up his family.'

Alaric watched her sharply but she wasn't fishing for details, just expressing genuine sympathy.

'My father had plenty of assistance. Staff. Tutors. You name it.'

Looking back on his boyhood it seemed his remote, irascible father had only appeared in order to deliver cutting lectures about all the ways Alaric failed to live up to his golden-haired brother. For a man who, according to under stairs gossip, had only slept with his wife long enough to conceive a spare heir, he'd been remarkably uninterested in his younger son.

'Still,' she said, 'he must have missed your mother. Even if he didn't marry for love, he would have grown to care for her.'

Alaric shook his head. No point letting her believe some fairy tale when the truth was publicly known. 'My father didn't waste any time finding another woman.'

'He married again?'

'No, he simply ensured there was a willing woman warming his bed whenever he wanted one. He was a good-looking man and he had no trouble attracting women.'

People said Alaric was like him.

Hadn't the disaster with Felix stemmed from Alaric's too-easy success with women?

There was no disputing the fact Alaric, like his father, had never fancied himself in love, possibly because he'd never experienced it. Ice trickled down his spine. Maybe it was a character flaw they shared. That they were incapable of love. Unlike Felix. Unlike Alaric's mother who'd reputedly died of a broken heart.

'I see.'

He doubted it. Tamsin, he was beginning to suspect, had a naïve streak a mile wide.

He'd bet she'd be horrified to learn the first girl to profess love for Alaric had simply been aiming to meet his father. That *love* had been code for sex and expediency in a quest for the power and riches she'd hoped to obtain in the bed of a man old enough to be her own father.

Alaric had learned his lessons early. If there was one thing he'd never be foolish enough to do, it was to give his heart.

CHAPTER SIX

'THANKS for coming, Alaric. It was good to talk before I put the expansion plans to the rest of the board.'

Alaric turned. He didn't let his eyes flicker to the scar disfiguring Peter's cheek and neck. He'd long ago trained himself not to, knowing pity was the last thing his old comrade wanted. But nothing could prevent the sour tang of guilt in his mouth.

'My pleasure.' He forced himself to smile. 'You know I always have time for the youth centre. I just wish there'd been something like it when we were kids.'

Peter shrugged. 'The army saved us both from turning into feral teenagers.'

Alaric thought of his rebellious teens, chafing at his father's aloof authoritarianism and his own sense of uselessness, kicking his heels between royal duties.

'You could be right. Just as well the military is royalty's accepted profession for superfluous second sons.'

'Hardly superfluous.'

Alaric shrugged. It was the truth, but he wasn't interested in discussing his family.

'I like your Tamsin, by the way. A bit different from your usual girlfriends.'

It was on the tip of Alaric's tongue to say she wasn't his, *yet*. 'She is different.' That's why she fascinated him. She was an enigma. Once solved she'd lose her allure and finally he'd get a full night's sleep.

They walked into the large indoor sports hall to find a crowd clustered below the climbing wall. There was no sign of Tamsin. Last time he'd seen her she'd been engrossed in some new computer programme with a couple of lanky youths.

Then he saw her—halfway up the towering wall.

Bemused, he stared. He'd left her without a qualm, seeing her so involved and with his staff to look after her while he attended his meeting. Had she been pressured into scaling the massive wall? The teens often challenged visitors in a test of courage.

'Way to go, Tamsin!' called one of the youths holding the rope that kept her safe.

Alaric strode over, fury pumping in his veins. At them for forcing her into this. At himself for allowing it to happen.

He slammed to a halt as he realised, far from being petrified, she was making steady progress up the wall.

She wore a helmet but her feet were bare and her trousers rolled up, revealing those shapely calves. The harness she wore outlined the lush femininity of her derriere and made his blood pump even faster.

Tamsin moved with the grace of a natural climber. Another metre and she reached the top. Roars of approval erupted, almost obliterating her exultant laughter.

Who'd have thought it? Prim and proper Dr Connors had the makings of a thrill seeker! He watched her climb down.

'That was fantastic,' she called over her shoulder. 'I...' Looking down she saw him. Her foot jerked beneath her.

'I've got you.' Alaric stepped close. 'Let her down.' They obeyed and a moment later she filled his arms.

She was soft and intriguingly curvaceous for such a slim woman. The warm puff of her breath hazed his neck and his grip tightened.

She fitted snugly in his hold, her breast soft temptation against his chest, the sunshine scent of her enticing. His pulse accelerated but he kept his eyes on her flushed face, rather than linger on the pronounced rise and fall of her breasts.

'Thanks. You can put me down.' She sounded delightfully breathless. Free of her glasses, there was nothing to hide the amber glow of awareness in her eyes. Alaric felt he was falling into sunshine.

He had an intense vision of her looking up at him like that, lips parted invitingly, eyes dazed. But in his mind she was sprawled beneath the royal blue canopy of his bed, naked on silk sheets, awaiting his pleasure.

Alaric's breathing grew choppy as he fought the most primitive of physical reactions. His lower body locked solid at the force of abrupt arousal. The sound of applause and excited comment faded as fire ignited his blood.

Tamsin moved, dragging her gaze from his and fumbling at the strap of her helmet. It dropped away before she could stop it and her hair frothed over his arm in a dark cloud.

The scent of wildflowers hit him.

Forget the bedroom. He wanted this woman on sweet alpine grass. He wanted to watch her eyes light to gold as he plunged deep inside and took her to ecstasy.

'Alaric.' Her voice was deliciously throaty. He wanted to hear her calling his name as she climaxed. 'Please…'

Reluctantly he lowered her to her feet. But holding her had cemented his resolve. Amazingly, for those few moments she'd banished the dark shadows. He'd been utterly consumed by sexual need. Just as when they'd kissed.

It was no longer enough to satisfy his pride by making Tamsin Connors beg for his kisses. Alaric craved the release he knew he could find in her sweet, supple body.

And he intended to have it.

'A moment of your time before you go in.'

Tamsin halted at the door to the castle's staff quarters. Slowly she turned, schooling her face to polite interest. They were alone, the security men melting away when they arrived back from the youth centre.

In the late afternoon gloom of the castle courtyard, Alaric's face was unreadable but the way he towered above her, his shoulders blocking her vision, reminded her of the night he'd kissed her.

Of the way it had felt an hour ago when he'd held her in his embrace.

A shiver tingled to her toes as she recalled the heat in his eyes and the answering fire in her belly, and lower, at the message that had passed wordlessly between them.

No! Her imagination ran riot. Prince Alaric would never look at her with desire. Her hormones made her see what wasn't there. He'd played at intimacy for their audience.

'Yes?' At least her voice was steady.

For a moment he simply gazed down. She sensed the intensity of his regard, despite the way his eyelids dropped to half-mast. That gave him a dangerously seductive look that made her pulse race into overdrive.

He leaned closer, his breath tickling her forehead.

'Why wear those glasses? You don't need them.'

Stunned, she stepped back, only to find she'd already backed up against the door. He followed, lifting a hand idly to rest on the wall near her head. Instantly Tamsin was torn between unease at the sense of being trapped and, worse, delight at being so near him.

Beneath her jacket her breasts felt fuller. She wanted his hand there, she realised with a stifled gasp, on her breast, moulding her flesh.

This was worse than anything she'd felt for Patrick. Far worse. Surely it wasn't normal to feel this lick of heat between her legs or the heavy swirl low in her belly?

'Tamsin?'

Flustered, she grappled for the thread of the conversation. 'My glasses?' She touched them, gaining a moment's reassurance from their familiarity. 'For magnification. I do a lot of close work.'

'They don't magnify much.'

How did he know that?

'You don't need them now. You took them off to play squash and to climb. Why not remove them when you're not working?'

'I'm used to them.' Even in her own ears it sounded lame, but it was true. 'I've worn them for years.'

'Then perhaps it's time you came out from behind them.' Alaric leaned forward, his words a whispered caress that tantalised her bare skin.

He lifted a hand and for a moment she thought he was going to grab her glasses. Instead he stroked her hair from her face.

After taking it down to fit under the climbing helmet, she'd only secured it quickly and now strands escaped. She felt them tickle her neck.

Or was that his warm breath? He'd lowered his head and they stood close.

'What difference does it make to you?' Her voice was uneven, as if she'd run up the zigzag road to the castle.

'None.' Again his fingers stroked as he tucked hair behind her ear. Did she imagine his touch lingered? 'I just wondered why you hid behind them.'

Tamsin stiffened. 'I'm not hiding!' She'd acquired the glasses when she'd worked on a particularly difficult manuscript at university. The text had been so tiny she'd suffered eye strain until she'd got them.

She watched one dark eyebrow rise questioningly. She was about to reiterate her words when something stopped her.

The memory of how comfortable she'd felt behind her new glasses. How easy not to notice when older students pointed and dug each other in the ribs as they whispered about her. How hurtful it was when they'd gone to the pub after lectures leaving her, the young kid, behind and alone.

When had she decided to use her glasses all the time? Had it even been a conscious decision?

Or had she slipped into the habit the same way she'd filled her wardrobe with clothes that were functional rather than fashionable? *Because there was no point pretending to be what she wasn't.* Because she was what she was: a brain rather than a face. Known for her intellect, never invited out or pursued for her looks or personality.

Was he right? Had she been hiding? Isolating herself as a defence mechanism?

'Tamsin?'

'Was there anything else...Alaric?' She stood straighter, looking him in the eye, her brain whirling with the implications of his words. She'd think about it later. She couldn't think when he was so close, so...distracting.

'As a matter of fact there is.' He smiled and her heart jerked as if pulled on a string.

Tamsin swallowed, telling herself it was a trick of the fading light that made his expression seem intimate, as if he wanted nothing more than to stand here with her.

'Yes? You have another outing planned?' It didn't matter that she'd enjoyed her afternoon. That she'd revelled in the company of the teenagers, seemingly antisocial and yet so enthusiastic. Alaric had only invited her to be seen with him. Because she was a decoy.

He must have been ecstatic when she'd swooned in his arms, reinforcing their fictional relationship. Heat rocketed to her cheeks at the memory.

Would he be angry or amused if he realised how she felt about him? That the thought of him touching her made her long for things far beyond her experience?

'Not an outing.' He paused. 'I'm hosting a winter ball. It's an important event on the calendar.'

'*Another* ball? But you just had one!'

His mouth lifted in a lazy smile that softened her sinews and made her slump, grateful for the solid door behind her. In the gathering dusk Tamsin read the amused glitter in his eyes.

'How puritanical you sound. Do you disapprove?'

'It just seems a little…'

'Excessive?' He shrugged. 'Last week's was a small affair, only eighty or so guests to meet a new consul. The winter ball is something different. In four hundred years it's been held as regular as clockwork every year but one.'

'During war?'

Alaric's expression sobered. 'No.' Tamsin waited what seemed a full minute before he continued. 'There was no winter ball the year my brother died suddenly.'

Tamsin's flesh chilled as his words, sharp as shattered crystal, scored her.

'I'm sorry, Alaric. So sorry for your loss.' When he'd spoken briefly of his family the other night she'd had the impression they weren't close. Except his brother. The way Alaric spoke of him she sensed a special bond there.

She lifted her hand to reach for him, then dropped it. He wouldn't welcome her touch. He'd never looked so remote.

'Thank you.' He nodded curtly. 'But the point is this event, above all, is one where I'd be grateful for your presence.'

'Of course.'

It didn't matter that attending a ball was the last thing she wanted, that she'd be way out of her comfort zone. She'd seen the pain behind Alaric's cool expression. For a moment she'd seen anguish shadow his eyes and the sight hit her a body blow.

If he wanted her, she'd be there.

She didn't pause to question her decision.

'Good. Thank you.' His lips tilted in a ghost of his usual smile and something seemed to unravel, deep inside her. 'A dresser will attend you tomorrow and you can make your selection to wear to the ball.'

'But I—'

'Let me guess.' This time his smile was real and her heart tumbled. *Oh, she had it bad.* 'You're going to insist on buying your gown?'

'Well, yes.'

'You'd only buy a ball gown as a favour to me.' He stroked a finger down Tamsin's cheek, effectively stifling the objection rising in her throat. That simple caress held her still, breathless with pleasure.

'Consider it a work-related expense. I need you there and you need a dress. Unless you have one with you?'

Tamsin shook her head. She'd never owned a ball gown.

He leaned in. For a heart-stopping moment she wondered if he'd kiss her. She should object but her willpower seeped away. Her damp palms spread on the door behind her for support and her pulse juddered madly against her ribcage.

'Leave it to me.' His lips were so close Tamsin almost felt them against her skin. She sucked in a difficult breath as he spoke again in that deep, seductive whisper.

'All you have to do is relax and enjoy.'

CHAPTER SEVEN

TAMSIN lifted a hand to her hair then changed her mind and let it fall. She didn't want to disturb the softly elegant knot with its glittering pins or the artfully loose tendrils caressing her neck.

The dresser who'd returned this evening had done far more than zip up the dress. She'd transformed Tamsin into a woman she barely recognised. A woman who looked attractive in a way Tamsin never had before.

At first she'd thought it was simply the ball gown that made the difference. Of red silk shot with amber and gold, it was unlike anything she'd owned. From the moment she'd put it on she'd felt…special. The last of her scruples about accepting it disintegrated as she twirled before the mirror.

The bodice, cut high and straight above her breasts to leave her shoulders bare, made her look feminine and elegant. Even the fact that she'd had to go braless, relying on the dress's hidden support in lieu of a strapless bra she didn't own, didn't dampen her excitement.

It was shallow of her to feel wonderful because she looked good. But Tamsin didn't care. It was such a novel experience! Excitement bubbled in her veins. She felt she could take on the world!

For weeks Tamsin had featured in newspaper and magazine articles beside Alaric. Worst of all, the ones that made her cringe, were the 'then and now' pieces. Showing Alaric with previous girlfriends, all gorgeous and sophisticated. Those photos were set against pictures of Tamsin, looking anything but chic, her expression startled or, worse, besotted as she stared up at the powerful man beside her.

She wasn't besotted. She wouldn't let herself be.

The theme of each article had been the same. What did Alaric see in her? Those pictures had confirmed every doubt she'd harboured about herself, especially since Patrick.

More than once she'd been tempted to call a halt to this charade. She didn't, not simply because she'd given her word, but because being with Alaric, the focus of his glowing looks, made her feel good.

Even it if was a sham, she *enjoyed* being with him. It was balm to her wounded soul. Was it so wrong to enjoy the pretence that he genuinely liked her?

Yet the temptation was dangerous.

Now for the first time Tamsin knew she looked like a prince's companion. Delight filled her that this time there'd be no snide conjecture, no damning photos. This time she looked… attractive.

Tonight she'd learned so much. Things she'd always told herself she was too busy to bother with. Things her mother, so profoundly uninterested in fashion, hadn't thought to teach her. Like what shade of eye shadow accentuated the colour of Tamsin's eyes without being too obvious. Like how to tame her hair into a sophisticated style.

Yet the dresser said it was the glow in Tamsin's skin, the sparkle in her eyes that made her look so good tonight.

Surely that had been a pep talk to give her confidence. Apart from the clothes and light make-up, she was the same. As she turned before the mirror, feeling the silk swirl around her legs, Tamsin experienced a prickle of unease. The colour in her cheeks was because of the dress, that's all.

For there was only one other possible explanation. That her inner sparkle was anticipation at the idea of spending the evening with Alaric, maybe even dancing in his arms.

She stopped abruptly, letting her long skirts settle around her. No! She wouldn't let it be so. To Alaric she was a convenient companion. She wouldn't spin fantasies about him. These past weeks as his companion had been surprisingly delightful. She enjoyed his company. *But that's all.*

The phone rang and she snatched it up, grateful for the interruption to her disturbing thoughts.

'Tamsin? How are you, darling?'

Instantly her spine stiffened. She'd hoped not to hear that voice again for a long, long time. She'd crossed Europe to avoid this man. To pull herself together after he'd hurt her so badly. Now he had the temerity to call her darling!

'Who is this?'

'Ah, sweetheart, it's Patrick of course. Are you still upset about the way we parted?' He paused as if waiting for her to speak. 'Didn't I apologise?'

He'd apologised all right, while smirking at his success and her gullibility in believing he could ever interest himself in a plain Jane like her! As apologies went it had been a masterpiece of form over sentiment. He hadn't been sorry and in that moment Tamsin had finally realised how blind she'd been to his true personality.

In love with the idea of love, she'd fallen for him like a ripe peach. Or from his perspective, like a dried up prune! Too late she'd discovered his taste really ran to curvy blondes who dressed to reveal rather than conceal.

'It's late for a business call.' She was proud of her nonchalant tone.

'You're assuming it's business?'

'What do you want, Patrick?' He thought he was God's gift to women but he surely couldn't believe her weak enough to care for him after what he'd done.

His sigh might have moved her once but now she merely felt a burst of impatience.

It was only when he mentioned the date testing on the sample she'd sent to her home institution that Tamsin grew interested. By the time he'd finished speaking her scalp prickled with excitement.

She'd *known* this was special! Now the dating proved it.

Yet doubt lingered. On the face of it she now had proof that Alaric should be Maritz's next king. But caution warned her to make absolutely sure. Just because the document's age was right didn't prove the content.

Besides, Alaric wasn't as eager as she'd expected. Did he really not want to be king? Look at the strict security he'd instituted around the chronicle. It was locked away the minute she'd finished work each day.

'Tamsin? Are you still there?'

'Of course. I'll look forward to reading the report when you email it. Thanks for calling.'

'I said it seems you've got an interesting cache of documents. I hear on the grapevine the prince himself gave you extra staff for the project. Plus old Schillinger says you've sent him copies of some fascinating pages.'

'That's right.' She frowned. There was no way Patrick or anyone else could guess the explosive revelations in the manuscript. Those pages were kept here under lock and key. Dr Schillinger's interest in the rest was purely linguistic.

'Perhaps if it's such a find you'd feel better with another expert there. Someone you know you can work with.' He paused as if waiting for her to speak. 'I have a lot on at the moment but for you'd I'd tear myself away and…'

'No! That's not necessary.'

Did he think she was still so besotted that she'd invite him here after the way he'd treated her? Had she really been such a pushover?

'Tamsin.' His voice deepened to a cajoling note. 'I hurt you and I've regretted it ever since. I made a mistake and I'm not too proud to admit it. If I came over there we could pick up where we left off. I'm worried for you. Sometimes on the rebound people behave impulsively.'

Was he referring to the press reports linking her and Alaric? He had a hide!

How had she fallen for his oily charm? The only person Patrick cared about was Patrick. It made her sick to realise she'd been so needy she'd let him walk all over her without seeing his selfish opportunism.

As for his wet kisses and perfunctory embraces… Tamsin shuddered. How had she ever thought him appealing?

She remembered Alaric's demanding, exciting kiss. The combustible heat that consumed them and made her feel like she soared close to the sun.

In comparison Patrick's pallid caresses faded to insignificance. Now so did he: a mean, conniving man who wasn't worth her time or emotional energy.

'No, Patrick. I appreciate your offer to *tear yourself away*.' Her lips curled at his attempt to muscle in on what he thought was a project to further his career. 'It's all under control. The staff are excellent and we've gelled into a great team. Of course, if ever we need further support I'll be sure to let you know.' *When hell froze over.*

'But I—'

'Sorry, Patrick. I can't talk. I have to go.'

She put down the phone then stroked unsteady hands along the soft fabric of her dress, trying to conjure again her earlier pleasure.

Her stomach churned from hearing his voice. Not because she missed him, but at the knowledge of how close she'd come to making a complete fool of herself. She'd once considered *giving* herself to that…toad of a man!

Tamsin was fed up with being second best. Being *used*.

First Patrick and now Alaric, who only wanted her as a decoy. It didn't matter that Alaric also made her feel exciting, dangerous, unfamiliar things. That he brought her to tingling life like a sleeper waking from long slumber.

She was tired of being manipulated by men who wanted her for their schemes. Men who saw her as a convenience to be exploited.

Not a real woman of flesh and blood and feelings.

She stared in the mirror, taking in the reflection of a woman who was her and yet not her. Same nose, same eyes, same person, but so different from the old Tamsin everyone took for granted.

She was tired of hiding. Of not being noticed as a woman.

The idea of leaving the protective comfort of her usual role, of daring to pretend to be feminine and desirable, filled her with trepidation. Yet Alaric was right. Tamsin had isolated herself.

She owed it to herself not to hide behind her work and her past any longer. She might be out of her depth tonight but she was no coward.

Deliberately she lifted her hand and removed her glasses, dropping them onto a nearby table. Straightening her shoulders she left the room, her head high.

Alaric viewed formal balls as a necessary evil. Until he turned from greeting an ambassador and her husband to see the next guest in line and the air punched from his lungs.

She was breathtaking.

Among the bejewelled and bedecked glitterati she was un-adorned, yet she glowed with a radiance that set her apart. She didn't need diamonds and platinum. Her skin was flawless, her lips a glossy pout that turned his blood molten hot with instant hunger. Her dark hair was a sensuous invitation to touch. It looked like she'd just pinned it up after rising from a bath or bed. As if it would tumble down at any moment around her bare shoulders.

And her eyes. She'd removed the glasses and her amber-gold eyes were even more vibrant, more beautiful than he remembered. They blazed with an expression he'd never seen.

He'd *known* she was hiding her real self. But nothing had prepared him for this.

The ambassador moved away and Tamsin approached.

Alaric stiffened. She was fully covered, more fully than many of the women present. Yet he knew an almost overpowering impulse to unbutton his military tunic and toss it around her bare shoulders.

He didn't miss the arrested glances from the men nearby. He wanted to growl out a warning to keep their distance. To look away.

'Tamsin.' His voice worked, though it emerged brusquely from frozen vocal cords. 'It's good to see you.' If his muscles weren't so stiff with shock he'd have laughed at the enormity of that understatement. He bowed over her hand, resorting to punctilious formality to prevent himself shepherding her straight out the way she'd come. Away from those admiring stares.

His gaze dropped to her bodice, tightly fitted to show off her slim frame and full breasts. Flaring skirts accentuated Tamsin's narrow waist and for an insane moment he found himself distracted, musing whether he could span her with his hands.

'Hello, Alaric.' Her voice was low and throaty, yanking his libido into roaring life.

His hand tightened around hers and he wondered what would happen if he swept her away right now and didn't come back. He was within an ace of scandalising everyone, had moved closer, when she spoke again.

'I'm sorry I'm late.'

Reluctantly he dropped her hand and stepped back, removing himself from temptation.

'You're not late at all.' His voice was unnaturally clipped. 'Please, go on in. I'll join you soon.'

She nodded and he turned away, forcing himself to greet the next guests in the reception line. Never had it been so hard to focus on duty.

It was easier than she'd expected to mingle at a royal ball. Tamsin smiled as she sipped a glass of champagne and listened to the conversation around her.

'You're enjoying yourself?' asked Peter, the friendly community centre coordinator she'd met just over a week ago.

'How could I not? I've met so many fascinating people and I love dancing.' She'd only discovered that tonight, as partner after partner had whirled her round the mirrored ballroom, her dress swishing about her and her blood singing in her veins. It had been heady and delightful.

She turned. Peter wore an officer's dress uniform. The gold braid and the neat row of medals across his chest gleamed in the light of the chandeliers. He looked the model of a dashing soldier of a couple of centuries ago, except for the scar on his neck and cheek.

He laughed. 'It's true, then, that all the girls love a uniform.'

'Sorry. Was I staring?' His smile dispelled any embarrassment. 'It's just so unusual. Uniforms have changed since the Napoleonic Wars.'

'Not in Ruvingia. Not for formal occasions.' He winked. 'Especially as they make us so popular with the ladies. But in the field we wear khakis like everyone else.'

A pair of dancers swung by: Alaric looking like he'd stepped from the pages of a fairy tale in a uniform like Peter's only with more medals pinned to his chest, and in his arms a delicate blonde woman glittering in azure silk and sapphires.

Something struck Tamsin in the ribs. Jealousy? The possibility appalled her.

Despite promising to join her hours ago, Alaric had only danced with her once. He'd held her at arm's length, propelling her around the floor as if she were an elderly maiden aunt. Not close in his embrace as he smiled down into her face like he did with the gorgeous blonde.

The pain in her ribs twisted, intensifying.

'The prince, too? Surely he doesn't have to wear khaki?'

'Alaric? You don't know—?'

The surprise in Peter's voice made her swing round to meet his suddenly sombre face.

'Don't know what?'

He shrugged and she had the impression he was buying time before answering. The instinct she'd always trusted with her work sent a tiny shiver down her backbone.

'You mean Alaric is a real soldier, too?' If Peter was surprised by her use of the prince's first name he didn't show it. 'I thought the uniform might be a perk of position. Like being a royal sponsor rather than a member of the regiment.'

Yet even as Tamsin spoke she recalled her first impression of Alaric. His controlled power and athleticism proclaimed him a man of action, not a tame administrator.

'Some perk!' Peter shook his head. 'He won his commission through talent and hard work. Much good it did him.'

Tamsin put her glass down. 'What do you mean?' Peter's grim expression spiked foreboding through her.

'There was nothing pretend about our work. Alaric was our commanding officer and a good one, too. But with command comes a sense of responsibility. That can weigh heavily on a man who genuinely cares, especially when things go wrong.'

He half lifted his hand towards his scarred face and Tamsin's heart squeezed in sympathy. She wished she'd never started this conversation.

'I'm sorry,' she said breathlessly. 'I shouldn't have brought it up.'

He smiled. 'Because of this?' He gestured to his face. 'Don't be. There are worse things, believe me.' He looked at the dance floor as Alaric and his partner swung by again. 'Not all scars are on the outside, you know. At least mine have healed.'

Tamsin's gaze followed the prince. So handsome, so powerful, standing out effortlessly from every other man here. The focus of so many longing female glances.

Yet Peter hinted at hidden scars. Could he be right?

She thought of the way Alaric's shadowed eyes belied his easy charm, hinting at dark secrets.

Out of nowhere came the recollection of Alaric's ashen face after he'd saved that boy from serious burns. The prince's expression had been stark with pain or shock. He'd frozen rigid, eyes staring blankly as if looking at something distant that horrified yet held him in thrall.

'Tamsin?'

'Sorry?' She turned to find Peter holding out his hand.

'Would you like to waltz?'

She met his friendly dark eyes and tore her thoughts from the man even now bowing to some aristocratic lady on the other side of the ballroom.

She spent far too much time fretting about Alaric.

'I'd love to.'

For the next hour she danced with partner after partner, revelling in the exquisite venue, the glamorous crowd, the pleasure of the dance. Resolutely she tried not to notice Alaric dancing with every pretty woman in the room. Finally, pleading exhaustion, she let her partner lead her to a relatively quiet corner for champagne and conversation.

He was an editor from a national newspaper, good looking and full of entertaining stories that made her laugh. Tamsin saw the

openly admiring light in his eyes and felt a warm glow inside.
Here was one man at least who didn't look on her as second
best!

Plus he was flatteringly interested in her work, suggesting a
feature article on the archives and preservation work.

'May I interrupt?'

At the sound of that deep voice her companion halted in mid-
sentence. 'Your Highness, of course.'

Reluctantly Tamsin turned. She'd told herself she was glad
Alaric hadn't shown her off as his fake companion tonight. She'd
wanted to be her own woman, hadn't she?

Yet his lack of interest stung.

Had he finally decided she wasn't up to the job?

Piercing indigo eyes met hers and heat sizzled through her,
making the hairs on her arms stand up as if he'd brushed fingertips along her bare skin.

She searched for the shadows she'd seen in his gaze once
before, the shadows Peter had hinted at, but there was nothing
wounded about this man. If anything there was a hint of steel
in his stare, a tautness about his mouth. He was commanding,
assured, supremely confident.

He bowed. The epitome of royal hauteur from his severely
combed hair to his mirror polished shoes.

'Tamsin, I believe this is our dance.'

She tried to tell herself she didn't care that he'd come to her
at last, but her heart gave a little jump.

'I'll be in contact later, Tamsin.' Her companion smiled and
took her wineglass, urging her forward. She had no excuse but
to go with Alaric.

A strong hand closed around hers and her heart hammered.
Ridiculous! She'd danced with the prince earlier. But then he'd
barely looked at her, his formality quenching her excitement.

Now his gaze pinioned her, so intent it smouldered.

What had she done to antagonise him?

'You've made a new friend,' he murmured as he curled long
fingers around her waist. His touch evoked a tremor of primitive
anxiety. As if she'd stepped too close to a slumbering predator.

Taking a deep breath Tamsin placed an arm on his shoulder, let him clasp her other hand and fixed her gaze on his collar. This was just a dance. For show.

'Yes, several. Everyone's been very pleasant.' Despite the heat flooding her veins as Alaric guided her on the floor, something in his tone chilled her.

'So I saw. You've flitted from man to man all evening.' His voice was harsh and she raised surprised eyes to his. Blue fire flashed like lightning in an approaching storm.

'Your instructions were just that I attend the ball.' Her breasts rose in indignation, straining at the taut fabric of her bodice. 'I hadn't realised I wasn't allowed to mingle.' After ignoring her most of the night, how dare he complain she'd socialised with the other guests?

'Is that what you call it?' He spun her faster till the room whirled around them. Yet in his firm hold Tamsin felt only a heady rush of excitement. As if she were on the edge of something dangerous that nevertheless called to her.

'Do you have a problem, Alaric?' She told herself she was breathless because of the speed with which they circled the room. Her skirts belled out around her and her breath shallowed but she didn't feel nervous. She felt…exhilarated.

'Of course not. Why should I?' He kept his gaze fixed over her shoulder. 'Though I'd be sorry to see you hurt.'

'Hurt?' The music ended and they spun to a halt, yet Alaric didn't let her go. They stood in the centre of the dance floor, his grip holding her still.

'We Ruvingians are hospitable to guests. I wouldn't want you to misunderstand and interpret friendliness for something more.'

Tamsin's breath hissed between her teeth as pain lanced her. 'What are you insinuating? That no one would normally want to spend time with a woman like me? That I'm too uninteresting? Or perhaps I'm too plain?'

All the pleasure she'd felt in the evening shattered in that moment, like fragile crystal smashed underfoot. She told herself she didn't believe him, but suddenly the brilliant glare of the antique chandeliers seemed to flicker and dim. The heady excitement of the evening faded to something tawdry and shallow.

She stepped back to break his hold but his grip tightened.

'Of course not. You're misinterpreting my words.'

The music struck up again and around them couples took to the floor, a throng of glittering, designer clad, beautiful people.

She didn't belong here.

'You can let me go, *Your Highness*. You've done your duty dance.' She primmed her lips rather than say any more.

He didn't move, though she saw his chest rise as he took a huge breath.

'I said—'

He muttered something savage under his breath in the local dialect. Something she had no hope of understanding. A second later he pulled her close and twirled her round into the dancing crowd.

This time there was nothing prim or proper about the way they moved. Gone was the staid distance between them. Instead Tamsin was plastered to Alaric's torso. His arm at her waist didn't steady her, it welded her to him. His breath feathered her forehead. His hard thighs cradled her then shifted provocatively between her legs as they danced, evoking a strange hollow ache in her womb.

This close she felt his every movement, partly because her hands were trapped against his chest. His heart pounded fast and strong beneath her palm and despite her anger and hurt, spiralling excitement rose.

'I've had enough dancing,' she gasped as he swung her round and back down the long ballroom. This was too much, too dangerous.

'Nonsense. You love to dance. I've seen the smile on your face all night.'

All night? That implied he'd watched her which he hadn't. He'd been too busy squiring so many socialites onto the floor or engaging them in close conversation.

'You may find it hard to believe, Your Highness, but not all women long to dance with you.' The room flashed by and her heart pounded faster and faster. 'I want to stop.'

'I told you to call me Alaric.'

His body moved against hers and she bit her lip at the surge of pleasure she felt. At the powerful throb building inside. She was pathetic. This was just a dance and with a man she assured herself she didn't like. Though as his arm dropped low on her back, pulling her even tighter, it felt like something altogether different.

'Alaric.' The word was barely audible. Whether from the pulse pounding in her ears or because she couldn't seem to catch her breath, she didn't know.

'That's better.' His voice was rough as his lips moved against her hair. 'I like it when you say my name.'

With one final turn he spun them off the dance floor. Before Tamsin could catch her breath he'd shoved aside a hanging tapestry and hustled her through a door into a narrow passage. A few steps on and another arched door opened on their left. They were through it and in a dimly lit chamber before Tamsin could get her bearings.

A key scraped in the lock, loud as the thrum of her heartbeat. Then she felt a solid wall behind her and Alaric's powerful body trapping her against it.

'What do you think you're doing?' It was meant to sound outraged. Instead Tamsin's voice was uneven, weak with the force of conflicting emotions.

She should abhor this forced intimacy, the press of his body. Yet a secret thrill of pleasure ripped through her.

'Getting you to myself.' Alaric cupped her face in warm palms and lifted her chin so she looked deep into eyes the colour of a stormy night sky. 'I spoiled your evening. I didn't mean to.'

He leaned forward, touching his forehead to hers, hands tunnelling her hair, sending threads of shivery sensation down her spine and across her shoulders. Suddenly it wasn't him holding her prisoner, but her body's response.

'Why?' she croaked, her mouth too dry for speech. How had they come to this?

She should move but she made no resistance as he caressed her scalp and rubbed his nose against hers.

Where was her anger? A deep shuddering sigh rose and she strove to stifle it.

'Because I was jealous.' Shock slammed into her. Yet she felt the words as well as heard them as his lips caressed her eyelids. He really had said it. 'From the moment you appeared tonight I wanted you with me. Only me.'

This couldn't be. Tamsin shook her head, or tried to. He held her so close she couldn't move.

'I don't understand.' She hated her shaky tone but she was at a loss. 'You avoided me most of the night.'

'Displacement activity. I either spent the evening glued to you, or I kept my distance, acting the polite host. There was no happy medium. In the circumstances I thought my self-control admirable.'

His hands moved, slid down her throat and spread across her bare shoulders. Something about his powerful hands touching her so tenderly made her breath catch. His palms circled back to her throat, warming her skin and making her pulse race.

'Every time I saw you smiling at a dance partner I wanted it to be me you smiled at. No one else. Do you have any idea how gorgeous you are tonight?'

He couldn't be serious!

She couldn't think logically when he caressed her like that. She needed to think, to understand.

'Please. Alaric, I…'

'Yes, let me please you. Like this?'

His hands dropped, skimming the silk of her bodice, down the sides of her breasts, till her nipples tightened and the breath seared from her lungs.

Logic didn't matter when his mouth was a mere inch away. She craved him with every fibre of her yearning, untried body. As if this were what she'd secretly waited for. Without volition she raised her face, hungry beyond rational thought for his passion.

His mouth hovered, a breath away from hers.

'I promised I wouldn't.' His husky voice stroked like suede, dragging at her senses. 'So ask me to kiss you, Tamsin.'

CHAPTER EIGHT

ALARIC'S heart slammed against his ribs as he awaited her response. Every nerve, every sinew strained at the need for control.

Part of him was furious that somehow, without him knowing how, she'd cracked the wall he'd built around himself. The wall he'd reinforced the day he'd learnt the need to keep his affairs short and uncomplicated by emotion.

Surely he knew the dangers of reckless affairs!

But this was different.

More than dalliance to hold other women at bay. Far more than a ruse to keep an eye on someone who might, though it surely wasn't possible, be in league with those wanting to undermine the government.

This was an urgent, blood deep hunger.

Somewhere in the ballroom he'd crossed an unseen boundary.

Had it been when he bundled her from the room in full view of scandalised eyes? Or when he'd hauled her close in contravention of every protocol, staking his unmistakeable claim on her? No, it had been earlier. When he'd read the shattered hurt dulling her eyes and known himself the cause. His pain then had been as sharp as any physical wound.

He'd never felt this intensely about a woman.

He didn't *want* emotion. He didn't *want* to feel. Emotions were dangerous, deceitful. Yet for now he functioned on a more primitive level. Raw instinct not reason drove him.

He inhaled deeply, intoxicated by the scent of her. Unthinking, he bent to the delicate curve where her shoulder met her throat, nuzzling flesh so soft it made him feel like a barbarian, demanding her acquiescence.

But he didn't care. Desperation smoked off his skin, clamoured in his pulse, clenched his belly.

From the moment she'd arrived, a demure siren among a crowd of overdressed mannequins, he'd hungered for her.

As he'd watched her laugh and whisper and dance with all those other men he'd experienced a completely alien sensation. A roiling, dangerous, possessive anger.

Jealousy.

The sight of her with that journalist, known as much for his feminine conquests as his provocative editorials, had been a red rag to a bull.

Alaric told himself he'd acted to break up any potential leak of sensitive information. They'd looked like conspirators, their heads close together, their voices lowered. The last thing he wanted was news of her theories about his inheritance splashed across the newspapers.

But in truth he'd stalked across to claim her because he couldn't bear to watch their intimate *tête à tête*.

He laved her skin with his tongue, filling his mouth with her essence. Tamsin shuddered against his hardening body and he did it again, unable to stop. She was delicious.

'Alaric!' Fleetingly he registered her trembling sigh was probably a protest, though it sounded more like encouragement.

'Mmm? I'm not kissing you.' His mouth moved on her skin, trailing up to just below her ear. 'This isn't a kiss.'

He closed his teeth on her lobe in a gentle, grinding bite that made her spasm and fall further into him. Fire flickered through his veins.

So responsive. So incredibly attuned to every caress.

Escalating desire bunched each muscle into lockdown. The press of her belly against his erection was exquisite torture. If she moved again...

'Alaric. No.' It was a throaty whisper that incited rather than protested.

This time he grazed his teeth against the tender flesh below her ear and was rewarded with a shuddering sigh as her head lolled back against the wall. She'd stopped trying to push him away, her fingers curling instead into his tunic as if to draw him closer.

He nipped his way down her throat, revelling in the sinuous slide of her body against his. Unable to resist any longer, he levered away a fraction so he could cup her breasts. High, ripe, lush, they fitted his palms perfectly.

Suddenly slim hands bracketed his jaw, urgently dragging his face up. An instant later Tamsin's lips met his, hard and frantic, delightfully clumsy in her ardour.

When her tongue invaded his mouth it was Alaric's turn to groan at the sheer intensity of sensation. She kissed like a sexy angel. Half seductress, half innocent. For a moment the illusion hovered that she'd saved herself for him alone. That he was her first, her only.

Then he sank into bliss as their tongues slid and mated and thought became impossible. She melded to him with a supple sensuality that drove him to the edge.

He caressed her nipples and she growled in the back of her throat, a decadent purr of pleasure that had him thrusting his knee between hers, parting her legs. In response she arched into his hands, pressing as if she too couldn't get enough.

He needed her. *Now.*

Tearing himself from her grasp he looked down. The gown's neckline was high across her breasts, and tight enough to make them inaccessible. But locating the fastening at the back was the work of a moment. As was lowering the zip enough to loosen the bodice.

He heard her suck in her breath but she didn't protest. Seconds later he peeled the bodice down enough to reveal her cleavage. Her breasts rose and fell rapidly, silently inviting.

With a swift yank of the silky fabric he bared her breasts, watching blush pink nipples bud in the cold air. Not even a strapless bra. Who'd have thought it of prim and proper Dr Connors?

Alaric wasn't complaining. He drank in the sight of pure white skin, full breasts, perfectly formed and deliciously uptilted as if begging for his attention.

His erection pulsed and he almost groaned aloud when she rocked her hips, her thighs widening suggestively. He needed that pelvis to pelvis contact, was desperate to sheath himself inside her. But first…

He lowered his head to her breast, skimmed a caress across her nipple and felt her hands claw his shoulders as if she could no longer stand without support.

He smiled as he kissed the impossibly soft skin around her aureole, revelling in her responsiveness as she gasped and shifted beneath his ministrations.

'Stop teasing.' Her voice was hoarse and uneven. Alaric looked up to see her brow furrow as she watched him. 'Just…' She paused and swallowed hard. 'Do it.'

Despite the wobbly order, Tamsin's eyes were dazed and her skin flushed with arousal. The combination of prim command, desperation and luscious wanton was delicious.

Eyes holding hers, he covered one nipple with his lips, enjoying the way her eyes widened as she watched him draw her into his mouth. Heat shot through him, catapulting him into a world of sensual pleasure as he devoured her sweetness. He sucked hard and she jerked like a puppet on a string, head and neck arched against the wood panelling. Her lower body moved restlessly against him, mimicking his own edgy need to thrust into her.

Not yet. Tamsin was pure delight. He couldn't get enough of her.

He moved to her other breast, daring a tiny erotic bite. She keened her pleasure, her body stiffening around his as if he'd generated an electric current. He breathed deep the sweet scent of feminine arousal and his blood surged south.

She was so hyper-sensitive, was it possible he could bring her to orgasm like this? The notion was almost too much for his threadbare self-discipline.

Another graze of his teeth, this time at her nipple, and another jolt ripped through her. Hungrily he suckled, feeding the demon inside that demanded more, demanded everything from her.

Fumbling, he scrabbled at her skirts, the slippery fabric sliding through his unsteady hands.

He couldn't wait any longer.

Rising, he plastered his mouth over hers, revelling in her kisses as finally his questing fingers found silk clad thighs. Stockings! He found the upper edge, the line where material met bare, smooth flesh and he faltered, heart pounding at the image his mind conjured.

He wanted to spread her on a bed and leisurely inspect the sexy picture she'd make before taking his fill. But he didn't have time, his need was too urgent. His erection throbbed so needily he wondered if he'd be able to get out of his trousers without injury.

He drove her head back with hungry kisses as he hiked her skirts. In a perfect world she wouldn't be wearing panties.

But this was no fantasy. His hands encountered cotton. Despite the sexy gown and stockings, Tamsin had chosen no-nonsense underwear. Underwear damp with arousal.

Spreading his hand to cup her mound, feeling her push hard into his grip, Alaric decided cotton panties were far sexier than silk, more of a turn on than Lycra or lace. Tamsin didn't need frills. She was potently, earthily sexy.

Her hand insinuated itself between their bodies to grapple with the fastening of his dress trousers.

She'd send him over the edge in a moment. He clamped an iron hand round her wrist.

'Don't!' he growled, his voice thick. He forced her hand back, high against the wall and kissed her again. He wanted this to last more than ten seconds. He'd bring her to climax, enjoy watching her take pleasure at his hands, and only then find release in her body.

His fingers slipped beneath cotton, drawn by her heat.

A roaring explosion cracked the night sky, penetrating his fog of sensual arousal. He stiffened, muscles freezing at what sounded like artillery fire. Dread engulfed him as adrenaline spiked in his blood.

By the time the second reverberating boom rent the air he'd opened his eyes and registered the flash of coloured light. Relief surged so strongly he felt weak.

Reality buffeted him and he dropped his head, gasping, trying to force down raw, conflicting emotions. Relief that he was no longer in the nightmare world of armed conflict. And lust—the almost insuperable need for completion. If only willpower could shift blood from his groin to his brain! Never had he so completely lost control.

'What is it?' Tamsin sounded as shaken as he.

Another couple of minutes and he'd have had her, ankles locked round his waist while he shuddered his climax into her. Even now he craved it. The effort of not taking her made him tremble all over.

If he did her gown would be rumpled and stained, proclaiming exactly what they'd been doing.

There'd be stares and rolled eyes about his behaviour but that was nothing. His shoulders were broad, his reputation bad and people's expectations low.

For Tamsin the gossip would be infinitely worse. He couldn't do that to her.

He'd failed Felix. Failed his men. But in this at least surely he could manage to do the right thing.

'Fireworks,' he murmured, his voice a strained whisper. He cleared his throat and released her hand, letting it slide down the wall. 'At the end of the ball we have fireworks and champagne. And a royal toast.'

He had to go. There was no chance to lose himself in Tamsin's slick, warm heat, no matter how much he craved her. Reluctantly he dragged his other hand from between her legs, felt her shudder at the movement and wished it could be different.

He let her skirts fall and stepped away, face drawing tight at the fierce pain in his groin. Desire and guilt and fury at the depth of his own need warred within him. He'd always enjoyed women but this…this was uncharted territory.

'Turn around.' The words emerged brusquely through gritted teeth. She stared up, her lips bruised to plumpness and eyes glazed, then she turned, her head bowed.

He stared at that expanse of naked back, the vulnerable line of her nape, and almost surrendered to temptation again. But a burst of green fire outside the window brought him back to the real world. To duty.

It took him a full minute to do up her dress, his hands were so uncoordinated. When it was done he moved away, wincing at each stiff-legged step as he paced to the window. He needed time before he made a public appearance. He needed to keep away from her before his resolve shattered.

'I'll have to go. I'm expected and my absence will cause speculation.'

He raised his hand to smooth his hair and caught the heady scent of her essence on his fingers. He dropped his hand, summoning every vestige of strength not to go to her when his body screamed out for completion. For Tamsin.

'Of course. I understand.' Her voice sounded flat, but then he couldn't hear clearly over his throbbing pulse and the crack of fireworks.

'Will you be all right?' Still he didn't turn around but stood silhouetted at the arched window, his back to her.

Why wouldn't he look at her?

She was the one embarrassed. He was the playboy with a reputation for loving then leaving each new mistress.

He'd known exactly what he was doing.

'I'm fine,' she murmured, wondering if the lie sounded believable. She was bereft, desperate for a look, a touch, *something*.

Tamsin shivered and slumped against the wall, hands splaying for support as she recalled how expert he'd been.

Her pulse raced out of control as she remembered his knowing, half-lidded look, watching her as he'd sucked at her breast. She squeezed her thighs together at the liquid heat between her legs. Who'd have guessed that every time he drew on her breast a taut line of fire would run down to her belly and lower, till she felt the empty ache inside?

Who'd have known she'd be so wanton as to rub herself needily against his hand? To delight in the sensation of his long fingers arrowing to her most private core?

Heat fired her cheeks at what she'd done, what she still wanted to do.

It was as if some alien woman had taken over her body. Some daring sensualist she'd never known, who acted on instincts Tamsin hadn't been aware of.

Was it remotely possible this was the real Tamsin, freed of the restraints that had ruled her life so long?

Or was this the result of a life without love or physical demonstrativeness? There'd been few cuddles growing up and no teenage kisses. With Patrick she hadn't ventured far into passion. Perhaps Alaric's caresses had unleashed a pent up longing for physical affection.

She released a shuddering breath. She'd determined to make a new start tonight, be a new woman, free of the crutches she'd used to distance herself from others. But she hadn't meant to go this far!

She hadn't thought…that was the problem.

Tamsin eyed Alaric's powerful frame, lit by a scintillating flash of red. She hadn't thought at all after he'd admitted to being jealous, to wanting her.

Had that been real? Or had it been an excuse to keep his distance because he genuinely hadn't wanted to be with her during the ball? The old Tamsin would have accepted the latter without a second's hesitation. Now she didn't know.

And this hot, heavy seduction scene? Could he have engineered it to provoke the kind of speculation he wanted? To create the illusion they were in a relationship?

But why go so far?

Yet if his desire had been genuine, and it had felt magnificently real when he'd ground himself against her, why the cold shoulder now? He'd reacted violently when she'd tried to touch him and his voice just now had been harsh.

Her lips twisted. If only she had more experience with men, with sex, she might understand!

Had he gone so far simply because she was so obviously, pantingly eager? For Alaric, was one warm female body in the dark as good as another?

The notion sickened her.

It was unfair to think it of him. Yet she remembered that first kiss and how he'd pulled up short when he'd knocked her glasses *and remembered who he was kissing.*

Tamsin bit her lip. All she knew was she wanted him to hold her and take her back to the place she'd been before he'd pulled away. She wanted him to smile and make her feel better.

Listen to her! She was a grown woman, not a child.

A knock sounded on the door and Tamsin started. Yet Alaric turned smoothly as if he'd expected it. Had this been a set-up?

He sent her a long, assessing look and her cheeks burned. Hurriedly she lifted her hands to secure her hair as best she could, then shook out her long skirts. But for the life of her she couldn't move away from the wall at her back. Her knees trembled too much.

'Enter.' Neither his voice nor his appearance gave any hint of what they'd been doing minutes before. *She'd* been the one half naked and wanting. Suddenly the fact that he'd remained fully clothed seemed suspiciously important.

Her throat closed on a knot of distress as she met his unblinking stare.

A steward entered and bowed deeply, his expression wooden. 'Your Highness. Madam.' He cleared his throat. 'I'm sorry to disturb—'

'It's all right.' Alaric's tone was clipped. 'Go on.'

Again the servant bowed. 'The guests are assembled on the terrace, Highness. The fireworks will end in five minutes.'

Alaric nodded, the picture of regal composure. 'Good. I'll be just in time for the toasts.' He turned to her and for a searing moment his gaze held hers, making her heart catapult against her ribs.

'Please accompany Dr Connors to her suite. She was overcome by the exertions of the ball. She doesn't know her way back from this part of the castle.'

The man nodded, his face betraying no emotion. Ridiculously that made Tamsin feel worse. Did Alaric make a habit of seducing women in antechambers? Given his reputation she supposed his servants were used to dealing with his cast off lovers.

A dreadful giggle rose in her throat. The joke was on them because she didn't fit the bill. She hadn't quite made it to the exalted ranks of ex-lover.

Now she probably never would.

'Dr Connors.' Alaric's bow was formal. He straightened and paused, as if waiting for her to speak.

'Your Highness.' A curtsey was beyond her. It was all she could do to stay upright, knees locked.

With a curt nod of acknowledgement he strode out the door, his bearing as rigid as a soldier on parade.

The fantasy was over.

It was time for Cinderella to leave.

At the knock on the door to his suite Alaric paused in the act of shrugging off his jacket.

Could it be her? Had she come to finish what they'd begun? His pulse rocketed, his body tensing in anticipation.

He'd been torn between visiting her now, tonight, and listening to the voice of responsibility that warned she'd been out of her depth. He'd taken advantage. He'd been so intent on seducing her he'd dismissed the need for discretion to protect her or to allow her time to think.

Yet he'd only come here to change from his uniform. He couldn't keep away after that taste of her sweet body.

Now she'd saved him the trouble!

'Come.'

It was an unpleasant shock to see his security chief enter instead. Disappointment surfaced and a disturbing premonition of bad news. The hair rose at his nape as he took in that sombre expression.

'I'm sorry to interrupt, sir, but you gave instructions about Dr Connors' phone calls. You need to hear this.'

The jacket fell from Alaric's hand to a nearby chair and he flexed his fingers. *He didn't want to hear this.*

The report on Tamsin had drawn a blank. The woman was so squeaky clean it was unbelievable. Recently Alaric had set aside his suspicion she might be connected with those trying to disrupt the government. He couldn't believe it.

After tonight he didn't *want* to believe it. He could still taste her cherry sweetness, smell the rich scent of her arousal.

He wanted to turn his back on whatever unpalatable truth awaited. But there was too much at stake.

He couldn't afford to trust his instincts when this was about far more than himself. What of the allegiance he owed Raul? If the document she'd found was genuine at the very least its public release had to be carefully managed. He couldn't fail in this as well.

'When was this call recorded?' He scrubbed a hand over his face, wearier than he'd been in months.

'Before the ball, sir. It was a while before I became aware of the contents. By then the festivities were under way and there was no time to inform you.'

'Very well.' Alaric gestured to a table, curiously unwilling to take the recording in his own hand. 'Leave it.'

His advisor looked as if he'd protest.

Between them hung the knowledge that a stable monarchy was at the core of the nation's wellbeing.

'You can go,' he ordered.

There was only a fractional hesitation. 'Yes, sir.'

The door closed and Alaric was alone. He exhaled slowly, reminding himself of his responsibilities.

Yet the imprint of Tamsin's body branded him. He could almost feel her breasts crushed against him, her hands clutching his hair as he demanded and she reciprocated with a fervour that blasted his control to smithereens. Her scent was on his clothes, his hands. His body was taut with unsated need.

No wonder it felt like betrayal when he took the CD and inserted it into the player.

Long after the recording had ended he stood, staring out into the stark blackness of the night.

Tamsin and Patrick. He knew of the other man from the in-vestigative dossier, though it had been unclear how intimate the pair had been. Now he knew.

They'd been lovers.

His gut roiled queasily at the thought of Tamsin in the arms of another man. In his bed. Alaric's jaw ached as he ground his teeth, trying to harness the overpowering need to do something rash, something violent. It was as well the other man was out of Alaric's way, safe in England.

The way he'd spoken to her in that call! He'd dumped her then expected her to welcome him back with open arms. Alaric registered a tiny flicker of satisfaction that she'd sent him packing. She'd adopted her most glacial schoolmistress voice to get rid of him.

And still Alaric couldn't obliterate the image of her naked in a stranger's arms.

So much for his fancy that her guileless yet fervent kisses were evidence of inexperience. He shook his head. He'd fallen for that buttoned up look, been swayed into believing her prickly reserve and her cover-up clothes meant she was an innocent.

Which showed how she'd impaired his thinking!

The woman was all combustible heat, a born seductress. She'd almost blown the back off his head, just with her cries of encouragement as he'd fondled her.

Alaric planted his palms on the window sill, anchoring himself to the solid rock of the old castle. Belatedly he forced himself to confront the other implication of what he'd heard. He'd deliberately shied from it.

The document she'd found appeared authentic. The date testing proved its age.

He would be the next king of Maritz.

Pain scored his fist as he pounded the sill. His gut hollowed. It was unthinkable! The nation deserved better than him.

Bile rose in his throat and he bowed his head, knowing if he let it, the pain would engulf him. Yet even then he wouldn't be free. He was destined to be alive, whole, unscathed. The ultimate punishment for his failure.

The metallic scent of blood from his grazed fist caught his attention, forcing him to focus. His breathing thickened as he imagined breaking the news to Raul.

Damn! His cousin should be monarch, not him.

Already he was his brother's usurper. How could he oust his cousin, too?

But they had no choice. They'd both been raised to shoulder their responsibilities and face even the most unpalatable duty.

Now, tonight, he had to make arrangements. Raul had to be updated and a second date test of the document organised. He'd have to call on more experts to help prove or disprove the chronicle. The royal genealogist had cautiously advised he couldn't rule out the claim to the throne. But that wasn't good enough. They had to be *certain*.

Yet Alaric had a hollow, sinking feeling each test would only prove his succession.

Fortunately the document was under lock and key. But there was still a danger news would get out before he'd found a way to manage the transition to monarch.

His mind conjured an image of Tamsin and that journo. They'd been so intent they hadn't heard him approach.

Surely she hadn't revealed anything to the newsman. Tamsin had too much integrity. Hadn't she? Doubt sidled through his thoughts and he squashed it furiously.

But finding her with the journo was too coincidental in the circumstances. Even if she was innocent, one unguarded word could shatter the fragile situation. She was so enthusiastic about her work she might inadvertently let something slip. Alaric must ensure that didn't happen.

He shook his head. He couldn't go to her tonight and lose himself in the mindless ecstasy he craved. There were urgent plans to make.

Alaric watched fat snowflakes drift past the window and an idea began to form. The need for Tamsin still gnawed at him, a constant ache. He'd gone beyond the point of no return and abstinence was no longer possible.

He assured himself it was purely physical desire he felt. Anything more…complicated was impossible.

He had to isolate her until arrangements were in place to deal with this mess. That would take time. But wasn't time with Tamsin what he craved?

There was benefit after all in coming from a long line of robber barons and ruthless opportunists.

Kidnapping was virtually an inherited skill.

CHAPTER NINE

'GOOD morning, Tamsin.'

Her shoulders stiffened and heat crawled up her cheeks as that low voice wound its lazy way into her soul.

Her assistant's eyes widened as he looked over her shoulder then darted her a speculative glance. Castle gossip had obviously worked overtime since last night.

Tamsin steadied herself against the archive room's custom built storage units. Finally she turned. She'd been expecting a summons. Even so, facing the man who'd stripped her emotionally bare took all her willpower.

She'd spent the night awake, trying to make sense of the evening's events. For the first few hours she'd half expected Alaric to come to her once his duties were over. Despite her doubts and her pride she'd have welcomed him.

It had only been as dawn arrived she'd realised he had no intention of visiting her. She preferred not to remember her desolation then.

'Hello...' She halted, her mouth drying as that familiar indigo gaze met hers. What should she call him? It had been *Alaric* until his steward had found them together. Then they'd been *Dr Connors* and *Your Highness*. The formality had been a slap in the face, even if it had been an attempt to hide what they'd been doing.

Here he was in her domain, alone, without any secretaries or security staff. *What did he want?*

Her blush burned fiery and she saw something flicker in his eyes. Awareness? Desire? Or distaste?

Tamsin had no idea what he felt. Last night his urgency, his arousal and his words had convinced her he felt the same compulsion she did. But later doubts had crept in.

'How are you today?' His voice held only polite enquiry but she could have sworn she saw something more profound in his expression.

Or was that wishful thinking?

'Well, thank you.' Again she hesitated. Despite his slightly drawn look, she wasn't going to ask him how he was. 'Have you come to see our progress?'

Grimacing at her falsely bright tone, ignoring her staccato pulse, she gestured for him to accompany her to her small office space. She'd feel better knowing every word wasn't overheard.

'Partly.' They reached her desk and Alaric spun round, his gaze intense. 'Why? Do you want to tell me something?'

Tamsin opened her mouth then shut it, frowning.

Last night there'd been no opportunity to tell him about the dating of the manuscript. Alone with him in the antechamber all thought of the document had been blasted from her mind by Alaric and the things he made her feel.

Her gaze skittered away as she recalled what they'd done. Even now desire throbbed deep in her belly and at the apex of her thighs. That persistent current of awareness eroded her efforts to appear unaffected.

She should tell him about the test results, yet she hesitated. Tamsin believed him now when he said he didn't want the crown. For whatever reason, the idea was anathema to him. It was a shame. She'd seen him in action these past couple of weeks and he'd make a terrific king. The easy way he related to people, truly listened to them. His sharp mind and ability to get things done. His need to help.

She read his taut stillness as he awaited her response.

Should she confirm his fears when in her own mind she wasn't fully convinced? Despite Patrick's news some things in the document still needed checking.

Tamsin shrugged stiffly and tidied her desk.

'The new staff have been worth their weight in gold. We're making good headway.'

'Excellent.' He paused as if waiting. 'And the chronicle? Anything interesting in your translations?'

'No.' It wasn't lying. She hadn't uncovered any more revelations.

Alaric's silence eventually made her look up. His expression was unreadable but there was a keenness, an intensity in his scrutiny that unnerved her.

'I should have more information for you soon.'

If she didn't uncover anything to justify her niggle of uncertainty by the end of the week, two days away, she'd break the news about the UK tests.

Strange, this sense that in being cautious she protected Alaric. She'd never met anyone so obviously capable, so patently self-sufficient.

Yet she couldn't shake the feeling that beneath it all, in this one thing Alaric was vulnerable.

'Good.' He reached out and fingered the spine of a catalogue.

Tamsin watched the leisurely caress, recalling how he'd stroked *her* last night. The touch of those large hands had been so exquisite she'd thought she'd shatter if he stopped.

She shivered and suddenly she was caught in the darkening brilliance of his eyes. Heat eddied low and spread in lush, drugging waves as she read his expression. The hungry yearning he couldn't hide.

Realisation slammed into her. Her heart soared.

It was real! Not her imagination. He felt it, too.

Tamsin struggled to inhale oxygen as the air thickened. Excitement revved her pulse, making her heart pound and her head swim. She swiped damp palms down her skirt. The heat inside ignited to a flash fire as his gaze followed the movement then rose, slow and deliberate, to her breasts, her mouth. Her nipples beaded and her lips parted eagerly as if he'd touched her.

'I need to see you, in private.'

'But last night...'

'Last night I should never have started something I couldn't finish.' His mouth twisted in a tight smile that echoed the rigid expression he'd worn as he'd left her in the antechamber. 'Do you really think a few stolen minutes hard and fast against a wall would have been enough?'

Alaric's words made her head swim. Or maybe it was the graphic image that exploded inside her brain. Tamsin's mouth dried as she saw his eyes mirror her excitement and frustration.

'And afterwards...' he paused '...I couldn't come to you.' Before she could ask why he spoke again, his voice darkly persuasive, his eyes glittering. 'But I'm here now.'

Murmured voices approached from the main archive room.

'I want you, Tamsin. Now. Away from interruption.' His voice dropped to a deep resonance that brooked no refusal.

Her breathing shallowed as she teetered on the brink. Part of her was shocked by his unvarnished words. But mostly she was thrilled. Abruptly she nodded, the movement jerky.

She wanted this. The intensity of what was between them scared her, but she would not to hide from it.

She'd done with suppressing her emotions and needs. She'd always love her work but it was no longer enough. She'd be a coward to turn her back on the marvellous feelings Alaric evoked. On the chance to live and experience the passion so blatant in his heavy-lidded look.

Tamsin had no illusions. Whatever he wanted from her, whatever he offered, would be fleeting. But it was genuine. If she had no expectations, except for honesty between them, how could she be hurt?

It was the lies that hurt. The soiled feeling of being used for ulterior purposes, as Patrick had used her.

The unabashed heat in Alaric's eyes, his single-minded focus were honest and headily seductive. Tamsin swallowed hard as excitement fizzed. After a life time of celibacy, she was ready to walk on the wild side.

Alaric had made it clear he didn't believe in love. At the time she'd felt sad for him but now she realised it was a bond between them. She didn't trust herself to try what passed for love again and Alaric was immune to it.

What they shared would be simple, straightforward and satisfying.

'Fifteen minutes.' His mouth barely moved as he murmured the instructions so her approaching colleagues couldn't hear. 'In the courtyard. Your warmest clothes.'

With a searing look he spun on his heel and was gone, leaving Tamsin's heart pounding like she'd run a marathon.

Fifteen minutes. It seemed a lifetime.

Alaric stamped his feet against the cold and refrained from glancing at his watch. She'd be here. He'd read her anticipation. This was one time Tamsin wouldn't object to an ultimatum.

His prim and proper Dr Connors was eager for this too.

He paused in the act of drawing on his gloves. Since when had he thought of Tamsin as 'his'? A sixth sense warning feathered his backbone.

Alaric ignored it.

Tamsin wanted him. He wanted Tamsin. Simple.

And the fact that his intentions weren't completely straightforward?

Alaric would go quietly crazy waiting on the interminable processes to confirm the succession. There was nothing he could *do*. A move to transfer power would be premature and potentially dangerous. Yet he itched for action, to work off the tension coiling within.

With Tamsin he could at least satisfy the lust eating him. This could be his last chance to enjoy freedom before the crown settled on his head. He'd make the most of every moment.

If he became king there'd be no more spur of the moment adventures, no dangerous sports. *No escape.* He shied away from that line of thought.

Tamsin wouldn't be hurt. He'd ensure she was well satisfied.

Despite her complex, fascinating personality, she seemed easy to read. He *wanted* to believe in her. Instinct said she was honest. Yet she'd kept from him the news of the chronicle's age, confirmed last night by her ex-lover. His thoughts snagged on the other man and tension rose.

He hadn't missed her prevarication today, the way her gaze had slid away guiltily as he'd given the perfect opportunity to broach the news.

He was determined to solve the riddle that was Tamsin Connors.

Anticipation coiled in his belly. He acted for the country, but this plan promised personal satisfaction.

Alaric drew on his gloves and glanced at the leaden tint just visible on the horizon. The sooner they left the better, or the forecast snowstorm would catch them too soon. He refused to endanger Tamsin.

If he were alone he'd revel in pitting his strength against the elements. Seeking out danger was one of his few pleasures. Action for the thrill of it. For the breathless affirmation of life in a world of bleak uncertainty.

Or perhaps, he realised in a sombre flash of awareness, in the expectation that eventually his luck would run out?

A death wish?

He gazed up at the bright bowl of the sky, vivid against the mountains, and felt the sizzle of expectation in his veins as he waited for Tamsin.

No. Despite the demons that hounded him, today he could truly say that given the chance he'd choose life.

'Your Highness?'

He swung round to see one of his security staff. 'Yes?'

'I have the report you requested several hours ago. It's only cursory. We'll have more in a day or two.'

At last! Information on this tiresome Patrick who'd rung Tamsin. And on the journo who'd hung on her every word.

He caught movement from the corner of his eye.

Tamsin emerged into the courtyard in a padded anorak and thick trousers. Gone was the glamorous woman who'd entranced him last night. Yet in the sharp light of a winter's morning her beauty defied the handicap of her bulky garments. Her face glowed in the crisp air. Unmarred by heavy glasses her clean, classic bone structure drew his appreciative gaze. Her eyes shone and the lush bow of her lips reminded him of last night's heady pleasure.

Even the way she walked, an easy stride that spoke of supple limbs and natural athleticism, fired his blood.

Besides, he'd discovered at the ball he preferred she hide her luscious body from all male eyes except his.

He was rather fond now of her shapeless outfits. He enjoyed picturing the hidden curves beneath. Especially as he had every intention of stripping those garments away for his pleasure very soon.

Alaric couldn't remember any woman getting so deeply under his skin. And he hadn't even slept with her!

'Your Highness?'

He swung back to the man patiently waiting.

'Thank you.' He nodded and took the envelope. No time now to satisfy his curiosity with Tamsin approaching. He stuffed the envelope into a pocket and rezipped his all-weather jacket. 'That's all for now. If anything urgent comes up I have my mobile phone.'

The other man bowed and stepped away as Tamsin reached him. Alaric turned, reminding himself not to touch, not yet, lest his brittle control snap.

Looking down into her bright eyes he realised this felt right. *She felt right.*

He smiled. Not a deliberate ploy to entice her but because for the first time in recent memory genuine happiness flared. He'd almost forgotten how good it felt.

'Where are we going?' They were the first words Tamsin had spoken in twenty minutes.

She'd been tongue-tied by the enormity of her feelings and the potency of what she saw in Alaric's eyes. When he looked at her, his gaze smoky and possessive, tendrils of awareness curled through her, spiralling tighter. Just the graze of his gloved hand on hers as he helped her take her seat had made her breathless.

Once they were under way disbelief, delight and sheer joy had kept her silent as she watched the forest slide past. Never in her wildest dreams had she envisaged a horse-drawn sleigh ride across pristine powder snow! It was a romantic fantasy.

They threaded their way through dense forest, emerging now and then into glades where the brilliant blue sky dazzled as it shone on diamond bright snow.

'We're visiting a small hunting lodge in the mountains. The road is impassable and the only way in is by sleigh.'

It sounded thrillingly intimate.

Alaric turned from guiding the horses and bestowed a single, lingering look. Instantly, despite the chill air, heat blazed through Tamsin. Beneath the layers of heavy blankets he'd tucked around her she was burning up.

'We'll be uninterrupted there.'

'I see.' Was that her voice, husky and low?

One black eyebrow arched and a crease arrowed down his cheek as he smiled. 'I knew you would.' His rich velvet voice held a hum of anticipation that matched hers. 'I've left orders that the lodge is absolutely off limits.'

His grin worked magic, loosening the final constricting ties of doubt. Under that look Tamsin felt buoyantly alive and strong, as if she could do anything. Dare anything.

Why be nervous? They were two adults. They both wanted this. Still her heart thudded against her ribs.

So what if she was a novice? Alaric had enough experience for them both.

Whatever the next few hours held, she wouldn't regret the decision to accompany him. Being with Alaric was like the thrill she'd felt scaling that climbing wall, recognising but defying the dangerous drop below. The glow of pleasure, knowing she'd dared the risk and triumphed, had been worth the initial doubt.

How different to the hemmed in half-life she'd led! How frightening to think that just weeks ago she'd have been too nervous, too wary to take this step.

Alaric turned back to the horses and Tamsin wriggled against the seat, luxuriating in an effervescent tingle of anticipation.

In the knowledge that at the end of the journey they would finish what had begun last night.

The whoosh and slide of the sleigh and the tinkle of harness bells echoing in the pine-scented forest reminded her they were completely alone. There were no staff, no members of the public seeking Alaric's attention. No one to look askance at his choice of companion.

Companion. For a moment the word jangled a discordant note. But even the memory of his original proposition, that she accompany him as a ruse, couldn't dim Tamsin's delight.

This was now. Just the two of them. *This was real.*

The admiration in his eyes made her feel like a princess. She intended to enjoy it while it lasted.

Looking up, Tamsin noticed slate grey clouds encroaching. 'That looks like bad weather coming.'

'It's nothing to worry about.'

It was on the tip of her tongue to protest. Surely those clouds presaged snow. But it was easier to sink back and ignore them. Alaric knew this place. Perhaps she was wrong and the clouds were moving away.

Finally they arrived in a clearing, hemmed in on two sides by the mountain. Below spread more forest and in the distance a vista of Alps and valleys.

'This is your lodge?' She'd expected something tiny. She'd almost allowed herself to forget Alaric was royalty. On the remembrance a tremor of doubt buzzed through her and she sat straighter.

'It was built by my great-great-great-grandfather Rudi as a retreat. For when he wanted to escape the court.'

She eyed the substantial building: traditional Ruvingian architecture but overgrown and embellished with mullioned windows, a forest of chimneys and even a turret. 'Let me guess. He didn't want to rough it.'

Alaric laughed and delight strummed her nerves. Soon…

'Rudi enjoyed his pleasures.' Alaric's glittering look made her press her thighs close against a needy hollow ache.

'You're cold. Let's get you inside.' Deftly he flicked the reins. Ten minutes later they were in a huge stable.

'You go ahead while I see to the horses.'

'Can't I help?' She'd rather watch Alaric's easy movements as he unhitched the horses.

'No.' His eyes held hers and heat pulsed. 'Go and get warm. Make yourself at home. I won't be long, I promise.'

The lodge was unlocked and she stepped into a flagged hall. Warmth hit her as she stared up at the staircase leading down on two sides. Antlers lined the room and a vivid mural ran around the top of the walls.

Tugging off her cap and gloves she paused in the act of undoing her jacket as she followed the scenes of revellers enjoying the bounty of the forest. There were plenty of buxom maids in attendance.

Her lips turned up wryly. Maybe Alaric's ancestor had been a connoisseur of women, too.

She hung up her jacket, letting her mind skim past the idea of Alaric with other women. She unzipped her boots and left them beside the antique tiled oven that warmed the hall. Someone had prepared the place for their arrival.

'Hello?' Tamsin wandered through sitting rooms, a library, a dining room that seated twenty, a kitchen and storage room, but found no one. Yet there was enough food to feed a small army.

Curious, she walked up the staircase. Its balustrade was carved with animals: hares, deer, hounds, even a boar. The whimsy appealed. Had old Rudi possessed a smile and a laugh as fascinating as his great-great-great-grandson's?

Alaric would be here soon.

Her heart gave a great thump and began to gallop. She moved on till she reached a pair of double doors and hesitated. There was something intimate about investigating the bedrooms. But Alaric had said to make herself at home.

Turning the handle she entered. Her breath caught as she turned to take it in.

The turret room.

It was round, windows set into curved, cream walls. Velvet curtains of azure blue were pulled aside, allowing sunlight to pour across thickly cushioned window seats and a gorgeous old Turkish rug in a kaleidoscope of colours. A fireplace was set ready for the match and opposite it was the biggest four poster bed she'd seen in her life. Drapes of blue velvet were tied back to beautifully turned posts and the headboard was carved with the arms of the Ruvingian royal house.

The reminder of Alaric's status stopped her, a splinter of harsh reality in her pleasant daydream.

Prince and commoner. It was too far-fetched. Too unreal.

'I hoped I'd find you here.'

Tamsin spun round as Alaric closed the door. Its click made her jump.

'I couldn't find anyone.' Her voice emerged too high. She watched his long silent stride. Something inside her shivered and her pulse danced.

'We're the only ones here.' His lips curved up but his eyes were darkly intent.

'I see.'

She wanted this, so why had her tongue stuck to the roof of her mouth? Why did she feel suddenly nervous?

'So you want to talk now?'

He raised an eyebrow. 'Talk? What about?'

'When you came to the archives you said you wanted…'

Slowly he shook his head as he paced closer. 'I didn't mention conversation.' He stopped so near she smelled warm flesh and horse and citrus soap. She breathed deep and put out a steadying hand to the post behind her.

She was quaking but not, she registered, in fear.

'You knew that.' His gaze snared hers and her stomach dipped. 'Didn't you, Tamsin?'

She nodded. No point prevaricating. She knew exactly what he'd wanted. Why he'd invited her here.

'Would *you* like to talk?' He gestured to a couple of chairs she hadn't noticed to one side of the room.

'No.' The single syllable was all she could manage.

'What do you want, Tamsin?' He purred her name and the final thread of resistance unravelled inside her.

She lifted her face to look him in the eye. What she saw there gave her the courage to be honest.

'I want to make love with you. Now.'

CHAPTER TEN

HER words blasted away Alaric's barely formed suspicion that she was nervous.

It wasn't nerves that made her eyes widen as he crossed the room. It was excitement. Despite her initial hesitation when he kissed her, and her occasional air of other-worldliness, Tamsin was no shrinking virgin. Last night's phone call from her ex-lover had made that clear.

Alaric breathed deep as anticipation roared through him. This was exactly what he needed. A mutually satisfying interlude with a woman who knew how to give and take pleasure generously. Tamsin's passion last night left him in no doubt this would be an erotically fulfilling encounter.

He shoved to the back of his mind the knowledge that he was taking advantage. That his motives bringing her here were complex and he was keeping things from her.

But he couldn't feel guilt. Not when he looked at Tamsin and knew only one thing drove him now: the purely personal need to claim her. Make her his.

'It will be my absolute pleasure to make love to you,' he murmured, his gaze trawling her tense form and coming to rest on her parted lips.

He'd waited so long for this. Too long.

He palmed her soft cheek, noting with delight the way she tilted her head up, instinctively seeking his mouth.

But he'd learned his lesson. Kissing Tamsin would unleash a desire so combustible he'd lose control in moments. This time he'd hold back to savour every exquisite detail for as long as possible. He had no illusions that the first time would be over almost before it began.

Just as well they had leisure for a second time and a third. And more. Tamsin would be here, his, for as long as he needed her.

'Let your hair down.'

She blinked at the rough growl edging his voice but lifted her hands. Rippling swathes of dark glossy hair cascaded around her shoulders. In the bright wintry light auburn tints gleamed. So rich. So unexpected. Just like Tamsin.

He took a slippery fistful. The scent of sweet summer meadows. Skeins soft as satin slid against his lips.

He was hungry for the taste of her. Hard with wanting.

'Now your pullover.' He wanted to strip her himself but he didn't trust himself to retain control.

Next time.

No, she wouldn't have a chance to get dressed before he had her again. His groin hardened as blood pumped faster.

For an instant Tamsin hesitated then she hauled the wool over her head. As she stretched her arms high a sliver of pale skin appeared at her waist. In an instant his hands were there, slipping beneath her grey shirt.

She stilled, half out of her pullover, as he slid fingers across warm flesh that trembled under his touch.

So deliciously sensitive. Her delicate little shudder of pleasure delighted him as his hands skimmed her waist and dipped below the waistband of her trousers to explore the curve of her hips.

By the time she'd discarded the pullover he'd tunnelled beneath her shirt, up, up, till all she had to do was lift her arms again and it was gone, too.

Alaric tossed it over his shoulder as he feasted on the sight of her. Her peaches and cream complexion was flushed to a soft rose pink. He'd never known a woman to blush all over. The novelty of it tugged at something deep inside and he felt an unexpected moment of protectiveness.

His breath sawed in his throat as he traced the tell tale colour from her cheeks, past her lips, down to the base of her throat where her pulse pattered hard and fast. He stroked lower, down the upper slope of her breasts.

Her nipples puckered in welcome beneath her ivory bra. Functional, with a minimum of lacy edging and a tiny bow between her breasts, on Tamsin the plain bra looked sexier than the most revealing demi-cup or lace-up corset.

Alaric's breath grew hoarse and heavy as he slipped his hands to her breasts. Warm, perfect, full, they filled his palms as she pressed forward, her eyelids flickering closed.

Fire exploded in his belly as he held her soft bounty in his hands. Gently he caressed and her head lolled back, her neck arched invitingly.

His mouth was a hair's breadth from her scented throat when he recalled his scattered wits. No kisses. Not yet.

He dragged himself back, wincing at the shaft of discomfort in his groin.

Alaric dealt with the snap on her trousers and the zip easily, pushing the fabric down, down those long, lithe legs till at his urging she stepped out of them. Even the act of stripping her long grey and black striped socks was a sensual indulgence as he crouched before her. The intimate heat of her sex was so close. The silkiness of her calves teased as he skimmed the socks down. The seductive arch of each foot distracted as he tugged the socks free.

Low before her he was tempted to lean in and explore her feminine secrets with his lips and tongue. But he was too close to the edge to risk it.

Instead he allowed his fingertips to skim her knees and thighs as he rose, lingering for a moment at her knickers, where her heat beckoned, over her belly, breasts and up to cup her jaw.

She was sensational. All soft curves, taut lines and delicate angles. Pure female seduction. Just looking at her almost tipped him over the edge.

Eyes bright as gold stared up into his, dazzling him. The impact of her sunburst gaze thumped through his chest and showered sparks through every nerve and muscle.

'You're wearing too many clothes.' Tamsin's voice was hoarse, almost unrecognisable. He felt a kick of satisfaction low in his gut that she was as desperate as he.

'Easily remedied.' With a violent movement he dragged his shirt and sweater up and off, flinging them behind him.

Though warm, the air was cool to his burning skin. Soft palms landed on his chest, fingers splaying. Tamsin explored his pectorals, scraping her nails tantalisingly over his hard nipples, trailing her hands to his belly.

In a flash his trousers were open and he shoved them down, balancing on one leg then another as he discarded underwear, socks and trousers in record time.

Belatedly he recalled the condom in his back pocket and stooped to retrieve it. There was a box of them in the bedside table but watching Tamsin's face as she took in his naked body, he knew those few metres to the table might as well be a hundred kilometres.

Tearing the wrapper with his teeth, he deftly rolled on the protection, pleasure spiking at Tamsin's expression of shocked excitement. The way she stared he could have been a demi-god, a hero, not an earthbound man with feet of clay. His blood beat hard and fast as his hands dropped away.

He stepped forward.

Alaric loomed closer and Tamsin backed up.

She hadn't intended to. It was instinctive, an unplanned bid to escape a man who suddenly seemed dangerous in a primitive, ultra-physical way she'd never known.

The reality of Alaric the man, of what they were doing, hit her full force.

He was so big, so heavily aroused; a sliver of anxiety pierced the fog of desire. He could bend her to his will and she wouldn't be able to resist. Whatever he demanded of her he could take.

An age old female wariness sped down her backbone. It had nothing to do with his royal rank and everything to do with Alaric as a virile, dominant male.

The cool slap of the high footboard against the back of her legs brought her up short. As did his puzzled expression.

'Tamsin?' He stood where he was, only reached out one arm to her. Like the rest of him it was powerfully corded with muscle. Yet as she looked she saw his fingers tremble.

She gulped down the panic that had bubbled out of nowhere and looked into his eyes, glazed with hot desire yet questioning. This time her brain kicked into gear.

When she'd watched him roll on the condom, his eyes had eaten her up with a fierceness that thrilled and terrified her. When he'd approached she'd let fear of the unknown swamp the surge of desire.

Now she saw that despite Alaric's raw hunger, he was the same man she'd come to know these last weeks. A man who'd been honest and straight with her. Who desired her.

A man she could trust.

Maybe every woman felt that tinge of fear the first time, confronted with such unvarnished lust and the stunning reality of naked male arousal.

Her lips curved up in a wobbly smile as she realised very few women were gifted with a first lover as gorgeous as Alaric. Just looking at him made her heart throb so fast she could scarcely catch her breath.

This was what she wanted. She refused to walk away from something that felt so good, so right.

She just needed courage.

Eyes holding his, Tamsin reached around and fumbled her bra undone, letting it fall with a shake of her arms.

Alaric drew a huge breath, his chest expanding mightily. His outstretched hand curled and fell away.

Her unbound breasts felt impossibly full, the nipples hardening to aching points as his heated gaze dropped. Fire scorched a trail across her breasts and lower.

Following the direction of his gaze, Tamsin hooked her thumbs in the sides of her panties. There she hesitated as her inbuilt urge to cover herself fought the need to offer herself to Alaric. A lifetime's habit was strong, but far stronger was the magic she felt when he looked at her with such longing.

She felt desirable. Desired. Feminine. Powerful. Needy.

Without giving herself time to think she shoved her underwear down, felt the slide of fine cotton against her legs and the waft of air against her skin. All over.

'You have no idea how badly I want you.' Alaric's voice was a rough blur of words that tugged at something low in her belly. Pleasure coursed through her as his eyes sparked blue fire.

A second later he lifted her up and onto the mattress.

His hands were so large they almost spanned her waist. His sure grip reinforced the physical differences between them. Yet this time her vulnerability didn't bring fear. A delicious flutter of excitement filled her.

With one fluid, powerful movement he pushed her up the bed and sank down on her. Senses on overload, she gasped for breath, but nothing could calm the spiralling excitement that drove her on. She was hemmed in, surrounded by him and nothing had ever felt so perfect.

Arms closing round his torso, Tamsin pressed her mouth to Alaric's neck, his shoulder, tasting the spicy salt flavour of him. Sinking into the mattress, soft velvet caressed her back while her breasts, belly and legs rubbed against satiny skin, powerfully bunched muscles and coarse hair that teased every nerve ending.

He was so...male. So intriguing.

So sexy.

He moved and she swallowed a gasp of pleasure at the sensation of his broad chest sliding against her breasts. Delight was a rippling wave engulfing her, surging again with each tiny move, each touch.

Driven by instinct, she'd invited this. Yet she'd been unprepared for the stunning reality of Alaric's body against hers. Theoretical knowledge only took a girl so far.

Alaric slid a fraction and his erection pressed against her belly. Instantly the hollow ache inside intensified and her hips strained up against him.

Thankfully her body knew what it was doing. Instinct would make up for her lack of practical knowledge.

Then Alaric's mouth captured her nipple and Tamsin lost the capacity for thought as wet heat tugged at her, drawing blood-hot wires of tension through her arching body.

She needed...she needed...

'I love it that you're so hot and ready for me.' His hoarse voice was the most thrilling thing Tamsin had ever heard and the possessive splay of his hand across her feminine mound would have brought her up off the bed if she hadn't been anchored by his strong frame.

She wriggled her hips and he moved, nudging her legs apart with one solid thigh. Eagerly she complied.

'Yes. Like that,' he growled, raising his head and spearing her with a searing look of approval.

Vaguely she noticed the way Alaric's skin stretched taut over that magnificent bone structure, his mouth a grim line of tension.

His hand moved, arrowing unerringly through damp curls and folds that felt plump and hyper-sensitive. Tamsin's body jolted as long fingers slid down.

She couldn't gasp enough breath. Her chest pounded and she stretched her arms up to grab his shoulders, digging into taut, hot flesh. He said something she couldn't hear over the roaring in her ears as he looked to where his fingers stroked again, further, faster.

Tamsin bit her lip against the sob of pleasure rising in her throat. But she couldn't stop the way her body moved into his caress. Confidently, needily.

When he met her gaze again there was a feral glitter in his eyes. He looked like a marauder, a ruthless barbarian intent on plunder. As if she were the bounty he intended to take for himself.

She loved it!

Slipping her hands along those wide shoulders, she clamped her fingers behind his head, desperately burrowing through his thick hair for a good grip. Pulling down, she raised herself and plastered a raw, breathless, open-mouthed kiss on his lips.

For one fragile moment he seemed suspended above her, unmoving. Then he sank onto her again and passion erupted.

Their kiss was fervent, impatient, and his caress between her legs changed. No longer Alaric's hand but something longer, throbbing with a will of its own as he clamped his hands beneath her buttocks and tilted her hips.

'I'm sorry. I can't hold off any longer.'

Tamsin barely processed his words when he shifted and she felt heat nudge the entrance between her legs. Fire flooded her womb at the spiralling whorls of anticipation created by that blunt touch. At last!

His lips closed on hers again, inviting her to join him in pleasure as his tongue pushed greedily into her mouth. At the same time his hold on her bottom tightened and his hips plunged against hers.

One long, slow thrust stretched her body till she was taut, impaled and impossibly full. Gone was the heady passion, replaced in that instant by the first flutterings of panic. Every muscle stiffened and her eyes snapped open.

Startled ink blue irises stared back. Alaric lifted his mouth from hers and sucked in a shaky breath as he pulled away.

Surprisingly, the sensation of his withdrawal instantly distressed her and she clamped her knees against his hips. She didn't want him gone! She just didn't want the scary feeling that he was too big for her. That despite their desire, this wasn't going to work.

'Alaric?' Tamsin didn't care that the word wobbled or that he could hear the entreaty in her voice. Pride had no place here. 'Please.' She didn't know what she expected him to do. She only knew she couldn't bear it to end like this.

A gusty sigh riffled her hair and his head dropped between his bunched shoulders. Tendons stood out on his neck and arms and inside she felt a pulse where the tip of his erection moved.

Response shivered through her at that tiny, impossibly erotic movement. Involuntarily she twitched, circling her hips and his breath stopped.

In answer he withdrew a fraction then slowly pushed forward. This time it didn't feel quite so scary. Or maybe that was his warm breath blowing on her nipple, teasing the aroused bud and distracting her from the slide of his body away then back again.

The next time he eased forward her hips lifted to meet him
and he sank a fraction further. But before she had time to register
the sensations he was gone again, pulling away and leaving her
frustratingly empty.

The fourth time he began to move she anticipated him, arching
upwards simultaneously, then gasping as a fiery spark of pleasure
flared at the point of friction. Her breath hitched and instantly he
stilled, his breathing harsh and uneven.

Tamsin waited but he didn't move. What now? Had he decided
this wasn't going to work? Her hands fisted at his shoulders and
she bit her lip against the protest that hovered on her tongue.

Then she saw the pulse at the base of Alaric's neck, thudding
out of control. He was waiting for her. Trying to accommodate
her fear, her discomfort. The rigidity of his body, the way his
broad chest heaved like overworked bellows told their own story
of the toll this took.

Suddenly this wasn't just about her. Tamsin felt ashamed by
her self-absorption.

Tentatively she slipped her hands down his body, feeling
muscles flinch at her light caress. Daringly she reached out and
smoothed her palms over his hips, down to his taut, rounded
buttocks that felt so good under her increasingly needy touch.
She wanted to explore him all over, she realised with a shock.

A spasm shook him as she tightened her hold and pulled him
towards her. For an instant he resisted then allowed himself to
be tugged closer, inside. Even further than before. This time
instead of panic, Tamsin felt a niggle of a strange new sensation.
A gnawing need for more. When he withdrew she followed.
When she urged him close he slid even deeper and a shaky sigh
of pleasure escaped her lips.

Gradually, a fraction at a time, their movements became rhythmic and fluid. Tamsin hated each withdrawal and welcomed each
thrust, even when it seemed he plunged impossibly deep. Yet
even that felt right. More than right. Fantastic.

Now she revelled in the way he drove so far within her.

Alaric's head lifted and his gaze locked with hers. It felt absurdly as if he touched a part of her no medical scan would ever identify. As if he caressed her very soul with his eyes, his body, his tenderness.

Tamsin's breath sucked out at the heat glazing Alaric's eyes and the reflection there of her own overwhelming need.

Lightning flickered as electricity jolted through her body. His tempo increased, her body tightened, achingly close to some unseen goal. A shudder raked him, raked her, and their rhythm rocked out of control into a fierce pounding beat that brought the world tumbling around them.

A gasping scream rent the air as Tamsin fell into pleasure. Everything swam around her except dark blue eyes, fixed on hers in the maelstrom of exquisite delight. Then, with a hoarse shout, Alaric followed her and she drew him close with trembling arms and an overflowing heart.

CHAPTER ELEVEN

A VIRGIN.

Alaric shook his head as if to dislodge the knowledge that weighted him. How had he convinced himself Tamsin was experienced?

He doused his head under the basin's cold tap but that didn't obliterate the voice of his conscience. He'd seduced a virgin. Deliberately set her up to fall into his bed.

He grimaced. He'd shown little consideration for her inexperience as he'd hammered her untried body.

It was no excuse that the feel of her virginal body tight around him had been the ultimate aphrodisiac.

Experienced as he was he had no defence against the pleasure she offered so unstintingly.

Would he have held back if he'd suspected the truth?

Nothing on earth would have held him back. He was as bad as that old roué Rudi, the ancestor who'd designed the place to keep his scandalous liaisons from prying eyes. Alaric's shoulders tightened. No, he was worse. The women Rudi had bedded had reputedly been experienced. Even his father had kept that rule.

Hell! This was a new take on *noblesse oblige*.

Alaric raised his eyes to the bathroom mirror, expecting, as ever, to see his sins marked on his face. But as usual he was the same. Unblemished. Outwardly whole. As if the darkness within were a figment of his imagination.

What right had *he*, of all men, to take her innocence? She deserved a man who could give her more.

Familiar pain lanced his chest, a physical manifestation of his guilt. The ghosts stirred and he waited for the inevitable chill to engulf him.

Yet there was only the remembered heat of Tamsin's sweet body. The warmth of her eyes, looking up as if he'd done something heroic rather than ravish her virginity. And around his heart was an unfamiliar glow.

Alaric shook his head again, splattering the mirror and his shoulders with icy droplets. This was no time for flights of fancy. He grabbed a towel and roughly dried his hair. With a final accusing glare at the mirror he left.

'You were gone a long time.'

He stopped mid-stride. He'd thought Tamsin would be asleep. Or was that his conscience hoping she'd be too exhausted to confront him?

His skin tightened as he looked up to find her propped against pillows, her hair a sensuous tangle of silk on pale shoulders. A flush coloured her cheeks and her lips were plump and enticing after those bruising kisses.

Alaric's belly went into freefall. His penis throbbed into life and he wished he'd thought to take his clothes with him into the bathroom.

Colour intensified in her cheeks as her gaze skated down. His arousal grew, as if eager for her attention.

'You're…ready again?' Her voice faltered and he winced, imagining her nerves.

'Don't worry.' He paced to the foot of the bed where his clothes lay scattered. 'I'm not going to pounce on you.'

'You're not?' He imagined a thread of disappointment in her tone and gritted his teeth. He looked for any excuse to have her again, even pretending she was eager for more.

'Of course not. You're a virgin and—'

'Was.' The flush intensified, spreading over her throat and down to where she clamped a snowy sheet against her breasts. Alaric's gaze lingered on the way they rose and fell. 'What's that got to do with anything?'

'Sorry?' He'd lost the thread of the conversation.

'The fact that I was a virgin. What's that got to do with not having sex again?'

He liked the way she said 'having sex' with a slight hesitancy. It reminded him of her innocently incendiary kisses and the initially faltering yet devastating way she'd taken him into her body.

He scooped up some clothing. Damn. It was her shirt. Where was his?

'Didn't you like it?' Now she sounded frosty. Good. They could do with reducing the temperature around here.

He grabbed something else off the floor. Her trousers, still warm from her body. Another reminder of the speed of their coupling. He should be ashamed. It was sheer luck she'd climaxed. Once he'd buried himself fully he'd been incapable of holding back to ensure her pleasure.

'Alaric? You didn't like it?'

He gritted his teeth. Thinking about what they'd done spun him to the edge of control. 'Men don't perform when they're not enjoying themselves.'

'Then why not again?'

He didn't meet her eyes. Coward that he was he turned to scan the room for his trousers.

'Wasn't once enough?' Surely his unskilled efforts didn't merit a repeat. 'Besides, you'll be sore. You're not used to sex.' The words were brutal but it was all he could do to keep talking when he wanted to vault into that bed, tug her close and take her again. The battle against his selfish, baser self was all consuming.

'I'm not sore.'

'You will be.'

'So you're an expert on virgins?'

'Of course not! I'm no expert on innocence.' He spun round, his temper flaring under the goad of her lashing words. *'Do you really think I'd have brought you here if I'd known the truth about you? This wouldn't have happened!'*

A half-smile stiffened on her lips and the bright flare of gold in her eyes dimmed. Too late he realised she'd been teasing, inadvertently zeroing in on his guilty conscience.

He raked a hand through his hair and breathed deep. His brain wasn't working and the words shooting from his mouth were all wrong. He couldn't think straight. Not with her sitting there all demure invitation, tempting him.

He'd thought to kill two birds with one stone. Keep Tamsin where she couldn't spill any headline news and sate his hunger. Suddenly, though, this had become something else altogether. The stakes, and his own culpability, had grown enormously.

There was a flurry of movement as she clambered out of bed, dragging a coverlet. Her chin was set belligerently but he couldn't read her face. She kept her expressive eyes downcast as she walked the length of the bed.

Automatically he backed away, knowing if she got too close he'd do something reprehensible, like grab her and plant kisses all over her petal soft skin.

At his movement she stopped so abruptly she seemed to shudder to a halt. Close up her mouth looked pinched tight, her face drawn.

He wanted to ease her hurt, tease her into smiling, but his light-hearted seduction skills had deserted him the moment he'd taken her in his arms.

His hands fisted as he watched her bend to retrieve some clothing. It was only as she rose that he caught the glitter of moisture at the corners of her averted eyes.

'Tamsin?' He stepped near and she stiffened. Pain scraped his heart. 'Don't cry. Please.'

'Don't be absurd. I'm not crying.' She sniffed and turned away, the bedclothes twisting around her. 'You've made it clear this afternoon was a monumental disappointment. If you don't mind I'd like to get dressed. Alone. I'll return to the castle as soon as possible.'

She shuffled away, hampered by the long trail of material which slid down to reveal the voluptuous curve of her spine.

'You've got it wrong!' He closed the space between them till he could smell the scent of her skin and the sunshine in her hair. Close enough to see her bare flesh prickle with cold. Or distress.

'Don't!' She breathed deep, her back to him. 'Please don't. I understand. I may be naïve but I'm not dumb. You wanted it to look like we were having an affair. To fool those other women. So you brought me here and…' Her averted head dropped low, revealing the vulnerable arch of her nape.

'I misunderstood.' Her voice was a whisper now and he had to crane to hear. 'I thought…you know what I thought. And when you said you didn't want to talk…'

Her head jerked up and around and she pinioned him with a furious amber stare.

'No! It's your fault as much as mine. You *know* what you implied. You let me think…' She bit her lip and swallowed hard. 'You didn't say anything *then* about only wanting experienced women!'

'Because it's not true.'

'So it's just me.' She blinked and turned away. 'I see. Well, I'm sorry I don't come up to your *royal* standards.' The wobble in her voice gouged a hole through his chest.

'I didn't mean that.' He planted a hand on her shoulder but she shrugged it off and moved to the head of the bed. 'Tamsin! You don't understand.'

'Leave me alone, Alaric. I was stupid ever to imagine you'd be attracted to a woman like me. I got carried away with the fairy tale, that's all. It must happen to you all the time. Women with stars in their eyes.'

She dropped her clothes on the bed in front of her and bent to step into her panties but the coverlet got in the way. With an exclamation of impatience she thrust it aside, letting it slide to the floor.

Frustration filled him. Self-contempt and annoyance at finding himself on the defensive. Plus a sexual hunger even greater than before. *One taste hadn't been enough.*

He reached for her again.

'Does it *feel* like I'm not attracted?' With his hands on her hips he jerked her back so his arousal pressed blatantly against her buttocks. He almost groaned at how right that felt.

The breath hissed from her lungs as he slid his palms over her belly and ground his hips in a slow rotation that left him lightheaded.

'I want you, Tamsin. I brought you here with the express intention of getting you into my bed.' He slipped one hand down to the moist heat between her thighs and felt her shudder as he homed in on that most sensitive of spots.

'Or not. Anywhere would do. The sleigh, the barn, the kitchen. I don't care. But I've been trying, unsuccessfully, to keep my distance because I realised too late how I've taken advantage. I'm responsible—'

'You're not responsible for me.' Her defiance was belied by her throaty pleasure as her lower body moved a fraction against his stroking fingers. Her responsiveness cracked his resolve further and he slid himself provocatively against her cushioning curves.

'I'm responsible for taking your innocence.'

'You're talking antiquated rubbish. It's my business when I choose to lose my virginity.'

'That doesn't diminish my culpability.'

'Oh!' With a violent jerk Tamsin freed herself and swung to face him. Before he could prevent her she snatched up the coverlet and hid all that firm, glorious flesh. 'You're infuriating! Do you always take the world on your shoulders?'

Alaric watched passion animate her features and felt desire cloud his brain. 'I knew what I was doing. You didn't.'

She rolled her eyes. 'You know, women even have the vote these days. We're capable of making decisions about who we want to make love to.'

Make love. It hit him with a jolt that for the first time the euphemism seemed more apt than 'having sex'.

Ridiculous. What they'd shared was carnal pleasure at its most raw. Pleasure so complete he could no longer resist its pull. Love didn't enter into it.

'All right. Who do you want to make love to?' Alaric loomed towards her. *His conscience could go hang.*

Tamsin shuffled back, eyes widening as she realised she was trapped against the bed.

'I want to go back to the castle.'

'No, you don't. You want to climb on that mattress and let me show you the things we didn't have time for earlier.' Heat sizzled under his skin just watching her shocked delight as she processed his words. The furtive way her eyes darted to the bed. 'I want it too.'

She tilted her chin defiantly and her grip tightened on the bedspread. 'It didn't sound like it a minute ago. Are you sure?'

'Totally.'

'Why?'

Why? The question flummoxed him. Couldn't she feel the erotic charge leaping between them? Didn't she understand what they'd shared had been remarkable, despite its brevity? So wondrous, so perfect no one in their right mind could walk away from it. He speared a hand through his hair in frustration. *Why did women always want to talk?*

The belligerent jut of her finely honed jaw said she wasn't going to make this easy.

'Because I've wanted you so long,' he murmured, finally giving himself up to the truth. 'Since I walked into the library and saw your sexy leg swinging above my head. Since I discovered a woman who challenges and intrigues and piques my curiosity. Who's passionate about something as complex as translating ancient books and as simple as a waltz. Who's not overawed by my title. Who's not charmed by wealth and prestige and isn't afraid to tell me what she thinks.'

'This isn't about duping those other women?' She gnawed on her lip and hurt shaded her fine eyes.

Alaric's mouth thinned and he silently cursed the fact he'd used that excuse to keep her close. If he'd known how unsure she was about her own desirability he'd never have done it. It had taken him too long to understand that her professional confidence hid deep vulnerability.

'It's got nothing to do with anyone but us.'

He lifted a hand and stroked the hair from her face, revelling in the way she swayed infinitesimally towards him. 'You're the most naturally sexy woman. Yet you hide your sensuality from everyone but me.' He smiled and slid a hand down her throat to where her pulse thrummed.

'Do you know what a turn on it is, being the only one in on your secret? Seeing your buttoned up shirts and long skirts, your sensible shoes and no-nonsense bun? Knowing that beneath is a siren who makes my pulse race with just one demure glance from those brilliant eyes?'

'I…' She shook her head as if words failed her.

He smoothed his index finger down her brow. 'Even that tiny frown you have when you're concentrating gets me. And the way you pout your lips over a knotty problem.' He breathed deep, trying to slow his escalating heartbeat.

'Every time I visit the archives and find you poring over papers I want to slam the door shut. I want to take you there, against the storage units. Or on that massive desk. You wouldn't believe how often I've imagined it.'

Colour flared in Tamsin's pale face and her mouth softened. Alaric bent his head, letting his breath feather her temple, torturing himself with the scent of her.

'You've imagined it too. I can see it in your face.'

For the first time Tamsin was bereft of speech. She just stood, staring up at him in mute appeal.

Unfamiliar sensations stirred. Something deep inside swelled, filling the tattered remnants of his soul.

'It's all right,' he murmured, wondering if he was reassuring himself as well as her. 'I'll make it all right.' He let his hand drop. 'But only if you want.'

Silence thundered in the air, pulsing like a living thing as their eyes meshed. Something unfamiliar twisted in his chest as he waited for her response. Something more than desire. Something far stronger.

'I want you too, Alaric.'

Relief speared him. She was his. For now.

That's all he wanted. He ignored the half-formed idea that there was more than simple sex between them.

Making love…

No. Emotional connections were too dangerous.

But sex...sex he could handle. Sex they would both enjoy. A final fling before he faced the burdens of the crown. Desperation edged his movements as he wrenched the coverlet from her slack hold. Rosy nipples like proud dusky buds pouted just for him.

He reached out to the bedside table and yanked open the drawer, unerringly finding one of the packets he needed.

'This time,' he promised with a taut smile, 'we're going to take things slow.'

Hours later Tamsin lay, limbs deliciously weighted, so exhausted she felt like she floated on a cloud above the huge four poster bed. The shift and rustle of logs burning in the grate was the only sound. Never had she felt so languid, yet so alert to each sensation. The tickle of hair across her shoulders as she burrowed beneath the covers, the awareness of her body. Especially those parts where Alaric had devoted such lingering attention.

She squeezed her thighs together, conscious of the achy, empty feeling just *there*. Not sore. More *aware*.

Her lips curved dreamily. It wasn't merely what they'd done together. Warmth like honeyed chocolate flowed through her as she remembered Alaric's words.

She wouldn't be human, wouldn't be female if she wasn't thrilled by the thought of him secretly desiring her, even though she couldn't compete outwardly with the glamorous sophisticates who were his usual companions.

He enjoyed her body as much as she enjoyed his.

For long moments she distracted herself remembering his powerful limbs, the curve and dip of his back and taut buttocks, the heavy muscle of his chest. She'd explored his body till he'd pinioned her to the bed with a growl that had awoken every sated nerve. She blushed all over recalling what he'd done then. How she'd delighted in it. So much that she'd cried his name as she'd shuddered in ecstasy.

After Patrick she'd wondered if she'd ever trust a man enough for intimacy. She'd assumed her first time with a man might be clumsy, uncomfortable and nerve-racking.

Instead she felt...treasured. Appreciated. Set free.

The fire in Alaric's eyes had incinerated the doubts and insecurities that had hemmed her in for so long. As if it was right to give in to the passions that simmered below the surface. To trust in herself and him.

He saw beyond her clothes and her job. He was attracted to *her*. He wasn't put off by the fact that she spoke her mind. He even liked her enthusiasm for her work! The news that he'd been intrigued by her right from the start made them seem like equals, despite the disparity in their social positions and experience.

This was true sharing. Something she'd never had.

Bemused, she snuggled into the pillows. If it wasn't for the proof of her exhausted body she'd think it a dream, too good to be true.

Forcefully she reminded herself this wouldn't last.

He was royalty. A tiny chill pierced her glow. He might even be *king*.

Tamsin pulled the bedclothes close as a disturbing thought surfaced. Could that be at the root of her nebulous doubts about Tomas's chronicle? It was the right date. Yet she had doubts.

Doubts or hopes? Selfish hopes that the chronicle was somehow wrong. That Alaric wasn't king.

Because if he became king there was even less chance he'd be interested in plain Tamsin Connors.

Her breath seized on a guilty gasp. Is that why she hadn't told him about the dating? The idea went against every professional principle. Yet deep in her heart a seed of disquiet grew.

Was it so wrong to wait a little to tell him about that? Enjoy this precious interlude before reality intruded?

This...relationship would end soon enough. Her mind shied from the idea of returning to her normal life without Alaric. But he'd given her a wonderful, precious gift. Honest passion and caring, shared unstintingly.

Nothing could ever take that away.

'Ah, Sleeping Beauty awakes.' That deep, rich voice slid like rippling silk right through her insides. Her breath caught at its beauty.

Slowly she rolled over. Backlit by the fire's glow Alaric's long frame was mouth-wateringly athletic in just a pair of black trousers. What was it about a bare male chest, tousled dark hair and a smile that drove sexy creases down his lean cheeks? Tamsin's breath sighed out in a whoosh.

Ink blue eyes met hers and heat trickled in her belly.

'What have you got there?' Her voice was husky and his smile widened. Every doubt fled as its warmth filled her.

He lifted his hand and a splash of fluid gold ran through his fingers. 'Here.' He sauntered to the bed and held up a silken robe.

She reached but he didn't release it, just stood, holding it by the shoulders, wearing a smile of secret challenge. Her gaze flicked to Alaric's bare chest. He had no qualms about nudity, but he was the most magnificent male. Whereas she...she was used to covering up.

His eyes beckoned.

'There's something I want to show you.' When he looked at her that way she felt she could walk across hot coals and feel nothing but the pleasure of his smile.

Shimmying to the edge of the bed she slid out, holding the covers as long as possible. It was stupid to feel shy after what they'd done together. Yet it was only the fact that his eyes remained fixed on her face that gave her courage to step from the bed and slip into the seductively soft silk.

'Excellent.' Why she should feel such pleasure at his approval she didn't want to consider. He smoothed the garment across her flushed skin, wrapping the sides closed across her breasts and stomach, tying the belt and caressing her unashamedly through the sensuous silk.

Her heart beat fast, lodging up near her throat as she sagged into his solid heat. She was exhausted, yet with a touch he overturned every sensible thought. She trembled, eager for his caresses. For more of his loving.

'Come and look.' He ushered her to the window then stood behind her. His arms wrapped around her waist, his body warmed her back and she sank against him.

The sky was dark and the vista almost obliterated by wafts of white. 'A snowstorm?'

His jaw scraped her hair as he nodded. 'We're not going anywhere today.'

Heat blazed and she grinned. Their idyll wasn't over. Yet she tried to be sensible. 'Won't your staff worry? Don't you have appointments?'

'Nothing that can't be delayed. They know we're safe. I texted them before we crossed that last ridge down into this valley. All we can do is wait.'

Tamsin tried to feel regret for Alaric's predicament, cut off from the meetings and important people he dealt with daily. But she couldn't repress a shiver of anticipation.

Before she could guess his intention, he hoisted her into his arms and carried her across the room. No other man had held her like this and she marvelled at the way she fitted so naturally in his embrace.

'We'll have to rough it here,' he murmured.

'Rough it?' The place was pure luxury.

Alaric shouldered open a door into a massive bathroom. The sound of running water made her turn. Set in an arched alcove, lit by flickering candles and topped by a mural of Venus bathing, was the largest bath she'd ever seen. Subtly scented steam curled above it.

On a table nearby were crystal flutes, an ice bucket cradling a foil topped bottle and a plate of plump fresh raspberries and peaches. He must have had the out of season fruit flown in.

'There's only one bath,' Alaric replied. 'I'm afraid we'll have to share.' His eyes gleamed and his roguish smile thrilled as he lowered her, inch by provocative inch to the floor. His hands warmed her hips as she swayed.

Tamsin blinked, overcome by emotion. By the devastating pleasure of this over the top seduction scene. *He'd done this for her.* His darkening gaze invited her to enjoy it all, and him, to the full.

Guilt lanced Tamsin. She should tell him about the chronicle. But with guilt came a renewed sense of urgency. This would be over soon. She knew a bitter-sweet yearning to hoard every precious moment. She'd tell him when they returned to the castle. When the fantasy ended.

She'd never felt so cherished. Invited to share his laughter as well as the passion that lurked in the curve of his lips, his hooded eyes and his tight, possessive grip.

'Thank you, Alaric.' Her voice was hoarse as she stared at this man who'd given her so much. Physical pleasure, but more too. Something that made her feel strong and special.

She stretched up on tiptoe and pressed her unsteady lips to his. Instantly he gathered her close, arms wrapping tightly around her, kissing her with tender persuasion.

Alaric didn't believe in love or commitment. Yet it would be so easy to fall for him. Totally foolish, definitely dangerous, but, oh, so easy.

CHAPTER TWELVE

'No, NOT like that, keep your palm flat.'

Alaric wrapped his hand round Tamsin's, holding it steady while the mare snuffled a chunk of carrot. Tamsin's gurgle of laughter echoed through the stable. He felt it as he stood behind her, his other arm pinning her close.

The horse whickered and mouthed Tamsin's palm. She crooned to it, rubbing her hand along its nose.

Alaric's belly clenched in response to her tone. It was like the one she used when they were naked and he discovered a new erogenous zone on her supple, gorgeous body.

He loved listening to Tamsin, he realised. Whether the soft gasps and cries of delight as they found ecstasy together, or the quiet, serious way she discussed other matters. Or her passion when she talked about books and dead languages and preserving the past. He even liked the schoolmistress voice she used to counter his teasing.

His groin stirred and he tugged her nearer, taking her weight. He was turned on by a woman whose eyes shone with delight over the size of his library!

This was new territory.

Normally his interest in a woman was skin deep. But these past few days with Tamsin he'd discovered a deeper pleasure, sharing her delight, not just with intimacy, but with the world around her.

He'd known joy unfettered by the cold shadows of the past. He even slept soundly, devoid of dreams.

Was it any wonder he didn't want her out of his sight? It was selfish, but the sunshine she brought to his soul was worth ignoring the responsibilities it would be his duty to shoulder soon. Already discreet arrangements were under way to ensure the crown's smooth transition if necessary.

Just a little longer…

A disturbing memory surfaced of Felix talking excitedly about finding the one right woman. *But his brother had made the mistake of believing in love.*

Alaric would never make that error.

'Why are you shaking your head? Aren't I touching it right?'

Alaric rubbed his chin against her hair. 'You *always* touch just right. It's one of your talents.'

Tamsin was a natural sensualist who loved giving and receiving pleasure. Her tentative forays into pleasing him reduced him to a slavering wreck. Imagine when she became expert at seducing a man!

A splinter of dismay punctured his self-satisfaction at the notion of Tamsin sharing herself with another.

Alaric's jaw tensed.

He wouldn't let it happen.

Not yet. Not for a long time. He wouldn't relinquish her until this liaison had run its course.

His left hand crept towards the apex of her thighs.

Her hand clamped his wrist and instantly he felt ashamed. Only an hour ago they'd finally emerged from bed. His attempts to restrain himself, allowing her time to recuperate from their lovemaking, kept failing abysmally. He needed to be more considerate. Until a few days ago she'd never been with a man.

His chest expanded on a rough breath of satisfaction. He couldn't help it. He tried to feel guilty for stealing her virginity but now all he experienced was pleasure knowing he was her first, her only.

It must be the novelty that made him feel he never wanted to let her go.

'Not in front of the horses,' she whispered as he nudged her ponytail aside and kissed her neck.

'You think they'll be offended?' He smiled against her fragrant skin, pulling her back from the stall.

'I…' The word disintegrated in a sigh of delight that stoked his ego.

'You've never been naked in front of a horse?' he teased as he laved her skin.

'I've never been near a horse.' She tilted her head to allow him better access.

'Tragic,' he murmured. 'So much to make up for. Horses, sledding, caviar, breakfast in bed. So many firsts.' He punctuated each word with a tiny bite to her neck and was rewarded by tremors of response that racked her body. He gathered her close. 'What were your parents thinking to deprive you so?'

Did he imagine a stiffening of her slender form?

'I was a very fortunate child. You can't call me deprived.'

No? Alaric thought of how she hid her bright, strong personality behind a dowdy façade. It wasn't a deliberate ploy, he knew now, but part of who she was. He recalled the way her eyes clouded when she'd thought she'd disappointed him. There was a strong streak of self-doubt in his lover and Alaric wished he knew why. With her intelligence and drive it was a wonder she wasn't over-confident.

'Ah.' He nuzzled her hair. 'So you were a pampered miss who got everything her way. All the latest toys on demand?'

She shook her head. 'My parents didn't believe in store bought toys. I amused myself. But I had access to books and solitude to read. I had a secure home and time to dream.'

Alaric's hands stilled in the act of slipping up her ribcage. 'Secure' didn't sound like 'happy'. 'Solitude' had a lonely ring. A familiar ring. His father had ensured Alaric and Felix grew up in impeccable isolation. But at least Alaric had had a brother to look up to.

'What did you dream about, Tamsin?' He cupped her soft breasts and felt her sink against him. 'A prince in a far-away castle?'

'Sometimes,' she whispered.

'Did he have dark hair and blue eyes and his very own sleigh?'

She twisted in his arms. A moment later her arms twined around his neck.

'Of course!' Her eyes gleamed and her lips curved in a gentle smile that tugged at something deep inside.

'What else did you dream about?'

Tamsin shrugged and her gaze dropped. 'I don't know. Adventure. Going out with friends. The usual.'

Alaric thought of the dossier at the castle. It described a girl without siblings or close friends, whose much older parents had busy careers. A girl living a solitary life.

Did she realise how much her words revealed about her loneliness? Something swelled in his chest. Something like pain or regret.

'I think we can organise some adventure.' He tipped her chin and looked into her now guarded eyes. 'We could climb the base of the cliff behind the lodge if it's not too icy.'

Tamsin's eyes lit with golden sparks. Her smile made him feel like royalty in a way he never had before.

'I'd love that! Thank you. When can we go?'

He grinned. He'd *known* she had an adventurous streak. How easy it was to make her happy!

It surprised him how much he wanted her to be happy.

Alaric lifted his hand and pulled her ponytail loose so he could feel her heavy tresses on his hands. He needed this constant connection. To touch and taste, as if he feared she'd vanish if he didn't hold her.

'Another hour to let the sun melt any fresh ice.'

'That gives us time.' Her hands slid down, trailing fire. She yanked his shirt loose and slipped her palms up his torso, flesh against sizzling flesh. His body hardened.

Alaric loved that she was a quick learner.

'Time for what?' His voice was husky as desire twisted in his belly.

'Another first.' Now her smile was mischievous and he felt its impact in some unnamed part of him. 'I've never made love in a stable.'

Heart pounding, Alaric slipped his arms around her and lifted her into his embrace. It felt right. Satisfying.

He turned and strode towards the clean hay in the far corner. 'Allow me to remedy that right now.'

* * *

It was the noise that woke Tamsin. A cry so raw and anguished it made her blood congeal in atavistic terror.

Startled, she lay, breathing deep, wondering what had shattered her slumber. Moonlight streamed through the windows and behind the fire screen embers glowed.

Instinctively she moved closer to Alaric. For the past three days there'd barely been a moment when they weren't touching, even in sleep.

Amazing how she missed that contact.

As she rolled over she realised he was burning up, his skin feverish and damp with sweat.

Tamsin touched his shoulder. It was rigid as if every sinew dragged tight. She leaned close and heard his breathing, sharp and shallow. Her hand slid across his muscled chest that rose and fell in an unnatural rhythm.

'Alaric?'

No response. Did she imagine his breathing was laboured? Desperately she tried to recall everything she'd read about asthma and restricted airways.

'Alaric!' She shook him, alarmed at how her hands slipped on his fever-slickened flesh. 'Alaric. Wake up!' She shook his shoulders.

Restlessly his head turned back and forth. He mumbled something. But try as she might she couldn't wake him.

Fear spiked. They were out of phone range and she couldn't summon help if his condition worsened. Tamsin bit her lip. It wouldn't come to that.

First she had to get his temperature down.

She slid back the covers ready to fetch a damp flannel when another cry rent the air. Her blood froze at the wordless horror of that shout. It tapered into a wail of such grief every hair stood on end.

There was a convulsion of movement. The covers were flung wide and Alaric's hard frame landed on hers with such force it knocked the air from her lungs.

'No!' Huge hands gripped her shoulders. 'You can't!' He choked on the words, his head sinking to her breast.

It took a moment to realise the dampness she felt there wasn't sweat but tears. A sob shook his big body and Tamsin reached up, cradling him close.

'Sh, Alaric.' His distress frightened her, evoking fierce protective instincts. She felt his pain as if it shafted through her body. 'It's all right, darling, do you hear me?' Tamsin squeezed as tight as she could while his shoulders heaved and hot tears smeared between them.

She hated feeling so useless.

She hated that he hurt so badly.

'It's OK. It'll be OK,' she crooned, rocking him as best she could. 'My darling. Everything's all right.'

Gradually, as she murmured endearments, the rigidity seeped from his body and his breathing evened a little.

'Tamsin?'

Still she rocked him, her arms clamped tight. 'It's all right. It was just a dream.'

For long moments he lay still in her arms, then without warning he rolled off her, leaving her bereft.

'Alaric? Are you all right?'

He raised his forearm over his face. In the pallid light she saw his mouth crimp into a stern line as he fought whatever demons plagued him.

Instinctively she moved closer, tugging the discarded bedding to his waist and nestling her head on his chest, one arm wrapped protectively across him. He'd always seemed so strong and confident, so casually in command.

Her distress at his pain was a sharp ache. Was this what happened when you connected with another person? When you shared your true self as well as your body?

'I'm sorry.' His voice was slurred. 'You shouldn't have to witness that.' His breath shuddered out. 'I didn't mean to frighten you.'

For answer she snuggled closer, lifting her leg to anchor his thighs, as if by surrounding him she could blot out his nightmare.

'Don't worry. Everything's fine now.'

'Fine?' The word cracked like a gunshot. 'It'll never be fine.'
He tore his arm from his face and she saw his fist pound the other
side of the bed. But behind her his arm curved tight, holding her
close.

'Did I hurt you?' His voice was a deep rumble. He stared at
the top of the four poster bed, as if unwilling to face her. 'Tamsin,
are you OK?'

'Of course I'm OK.'

'No questions?' he asked after a minute. 'Surely that enquiring
mind of yours wants answers?' His mouth was a grim line in the
half-dark.

A month ago his expression would have deterred Tamsin. But
now she knew the tender, caring man behind the royal title and
the rogue's reputation. She sensed his deep hurt.

She stretched up. Her breasts slid over his chest but she managed to ignore the inevitable tremor of awareness. She leaned
over him till her hair curtained their faces in darkness. Holding his
jaw in her hands she planted a whisper-light kiss on his lips.

He tasted of salt and heat and suffering.

His mouth was warm beneath hers as she repeated the action,
allowing all she felt for him loose in that simple caress. Feelings
she hadn't censored.

When she lifted her head one large palm covered the back of
her skull and urged her down for another kiss. One so piercingly
sweet she ached with the beauty of it. His other arm roped around
her hips, drawing her in as if to ensure she wouldn't escape.

As if she wanted to go anywhere!

Never had they kissed like this: a sharing of the soul, not the
body. Emotion escalated, filling every lonely part of her. She
clung, wanting to explain how she felt but not having the words.
Letting her body say what she couldn't.

From nowhere tears welled and spilled unheeded.

'Tamsin?' His thumb stroked her cheek, blurring the hot trail.
'Don't cry. Not over me.'

Too late. She was in too deep. Asking her not to care was like
asking her to set fire to a library. Impossible.

Fervently she pressed her lips to his, blotting out whatever he was going to say. He kissed her till she sank into languorous pleasure. Finally he pulled back.

In the dark she felt his gaze. With a sigh he settled her on his chest and wrapped her close. Beneath her ear his heartbeat thrummed steadily.

'I owe you an explanation.' His voice was husky.

'You don't owe me anything. It was just a nightmare.'

'I was selfish, sleeping with you. What if I'd hurt you? I should have let you sleep alone.'

'It's you I'm worried about.' She hesitated, trying to summon an even tone and force away the chill that invaded at the idea of sleeping alone. 'You have these dreams often?'

His silence answered for him.

'You're afraid you might lash out in your sleep?'

'It's too dangerous. I risked your safety.'

'I told you, Alaric, I'm—'

'OK. So you say. But you don't know.' His words tailed off and the desolation she heard cut to her heart. 'Everything I touch turns to ashes. *Everyone.*'

Tamsin froze at the profound despair in his voice.

'Tell me.' She cuddled closer, her mind whirring while she tried to sound cool and detached.

'Talking about it will help?' Sarcasm threaded his voice. She ignored it, guessing he fought deep-seated pain any way he could.

'Bottling it up is no solution.' Look at the way she'd turned inwards, isolating herself rather than take the risk of being rejected. 'Whatever the problem, it will fester if you don't face it.'

'Now you're calling me a coward.' There was a huff of amusement in his voice that made her smile sadly. Alaric was excellent at using humour and his killer charm to deflect attention from the inner man.

How had she not seen it before?

'What have you got to fear? Unless you think I'll do a kiss and tell interview?'

'I can't imagine anything less likely.' He stroked her hair and Tamsin's tension eased a little. She had his trust at least. That was a start.

Silence fell.

'It's not about me,' he said eventually. 'It's the people I failed. That's who I dream of.' He sounded so stern, so judgemental, not like the Alaric she knew.

'I can't imagine you letting anyone down.'

His laugh was bitter. 'Don't you believe it. I was an unruly kid, always in trouble, a constant disappointment to my father. I heard often enough it was lucky I was just a second son. I didn't have what it took to rule.'

Tamsin bit her tongue rather than blurt out that his father sounded like a brute. A man who hadn't loved his wife, or, it seemed, his child. The more she heard the more she disliked.

'Then he'd be surprised to see Ruvingia flourishing now.'

Alaric said nothing. She sensed the reference to his father had been a distraction.

'Alaric? Tell me about your dreams.'

His chest rose beneath her like a wave cresting to shore. Tamsin clung grimly, willing him to share the source of his grief. It ate at him, destroying his peace.

At last he complied. 'I see them all die,' he whispered, 'and I can't save them.'

Tamsin's blood chilled at his haunted tone. 'Tell me.'

'So you can absolve me?' But his scepticism held anguish. Finally when she didn't answer he explained.

As a career army officer he'd jumped at the chance a few years ago to put his skills to good use, volunteering as a peacekeeper overseas. No sooner had he signed on than his whole unit had followed him.

They were posted near an isolated village, protecting a wide area from insurgents. Short bouts of dangerous activity were interspersed with long quiet periods which allowed time to get to know the locals. One little fatherless boy in particular had hung around, fascinated by the foreigners and especially Alaric. From his tone it was clear Alaric had been fond of him too.

When a report came of trouble in an outlying zone Alaric responded immediately, taking men to investigate.

'It was a ruse. But by the time we got there and discovered that it was too late.' They'd returned to their base to discover the village had been attacked. Both soldiers and civilians had been wounded and some had died, the little boy among them.

'He died in my arms.' Alaric's voice was hoarse. 'I couldn't save him.' A sigh racked his body. 'There were too many I couldn't save.'

'There's nothing you could have done.' Her heart broke at the pain ravaging him.

'No?' Glittering eyes clashed with hers. 'I was the officer in charge. If I hadn't split my men the village would have been safe. If I hadn't responded so quickly to an unconfirmed report—'

Tamsin cupped his jaw in her hand. 'You don't know what would have happened. Maybe the attack there would have been worse. You did your best.'

'You don't understand. I was there to protect them and *I failed.* I failed my men too. They were only there because of me. Some didn't survive. Others still bear the scars.' He halted, swallowing. 'Except me. I came home without a scratch.'

Tamsin's heart clenched at the guilt and self-loathing in his voice. She remembered Peter, his livid scar and how he'd talked of Alaric's sense of responsibility. Now it made terrible sense.

'Far better if I'd died too.'

'Don't say that!' Her fist clenched on his chest.

For a moment Alaric let himself enjoy the pleasure of her innocent belief in him. It was novel to have anyone so vehemently on his side.

The whole truth would rip the scales from her eyes. Part of him wanted to keep her in ignorance.

But he didn't deserve her charity.

'I came back to Ruvingia.' He'd been at a loose end, unable to settle, finding it hard to carry out the most routine official duties whilst memories of the deaths plagued him. 'I spent my time amusing myself. Fast cars, parties, women. Lots of women.' Sex had at least brought the oblivion of exhaustion, allowing him to sleep.

'My older brother, Felix, welcomed me.' His gut twisted, remembering Felix's patience with his wayward and tormented younger sibling. 'He was full of plans, even talking of marriage, but I wasn't interested. I was too wrapped up in my own troubles to listen.'

Some days it had been almost too hard to see Felix, so successful, capable and grounded. The epitome of what Alaric had aspired to be but not achieved.

Felix wouldn't have let those he was responsible for die. Felix would have found a way to save them.

'Alaric?'

'There was a girl,' he said, eager now to get this over. 'A beautiful girl. I first noticed her at a function when I saw Felix watching her.' He hefted a breath into tight lungs. 'Two days later she was in my bed.' Another of the stream of women he'd used to lose himself for a while.

Tamsin's body stiffened. Grimly he ploughed on, knowing by the time he'd finished she'd never want to look at him again. He ignored the shaft of pain that caused.

'I didn't love her. I never pretended to. And she… I think my reputation appealed. She wanted the thrill of being with someone notorious.' He grimaced. 'It was mutually satisfying. Till Felix discovered us and I found out she was the woman he'd already fallen for. The one he'd wanted to marry after a proper courtship.'

Tamsin gasped. 'You didn't know?'

'I knew he planned to marry but I assumed it would be an arranged marriage. He hadn't mentioned a name and frankly I wasn't interested.' Alaric paused, forcing out the truth. 'But I knew he was attracted to Diana. Most men were.'

Again he wondered if his pleasure in winning her had been fuelled in part by the need to best Felix. To prove that in this one thing, the ability to get any woman he wanted, Alaric was superior.

Could he have been so shallow? So jealous? What did that say about him?

He'd never before thought himself envious of Felix. But now he couldn't banish telling doubts about his motives.

'Felix was furious when he found out. I'd never seen him like it.' Alaric remembered not only his anger, but his pain. The disillusionment of finding out the woman he'd put on a pedestal had sullied herself with his scapegrace brother. 'He accused us of betraying him.' That memory alone crucified Alaric. Felix was the only person with whom he'd been close. The only person who'd ever really cared.

'And Diana?'

'She was angry she'd made such an error. She hadn't realised he intended marriage. She didn't love him but she liked the notion of being a princess.'

'So what happened?'

Typically, Tamsin was intelligent enough to sense there was more. He let his arm tighten round her soft body, knowing it would probably be for the last time.

'Felix changed. He became short-tempered, not just with me, but everyone. He grew erratic, increasingly unreliable and he began drinking heavily.' The memory of that time, and his inability to stop his brother's slide into depression, chilled Alaric.

'One day I found him climbing into my sports car, determined to drive himself to a function. He reeked of whisky.'

'Oh, Alaric.' Tamsin's palm flattened on his chest and he covered it with his own.

'I couldn't stop him but I couldn't let him go. I jumped in just as he accelerated out of the courtyard.' He drew a deep breath, letting the familiar, corrosive pain claim him. 'We argued.' And each word of Felix's accusations was branded in Alaric's memory, reinforcing every doubt he'd ever harboured about himself.

'Felix lost control on a hairpin bend and I grabbed the steering wheel. We didn't make it around the next curve. We went into the embankment.' His breath grew choppy and sweat prickled his skin. 'I'd buckled my seat belt and the airbag saved me. Felix wasn't wearing his belt. He died instantly.'

Alaric forced himself to relinquish his hold on Tamsin, knowing she'd move away now.

* * *

Tamsin held her breath, shocked at his story. Stunned by the blankness in Alaric's voice. How much he'd suffered! He'd hidden it all behind that charming mask.

It was obvious he'd loved his brother. Given the little she knew, perhaps Felix was the only person who'd ever cared for Alaric.

'I'm so sorry.' The words were pathetically little.

'So am I. Every day. But that doesn't change the fact I'm to blame.'

'Don't say that!'

'If I hadn't seduced Diana, none of it would have happened. If I'd stopped him—'

'If Diana had loved him back, nothing you did could have caused a rift between them.'

There was silence for a moment as if Alaric considered the idea for the first time. Then he shook his head.

'I should have been more careful, less eager to get her into my bed.'

Tamsin couldn't argue with that. 'Your brother blamed you because he was disappointed. It wasn't your fault he loved someone who didn't return his feelings.'

'But he didn't need me undermining him. He deserved my loyalty. I should have been there to help him. Protect him from himself when he turned to drink. I couldn't even do that. *I failed him when he needed me.*' His voice hollowed and Tamsin's throat ached as she stifled tears at his pain.

From the first she'd noticed his tendency to set high standards for himself. Look at the way he'd talked about *taking her virginity.*

Did that overblown sense of responsibility come from being told constantly by his father that his best wasn't good enough? She sensed the weight Alaric bore didn't stem solely from tragic recent events, but from unhealed scars he'd carried a long time.

It didn't surprise her that he wasn't thinking clearly. He'd had one shock piled on another.

Alaric's bitter laughter shredded the silence. 'And here I am, about to take the crown. To do my duty and promise to serve and *protect*! How can I be sure I won't fail again?'

Tamsin's heart broke at his pain and self-doubt. He truly didn't see how capable and competent he was.

No wonder he spent his time dallying with socialites and risking his neck in extreme sports. No wonder he never wanted to be still. He was running from this trauma.

Fury rose in her that those closest to him hadn't seen this. That they hadn't helped him.

Her mind boggled at the weight of guilt he bore. How did he function, much less put on that devil-may-care air? He believed he'd failed his duty to his comrades and his brother. That he was to blame.

That explained why he was appalled at becoming responsible for a nation. And why he didn't want to get close to anyone. He felt himself unworthy. She'd bet, apart from his brother, his comrades were the closest he'd come to a family.

Tamsin breathed out a huff of relief that she hadn't told him the chronicle's date had been verified. Wild horses wouldn't drag that from her now.

'Oh, darling.' She pressed closer, kissing his chin, neck and face. 'You have to forgive yourself. Believe me, you're a victim too.'

He shook his head. 'Tell that to men who came home scarred. Or the mother of an innocent boy who died.'

Tamsin framed his face with her palms. His pain tore at her and she couldn't bear it. 'Your ego is out of control if you think you caused all that! Your brother would be horrified to know you blamed yourself. Do you really think he'd want that? You're a good man, Alaric. I'd trust you with my life.'

'Sweet Tamsin.' He raised a hand and brushed a furious tear from her cheek. 'Don't waste your tears on me.'

'I'll cry if I want to.' He was so stubborn! So eager to shoulder guilt.

Yet his loyalty and honour were part of what made him the man she cared for. *The man she loved.*

Knowledge sideswiped her with a force that left her speechless. Somehow, without her realising, he'd changed from fantasy prince to the man she loved.

Her heart gave a massive jerk and thundered out of control. Her hands shook against his lean cheeks.

She'd thought she risked her pride in coming here, only to discover she'd risked much more.

She'd given her heart to Alaric.

A man with no thought of long term relationships. Who distrusted love. Yet for now even that couldn't dim the incandescent glow filling her.

'We can talk about this later. Now you need sleep.'

'I'll move to another room.'

'Don't even think about it! I'll just follow you.' She slid down into the bed. 'Shut your eyes and rest. I'll stay awake. You won't hurt me.'

'I could get used to you trying to dominate me,' he murmured in a pale imitation of his usual teasing. 'I'm too tired to resist.'

His breath was warm on her skin, his hand splayed possessively at her waist as he tucked her close. But there was nothing sexual about the way they lay. This was about comfort and peace and love.

Even if he didn't believe in it, Tamsin hoped Alaric felt the love drenching her skin, filling her heart, wrapping itself around him.

Later, she knew, her predicament in falling for this man would devastate her. But for now it filled her with a peace she'd never known.

CHAPTER THIRTEEN

THE pink flush of dawn lit the sky as Tamsin crept downstairs. Though Alaric had slept for hours she didn't want to wake him.

She shivered and pulled the silk wrap tighter as she reached the ground floor. The lingering warmth from the central heating made the chill bearable.

Yet nothing dispelled the cold squeezing her heart. How could she even begin to help Alaric?

Or herself. Her situation was impossible.

She was in love.

With Prince Alaric of Ruvingia.

A man with no history of commitment. A troubled man who scorned the notion of falling in love. A man so far beyond her sphere any idea of a relationship was laughable.

Alaric was used to the best in everything. Could he ever settle for someone as ordinary as her? It was ridiculous to hope, but she couldn't stop herself.

Would he ever tie himself to a woman? Especially a woman who wasn't witty or glamorous or well born?

She'd come here knowing she was a short term diversion. At first the bright promise of his offer had been enough. Now she realised she'd been dragged out of her depth.

She loved him.

Tamsin hugged the bitter-sweet knowledge to herself, alternately thrilled and horrified.

Yet as she'd lain, overwhelmed by the realities she faced, part of her brain had pondered the one useful thing she could do: prove once and for all if Tomas's chronicle was legitimate. Lately she'd harboured doubts. Were they well founded or, as she'd begun to suspect, an excuse not to break the news that would take Alaric even further from her?

She thrust open the library door, flicked on the light and headed for the desk. She worked best with pen and paper. Perhaps if she listed her concerns she'd get them straight in her head.

She'd happily give up the kudos of rewriting history with her find if it meant bringing Alaric peace of mind.

He was more important than any professional coup or the chance to rub Patrick's nose in her success. Nothing mattered more than his peace and happiness.

How much had altered these past months!

Despite her selfish fear about the yawning void it would open between them, Tamsin couldn't help regretting that he didn't want the crown. The respect and admiration between Alaric and his people was tangible even if he didn't see it. He'd make an excellent monarch with his dedication to duty and practicality. If only he could see beyond his pain.

She opened a drawer and found a notepad. She withdrew it then paused, an envelope catching her eye.

Tamsin Connors. It was addressed to her?

Her brow puckered as she reached for it. No stamp. No address. Just her name. What did it mean? A trickle of sensation slid down her spine.

'Tamsin!'

Startled, she turned to find Alaric filling the doorway, his face pale and set. Her gaze traversed his perfect, muscular torso and a familiar weakness hit her knees. He wore only jeans, zipped but not buttoned.

No man had a right to look so magnificent! Her pulse gave a queer little leap and hurried on.

'What are you doing?' The hoarse edge to his voice reminded her of his revelations last night. She moved towards him then stopped, uncertain.

'I came to find pen and paper. I had an idea about the chronicle. I wanted—'

'Come back to bed.' He held out a hand, his eyes boring into hers as if to force her to obey. Despite his outstretched hand it wasn't an invitation. It was an order.

'What's wrong?' The room hummed with tension.

'Nothing. I just want you with me. This can wait.' He smiled, but it didn't reach his eyes.

'I'll be up soon,' she assured him. 'I only want to jot some points. Besides, I found this.' She looked at the envelope, frowning as she read her name again.

Before she realised what he intended, Alaric had crossed the room. He stood before her, his palm open as if inviting her to pass the envelope over.

'Leave that. It's not important.' His clipped tone surprised her and she stiffened.

Tamsin looked from those blazing indigo eyes and the stark lines accentuating the stern set of Alaric's mouth to the envelope in her hand. A frisson of foreboding rippled through her. Suddenly the envelope didn't seem quite so innocuous. She wanted to drop it on the desk but her fingers locked tight.

'Why don't you want me to open it?'

Silence. He moved close but didn't touch her. That tiny distance made her feel colder than the chilly dawn air.

'Because it's not for you. It's about you.'

For what seemed an age Tamsin stood, unmoving, staring blankly at her printed name. About her?

Realisation, when it came, rocked her onto her heels.

'You mean an investigation? *Of me?*' For the first time she noticed the date under her name. The day they'd left the castle. Alaric must have brought it with him.

Her head jerked up and their eyes met. His were blank.

Tamsin's heart tripped. She'd grown used to the other Alaric. Warm, generous and fun loving. Caring. She'd almost forgotten the cool control he could summon at will.

'Yes,' he said at last. 'I had you investigated.'

Something squeezed around her lungs and it took a few moments to catch her breath. 'What's in it?'

'I don't know. I haven't read it.'

'Do you have dossiers on every employee?'

It must be a routine security check. But why was it done so recently rather than before she'd come to Ruvingia?

'Not like that.'

Tamsin's heart plummeted. She slipped her finger under the flap and drew out the papers.

Alaric didn't move a muscle. His eerie stillness only increased her fear.

The first page puzzled her. It was about the journalist at the ball. It was only when she turned the page and read a note that there was no evidence of previous contact between him and Tamsin that she understood.

The paper fluttered to the floor.

Other pages were about her and Patrick. Heat rose in Tamsin's cheeks as she recognised office gossip about them. How could Alaric have ordered someone to pry into her life?

'Why didn't you ask, if you wanted to know about the men in my life?' Her mouth twisted bitterly.

Alaric was the only man in her life! Somehow, now, the idea didn't thrill her so much.

'Do you normally vet prospective lovers?'

Alaric shook his head. 'It's not like that.'

'How did you know about Patrick anyway? I didn't mention him to anyone here.' She turned to the last page. What she found turned her heart to a solid lump of ice.

'You had my phone tapped!' She could barely believe it. 'Surely that's not legal, even if you are the prince!'

'It is, if it's a matter of state security.'

'State security! I'm a curator, not a spy!'

'You turned up out of the blue—'

'You invited me here, remember?'

'At a volatile time,' he said as if she hadn't interrupted. 'There's no king. Parliament is in recess till after the coronation, which by law can't take place for several months. It's a time ripe for factions building on past dissension to try toppling the democracy.'

He looked utterly implacable and something inside Tamsin shrivelled. Gone was her tender, vulnerable lover.

'Suddenly you appear, claiming to have proof that I, not Crown Prince Raul, am the legitimate heir. Can you imagine how catastrophic it might be if that news reached the wrong people before we had time to prepare?'

Tamsin stepped behind the desk, needing space to clear her head. Her eyes widened as she saw Alaric's severe expression. The tiny voice that cried this was all a mistake fell silent under the impact of his stare.

'You thought I lied about what I found?' The edges of the room spun as she grappled with the depths of his distrust.

'I acted in the interests of my country.' His tone was stiff, as if he was unused to being challenged.

'You thought that and *still* you took me to bed?'

No, Tamsin. That's why he took you to bed! To distract you, keep you from doing any more damage.

Neutralise the threat. Wasn't that what they called it?

She braced herself against the desk as pain gutted her and she doubled up. Blood roared in her ears like a deafening tide. In a series of snapshots, Tamsin recalled so many tell tale moments.

Her carefully monitored access to the chronicle.

The presence, wherever she went, of staff, no doubt reporting her movements.

Alaric asking her to be his companion, just the day after she'd told him about the chronicle. It had been a ruse, not to keep women away, but to keep an eye on her!

Alaric's fury at the ball when he'd found her with that journalist. He'd lied. He wasn't jealous, just angry she might have revealed something. Or maybe, she thought of what she'd read, Alaric suspected them of being in cahoots.

Pain blurred her vision and cramped her breathing. Her breath sawed in aching lungs as she fought to stay upright.

A hand reached for her and she jerked away.

'Don't touch me! Don't...' She drew an uneven breath. 'I can't bear it.'

To think she'd felt guilty, not telling him immediately about the test results, agonising over whether she could find something to prove or disprove the document once and for all. *And all the time he'd known!*

Her own small omission was nothing compared to his elaborate machinations!

'Tamsin. Have you heard a word I've said?'

'I don't want to hear!' She stumbled to the window, arms wrapped tight around her middle.

'Bringing me here was a ploy, wasn't it?' She stared dry eyed across the snow as cold facts solidified in her shocked brain. 'No wonder the pantry was well stocked. You planned to keep me here, out of harm's way.'

Bitterness scalded her throat. He'd succeeded. For days she'd delighted in the mirage Alaric had created. She'd barely given a thought to her work.

He'd been so sure of her. Had it been a lark, or an unpalatable duty, seducing her?

Tamsin's breath hissed as another piece of the picture slotted into place. The man at the sleigh, handing Alaric an envelope before they left. Alaric's dismissal of her concerns about a change in weather.

'You knew heavy snow was forecast.' She didn't turn. She couldn't face him. Not when the knowledge of her naivety filled her and every breath lanced pain. 'Didn't you? You wanted me cut off here.'

'I knew,' he answered at last, his words dropping like stones into an endless icy pool.

No apology. No regret.

She squeezed her eyes shut. *What they'd shared meant nothing.* Nothing to him but expediency.

It must have galled him to go to such lengths. No wonder he'd been disappointed the first time in that big bed. She hadn't even possessed the skills to please him.

Had he closed his eyes when they'd made love—no, when they'd had sex—and thought of another woman? Someone gorgeous and alluring?

How had she thought, even for one moment, that she'd snared the interest of Alaric, Prince of Ruvingia? Tamsin cringed inside but she kept her spine straight.

'You're an excellent actor.' She ignored the tremor in her voice and stared at the gorgeous alpine vista. 'You had me convinced. Congratulations.'

'Tamsin, it wasn't like that. Not all of it. To start with, yes, I wondered about you. About the way you hid behind that spinster look. About the odds of you finding such a document so conveniently.'

'It wasn't convenient!' She'd spent long hours working in the archives. And all the time he'd thought she'd lied.

'But later it wasn't about the papers, Tamsin.' His voice was nearer, as if he'd followed her to the window. 'It was about how you made me feel. And how you felt.'

'How I felt?' Her fury boiled over and she swung round. 'Are you saying I *asked* you to dupe me? That I *invited* you to make a fool of me?' As she spoke the final, fragile shell of happiness round her heart crumbled.

She'd believed. She'd actually believed in him! How many times before she finally learned her lesson? Was she so imbued with romantic fantasy that she was doomed to fall again and again for men's lies?

Even as she thought it she realised that wasn't possible. She'd survived Patrick's deception but this was far worse. She'd fallen in love with Alaric.

Now she hated him too.

'I'll tell you how this feels, *Your Highness*. It feels like hell! There was no excuse for what you did. None!'

'Tamsin, you have to listen. That's not really why I brought you here.'

She backed away from his outstretched hand as if it were poisoned.

'Not really?' Her voice dripped sarcasm. 'So the phone tap wasn't real? And the goons patrolling the grounds to make sure I didn't meet anyone in secret?' She flung an accusatory hand towards the papers on the floor. 'And the investigator's report—I suppose that was make-believe?'

Did she imagine he stiffened as each accusation lashed like a whip? Or that his face paled beneath its tan?

No! She could afford no sympathy for this man. Already it felt as if she bled from an unseen wound. The sort of injury that would never heal.

'You know what hurts most?' She stood rigidly straight. 'That you discovered how Patrick used me and decided to try the same tactic yourself. And that I fell for it.'

His brow puckered in a marvellous show of apparent innocence. 'I don't follow you.'

'Your report didn't detail that juicy titbit?' She'd skimmed the text, unable to take in every word. 'I don't believe you.' She sucked air to her lungs.

'Patrick set out to make me fall for him. He conned me into helping him *manage his workload* till I found him passing off my work as his. Using it to get a promotion at my expense. When he got it he dumped me and took up with a sexy blonde who knew how to please a man.' She almost gagged, remembering Patrick's satisfaction as he'd said that.

'And now you, you...' She blinked dry, scratchy eyes. 'I can't believe I fell for it again. That I actually *believed* you were attracted to me.'

She couldn't go on. Bile rose in her throat and her stomach churned queasily. Being sick in front of Alaric would be the final humiliation.

Tamsin stumbled to the door, thrusting aside his hand, ignoring his call for her to stop as pain, nausea and despair took hold.

The cold seeped into Alaric's bones as he stood, staring at the library's empty fireplace. It wasn't the chill air that froze his half-dressed body. It was the memory of Tamsin's distress. *The pain he had caused.*

Guilt flexed its claws, raking his belly. Lacerating the peace he'd discovered these past days with Tamsin.

Seeing her anguish, hearing her desperate attempt to keep her voice steady, Alaric had wanted to gather her close and comfort her. Force her to accept his embrace. Accustomed as he was to causing pain, he couldn't bear this.

Letting her leave had been the ultimate test of endurance when every instinct roared for him to go to her.

Yet he had to give her time alone. Enough to calm a little so she'd listen.

She felt betrayed by him.

He turned to pace, unable to remain inactive. If only he'd known her history with the Englishman! How much more damage had Alaric done to her bruised self-esteem?

She thought he'd used her for his own ends too.

But it hadn't been like that.

Yes, he'd been selfish. He'd seduced an innocent. But his motives, though not pure, hadn't been as despicable as the Englishman's. Her work had been a catalyst for intimacy. Yet it had also provided a convenient excuse. How much easier to explain away his fascination with a drably dressed bookworm than admit she intrigued him? That he wanted her in ways he'd never wanted anyone? Ways that had as much to do with emotions as with sexual gratification?

Air punched from his lungs as an unseen blow pummelled his solar plexus.

Emotions.

He'd spent so long distancing himself from intimacy except the sort he found in the beds of accommodating women. It was a shock to realise how much he felt for Tamsin. How much he *cared.* He'd thought it impossible, but it was true.

Instantly fear rose. Its familiar, hoary hand clenched his heart and iced his blood. No matter how he fought he couldn't blot out the voice in his soul.

He tainted everyone he touched.

He should never have allowed himself near Tamsin, so bright and generous and trusting.

His darkness spread like a miasma, infecting everyone he cared for. Now it had soiled that brief bright moment of delight. It had engulfed Tamsin too. He'd let her down.

But how to look into her bright eyes and listen to her soft, serious tones and not give in to temptation? For all his inner darkness, he was a man, not a machine. Resisting her innocent sweetness, her tart asperity and her zest for living had been impossible.

He'd craved an end to the darkness and he'd got that from her. No wonder he'd been insatiable, unable to bear her out of his sight. Before her his smiles and banter had carefully masked bleak emptiness. She'd filled that void with light and warmth.

Alaric recalled her soft murmurings as she'd listened to his story. Instead of shunning him when she'd heard what he'd done she'd called him 'darling' as naturally as if it might even be true. The sound of it had lodged somewhere near his heart and he'd cherished it.

He'd be damned if he'd give that up.

Twenty minutes since he'd let her walk away. A sensitive man might wait longer before confronting her. But his need was too urgent. He strode from the room.

The turret bedroom was empty. Alaric refused to think of it as *their* room, though the hint of her scent and the sight of rumpled sheets hit him in the chest like a ton of bricks. Setting his jaw, he searched the other rooms. Empty.

Fear ratcheted up in his belly.

It was only as he paused by a window that he realised where she'd gone. Her tracks led to the cliff where he'd given her a climbing lesson.

His heart almost failed as he remembered telling her that was the quickest way to the castle. It was an easy climb if you were experienced, but for a novice…

He'd hurt her so badly she'd rather face the mountain than him?

Alaric was no stranger to anguish but as he raced downstairs his torment was worse than anything he'd known.

If anything happened to her…

The cold numbed Tamsin's hands as she trudged through the snow. She'd forgotten her gloves in her haste but she wouldn't return for them. Not yet. Not till she'd found the strength to face Alaric without crumbling in a heap.

The nausea had eased a little but the pain was so raw, so sharp, she could barely breathe.

She shoved her hands in her anorak pockets and averted her eyes from the place where he'd taught her to climb. He'd been so tender and patient.

A sham!

Quickening her step she passed the small cliff and came to the base of a steep mountain slope. She'd have no trouble retracing her steps but for now she wanted solitude.

If she could she'd run away and never face him again.

The thought made her stumble to a halt.

She'd run across Europe rather than face Patrick. She'd spent years hiding herself rather than risk the chance of rejection. She'd thought there was strength in independence. But she hadn't been independent. She'd been a coward.

If she were truly the new, independent woman she'd been so proud of the night of the ball, she'd face Alaric.

She was furious and hurt by how he'd used her. But almost as bad was knowing she'd made the same mistake again. Fooled twice by manipulative men. Only this time her mistake was ir-redeemable. She'd fallen for Alaric, heart and soul. Despite his ruthless actions he was so much more than the flawed man he thought himself.

Something, an awareness, made her turn. An hour ago the sight of Alaric chasing her through the snow would have thrilled her, a precursor to some new lovers' game.

Now it was despair she felt, for even knowing how he'd used her, her heart leapt at the sight of him. Her blood roared in her ears. Would she always react to him like this?

'Run!' He was so near she saw his eyes blaze fire.

For a moment she saw stark fear in those glittering depths, then his hands closed on her and she was running, stumbling, carried by the force of his charging body. He kept her on her feet, urging her, tugging her at an impossible speed through the snow.

It was only as he spoke again that she realised the whispering roar wasn't her blood. She saw his lips move but the sound was obliterated by the thunder of tonnes of snow and rock falling off the mountain.

Avalanche! She read his lips but it was his urgent hands, his grim expression, that gave her strength to run.

Ahead a curve in the line of the mountain promised safety. They couldn't possibly make it. Then with a tremendous shove at her back Alaric propelled her forward.

She sprawled, hands over head as snow and scree dropped around her. The thud of the avalanche reverberated through the valley, snapping her teeth together. But the fall here on the periphery of the slide was relatively light.

Finally it was over. Gingerly she moved, burrowing her way up, grateful for the sight of sky above. She dragged in a deep breath scented with pine and ice and adrenaline.

Without Alaric she would have been buried under the massive fall. She turned to thank him.

To find only a huge tumbled mass of ice and boulders.

CHAPTER FOURTEEN

'THE prince is being released from hospital.' Tamsin's colleague gave her a sidelong glance. 'He'll be back at the castle soon.'

'That's excellent news.' Tamsin pinned on the cool, professional smile she'd perfected. It concealed the fluttery reaction in her stomach at the mention of her employer, her ex-lover. The man she dreamt of every night. 'I didn't think he'd be out so soon.'

After fracturing his collarbone, a leg and an arm, as well as sustaining concussion, the pundits had said Alaric would be under medical supervision far longer.

'Apparently the doctors didn't want to release him but he refused to stay any longer.'

Tamsin nodded, remembering Alaric's determination and strength. He had so little regard for himself he'd probably ignored medical warnings. A twinge of worry stabbed her. Would he be all right?

She still got chills thinking of those long minutes as she'd scrabbled beneath the debris to the seemingly lifeless form she'd finally found. Her heart had plunged into freefall as she'd searched for a pulse.

In that moment it didn't matter how he'd used her, how he'd cold-bloodedly taken her into his bed. All that mattered was that she loved him and he might die.

It had felt like *her* life blood oozing across the snow.

The metallic taste of fear filled her mouth as memory consumed her. Her helplessness, till she'd found Alaric's mobile phone and, miracle of miracles, discovered it still functioned. She'd felt only a desperate satisfaction that, despite what he'd led her to believe, there was perfect phone reception. Within twenty minutes medical staff had arrived by helicopter.

'Perhaps he'll visit the archives to see how we're getting on.' No missing her colleague's arch tone of enquiry. Not surprising given Alaric's previous impromptu visits.

But he'd only come because he didn't trust her.

Had he fretted all those weeks in hospital, wondering if she'd talked of what she'd found? The surveillance seemed to have stopped. She'd lost the claustrophobic sense of being watched.

'I suspect the prince has more important things to do.'

Even she had heard the speculation about Crown Prince Raul's delay in finalising his coronation, and how much time he spent closeted with his injured cousin. No doubt they were organising for Alaric to be crowned when he recovered.

He'd make an excellent monarch. Stoically she ignored the fact that his coronation would hammer the final nail in the coffin of her wishful dreams. Dreams that even his actions hadn't quite managed to stifle.

Tamsin looked at her watch. 'Time to pack up, don't you think?' She ignored her companion's curious look. For well over a month she'd faced down blatant interest about her relationship with Alaric.

Only when she was alone in the room did she slump in her chair, her heart pounding at the thought of Alaric here, in the castle again.

His pain still haunted her. Her heart ached for him and all he'd been through. Once she'd believed she could help him. As if *she*...

She bit her lip. She'd done with fantasy.

These past weeks had been a hell of worry about Alaric and constant scrutiny from the curious. Yet she'd endured. She'd put up with the gossip and completed the initial period of her contract, determined to fulfil her obligation.

Did her resolve stretch to seeing him again?

Tamsin shot to her feet, too edgy to sit. They'd find someone to replace her when she didn't renew her contract. Patrick perhaps. Strangely she felt no qualms about the idea of him here in what had been her territory.

She wouldn't return to Britain. But there'd been that offer last year of a job in Berlin, and a hint about work in Rome. She'd delayed following up either opportunity. Her lips twisted as she realised it was because in her heart she wanted to be close to Alaric.

Pathetic! There was nothing to stay for. The sooner she moved on the better. Starting with a weekend in Berlin or Rome. Either would do.

Would it be easier to heal a broken heart in new surroundings?

Out of nowhere pain surged, cramping her body and stealing the air from her lungs. It took a full minute to catch her breath and move again.

Tamsin refused to acknowledge the fear that nothing would heal what ailed her. She felt a terrible certainty that the love she still felt for Alaric, despite everything, would never be 'healed'.

'The answer is still no.' Alaric hobbled across the hospital room. He set his mouth against the pain when he moved too fast. 'I won't do it. That's final.'

'Do you think I liked the idea of an arranged marriage, either?' Raul sounded weary. They'd been over this time and again. 'It's your duty, Alaric. If you accept the crown then you accept the responsibilities that go with it.'

'Don't talk to me of duty!' Alaric's clenched fist connected with the wall but he barely felt the impact. 'I don't want this, any of it. I'm only accepting the crown because, like you, I've been brought up to do my duty.'

Strange how things had changed since the accident. His fear of failure had dimmed. He no longer got that sick feeling in his belly at the thought of ruling the nation. He could face the idea of leadership again with equanimity, though being monarch wasn't his choice.

In hospital he'd had plenty of time to think. To his surprise he'd realised how much he'd enjoyed the work he'd begun in Ruvingia. It had been satisfying solving problems and organising innovative community renewal. He'd like to follow through the improvements they'd begun in his own principality.

But as king he couldn't be so hands on. His life would be all protocol and diplomacy.

At least he knew now he could face what was required of him.

What had changed? Even the nightmares had receded a little. Because he'd broken the curse of good luck that had seen him emerge unscathed from tragedy? Because he'd shattered his body and almost lost his life, proving his mortality? No, it couldn't be that simple.

He'd been overwhelmed by the genuine distress of his people after the accident. The number of communities and groups who'd sent representatives had stunned him. They'd wished him well, and, as he recovered, sought his renewed input to their projects.

Yet Alaric knew the real change had come from his brief glimpse of happiness. The peace and sense of connection he'd felt in his short time with Tamsin. Surely that's what had hauled him back from the brink of self-destruction, giving him hope for the first time in years.

Six months ago he'd have embraced death with equanimity. But lying in hospital as doctors fussed over him; Alaric had discovered he wanted to live so badly he could taste the need.

He *had* to live, to see Tamsin and set things right.

The night he'd shared his past with her had cracked something wide open inside him. Not just his guilt and fear. But a lifetime of barriers. Barriers that had kept him cut off from love, preventing him building a real relationship.

'Alaric.' His cousin's voice yanked him from his reverie. He turned and met Raul's sympathetic look. 'I know this is hard on you.'

'Hard on us both.' Raul had been raised to be king. It was a measure of his integrity that he'd taken so well the stunning news that Alaric should be monarch. The final testing and double checking of Tamsin's document and other contemporary sources had proven her right. Alaric was destined to be king, not Raul.

Raul shrugged. 'There's no way out of the wedding. You think I haven't double checked? It's a binding agreement. The Crown Prince of Maritz is betrothed to marry the Princess of Ardissia. No negotiation.'

'Even though we don't know where she is?' If Alaric had his way they'd never locate her.

'We will soon. And when we do…' Raul shrugged.

'A royal wedding.' A loveless marriage. Surely the only sort he wanted or deserved. Yet his blood froze.

He remembered Tamsin's smile, felt the radiant warmth it brought his blighted soul. He heard her soft cries of delight as he pleasured her, smelled her fresh summer scent.

She hadn't come near him since the accident. She *hated* him for what he'd done to her.

His chances of persuading her to forgive him were slim.

But to marry another woman…

Alaric stiffened, realising there was only one way forward. It would be perhaps the most difficult thing he'd ever done, but he had no choice.

'I *beg* your pardon?' Tamsin couldn't believe her ears.

'None of the documents held in safekeeping can be released without His Highness's permission.' The secretary sounded uncomfortable.

'But it's *my* passport!' Tamsin shot to her feet, the phone pressed to her ear, then drew a calming breath. 'There must be a misunderstanding. The passport was held for safekeeping only.'

'You're planning to travel?'

Tamsin frowned. She shouldn't have to report her plans. But maybe it would stir this bureaucrat into action.

'I fly to Rome this weekend.' An overnight trip to discuss a possible job. She told herself she'd be enthusiastic about it once she got to the sunny south. 'So when can I collect it?'

Another pause. 'I'll have to get back to you on that. The prince gave specific instructions…'

A chill fingered its way down Tamsin's spine. *Alaric's* instructions? Impossible! He couldn't want her here.

Yet he'd manipulated her before. Was it possible he was doing it again? Fury sparked. She would *not* be a pawn in his games again.

The secretary was talking when she dropped the phone into its cradle.

Fifteen minutes later Tamsin entered the royal antechamber. Ironically she'd made it through security easily. Chancing to meet the servant who'd come to fetch Alaric the night of the ball, she'd asked for directions, letting him believe Alaric had sent for her.

As she entered the room a man, busy at a desk, looked up.

'The prince is not receiving visitors.'

Tamsin's eyes narrowed as she recognised his voice. The secretary who'd stonewalled her on the phone.

'This can't wait.' She kept walking.

'Wait!' His eyes flicked to the double doors on the other side of the room. 'If you take a seat I'll check the prince's schedule.'

Her pace quickened. She was sure now that Alaric was in the next room. Tamsin wasn't about to be fobbed off. Whatever was going on she'd get to the bottom of it. Now.

'Thank you. But I'll make my own appointment.'

From the corner of her eye she saw him scramble to his feet, but he was too late. She wrenched open the door and catapulted through it, her heart pounding as adrenaline surged. She'd hoped to avoid confronting Alaric again, yet part of her longed to see him one last time.

Two steps into the room she stumbled to a halt, eyes widening at the tableau before her. Alaric was there but so were many others, all formally dressed and wearing sober expressions. There was a sprinkling of uniforms, clerical robes and a few judges in old-fashioned costumes.

In the centre sat Alaric, one arm in a sling, writing at a vast desk. He put his pen down and looked up.

Lightning blasted her senses as his piercing eyes met hers down the length of the chamber. Her body quivered with the impact of that look.

Tamsin swayed and shut her eyes, aghast at her weakness. She had to get away from him once and for all. Going to Rome was the right thing.

A hand grabbed her elbow. 'My apologies for the intrusion, Highness.' The hand tugged and Tamsin opened her eyes.

The secretary's words had made everyone present turn to look. Silence reigned for a moment and despite crawling embarrassment she stood straight, facing the curiosity of the gathered VIPs.

What had she stumbled into?

'It's all right.' Alaric's voice drew her gaze to where he sat, so handsome in dress uniform. 'Dr Connors is my welcome guest.' Did she imagine his voice deepened seductively?

No! There was nothing between them. There never had been. She had to remember that.

'Of course, Your Highness.' The man released her, bowed and melted away.

Silently Alaric gestured her to a chair and she went to it gratefully. Yet she didn't sit. By now she knew she'd interrupted something important. The judges stepped forward with deep bows and signed the document Alaric passed to them. Then several others, all with a slow formality that proclaimed this a significant occasion.

Finally Alaric stood. Tamsin's heart clenched as he limped from his chair. He was pale, his face pared down. She wanted to smooth her palm across his face, trace the high slant of his cheekbone and reassure herself he was all right. Her hands trembled with the force of what she felt.

The day of the accident she'd stayed as close as she could, scared to let him out of her sight till finally the doctors pronounced him out of danger. Since then she hadn't seen him, knowing it was better that way. Yet she'd scoured the news reports for updates on his recovery.

He must have come here straight from the hospital.

Anyone else seeing his straight backed stance would think him fully recovered. But to Tamsin's eyes there was a stiffness around his neck and shoulders and a tension in his jaw that betrayed pain.

What was so important he'd left the hospital for it? Couldn't anyone else see he needed rest?

Impotent anger surged. It was no use telling herself he didn't need her sympathy. She couldn't squash her feelings.

Alaric turned to the man beside him. A tall, handsome man with familiar features. Alaric said something she couldn't hear and bent his head in a bow. But before he could complete the action the other man spoke sharply and put a hand on Alaric's shoulder.

Alaric raised his head and for a moment Tamsin saw something flash between the two. Wordless understanding. Then Alaric spoke, making his companion laugh and reach to shake his hand vigorously.

There was a burst of applause and cheers in Ruvingian that Tamsin wished she understood. The two men turned to face their audience, accepting the accolade with an ease that spoke of long practice.

She watched Alaric avidly. This might be the last time she saw him and she wanted to imprint every detail. The way he smiled. The light in his eyes as he nodded at something his companion said. Familiar hunger swamped her. It was like watching a feast through a window and knowing though you were starving you couldn't reach out and eat.

Instead she tasted the ashes of hopeless dreams on her tongue.

At a word from Alaric, the crowd began to leave. They were too well bred to stare, but she felt their surreptitious glances. Heat gathered in her cheeks but she stood her ground. She wasn't into hiding any more.

Last to leave was the tall man who'd stood with Alaric. He too was in his early thirties. He wore his hand-tailored suit with an easy elegance that might have made her stare if she hadn't been so conscious of Alaric behind him.

'Dr Connors.' The stranger lifted her hand to his lips in a courtly gesture that would stop most feminine hearts. Over his shoulder she caught Alaric's sharp stare and fire sparked in her veins.

'It's a pleasure to meet you. I'm Alaric's kinsman, Raul.'

Tamsin blinked and focused on the man who she now saw bore a striking resemblance to Alaric. Jade green eyes instead of indigo and a leaner build, but the same angled cheekbones, strong jaw and lush dark hair. The same indefinable air of power and authority.

'Your Highness.'

He smiled, unfazed by the tension emanating from his cousin's rigid form. Tamsin could feel it from where she was but Prince Raul merely released her hand slowly. 'I'll look forward to our next meeting.'

Then he was gone. She was alone with Alaric.

CHAPTER FIFTEEN

'HELLO, Tamsin. It's good to see you.'

Alaric's voice was low and smooth, evoking memories of heady passion and soft endearments. In that moment her indignation bled away, replaced by longing and regret.

'Hello, Alaric.' Her voice was breathless, as if she'd run across the castle compound and up four flights of stairs instead of being escorted in a state of the art lift.

Silence fell as their eyes locked. Tamsin wanted to look away but couldn't, mesmerised by something in his gaze she'd never seen.

Despite the sling and a slight limp as he walked towards her, Alaric was a formidable figure: handsome, virile and powerful. Tamsin's nerves stretched taut as she fought not to respond to his nearness. Yet her stomach filled with butterflies and her knees trembled.

If only she couldn't remember so clearly the bliss she'd found in his arms.

But seeing him at the centre of that gathering, easily dominating the proceedings, had reinforced everything she'd told herself the last six weeks or so. That they belonged to different worlds.

'What was that, just now?' Jerkily she gestured to the desk where so many people had come forward to sign that large parchment. 'Some sort of ceremony?'

'Royal business,' he said, watching her so intently it seemed he noted every move, every expression. Was he wondering how he'd brought himself to make love to her?

Heat rushed into her cheeks. When he didn't explain further, Tamsin understood. His silence reinforced that she had no business enquiring into matters of state. The gulf between them was unbreachable.

He seemed taller, looming over her, making her feel vulnerable. His eyes were darker. They looked almost black. Try as she might she couldn't read his shuttered expression.

He stepped near and instantly her nerve ends tingled in awareness. Automatically she inched back a step, then, realising what she was doing, planted her feet.

'How are you, Alaric?'

'As you see.' His lips twisted ruefully. 'I survived.'

'Will you recover fully?' She gestured to his stiff leg.

'I'm told so.'

Her heart thudded in relief and she clasped her hands, unable to tear her gaze from those unfathomable eyes.

'It's my fault you were injured—'

'Don't even *think* of apologising!' The words shot out like bullets. He leaned towards her, his eyebrows lowering like storm clouds over flashing eyes.

'I'm the one who's sorry.' His mouth flattened. 'I tried earlier, at the lodge, but you wouldn't accept my apologies.'

Tamsin frowned. She couldn't remember that. But the scene was a blur of misery and grief.

He shifted as if it pained him to stand. 'I had no business seducing you. You are a guest in my country, an employee.'

Tamsin didn't know why her heart shrivelled at his reminder of their relative stations. It was true yet for a bright brief period it hadn't seemed to matter. That had been an illusion. Part of his seduction technique.

'I should never have—'

'Please!' She couldn't bear him to go on, enumerating everything that had happened between them. She'd relived every moment these past weeks and it brought no solace, just aching regret like a cold lump of lead in her chest.

'Don't go on. I accept your apology.' She turned to face the glowing fire in the ornate fireplace rather than meet his intense gaze. 'You believed you were protecting your country.'

It had taken her a long time but finally she'd seen a little of his perspective. A perspective reinforced by the scene she'd just witnessed. He had responsibilities for a nation that weighed heavily.

Tamsin understood his motives but that didn't excuse his tactics. She cringed at the thought of others listening to her conversation with Patrick. And as for Alaric letting her think he really cared, really desired her...

'You're very forgiving.'

She avoided his eyes. 'I've had time to consider.'

'But there's no excuse for—'

'No, but I don't want to discuss it.' Pain clawed at her. She didn't want to revisit the details. Like how he'd bedded her as part of his scheme. Or how she'd given her heart to him.

At least he didn't know that. How much more sorry for her he'd be if he knew she'd fallen in love.

Listening to his mellow baritone was delicious torture. Being here with him was what she'd dreamed of and yet it was dangerous.

She wanted what she could never have. She'd fallen for an illusion, believing in a relationship that could never be. Pain seeped from her cracked heart.

'You saved me the trouble of coming for you.'

At his words her head jerked round. Alaric had intended to come for her? For a foolish instant hope quivered in her heart, only to be dashed by harsh reality. No doubt he'd planned to deliver his apology and suggest she leave, rather than stay and embarrass them both.

'I've come for my passport.' The words came out full of strident challenge.

Did she imagine a stiffening of his tall frame?

'You want to leave?' He frowned.

'Yes!' How could he even ask it? 'But I need my passport and I'm told I need your permission to get it.'

'What if I asked you to stay?' His eyes probed, laser bright.

'No!' Her response was instantaneous. He couldn't be so cruel as to expect her to remain. Seeing him, always from a distance, would be unbearably painful.

A sound broke across her thoughts and she looked up. Alaric's mouth had twisted up at one side.

Surely he wasn't laughing at her?

Indignation and fury warred with hurt. A voice inside protested Alaric would never be so deliberately cruel. He wasn't callous like Patrick.

But she knew to her cost men *were* cruel.

She spun on her foot and marched to the door. She'd get a lawyer to retrieve her passport.

Tamsin was reaching for the door handle when something shot over her shoulder. A hand slammed onto the door, holding it shut. Alaric's arm stretched in front of her and her skin prickled at how close he stood. His heat was like a blaze at her back.

'No!' The single syllable cracked like a gunshot. 'You're not leaving. Not like this.'

Alaric's chest ached as he forced himself to drag in oxygen. His pulse thundered, pumping adrenaline through his body. The sight of Tamsin storming out of his life had been impossible to bear.

'I refuse to stay and be the butt of your humour.'

He stared at her glossy hair, her slim shoulders and lithe body and felt heat punch his belly. She thought he'd laughed at her?

'Tamsin, no. It's not like that.' It had been more a grimace of pain than anything else. Pain that slashed bone deep. 'If I was laughing it was at myself.'

'I don't understand.' She didn't move a muscle, but neither did she try to wrestle the door open.

'I told Raul I was going to ask you to stay. I was just remembering his response.'

'You talked to your cousin about me?'

She turned, looking up with wide amber-gilt eyes that melted his bones. He shuddered with the effort of controlling the emotions threatening to unravel inside.

'He thought I'd have no trouble persuading you. Then, as soon as I suggested it, you instantly objected.' Objected! *She'd turned ashen. As if she couldn't think of anything worse than being with him.*

Fear petrified him, as strong as in that soul-wrenching moment when he'd seen her in the path of the avalanche.

What if he couldn't persuade her? Had he hurt her so much he'd destroyed his last tentative hope?

He refused to countenance the thought.

'I don't understand.' She blinked and looked away, as if she couldn't bear to look at him. He didn't blame her.

His self-control splintered. He lifted his hand, stroking knuckles down her velvet cheek. His fingers hummed as a sensation like electricity sparked beneath his skin. She gulped and a tiny fragment of hope glowed in the darkness of his heart.

'I don't want you to leave. I won't allow it.' He cupped her chin and lifted her face till she had no option but to meet his gaze. The jolt of connection as their eyes clashed shook him to the core.

'You have no right to talk about allowing.' The belligerent set of her jaw spoke both of pain and strength. His heart twisted as he recognised one of the things that drew him to her was her indomitable spirit.

'No. I have no right.' The pain of these past weeks returned full force. 'But I'm too selfish to give up. *I'll make you stay.* Whether I have to persuade you or seduce you or imprison you in the highest tower.' Her lips parted in shock. The urge to kiss her soft mouth was almost more than he could bear.

'You're crazy.' She stepped away, only to back into the door. Alaric paced forward till a hair's breadth separated them. Tamsin drew a strained breath and the sensation of her breasts brushing against him made him groan. It had been so long since he'd held her. Too long since he'd kissed her.

'No!' She held him at bay.

She didn't want him after what he'd done.

'Tamsin, I…' He hesitated, groping for words to express unfamiliar feelings. Feelings he hadn't believed in before her.

'Let me go, Alaric.' She looked away, blinking. 'I don't know what new game this is but I've had enough.'

'Sh, darling, I know.' Gently he brushed a strand of hair off her face, his heart twisting as she flinched from his touch. But he couldn't resist tracing the line of her throat down to the pulse hammering at her collarbone.

'It's not a game. It's gone far beyond that. Once, in my complacency, I planned to seduce you.' Pain wrapped gnarled fingers around his heart as he read her anguish.

'I told myself it was for the benefit of the nation I kept you close, kept you with me, even kidnapped you.' He drew a breath that racked his body. 'But from the start I lied, not just to *you* but to myself. I plotted to get you into my bed *because I wanted you*. I needed you as I've never needed anyone. I couldn't stop thinking about you. Not your chronicle and your news about the throne, but you.'

He tunnelled his good hand through her hair, revelling in its silk caress and the warmth of her close to him. For the first time since the accident he felt *complete*.

'You don't know how I've missed you.' His voice was a hoarse groan and her eyes riveted to his. He was drowning in warm, amber depths.

'I fell for you, Tamsin. That's why I kidnapped you. The rest was an excuse.' She shook her head but he pressed on. 'At first you were a problem with your unwanted news. But you were a conundrum, too, a woman I couldn't get out of my head. You intrigued me. I've never met anyone like you.'

'Because I'm a misfit, is that it?' Her eyes shimmered, overbright.

'You? A misfit? The way you charmed ambassadors and aristocrats and commoners alike at the ball? The way you bonded with those teenagers at the community centre? I hear you've kept visiting and they love it. And your staff in the archives have nothing but admiration and liking for you.'

'You've been spying on me again?'

'No!' It had gone against the grain the first time. He'd never do that again. 'Their permanent employer wants them back and they petitioned my staff to remain. While you stay they want to.'

He watched her eyes widen. She genuinely had no idea how special she was with her talents, her intellect and above all her passion.

'I used every excuse I could think of to keep you with me, Tamsin. But the truth is I did it all because I wanted you.' Even though he didn't deserve her, he was too selfish to let her go.

'I still want you. I need you.' Saying it aloud for the first time Alaric was stunned by the force of his emotions. Emotions he'd never thought to experience. Emotions strong enough to obliterate a lifetime's cynicism.

She shook her head so vigorously her hair came down to swirl like a dark cloud around her. He wanted to bury his face in it, inhale her sweet scent and lose himself.

But her pain, like a razor wire fence between them, held him back.

'I'm a novelty. A change from your sophisticated women.' Bitterness laced her voice. 'You don't need me.'

'You *are* different.' He reached for her hand and planted it over his chest, pressing it to his pounding heart. 'For the first time in so long I *feel*, Tamsin. It scared the life out of me. That's why I kept telling myself it wasn't real.'

'No!' Her shout startled them both. 'Please, don't. This isn't real. You feel guilty, that's all.'

Alaric looked into Tamsin's taut features, searching for a softening, some proof she cared. But there was nothing, only pain. The tiny flame of hope flickered perilously and his chest hollowed.

Had he lost his one chance of happiness?

'I love you.' He swallowed and it was like every broken dream scored his throat. He'd never thought it possible to feel so much and it scared him as nothing ever had.

'I realised that as I lay in hospital and replayed every mistake I'd made. That's why I signed myself out early, to come and tell you. *I love you.*'

She stood like a statue, her brow furrowed and her mouth a tight line.

He'd never felt like this, never told any other woman he loved her.

He'd expected a better response!

Alaric was tempted to kiss her into compliance. He could win her body. Yet he wanted her mind too. Her heart.

'You don't believe me?'

'I…don't know. It seems so unlikely.' She looked so dazed his heart squeezed in sympathy. Or was that fear?

'Then believe this. That scene you walked in on? I wanted it over before I came to you today.' His lips twisted, thinking how Tamsin always managed to turn his plans on their head. 'The reason for all the witnesses was because I wanted there to be no question about my actions.' He drew a slow breath and squeezed her hand. 'I just signed away my claim to the throne of Maritz. Raul will be king after all.'

'You did *what*? Oh, Alaric! You'd make a wonderful king. You mightn't be able to see it but I can. And I'm not the only one. The—'

He silenced her with a finger on her lips, telling himself soon he'd feel their soft caress with his mouth.

'It's all right, Tamsin. I didn't do it because I feared to take the throne.' That was well and truly behind him, though it warmed him to have her as such a passionate advocate. Hope flared again and excitement sizzled in his bloodstream.

'I discovered the king is obligated to marry a princess from Ardissia. I'd have to take on the throne and a ready-made wife. When it came to the crunch I couldn't do it. I'd accept the king-ship and all its responsibilities but I can't marry another woman. Not when I love you.'

'*You did that for me?* You hardly know me!'

'I know you, Tamsin. I know the real you.'

He'd never known a lovelier woman.

He looked down into her stunned face. Her hair was loose around her shoulders. Her intelligent eyes were bright, her skin glowed and the delicate curve of her cheek made him want to stroke her till she purred. She wore a fitted russet suit he'd never seen before. It skimmed her curves in a way that made his hor-mones rev into high gear.

'You've bought new clothes.' He frowned. He wasn't sure he wanted her looking good for anyone but him.

'You really abdicated?' She cut across him, staring as if she'd never seen him before. 'But that's…'

Her lips curved in a tremulous smile that snared his heart all over again and sent heat scudding through every tense muscle. 'I can't believe you gave up a crown for me.'

'In the end it wasn't the crown I objected to.' He hauled her close with one arm, his pulse racing. 'It was the bride. I prefer to choose my own.'

Cool palms slid around his neck as she pressed close, her eyes a blaze of molten gold. It was like staring into the sun. Surely she couldn't look at him like that and not…

He took his courage in his hands.

'Tamsin, could you forget the past and start again?'

For what seemed an age she stood silent. He held his breath.

'I don't want to forget,' she murmured. 'You've given me so much.' Her smile warmed every corner of his soul and his pulse tripped into overdrive.

'Tamsin.' His voice was so husky he had to clear his throat. 'Could you live with a man who's made mistakes? Who still has to learn to how to settle down? A man with a scandalous reputation?' He lifted her palm to his lips. 'A man who has occasional nightmares about the past?'

'I could.' She looked so solemn, as if making a vow. 'If you're *sure*?'

The doubt in her eyes made him vow to prove to her, daily, how much she meant to him. 'Never more so, my love.'

'A scandalous reputation sounds intriguing.' Her expression grew tender. 'And as for nightmares…they'll pass with time and help.'

She leaned up on tiptoe, her mouth brushing his in the lightest of kisses.

'I love you, Alaric. I fell for you the night we met. I still can't believe—'

He slanted his mouth over hers, relief and triumph and love overwhelming him.

She was his! He'd silence the last of her doubts. He'd devote his life to making her happy.

Much later, when the flare of passion threatened to roar out of control, Alaric stepped away.

'What are you doing? Alaric! Your leg!'

Ignoring the pain he finally managed to settle on his good knee. He held her hand tight in his, their fingers threaded together.

'I'm proposing. I want to do this right.'

'Oh.'

She looked stunned. He'd finally found a way to silence her. But she confounded him by dropping to the floor in front of him.

'Yes,' she said, her voice breathless.

'I haven't asked you yet.' He couldn't prevent the grin that split his face. Joy welled in an unstoppable flood.

'I'm saving time. You have to get off that knee.'

'In that case…' He pulled her off balance as he toppled back onto the thick carpet. She sprawled over him and his unruly body stirred.

'Alaric!' Tamsin gasped as he pulled her down hard over his groin. 'We can't. We shouldn't. You're just out of hospital!'

'We can. We will.' He kissed her soft lips and sighed his pleasure. 'You can spend your life reforming me.'

'Never. I love you just the way you are.'

She kissed him and Alaric silently gave thanks. In Tamsin he'd found the one perfect woman to make his life complete. He'd found love.

EPILOGUE

THE Gothic cathedral glowed as afternoon sunlight poured through the stained-glass windows. The scent of candles mingled with expensive perfumes and the fragrance of fresh flowers that were massed everywhere.

It was like a dream, walking down the aisle, the focus of every look. The place was crowded. Aristocracy from all around Europe, diplomats and community leaders, plus members of the public who'd been lucky enough to win a ballot to attend. But among them Tamsin spotted familiar faces: her colleagues, friends from the youth centre, Alaric's old comrades, smiling as they nodded encouragingly. Even her parents, looking proud and slightly bewildered.

But she'd barely been able to tear her gaze from the man who watched her every step with an intensity that sent heat and excitement spiralling through her.

Alaric. Tall, proud and handsome in his uniform.

His cousin Raul had stood beside him, stunningly good looking with his killer smile and black as night hair. Yet Tamsin had barely spared him a glance, her whole being focused on the man she was to marry.

Seeing the love in Alaric's eyes had made it all real as nothing else had. The luxuriously embroidered crimson velvet gown and its long train had felt unfamiliar and daunting as it trailed impressively behind her. The weight of the delicate beaten gold diadem had made her nervous, as had the filigree collar of gold and rubies circling her throat.

When she'd entered the cathedral to the triumphant blare of trumpets and swelling organ music she'd felt like an impostor, a little girl pretending to be a princess.

But from the moment Alaric's gaze had locked with hers joy had sung in her heart and the world had righted itself.

This was so right she almost cried with happiness.

Now, with the ceremony over, they faced the congregation. Alaric stood behind her and in defiance of all protocol wrapped his arms around her, pulling her close.

'Tamsin?' Pleasure skated through her at the intimate purr of his voice saying her name.

'Yes?' She struggled to focus on the smiling throng and not Alaric's hot breath feathering her neck.

'No regrets?'

'Never!' She twisted round in his arms to see his indigo eyes dark with love. Neither heard the jubilant roar of the crowd as she kissed him full on the mouth and he responded emphatically.

Afterwards everyone present attested Prince Alaric and his bride had broken tradition and married for love.

THE ROYAL MARRIAGE

BY
FIONA HOOD-STEWART

Fiona Hood-Stewart was born in Scotland and brought up internationally. She went to boarding school in Switzerland, and then to several European universities. When Fiona married, she moved to South America where she ran her own design business before turning to fashion, for which she created her own label and opened several boutiques in Brazil and the US.

However, like the characters in her novels, Fiona has always been mystically drawn back to Scotland. She is well acquainted with all the locales that are visited in all her novels, which she infuses with her own life experiences. As she speaks seven languages fluently, Fiona has a unique insight and exposure into customs and lifestyles of foreign countries.

Fiona divides her time between Europe and her ranch in Brazil. She has two sons and travels frequently to Paris, New York and can be seen at the races in Deauville in France, or at Royal Ascot in the UK.

Fiona credits her mother with putting her on the path to becoming a writer. "My mother always read aloud to me as a child. She didn't approve of television and I spent many hours with my nose in a book. As a child I read everything I could get my hands on."

CHAPTER ONE

As THE four-by-four SUV raced over a bumpy road in the arid north-eastern Brazilian countryside, HRH Prince Ricardo of Maldoravia asked himself—not for the first time—what had induced him to accept an invitation that could only lead to trouble.

He glanced at the SUV's driver—a small, wiry individual in designer sunglasses, brown as a nut, with a wide smile and an attitude when it came to dealing with the local police. They seemed to enjoy stopping a car on the road for no apparent purpose other than to check papers, then hum and ha for a while, before sending its occupants on their way. Ricardo then glanced at his watch: three-thirty-five. The intense heat outside had penetrated the interior of the SUV, despite its tinted windows and the air-conditioning, which was on full blast. From his limited Portuguese, he understood the journey would take at least another hour. And that, he realised, could signify anything: time here had a different meaning.

He leaned back and stretched his legs as far as they would go. He must, he concluded wryly, be crazy to have accepted his late father's old friend's invitation. Gonzalo Guimaraes and his parent had studied together at Eton and Oxford many years ago, and although their lives had taken very different routes—Ricardo's father becoming ruler of the small island Principality of Maldoravia in the Mediterranean, and

7

Gonzalo heading back to his vast Brazilian *fazenda*—the two men had enjoyed a lifelong friendship. And in all those years Ricardo had never known Gonzalo to ask for any favours. Which was what made the request for Ricardo to visit him in his fiefdom all the more intriguing.

They were driving along the coastline now, and the landscape had changed: rolling waves, white sand and scattered coconut trees swayed with samba-like rhythm in the summer breeze. Two skimpily dressed men sat by the roadside, seemingly oblivious to the blazing sun. Another led a packed mule at a gentle pace. Speed was apparently not a factor in this part of the world. At one point Ricardo could see a little bronzed boy of about ten holding up a snake with the hopes of selling it to one of the few passers-by heading along the dust-bitten road.

So, although he had misgivings about the trip, Ricardo was fascinated. It was not the first time he'd visited Brazil—he'd made a brief visit to Rio a few years ago, for Carnival. But what he was seeing here and now was a very different country, one locked in a time warp where not much had changed and where the outside world meant little.

An hour and a half later they turned left down an earth road and the driver pointed to huge gates surrounded by coconut trees. Beyond them Ricardo spied a small bridge. Thick vegetation hid whatever else lay beyond. At the gates several dark-suited guards came out and greeted them. One bowed and, through gold teeth and in broken English, bade him welcome. Then the gates opened electronically and the vehicle proceeded at a more sober pace up a driveway bordered by a vivid mass of multi-coloured hibiscus and bou-

gainvillaea. To the right more coconut trees framed
the cerulean ocean. The driveway, Ricardo noted, was
in considerably better repair than the highway.

About a mile and a half farther on a sprawling mansion came into view—a maze of whitewashed walls
and low-lying red-tiled roofs emerging from a panoply
of lush vegetation. It was strangely harmonious, as
though the architect had felt entirely in tune with his
surroundings.

'We here,' Lando, the driver, proclaimed triumphantly as he stamped on the brakes and the SUV
came to a standstill. Ricardo smiled thankfully. He
wondered why Gonzalo didn't have a private airstrip,
which would have made life a lot easier; he could
certainly afford it.

Then servants appeared, doors opened, and as
Ricardo exited the vehicle he saw Gonzalo, a man of
medium height, brown and wiry—rather like the
SUV's driver—in a short-sleeved white shirt and beige
trousers, his thick white hair swept back, coming down
some shallow steps to greet him.

'My friend,' he said, with a broad smile of greeting,
'welcome to my home.'

'Thank you. I'm happy to be here.' The two men
shook hands warmly.

'I'm sorry we couldn't send the plane to pick you
up in Recife, but there has been a problem with our
radar system and in this back-of-beyond place we have
to wait two days for the specialist to arrive. Usually
my own team can take care of minor problems, but
I'm afraid this time it was too complex. Come in out
of the heat,' Gonzalo insisted.

Ricardo obeyed gladly and stepped inside a huge

cool marble hall. 'It certainly is hot out there,' he re-marked.

'At least forty degrees today,' Gonzalo agreed, lead-ing the way into a vast living room decorated with modern white sofas, Persian rugs, exotic plants and tasteful antiques. The panoramic view over the ocean was magnificent.

'You have a beautiful place here,' Ricardo said, gazing out, impressed. There was something wild and untamed about the landscape—something he couldn't define but that he found viscerally disturbing.

The two men sat down on the sofas and two uni-formed maids materialised with coffee and fruit juice.

'This fruit is *umbu*,' Gonzalo said as Ricardo tasted the refreshing juice. 'It is typical of the north-east of the country. We have a great variety of fruit here.'

'Delicious.' Ricardo was still wondering what it was that had triggered Gonzalo's urgent message. He was travelling incognito, having left his usual retinue be-hind in Maldoravia, and he was enjoying the freedom this allowed him. Right now he was content to bide his time. So, instead of showing overt curiosity as to why Gonzalo had summoned him, he sipped his juice and waited. Three years as ruler of the Principality had taught him patience. He had no doubt that all would be revealed in good time.

Several minutes later Gonzalo was conducting him up a wide marble staircase, past walls covered with bright colourful paintings that Gonzalo explained were from local and other South American artists, to a large suite of rooms. There the maids were already unpack-ing his belongings.

'I suggest you take a rest,' Gonzalo said. 'When it is cooler we can meet for drinks downstairs and chat.'

'That sounds perfect,' Ricardo replied.

A few minutes later he was under the shower, enjoying the rush of ice-cold water. When he got out he sleeked back his dark hair and twisted a bath towel around his waist. He was a tall, well-built man. At thirty-three, several years of working out had left him with a trim, sculpted body. His dark brown eyes surveyed the reflection of his finely chiselled face in the bathroom mirror as he debated whether he needed another shave.

Water still trickled down his tanned back as he moved across the marble floor towards French windows and opened the doors. As he stepped out onto the balcony he was met by a pleasant breeze. The scorching heat of earlier in the day had subsided. Leaning on the balustrade, he looked out towards the rolling sand dunes and the bright blue sea, intrigued. From here, the next port of call, he reflected thoughtfully, was Africa. There was clarity and luminosity now that the heat haze had subsided, leaving the coconut trees and the rich vegetation distinct.

Ricardo stretched. He was about to turn back inside and lie down when a movement in the far distance caught his eyes. Shading them from the setting sun, he watched a straight-backed female figure astride a handsome white horse approaching along the beach at a gentle canter. It made a pleasant picture. As she drew closer he could make out her lithe movements, and her long dark hair flowing wildly in the wind. The woman and the animal blended as though they were one.

Ricardo stood glued to the spot, watching as she reined the horse in, then dismounted easily onto the sand and shook her hair back. The horse stood obediently as she removed her jeans and shirt, revealing long bronzed limbs and a perfectly proportioned body encased in a tiny white bikini. Then, like a top model on a Parisian catwalk, she glided towards the water and entered the spray, dipped under a wave and then emerged. He could hear her laughing and calling to the horse. A smile broke on his lips as the animal trotted into the water and together they frolicked. It was a magical scene, unreal. A beautiful deserted landscape, a girl and a horse so in tune with one another. Like something out of a movie.

He wondered who she was. He knew little about Gonzalo's family—only that he had been a widower for many years. He had never met any of Gonzalo's children. Certainly he had never heard his own father mention any.

He stood straighter and observed the girl lead the horse out of the water, back to where she'd left her clothes. Even at this distance it was confirmed to him that her figure was almost perfect, and he experienced a rush of raw sexual attraction. Then, throwing her garments up on the horse, the girl leapt into the saddle.

Ricardo drew in his breath as she galloped off into the rich crimson sunset.

'You must naturally be wondering why I asked you to come here at a moment's notice,' Gonzalo remarked as, later, the two men sat on the lushly decorated veranda, which was furnished with dark rattan chairs upholstered with comfortable white cushions, low coffee tables and tropical plants.

It was pleasantly cool now. A gentle breeze blew in from the sea and a delicate crescent moon shone above them at a right angle. Night had fallen quickly due, Ricardo knew, to the proximity of the Equator.

Brightly etched stars dotted the inky sky even though it was still early. He could even distinguish the Southern Cross.

'I must confess to curiosity,' he said, taking a sip of whisky, studying his host.

'Then I shall not beat about the bush,' Gonzalo replied, with a wise, knowing smile that held a touch of sadness. 'I am an old man, Ricardo, and unfortunately my health is not in the best of shape.'

'I'm sorry to hear it.'

'So am I. Not for myself, you understand, but for one that I must leave behind when the time comes to pass on.'

'I wasn't aware that you were married.'

'I'm not now. I have been a widower for many years. I had no children from my first marriage. But years ago I had an affair with a young woman—a young English film star whose movie I financed. We were married in secret, as she didn't want the publicity to affect her career, but she was killed in a plane crash just two months after our daughter was born.'

Ricardo said nothing, merely crossed one leg over his knee and waited. Some favour was about to be asked, he was sure.

'Last month my doctors in New York told me that I have less than a year to live. It's cancer, I'm afraid, and it's terminal. I have only a few months left.'

'I'm deeply sorry,' Ricardo said, truly sad for his father's old friend. 'What can I do to help?'

Gonzalo took his time, swivelled his glass in his fingers, then looked Ricardo straight in the eye. 'Marry my daughter.'

'Excuse me?' Ricardo sat straighter. He had expected a request—but hardly this.

'I would like you to consider marriage to my daughter. A marriage of convenience. It is not unusual in your world. The Maldoravian royal family have always had planned marriages, as far as I can gather.'

'Maybe, but—'

'Even your own parents' marriage was arranged, dear boy. And I gather a marriage of convenience was what your father had planned for you, was it not?'

'That's all very well,' Ricardo countered. 'But my father is dead and times have changed, Gonzalo. I lead my own life now.'

'And from all I've heard you are enjoying it very thoroughly,' Gonzalo replied with a touch of dry humour. 'But you are thirty-three years old, Ricardo, and the succession must be thought of. Is there anyone you would consider as a future wife?'

'Well, actually, I haven't got around to thinking of marriage yet,' Ricardo replied, a picture of Ambrosia, his exotic Mexican mistress, forming in his mind. He had no intention of giving her up, even though marriage would never come into it. 'There is still time ahead of me.'

'Perhaps. I am not asking you to change your lifestyle, merely to consider an arrangement that could be advantageous to both parties. After all, you need an heir—and a wife who is both suitable socially and a virgin. Also, it has come to my knowledge,' Gonzalo added with a speculative look before Ricardo could interrupt, 'that your uncle Rolando has made some unfortunate deals for the Principality.'

This last was true. But how this knowledge, which had been kept very secret in the family, could have reached Gonzalo was beyond him. Ricardo experienced a twitch of irritation. Time to tread very carefully, he realised, on the alert now.

'There have been one or two unfortunate incidents,' he said guardedly, 'but nothing serious.'

'No. But I remember your father telling me that it is written in the Maldoravian constitution that until you marry you are still obliged to accept your uncle's participation in the Principality's government, aren't you? And, should you die without issue, he will automatically become ruler. A daunting thought,' Gonzalo murmured, letting his words sink in.

'That is true.' There was an edge of bitterness to Ricardo's voice. His uncle had been nothing but trouble with his profligate lifestyle. The fact that he was second in line to the throne was subtly brought home to Ricardo by his Cabinet on every possible occasion.

'What I propose,' Gonzalo continued smoothly, 'is a scheme that could help you organise your affairs satisfactorily and help me die in peace.'

'Gonzalo, I would love to help you, but—'

'Your father and I used to talk of this sometimes— jokingly, you understand. But now time is of the essence. My daughter, Gabriella, is nineteen. She will inherit my entire fortune—which, though I say it myself, is sizeable. I cannot leave her unprotected. I fear for her future. I would like to know that she will be marrying someone who will respect her and take care of her affairs, as I know you would. There would be many other advantages to the match, of course, but those we can discuss in due course.'

'I think I had better make it quite clear,' Ricardo replied coldly 'that I consider marriage a big step. I do not view it as a business arrangement, and I am afraid that I must therefore decline. If there is anything

I can do to help protect your daughter in other ways, then you can count on me. But I'm afraid marriage is out.'

Gonzalo smiled. 'I expected this reaction. It proves you are truly the kind of man I thought you had grown into. Your father's son. But enough for now. Let us relax and talk of other matters.'

At that moment the clipped echo of high heels on marble interrupted the conversation. Ricardo turned. Gonzalo's head flew up and a warm smile lit his eyes.

'Querida,' he said, rising, as did Ricardo. 'Come in and let me introduce you to His Royal Highness Prince Ricardo of Maldoravia.'

He was certainly handsome, even if he was quite old, Gabriella reflected as she glided into the room, eyeing Ricardo askance out of the corner of her eye. But she knew exactly what her father was up to and had no intention of co-operating. Why he had suddenly become fixed on marrying her off to someone when she had very different plans for her future was beyond her. She would let this man know exactly what she thought of the whole scheme. But for now she would play their game, get her own show on the road, and then, when the time came, she would twist her father round her little finger—as she always had.

'Ricardo—this is my daughter, Gabriella.'

Stopping in front of Ricardo, she extended long, tapered, tanned fingers. 'Good evening,' she said coolly. 'Welcome to the Fazenda Boa Luz.'

'Good evening.' Ricardo spontaneously raised her fingers to his lips, recognising Gabriella as the girl he'd seen earlier on the beach. He had rarely beheld a more beautiful young woman. She carried herself with such grace and elegance that it was difficult to believe someone so young could have acquired this kind of poise.

Gabriella sat down gracefully next to her father. Her flimsy white spaghetti-strapped chiffon dress emphasised the delicate curves of her slim, sinuous body. The single diamond at her throat shone against her tanned skin. Her long black hair cascaded silkily to her waist and her large green eyes shone, but her straight, chiselled nose looked almost disdainful as she crossed her legs. The chiffon parted, revealing never-ending limbs. She was a picture of studied elegance.

Ricardo wondered if she knew of her father's plan. There was a proud, rebellious glint in her eye that reminded him of the rolling waves and untamed natural beauty he'd observed earlier in the day. Another rush of heat gripped him. He took a long sip of whisky and disguised the desire that had sparked within him.

Just as conversation was about to resume, a uniformed servant appeared. 'There is a call for you from Brasilia in the study, Seu Gonzalo,' he murmured to his master.

'Ah, yes. Will you excuse me?' Gonzalo got up and disappeared through the wide double doors.

Ricardo and Gabriella sat in silence. She made no effort to engage him in conversation, simply smiled at the servant as he placed a flute of champagne before her on the low coffee table.

'Do you live here all year round?' Ricardo asked at last, letting his eyes course lazily over her. This girl was far too confident for her own good.

'No. I travel and study. I was at school in Switzerland until six months ago.'

'I see. What do you plan to study?'

'There is no need for you to make polite conversation with me,' she replied, her gaze haughty. Her English was perfect, except for a slight sexy lilt. 'I know exactly why you are here and I despise you for it.' Her eyes blazed suddenly like two glittering emeralds.

'You do?' Ricardo raised an amused brow, intrigued by her candour.

'Yes. You have come here to inspect me, as you might a filly, because Father wants you to marry me. I don't know why he has taken this idea into his head, but you could have saved yourself the trouble of your journey. I find it rather amusing that you should travel halfway across the world on a fool's errand.'

'You don't say?' Ricardo's voice was smoothly sardonic. His brow rose once more and he leaned back against the cushions, preparing to enjoy himself. Both beautiful and amusing. And in need of a sharp lesson. Had he been at home in his palazzo, his retinue would have rolled their eyes, aware of the danger signs. HRH was charming, but when crossed…

'Yes,' Gabriella continued obliviously. 'My advice to you is that you tell him right away that you don't agree to the plan. It'll make this so much simpler for all of us.' She took a long sip of champagne, sat back languidly on the sofa and flicked an invisible speck of dust from the skirt of her dress.

'Then you will be glad to know that I already have,' Ricardo replied smoothly, masking his amusement.

'You did?' The sophisticated camouflage dropped for a few surprised seconds, and he watched, intrigued, as her pride wobbled and the wind was neatly taken out of her sails.

'Yes. Like you, I find the whole idea of a planned

marriage with a stranger intolerable, and I entirely agree that it is far better to scotch any illusions your father may have right away. I'm glad we both feel the same way,' he added with a warm smile.

'Uh, yes, of course. But didn't you know why he'd asked you to come?'

'Actually, no. I only learned the reason a few minutes ago. But don't worry. I made quite sure there could be no doubt as to my reply. I have no desire to get married. Much less to an unknown nineteen-year-old,' he finished lazily.

Gabriella seethed inwardly. How dared he talk to her like this? She sent him back a bright brittle smile that revealed a row of perfect white teeth. 'That's wonderful. I'm so glad we see things eye to eye. Lucky, isn't it?'

'Isn't it? So, you see, now we can relax and you can tell me all about this place. After all, as you so rightly pointed out, I have came all this way on a wild goose chase, and I might as well spend a few days getting to know the region. I've never been to this part of Brazil before.'

'Naturally you must stay,' Gabriella replied, quickly retrieving her poise, once again the perfect hostess.

This man, she realised uncomfortably, was nothing like the picture she'd created in her imaginative mind. He was neither fat nor ugly, nor did he leer. Well, actually, she'd known that already, from having read about him in glossy magazines. But still. Not only was he devastatingly and disturbingly handsome, but there was something about him that attracted her in a way she'd never experienced before.

And he had the nerve to make it quite clear he wasn't interested in her!

That had never happened before. Since her early childhood Gabriella Guimaraes had been brought up to consider herself a rare beauty, a wealthy heiress, and a great catch. It came as a disconcerting blow to realise he was watching her rather as he might an amusing puppy. Well, that would not last long, she determined. A glint entered her emerald-tinted eyes as she leaned forward to reach for her glass, making sure she revealed a little more bronzed leg. He might not want to marry her, but she would make damn sure he knew exactly who he was dealing with. Gabriella Guimaraes was used to crooking her finger and watching all the young men she knew crawl, drooling, at her feet. She was not about to see that change.

Prince or no Prince.

CHAPTER TWO

THE horses moved abreast of one another, one white, one chestnut, galloping across the wet sand and kicking up a spray as they raced along the beach towards the setting sun, which was etched like a stark ball of fire on the pink horizon.

Ricardo had spent a pleasant day driving around the estate with Gonzalo. Then they'd returned for a late lunch of *ensopado de camarao*, a delicious dish of shrimp stew prepared with coconut milk, accompanied by white rice, black beans and *farofa*—a preparation of manioc flour and butter—and washed down with a Caipirinha—sugar cane alcohol with crushed lime and ice.

Then, after a siesta, Gonzalo had suggested Ricardo and Gabriella take a ride.

'Take your swimming shorts,' Gonzalo had said to Ricardo, 'and you can have a swim—either in the ocean or at the *cachoeira*. Gabriella will show you. She goes there regularly.'

And now here they were, galloping along the ocean's edge, the scent of the sea filling their nostrils, a soft wind caressing their skin.

'Follow me.' Gabriella twisted around in her saddle and called out suddenly. Then, changing direction, she headed up the beach and galloped inland, towards a tropical landscape of heavy vegetation that reminded him of the rainforest. Soon they were moving at a slower pace along a path through a maze of tropical trees interspersed with glimmers of red sunlight. Ricardo followed, watching the slim figure in the saddle before him, her hair catching the glinting light.

Then, when he least expected it, the thick vegetation gave way and they rode into a clearing. To his surprise Ricardo saw a small natural lake, at the far end of which a waterfall cascaded over stark rocks into silent dark green waters. It was extraordinarily beautiful.

'Isn't it lovely?' Gabriella exclaimed proudly, leaping off her horse. 'This is where we'll swim.'

'It's amazing,' Ricardo agreed, following suit and leaving his horse to graze as she had, watching her as once again she slipped off her clothes. He stood a moment appreciating the view: her body was spectacular, bronzed and smooth, her limbs long and lithe, her yellow bikini tiny. Yet there was nothing provocative in her stance. She was graceful and sexy, yet he got the impression she was not fully aware of just how sexy she actually was. He took a deep breath, then removed his own jeans and joined her at the water's edge.

Gabriella flashed him a quick, challenging smile. 'Race you to the other side,' she said, diving expertly in.

With no hesitation Ricardo followed. They were head-to-head when he realised Gabriella was an excellent swimmer. But soon he was several strokes ahead, and waiting for her when she reached the other side.

Her head emerged from the water, hair sleeked

back, eyes flashing. Ricardo grinned wickedly as they faced one another. A rush of desire coursed through him as she stood with the water barely reaching her hips, arched, then sank and dipped her head back in the water again, revealing the perfect curve of her small, firm breasts.

'You're not a bad swimmer for a prince,' she remarked with a pout as she straightened up again.

'What has my being a prince got to do with my swimming abilities?' He laughed, watching as she waded into even shallower water, her movements emphasising the curves of her exquisite figure.

'Nothing.' She shrugged, laughing too. 'I just thought that a prince would stay in a stuffy palace and be terribly correct. You don't seem prince-like at all.'

'Well, I'm glad I've restored your faith in princes,' Ricardo replied, amused. 'I do that too—being correct and stuffy, I mean—but not right now.' Instinctively he moved closer to her, the desire to touch her, to feel that delicious skin and that body in his arms overwhelming.

'I imagined you differently,' she said, sinking into the water and floating on her back.

'Really? How?'

'Well, you are quite old, of course, so I thought you'd be more serious. Hey, I'm going to stand under the waterfall. Want to come?'

'Why not?' Together they moved towards the rush of water. 'Usually I swim naked here,' she said with a touch of regret. 'It feels great.'

'Don't let me inhibit you.'

She moved from under the spray and looked at him

speculatively, her eyes filled with haughty challenge and a touch of doubt. Then she tossed her head and sent him a challenging glare. 'Okay. Hold on to this for me, will you?' Wriggling provocatively under the water, which barely covered her breasts, she slipped off the brief bikini and handed it to him. Then, before he could react, she was swimming away—a lissome, bewitching mermaid, playing a nimble game of hide-and-seek in the deep dark waters.

Ricardo watched her, fascinated, desire clouding his reason. Without hesitation he removed his swimming shorts. Tossing them to where Gabriella's bikini lay, he swam after her, catching her waist and turning her abruptly about.

'This is a dangerous game you're playing, little girl,' he murmured, his voice husky with pent-up desire as he drank in her full parted lips, her challenging yet hesitant eyes, her laughing head thrown back. But as his arms came around her he felt her stiffen, saw her sea-green eyes turn dark with doubt.

But it was too late.

Before she could move he drew her more firmly into his arms, felt the soft curve of her breast meet his hard chest, heard the quick indrawn breath. Instinctively his hands glided down her back. His cupped her firm, beautifully curved bottom and pressed her closer against him, until she felt the hardness of his desire. He saw her lips part in surprise, felt her gesture of restraint, saw the doubt in her eyes and knew he should stop. Instead his lips came down on hers, parting, seeking, provoking a soft yet anxious response as expertly he kissed her.

Gabriella had wanted to provoke him, but this was not at all the reaction she had expected. She had been kissed before—usually at a school dance—but had always found it boring. She was used to being in control, the one who decided when it would begin and when it would end. But now she was out of her league. She had never stood naked in a man's arms before, and as Ricardo's hand reached her breast she let out a gasp. She had never meant for anything like this to occur. Yet it was so new, so wonderful, so delicious, so incredibly sensual that all she could do was wind her arms about his neck and feel, letting her body cleave to his. It was an incredible sensation. Never had she been so close to a man. She knew she was the one who had sought the situation and that it was too late to draw back, even had she wanted to.

They kissed again. The movement of the water had brought them back beneath the rushing waterfall. Gabriella gasped as his thumb grazed her taut, aching nipples and her body arched with a new and pounding desire. She let out a tiny cry of delight as he played with her, slowly, expertly, drawing something from deep inside her that she couldn't describe, it travelled so deep. Then his fingers coursed down, seeking between her thighs, and she drew back, breathless.

'No,' she murmured, swallowing, catching her breath and shaking her head as she broke out of his arms.

Their eyes met—his clouded with desire, hers sparkling with new sensations mixed with misgiving.

'Gabriella, you wanted this,' Ricardo murmured, reaching his hand out and drawing her back towards him, thinking in the back of his mind that her father obviously had false illusions about her if he believed she was a virgin.

'I—I… No. We mustn't.' She shook her head again, let her fingers course down his chest and let out a sigh.

'Why not? You were obviously enjoying yourself,' he said, with a touch of arrogant masculine pride.

'My father would kill us.'

He looked down into her eyes, drowning there. His hands returned to her breasts and he caught her short gasp. 'You want this as much as I do. Don't deny it,' he muttered, slipping his fingers between her thighs and drawing her back into his arms.

She was delicious, the most delicious woman he had known for years. Only in his very early youth had he experienced the range of sensations that gripped him now. Lifting her legs around his waist, he felt her arms encircle his neck, saw her lips part and her wet skin shining as their shadows reflected in the still water. Her eyes were filled with longing and her breasts peaked with unrepentant longing. It was too much to resist. Guiding himself, he'd prepared to thrust inside her when she let out a sharp cry. Immediately he stopped and withdrew. But, catching her waist, he pulled her back to him.

'I—I can't,' she cried, turning her head away. 'I've never—I…'

'Why didn't you tell me that you were a virgin?' Ricardo asked, his expression dark with anger.

'I…' She swallowed, looked away again, then tilted her chin, her proud profile stubborn. She shrugged.

'I am not in the habit of deflowering virgins,' he

snapped. His hands dropped and he moved away to the wake's edge. Leaping out, he dressed quickly and mounted his horse. 'If this is the way you behave with men, I would counsel you to be more careful. One day you may come across someone who isn't quite as controlled as I am.' With that he wheeled his horse around, leaving Gabriella standing in the water.

She let out a ragged sigh. What had she been thinking of? She felt a rush of tears surface. It was all so difficult. Her father was determined that she should marry—that she shouldn't go to model in London, as she wanted to. Her whole life was a mess. And now this man, whom she'd been so determined to reject, was turning out to be the most enticing, attractive being she'd ever met. It wasn't fair.

Lifting herself out of the water, she sat for a moment on the edge of the pool, then reached shakily for her bikini on the grass. How could she have been so brazen as to take off her clothes in front of him and allow this to happen? She closed her eyes and felt a rush of heat suffuse her face. He must despise her— think that she was an easy lay. Or at the very least a tease, now that he knew she was a virgin.

Slowly Gabriella got up, whistled to Belleza, her horse, threw her clothes up over the saddle and mounted reluctantly. By now Ricardo would be almost back at the house. What would he do? Tell her father? No, probably not. But how would she face him at dinner? It was all so embarrassing. And, to make it worse, the whole thing was her own fault.

Letting out a deep huff, she rode slowly back to the beach and headed for home.

* * *

He could hardly leave tonight, Ricardo concluded, but tomorrow morning he would make a reasonable excuse and be on his way. The situation had got out of hand. He should have known she was a child playing with fire, and he blamed his own rush of passion for what had happened. She hadn't known what she was doing. But it was hard to forget her natural instinctive reaction—the hot, charismatic longing that had vibrated between them. As he showered, Ricardo tried to clear his mind and think reasonably. It was just physical, nothing more, he reminded himself as he dressed for dinner.

Gabriella dressed carefully, choosing a pale blue designer shift that fitted perfectly, all chiffon and lace, bought on her last trip to Milan, and thin, high-heeled satin sandals to match. Instead of leaving her hair loose she brushed it back in a strict ponytail that left her elegant rather than sexy. Diamonds sparkled in her ears. Taking a deep breath, she took a last look in the mirror then headed downstairs to face what would inevitably be an embarrassing encounter.

Ricardo rose as she entered the living room. She glanced at him sideways, unsure of his reaction. But to her surprise he acted as if the afternoon's interlude had never taken place. Gabriella experienced a rush of gratitude. She let out a tiny sigh of relief and sat next to her father, taking his hand in hers and giving him a hug. It felt secure to be next to him, to know he would always protect her, whatever happened in her life.

'So, my love,' Gonzalo said fondly, patting her cheek, 'did you two have a nice afternoon?'

'Very pleasant, thank you,' she answered demurely.

Ricardo watched her, resisting the desire to smile. She was a piece of work, he realised, amused despite his anger at her foolish behaviour. She was very young, and perhaps she had over-estimated herself— had no idea of just how patently sexy she was. He found himself feeling indulgent towards her as she cuddled next to her father, looking much younger despite her sophisticated outfit and the ponytail.

Dinner was announced and they rose. Then suddenly Gonzalo stopped, lifted his hand to his chest.

'Daddy?' Gabriella held him, sending Ricardo a panicked look. 'What's wrong, Daddy?' she cried.

Ricardo rushed to the other man's side, saw his face turn white. 'We must lie him down on the couch immediately,' he said, taking Gonzalo's weight and laying him among the cushions.

'Daddy, what's wrong?' Gabriella cried, grabbing her father's hand.

Gonazalo's eyes closed and his breath came fast. Then his lips opened. 'Promise me,' he whispered in a weak voice. 'Give me your hand,' he said to Ricardo.

Ricardo frowned and took the old man's hand, felt him place it over Gabriella's. 'I am leaving you, little one,' he whispered. 'I want you both to promise that you will marry within a month.'

Gabriella's eyes flew in panic from her father to Ricardo.

'But you can't go—you can't leave me, Papa,' she cried, panic-stricken, tears pouring down her cheeks.

It was a split-second decision. But as Ricardo looked from father to daughter, saw the anguish in the dying man's eyes, the lost distress in the girl's, he knew there was no choice.

'I promise,' he said, loud and clear.

'My Gabinha,' the old man whispered, his voice weaker by the moment. 'Answer me.'

'I—Daddy, don't leave me,' Gabriella wept.

'Promise me, my darling.'

'I…I promise,' she whispered, her head falling.

Ricardo watched as Gonzalo let out his last breath and Gabriella, her hair splayed over his chest, wept uncontrollably. A few minutes elapsed before slowly he lifted her and held her silently in his arms, aware that he had just made the biggest commitment—and perhaps the biggest mistake—of his life.

CHAPTER THREE

'WE CAN'T get married,' Gabriella insisted, not for the first time. 'It's absurd. We were under pressure. Daddy can't have meant it. He was just—' She cut herself off and turned away.

It was three weeks now since Gonzalo's funeral, and they were on Ricardo's private plane, a G5, flying to the Principality of Maldoravia, which he'd virtually abandoned for the past month. He needed to decide what the next step was. Not an easy task, he reflected, glancing at Gabriella, who had lived through the past weeks' events in a daze, allowing him to take charge of both her personal and business arrangements.

They had spent several days in the Presidential suite at the Copacabana Palace Hotel in Rio while Ricardo went over all Gonzalo's personal affairs with the lawyers and trustees appointed to administer them—only to discover that he was bound to Gabriella by the terms of Gonzalo's will. Sly old dog, he'd clearly known he'd get his way! Gabriella had sat by, barely registering what was happening, too caught up in her grief to care. He'd felt deeply sorry for her, and worried too. Her life had changed at the flick of a switch. It couldn't be easy, he recognised. She had lost quite a bit of weight too, he noted, eyeing her in the opposite seat and wondering how to get her to eat more than a couple of forkfuls of lettuce. Still, the subject at hand had to be faced.

'Gabriella, like it or not, we made a promise to a dying man. We must keep our word.'

'It was emotional blackmail,' she argued, crossing her arms tightly across her chest. 'It's not fair on either of us.'

'Nevertheless, I would not be a man of honour if I did not keep my word,' Ricardo said with a sigh. They'd had this discussion several times in the past days.

'That's rubbish and you know it. You could very well take care of my affairs and leave it at that.'

'You read the will yourself,' he said wearily. 'You can receive nothing—no income, or any part of your inheritance—until our marriage has taken place. Why not make it easier on yourself? Or is the prospect of marrying me really such a dreadful one?' He raised a brow and looked at her, an amused gleam flashing in his dark eyes.

'It's not you,' she said looking away. 'It's that I don't want to marry anyone. Not yet, anyway. I'm nineteen. I want to live. Not be tied down by a husband.'

Despite her unflattering words Ricardo sympathised with her, and wished as he had several times over the past few weeks that the dramatic circumstances of Gonzalo's imminent death hadn't changed his life and hers. But they had, and it was too late to retract.

'I understand how you feel,' he said matter-of-factly, 'but the fact remains that we have to get married, Gabriella. I gave my word and so did you. There are also the terms of your father's will. What happens after that is a different matter.'

'What do you mean?' she asked, frowning.

'Well, what I meant was that we can find a solution for this marriage which will allow us to live together without—how can I put this…?' He was already regretting his words. 'Without being a burden on one another.'

'Perhaps you could explain better,' she said, her eyes narrowing. 'I'm afraid I don't quite get the picture.'

'No. Well, never mind. I hope to make you very happy,' he answered quickly.

'No, you don't.' She shook her head vigorously and leaned forward, her eyes ablaze. 'I know exactly what you want. I've seen it over and over with my father's friends. You want to marry me, make me have a bunch of children, and then, while I sit in your wretched palace, taking care of them, you'll be off having fun with beautiful sexy girls. Do you think I'm stupid?' she said, hair flying as she rose and whirled to face him. 'Do you think that I don't know how men like you live? That my father was a saint and didn't have a bunch of mistresses all half his age? Well, I have news for you, Your Royal Highness. I am not going to be subjected to the kind of arrangement you—and obviously my father too—seem to think right for me. I have other plans for my life, and they don't include becoming a brood mare.'

'I never said that,' Ricardo replied, astounded at the onslaught. He'd expected opposition, but hardly this.

'But you implied it,' she spat.

'No, I didn't,' he replied through gritted teeth. 'I happen to take the commitment of marriage very seriously. And neither do I want an unwilling bride.'

'Then don't marry me,' she flashed. 'It's as simple as that.'

'I am responsible for all your affairs now. I have told the trustees of your inheritance that we will marry as agreed. Believe me,' he added, an edge to his voice, 'I have as little desire to go through with this damn wedding as you apparently have.'

'Thanks,' she said, flopping back in the seat, her eyes still glinting. Crossing her arms angrily, she stared out of the window at the clouds.

'Gabriella, do not try my patience any further. I have tried to be of as much solace to you as possible over the past weeks. But frankly you are being impossible. Why not try and make the best of the situation? We'll manage somehow.'

'Oh? Is that what you think?' Her eyes blazed again as she let out a ragged breath and her lip trembled. 'I've lost the only man I ever cared for. Life will never be the same without my father. But you can't understand that, I suppose?'

'Of course I understand,' Ricardo replied, his tone softening as he leaned forward to take her hand. 'I know this has been all very unexpected and traumatic for you. But why not make the best of the situation instead of the worst? This is a marriage of convenience, after all. I'm not asking for more than you're prepared to give—merely for you to comply with what we have both committed to.'

Gabriella shrugged, swallowed, looked down at his

fingers covering hers and suppressed the thrill that rushed up her arm and coursed to the pit of her stomach. How could she tell him that it would be hell to be married to him knowing that he was only doing it for the sake of his word given to a dying man? That he affected her in a way no other man ever had? She shuddered, remembering, as she had more than once over the past weeks, that episode at the waterfall. Slowly she drew her hand away. 'I'll think about it.'

'Not for too long, I hope,' he replied dryly. 'The month comes to an end in five days. Unless we are married by then you will lose your entire inheritance. I have already put the wedding plans in motion. Your gown is being prepared as we speak, and tomorrow we shall have the first rehearsal. There will be a lot of protocol for you to learn in a very short time. After all, this will be a state occasion.'

'How could you?' she whispered, her eyes filling with tears. 'And Papa? He loved me so much—always gave me everything I wanted or asked for. How could he do this to me? Threaten to leave me with nothing if I don't obey?'

'He is not leaving you with nothing, merely making sure that you are not taken advantage of,' Ricardo repeated for the umpteenth time. 'You are a very wealthy young woman, Gabriella.'

'That's a totally ridiculous, outmoded and chauvinistic way of looking at things,' she exclaimed. 'And you,' she added accusingly, '*you* think just the way he did—that because I'm young and a woman I'm incapable of dealing with my own affairs.'

'Actually, you're right, I do,' Ricardo replied

coolly, tired of arguing. 'Have it your own way, Gabriella. But unless you want to remain penniless you had better get used to the idea of being married in three days' time. Anyway, I have made all the arrangements. The ceremony will take place in the Cathedral of Maldoravia on Thursday afternoon.'

'And what if I refuse?'

'Then you'll have no choice but to go out into the world on your own, without any visible means of support, and I shall inherit your entire fortune,' he said bluntly, hoping it would have the right effect.

'Well, that's fine. If you feel quite happy with that then go ahead. I don't want the damn money. Take it.' She jumped up from her seat and glared down at him. 'I don't care about the fortune. I'll go to London and model and make a fortune of my own. I—'

'Gabriella, have you the slightest notion of how many girls try to model, and what the percentage is of those who actually succeed? Not many, I assure you. Now, sit down and stop carrying on like a spoiled brat.'

'I am not a spoiled brat,' she spat. 'I have rights.'

'Well, unless you comply with my arrangements— and the terms of your father's will—as of Saturday morning those rights fly straight out the window,' he said, in a firm, cold voice that sent shivers down her spine. 'I assure you, Gabriella, that if you do not behave properly I will not lift one finger to assist you.'

'Oh! How could you?' she threw at him, trembling, her hair thrown back and her eyes the colour of emeralds. 'I hate you, Ricardo. I really loathe and detest you.'

'Well, that bodes well,' he muttered, picking up a financial magazine and leaning back in the wide leather seat while Gabriella stomped off to the other end of the plane to nurse her temper.

The following couple of days were filled with activity. From the moment she set foot in Maldoravia Gabriella was taken in hand by personal assistants, servants, and Ricardo's charming aunt, the Contessa Elizabetta. She barely saw Ricardo, but although she felt rather lost and forlorn, she also could not help being excited at all the preparations taking place. There were fittings for her wedding gown, her trousseau, her going-away outfit—all of which she tried hard to seem uninterested in. But her innate sense of and love for fashion made that difficult.

On Wednesday afternoon she sat with the Contessa and her new personal assistant Sara—an Englishwoman of thirty, who had been hired at the last minute for her efficiency and for the fact that she had worked at Buckingham Palace and at several other royal establishments and knew the ropes. Gabriella had eyed her suspiciously at first, and said that she didn't need an assistant. But with supreme tact and charm Sara had won her over. Now both the older women exchanged glances and the Contessa raised her brows as Gabriella stared out of the window and for the thousandth time expressed her views.

'It's just not fair. I don't know how he can do it. And to say he'd simply inherit my money and be done with it. I mean, can you imagine?'

'I think Ricardo is merely trying to help you, my love,' the Contessa replied soothingly.

'Well, I don't care. Sara?' Gabriella said, turning round to face her assistant, who sat next to the Contessa wearing an elegant beige suit. 'Don't you think I could be a success as a model? I mean, look at me. I'm exotic, I'm tall enough, and I have all the right measurements,' she pleaded.

'Yes. But, you see, the trend at the moment in London is for sylph-like blondes. I'm afraid you might considered a little too…uh…' Sara searched for a suitable word '…too voluptuous. Perhaps in the future your look will return, and then you could consider it. In the meantime, if we could just go over tonight's seating arrangements?' she went on, producing a file and flipping through it. 'I think you would feel more at ease.'

Gabriella rolled her eyes and flopped into the nearest armchair. 'You really mean me to marry him, don't you?'

'Well, my dear, I don't see what other solution there is,' the Contessa said kindly, patting her coiffed silver hair with a bejewelled hand. 'After all, I can think of worse fates than being married to Ricardo.'

'I'm glad you can,' Gabriella muttered under her breath.

'He's very handsome—and quite a catch. I can think of all sorts of women who will be wild with jealousy,' the Contessa replied in an encouraging tone.

'Ah! You see! I knew it. Other women. That's precisely what I'm worried about. He says he wants a marriage of convenience,' Gabriella said, curling her legs under her and leaning further back into the armchair. 'That means he will have all sorts of horrid mistresses and I shall be left to wither in this—' she waved her hand expressively '—in this dungeon.'

'I would hardly call the Palazzo Maldoravia a dungeon,' Sara countered, hiding a smile. 'Your apartments are equipped with the finest furnishings, and the Jacuzzi works wonderfully. I had it tested myself.'

'It might as well be a dungeon for all I care,' Gabriella muttered.

Thursday dawned a beautiful sunny spring day. From the windows of her rooms in the Palazzo, Gabriella looked out at the perfect sky. The Mediterranean glittered clear and blue below, like a magical pond.

And now what was she to do? she wondered, opening the French doors and moving towards the balustrade of the balcony. Her black hair blew in the light morning breeze and the scent of jasmine filled her nostrils. At any other time she would have been enchanted. But right now the idyllic scene was lost on her. For the first time in her life Gabriella Guimaraes had come to the true realisation that she was not in control of the situation—and that, more than anything else, was driving her crazy.

That, and the fact that she was deeply and dangerously attracted to her future husband and damned if she would let him know it. What could be worse, she wondered, than to marry a man you found devastatingly attractive when probably right now he was making love to another woman?

'Oooh,' Gabriella seethed, throwing her head back

as she clutched the stone parapet and stared at the sky. She would never abase herself, never forgo her pride, never give in to him, never, ever submit to the kind of humiliation she had seen too many women go through.

As her father's only daughter, she had accompanied him in adult circles from her earliest childhood. Very soon she had seen what too many women's plights were, had listened to confidences beyond her years and seen men she knew were married parading their beautiful mistresses in full view of society. Why, she would rather live in hell than become one of them! It was absurd. For, although he was always charming, she knew that Ricardo only treated her like that because he was too polite to do otherwise, that deep down she was nothing but a duty, an obligation to be dealt with, another piece of business to be resolved. It was too infuriating. Too humiliating for words.

She turned back towards the room, hands clenched, her well-manicured nails digging into her palms at the thought of Ricardo and his behaviour over the past weeks. He had been wonderful and kind and the best friend anyone could have wished for when her father died. And she appreciated that—was grateful. But that was how he thought of her. A little girl he was sorry for because she was alone in the world. An obligation he had to fulfil.

She had racked her brains to find a solution, had again tried to persuade him to change his mind about the wedding that was to take place later today. But in vain. Ricardo had merely admonished her to pay attention to the protocol that had been instilled into her from the moment she'd stepped foot in the Principality. She sighed, stared out at the sea again, and her shoulders slumped. For the first time in her life she felt defeated. Instead of an excited bride she resembled a young queen preparing to face the gallows.

'He might as well be a frog,' she muttered under her breath. But deep down she knew that was not quite true, that it was precisely his undeniable attraction that disturbed her. If she were truthful she would have to admit that she even felt a fondness for the man he had proved himself to be—found his virile presence next to her disturbing yet reassuring. And for some reason she could not feel quite at ease in his company—particularly as flashes of that swim at the waterfall kept haunting her imagination, leaving her weak and wanting in a way she had never experienced previously.

Determined to get a grip on herself, and not allow him to perceive any of her weaknesses, Gabriella turned again back into the room and headed for the shower. There was no use trying to delay things any longer. She would marry him because, for now, there was no other way out. But he would find that he had a wife to be reckoned with.

In his office downstairs in the Palace Ricardo was experiencing his own set of doubts. His councillors were actually pleased that he was embarking on matrimony. They'd often mentioned the succession, and hinted at how providing an heir as soon as possible would eliminate the possibility of his uncle Rolando ever becoming Prince. But Ricardo had no illusions about his marriage. It was not going to be easy. Gabriella had made it plain that she meant to be as uncooperative as possible.

He raised his brows and let out a sigh. If he had not been a man of honour he would most definitely have got out of the duty that Gonzalo had forced upon him. He had even studied all the clauses of the will to see if there was any out. But none had presented itself. There was nothing for it but to bite the bullet and go through with it. He just hoped that Gabriella would behave. He'd had her primed in all the etiquette by his aunt, Contessa Elizabetta, and by the efficient Sara Harvey, whom thankfully she had taken to.

The Contessa was attractive and sympathetic, and had listened to Gabriella's complaints—at the same time managing to prepare her for what was going to be a state occasion at very short notice. Gossip was rife, he realised ruefully. Everyone wondered if the young girl was pregnant. An amusing assumption under the circumstances, he reflected, pushing away the papers he'd been studying and getting up from behind the huge mahogany desk.

Pregnant. Ricardo almost laughed. There was nothing amorous in their relationship. Far from it. In fact he wondered how they were going to fare in that department. He had never come close to kissing her again, and the day by the waterfall was nothing but a distant memory.

But one that would not quite disappear.

Still, despite that one occasion, Gabriella had kept him at arm's length. This stuck in his craw. Most women found him devastatingly attractive. But

Gabriella had made it plain that she had no desire for any intimacy, and on the few occasions when he'd tried to get things on to a happier footing she had rejected him outright. He grimaced, then glanced at the message from Ambrosia, to which he still hadn't replied, and rose from behind the desk. He would deal with that problem in due course. Right now it was time to prepare for his wedding—hardly the moment to be ringing his mistress. The future would take care of itself. He could do no more than perform his duty.

The rest was up to fate.

'Gosh, you're absolutely beautiful!' Princess Constanza, Ricardo's attractive younger sister, had just arrived for the wedding with her husband, the handsome Count Wilhelm of Wiesthun, and their two enchanting young children, who were to be attendants at the ceremony.

Gabriella turned away from the mirror. She was standing still while the designer's assistants gave the finishing touches to her magnificent yet simple satin wedding dress, a confection from Paris. Despite her unease she smiled at the attractive young woman at the door, and the pretty children.

'Hello, hello.' Constanza wafted in, a chestnut-haired woman of twenty-eight in a chic pale pink satin designer suit. She went over and kissed Gabriella on both cheeks. 'I heard all about what happened. You poor, poor thing. I was so sorry to hear about your father. And now you're stuck with Ricardo,' she remarked, grimacing and flopping onto the chintz sofa. 'He can be perfectly odious—even though he's a super brother.'

Gabriella eyed her and smiled. 'Are those your children?' she asked, watching the two little faces peeking at her from behind the sofa.

'Yes, little rascals. They're looking forward to being your attendants. I just hope they'll behave. Particularly as we weren't here in time for the rehearsal. Come, children,' she said, turning and pulling them out, giggling, from their hiding spot. 'Come and meet your new aunt.'

Gabriella's face lit up. Like most Brazilians, she adored children. Crouching, she beckoned to the lovely little girl and boy. 'Hello.' She reached out her hands to them. 'Oh, you're so beautiful,' she exclaimed, stroking the little girl's golden curls and smiling at the little boy, who grinned back shyly. They were already dressed, the girl in a pale blue satin bridesmaid's dress that was a tiny replica of her own, and the boy in a page outfit with velvet knee britches and a lace ruffled shirt.

'Ricky is three, and named after you know who.' Constanza rolled her eyes. 'And this is Anita, who's four.'

'What lovely names. Are you really going to help me at my wedding?' Gabriella asked them in a conspiratorial tone. Both children nodded seriously. 'I'm counting on you,' she said, straightening, and took their hands.

At that moment the Contessa hurried in, suitably attired in a rustling blue silk dress and coat. Several rows of large pearls hung about her neck and her ears gleamed with diamonds of the first water. She was followed closely by Sara. 'Ah, Constanza, there you are. I was worried your plane might be held up due to that storm in Germany. I see all is arranged. Now, Gabriella,' she said, turning towards her, 'run downstairs, my love. Ricardo wishes to see you.'

'But it's bad luck for the bridegroom to see the bride on their wedding day before the ceremony,' Constanza exclaimed, sitting up abruptly on the couch. 'He must know that.'

'Rubbish,' her aunt dismissed with a wave of her bejewelled hand.

'If it was me I wouldn't go,' Constanza said, jumping up and straightening the folds of the wedding gown.

'Oh, who cares? It really doesn't matter,' Gabriella muttered.

'At least take the gown off and slip something else on,' Constanza urged.

Their eyes met and, despite her desire to remain cool and aloof, Gabriella nodded.

Slipping into the walk-in-closet, she carefully removed the gown and hung it on a hanger, where its train spread out across the thick-piled beige carpet. She swallowed and her eyes filled with tears. At any other time it would have been the gown of her dreams. She turned quickly away and slipped on a pair of sweats and a short T-shirt that revealed her midriff. Serves him right. She sniffed, raising her chin belligerently and making her way down the wide, ornate corridor painted with frescoes and gold leaf. Tough luck if he didn't approve of her. She was damned if she was going to be everything he wanted.

He'd soon learn.

*　　*　　*

A knock on the double-panelled gilt door made Ricardo start. He'd been daydreaming for a moment.

'Come in.' He turned and faced the door, which a liveried servant was opening.

'You requested my presence?' Gabriella said with mock sweetness, thrusting her thumbs into the top of her sweats and standing at an angle, her foot drumming the floor.

Ricardo watched her, half-amused, half-irritated. She certainly did not look like a blushing bride preparing for her wedding, which was to take place within hours. He was about to make a pithy comment about her T-shirt when he realised with a touch of humour that she had done it on purpose, to provoke him. He smiled inwardly. Let the wedding take place. Then he would make very sure she never went around looking like this any more. As his wife it would be utterly inappropriate.

'I asked you to come down because I wanted to give you something.' He turned towards the desk and picked up a flat red leather jewel case, which he opened. On a white satin bed lay a splendid diamond necklace and earrings. 'This necklace has been worn by the brides in my family for several generations,' he said, moving towards her. 'It is appropriate that you should wear it too.' He lifted the necklace and laid the box down on a nearby table. 'If you turn around I'll put it on for you.'

She hesitated. He looked so devastatingly handsome. She hadn't expected him to be attired in dark dress uniform with gold braid and buttons, a sword hanging at his side. He looked rather like a prince out of a fairy tale. And it made him seem more remote and unreal.

Should she accept his gift or reject it?

But before she could react he came up behind her and slipped the necklace around her neck. She felt the cool of the white gold and the touch of his fingers on her skin, and a shiver coursed through her as he closed the clasp. Her eyes closed and she let out a sigh. Then his fingers touched her hair. She could feel the warmth of his breath on her neck and stood perfectly still as his fingers trailed down her back and she felt him drop a kiss on the back of her neck.

'There.' He drew back reluctantly. 'Turn around and let me see how you look.'

She turned about obediently, wishing she could find something snappy and intelligent to say, something to set her back on track. But the touch of his fingers and the kiss had been profoundly disturbing.

'Very nice,' he said approvingly, giving her a critical look. 'Or it will be once you are appropriately dressed. You will do very nicely, Princess Gabriella. You are aware that you will be assuming the title from the moment we are married? In other words, in about an hour and a half,' he said, glancing at the flat gold watch on his wrist. 'Try to be on time, okay? Now, where is Constanza?' he said, turning away with a frown. 'I need a quick word with her.'

If looks could kill Gabriella's would have meant his instant demise.

'I believe she's still upstairs,' she muttered through gritted teeth, wishing she had the guts to tear the necklace off and throw it at him. But dignity saved her.

Instead, her eyes flashed in green anger and she spun about without a word. So he thought he could treat her like another of his servants, did he? Well, he had another think coming. She whirled back up the stairs, leaving Ricardo with a pensive look on his face.

He didn't seem to be getting very far with Gabriella.

He hoped that he wasn't making a very grave mistake.

For both of them.

CHAPTER FOUR

As the royal yacht sailed out of Maldoravia's harbour and into the sunset, Prince Ricardo and his bride, the beautiful Princess Gabriella, waved from the deck in a charming manner.

So went the report in the *Maldoravian Gazette*, the Principality's leading newspaper. What the local and international journalists were not aware of was that the newly married couple were barely on speaking terms.

The yacht had sailed to the Italian coast, from where a helicopter had taken them to the nearest airport. From there an official plane had flown them to Ricardo's private Caribbean island next to the Dominican Republic, where they would remain for their honeymoon.

The wedding with all its pomp, the crowds that had waved in the streets as they'd driven from the Cathedral back to the Palace, their journey and their arrival on the island all seemed like a distant dream to Gabriella—as though she'd been an automaton and it had happened to someone else.

Now they were being guided by Ricardo's personal assistant, Baron Alfredo—an elderly white-haired man who had served his father—up to the huge master suite. Gabriella drew in her breath when Alfredo opened the double doors of a huge room and she saw the king-size bed. It had not occurred to her that they would be sleeping in the same room.

What an idiot she was, she chided herself as they stepped inside. Of course they would be expected to sleep together. The whole world believed that they were living a whirlwind romance. She opened her mouth to protest, but then, seeing the Baron's benign smile, closed it once more. She would have to wait until he'd left them alone.

As soon as the door closed behind him Gabriella moved towards the huge panoramic window overlooking the sea and took a deep breath.

'Ricardo, we shall have to come to some kind of arrangement,' she said, turning and facing him, head high, unaware of how lovely she looked framed against the backdrop of the sea and sky.

'What do you mean?' he asked, taking off his jacket and depositing it on the back of a rattan armchair.

'Well, this…' Gabriella gestured with her hand about the room. 'You don't really expect me to sleep in the same bed, let alone the same room as you?' she said hotly.

'Naturally we must share a room and a bed,' he replied in a casual tone, eyeing her calmly. 'Like it or not, Gabriella, you are now my wife. It would look very odd if we were to sleep in separate bedrooms. Particularly on our honeymoon,' he added dryly, his eyes encompassing her as he spoke. 'I think an international scandal is better avoided, don't you? I have no desire to be fodder for every tabloid on the planet.'

Gabriella was about to retort that she didn't give a

damn about tabloids, or anyone else for that matter, when the truth of his words sank in. She sat down abruptly on an ottoman and stared out of the window at the coconut trees. She felt a sudden pang of nostalgia, for the scene reminded her very much of home.

'Ricardo, we *have* to come up with something,' she said at last, trying to sound reasonable and grown-up. 'It—it would be impossible to sleep here together. I mean...' She looked away, waved her hand again in a vague gesture, embarrassed for one of the few times in her life.

Ricardo watched her, eyes narrowed, assessing the situation. 'Are you worried about sharing a bed with me, Gabriella?' he asked softly.

'No—yes. Oh, I don't know,' she exclaimed, irritated, rising but still staring out of the window, her back to him.

He stood for a moment watching the line of her tense body, her beautiful figure outlined under a soft linen dress which fitted her to perfection. All at once he recalled her lithe young form gliding through the dark waters of the Brazilian lake, and he moved behind her, slipping his arms around her waist. 'You know, we could deal much better than we have up until now, *cara mia*,' he murmured. 'Why not recognise that we are stuck with one another and make the best of it?'

'That is hardly a romantic statement,' she said pithily, her shoulders stiff. But Ricardo's hands reached up and he massaged them.

'True. But then we are not a very romantic couple, are we?'

'That's the understatement of the year,' she muttered, trying to hold out against the delicious ripples coursing through her as his hands caressed her.

'Nevertheless, it's reality,' he replied, his hands moving lower. 'Of course, that is not to say that we cannot become an extremely romantic couple. It's up to you, *cara*.'

'Oh, you don't understand,' she said, pulling away. 'How could you? After all, this is just an obligation you're fulfilling, and taking me to your bed is merely a part of it.' She drew back and swallowed the tears that surged in her throat. 'I'm going to swim. I need the exercise.'

'Very well,' he said, watching her closely. For a moment he considered taking her in his arms and forcing her to submit, then thought better of it. Better to let her simmer down. 'I shall see you at dinner.' With that he turned on his heel and walked out.

The ocean was deliciously warm and reminded her of Brazil. Gabriella let the water run over her and for a few moments forgot the circumstances of her marriage, giving way to the physical enjoyment of sea, sun and sand.

From the terrace overlooking the beach Ricardo watched her thoughtfully, wondering exactly how he was going to manage his marriage. The sight of her once more in a tiny bikini in the surf sent another rush of desire through him. What would tonight bring? he wondered. With a smile he turned back into the spacious living room. She was his wife. What was it the papers were calling her? 'The most beautiful princess in Christendom'? Well, so she was. What was comical was that he, Europe's most courted bachelor, was married to a woman who right now didn't want to give him the time of day, let alone share a bed with him.

A confident smile broke on his lips as he watched her. Give it some time. Wasn't that what Aunt Elizabetta had counselled? He'd never imagined he'd be taking advice about the conquest of a woman from his elderly aunt, but maybe she was right: give Gabriella some time to get used to her new way of life and the rest would fall into place naturally.

He watched her another few minutes, enjoying the scene, aware of the pulsating desire he was experiencing for her. He *would* give her a little time, but not too long. He wanted her and he would have her. With another confident smile he turned back into the living room, then made his way to the study to make the phone calls that, even on his honeymoon, he could not escape.

Dinner was served on the terrace under the stars. In any other circumstances it would have been the most romantic of settings. But the bride sat in an exquisite green silk designer dress, picking vaguely at the delicious food prepared with great care by the cook and her team, and the conversation was stilted. But the champagne was chilled. Gabriella took a long gulp, ignoring the fact that she very rarely drank alcohol.

Ricardo sat looking coolly sophisticated. At the end of the meal he nursed a brandy as if he had the whole night before him. Nervous, despite her determination to keep up as good a front as him, Gabriella accepted more champagne, twirled her flute and gazed out into the starlit night.

At this rate she would fall asleep, he mused. During the past few weeks he'd only seen her drink lemonade or water. He doubted she'd ever consumed this amount of champagne before. For a moment he thought of telling her to stop, but then decided to leave well alone. The worst that could happen was that she would have a bad head tomorrow morning.

But as the champagne took effect Gabriella's thoughts turned to all that had happened during the past weeks—the changes in her life and the fact that now she had a husband. She peered at him over the rim of her glass, blinking when she saw double.

'Are you feeling okay?' Ricardo said, rising and moving to where she stood leaning precariously on the balustrade, her hair swept back into a silken mass falling down her bronzed back.

'Fine. I'm fine. Just fine,' she mumbled.

'Are you sure?' He turned her around, saw the tears in her eyes and frowned. 'Gabriella, tell me what is wrong, *cara mia*?' His hands slipped to her shoulders.

'Everything,' she hurled at him. 'This is all your fault. If you hadn't insisted we get married none of this would have happened.'

'We're not getting into that all over again, are we?' he said with a sigh. 'It's done now, and we have to live with it.'

'No, we don't. I don't want to live with you,' she cried, a catch in her voice. 'I don't want to be your wife. I don't care what the papers write about us. It doesn't matter. I want out of this marriage. I hate you, and I refuse to be paraded about as your trophy. Like some exotic animal.' Her eyes blazed wet with tears and she downed another gulp of champagne.

'Is that how you think of yourself?' He looked down at her quizzically, a gleam in his eye.

'No,' she spat, 'it's how you think of me.'

'Now that you mention it, there are times when you resemble a tigress,' he commented, still eyeing her with amused if arrogant benevolence.

'How dare you?' she cried, wriggling in his hold. 'It isn't funny. I am not here to amuse you or be treated as your pet dog.'

'Dog? I thought you were a tigress. And tigresses needs to be tamed,' he said, his voice husky with desire as he gripped her shoulders, drawing her firmly towards him. Then before she could move he slipped his arms about her and brought her into him. One hand laced her hair and he drew her head back until her eyes blazed into his. 'The last time I kissed you you didn't dislike it that much, Gabriella. Let's see how you enjoy it this time.' His voice rang low and deep with desire.

Before she could react his lips were closing on hers. Gabriella fought weakly in his arms, but to no avail. Then as his tongue sought hers she experienced a rush of intense heat spiral from her head to the pit of her stomach, and her hands went limp and her breasts throbbed unbearably. Unconsciously she arched, as Ricardo expertly deepened the kiss, and his other hand slid down her back until it reached the delicious curve of her full, rounded bottom. Caressing her, he did what he had done that day at the lake and pressed her closer, forcing her to feel the intensity of his desire.

Every last shred of Gabriella's resistance gave way. She hated Ricardo, detested him, despised everything about him. Yet as their bodies entwined all Gabriella could think of was the scent of him, the raw, unadulterated attraction that overwhelmed her like a spell. She could feel his fingers unzipping her silk dress and knew that she longed to be free of it, to feel him skin to skin. She could barely breathe with the need of him.

'You are beautiful, Gabriella,' Ricardo muttered, slipping the straps of her dress from her shoulders so that it fell to her waist and revealed her small, taut breasts. He gazed down at her perfect body as she threw her head back and leaned against the balustrade. Her eyes closed as his thumb trailed down her throat and he grazed her aching nipples. When he lowered his lips to them she let out a tiny cry of protest and longing.

Ricardo savoured her, revelling in her scent, her skin, in those perfect breasts reacting so innocently yet so intensely to his touch. He knew this was the first time she'd been properly held in a man's arms, knew that although she was full of untamed, unfettered passion, it was up to him to take it slowly, to make it an unforgettable experience whatever happened to them in the future. Her reactions were spontaneous and natural—so much so that he almost laid her on the chaise longue to take her there and then. But sanity intervened and he pulled himself together. It was impossible, he reminded himself through the haze of desire gripping him. Even though she was so full of raw, wild passion, he must hold back.

A noise from inside the living room brought him back to earth with a bang. Hastily he pulled the dress up over her breasts and drew her into his arms, holding her close.

'What is it?' she whispered, opening her eyes.

'Probably just Marco the butler, making sure everything is all right for the night,' he whispered. 'Can you manage?' He smiled down at her now, their eyes meeting in complicity as she struggled to get the straps of her dress back in place and look demure. Then Ricardo turned and stepped back inside the French doors.

Gabriella heard him talking to the butler and dismissing him for the night. She blinked and tried to focus. What had happened to her? How had she allowed him to take her in this fashion? She shook herself and stood erect, her shoulders thrust back, then moved to one of the wrought-iron terrace chairs and sat dizzily down. Her head throbbed and she closed her eyes—only to feel the world spin.

'Oh,' she groaned, dropping it in her hands.

'Are you all right, *cara mia*?' Ricardo moved across the terracotta tiles to where she sat and crouched next to her. 'I think the best place for you is bed—after you've taken a couple of stomach-calming tablets and some water to ensure that you don't feel too bad in the morning.'

Then he swept her into his arms and carried her indoors and up the staircase to the huge bedroom.

Gabriella wanted to struggle, wanted to protest, but felt too dizzy. She must not allow him such liberties, she told herself in the recess of her hazy brain. Somewhere in the back of her mind she felt unhappy, disappointed that this was how she was going to spend her wedding night. But even in her woozy state it occurred to her that if she allowed the marriage to be consummated then she would be caught for ever. The only way she could insist on an annulment was if she didn't allow him to make love to her.

But all these were fleeting wisps of thought that touched the edges of her mind then disappeared as he lay her down among the pillows. She was too weak to protest when he began undressing her, too sleepy to…

Once he'd changed Gabriella into a pair of his pyjamas and tucked her safely into bed, Ricardo looked down at her sleeping form and smiled. Poor Gabriella. She had been through a lot. Silently he undressed himself and, after brushing his teeth, got into bed next to her. Turning off the light, he heard the soft pattern of her breathing next to him and sighed.

This was not going to be easy, he realised, turning on his side. Better try and get some rest. Tomorrow was another day, and he would take it as it came. But it was hard to sleep knowing that she lay curled next to him. Hard not to take her into his arms and make love to this woman who was legally his.

The next morning Ricardo was awoken by a discreet knock on the bedroom door. Glancing at Gabriella's sleeping figure, he rose quietly and slipped into the anteroom.

'Yes, Alfredo, what is it?'

'There was an explosion in the marketplace of Maldoravia fifteen minutes ago, Your Highness. They still don't know if it was a bomb planted by a terrorist group or simply an accident caused by a faulty electrical system in one of the surrounding buildings. As you know, some are very old and the wiring is unsafe. Anyway, Your Highness, it will require your immediate presence back in Maldoravia.'

'Of course. I'll leave at once.'

'Will you be travelling alone?'

He hesitated a moment, then took a decision. 'Yes. There is no point in worrying the Princess. I'll go, and return as soon as I can.'

'Very well.' The Baron gave a small bow and Ricardo closed the door.

Back in the room, he showered and dressed quickly. For a moment he glanced down at his sleeping wife, wondering whether he should wake her. But on second thoughts he decided she was better off resting. He would deal with business and return as soon as was possible.

Leaving the darkened room quietly, he closed the door softly behind him and was on his way.

It was past eleven o'clock by the time Gabriella stretched and yawned and realised that she was not in her own bed. She opened her eyes warily. Then all at once the events of the previous evening hurtled in, and she closed her eyes again with a groan. How could she have behaved in that manner? How could she have let him have his way? How...?

Suddenly it dawned on her that she wasn't lying ravished in a heap—rather that she was comfortably ensconced in a large pair of striped pyjamas which, although practical, were certainly not designed for seduction. She sat up among the pillows, crossed her legs and blinked. There was no sign of Ricardo, though from the dent in the pillows and the thrown-back covers it was obvious that he had slept in the same bed. Rising drowsily, she padded across the marble floor and, rubbing her eyes, went to the window. Perhaps he was downstairs. He must be. She felt a niggling feeling of guilt for having misjudged him. He had not taken advantage of her. Somehow the fact that she had automatically imagined he would made her feel ashamed.

For a moment she watched the coconut trees swaying in the warm morning breeze, then, turning on her heel, she walked into the bathroom and into the shower—where she stood for a good fifteen minutes as the cold water jet cleared her head and her brain. This was not turning out to be quite as simple as she'd imagined. She could not just be difficult, make him realise life was going to be hell and get him to agree to an annulment or a divorce. There was more to it than that. More than she had, as yet, put her finger on. But she was determined to get on top of it. She needed to control the situation, have it her way.

And that, right now, was what seemed to be eluding her.

'What do you mean, he left?' she asked, astonished, half an hour later as she walked into the large tropical living room where Baron Alfredo was awaiting her.

'Your Highness, the Prince was obliged to leave on state business early this morning. An explosion occurred in Maldoravia. The cause is undetermined as yet, but His Royal Highness decided to return home at once.'

'Oh.' Gabriella sat down on the couch with a bang. She should be profoundly relieved that Ricardo had been called away, but instead she felt strangely empty.

'His Royal Highness insisted that you rest and enjoy the holiday. He will be in touch later.'

'Thank you,' she replied with a brief smile. She must think—must decide what to do before it was too late. Ricardo was away. This might be her only chance to turn things in her favour. But what could she do? After all, she was stuck on this wretched island. Anything she did, any move she made, would immediately be reported back to Ricardo. Yet it could be her one opportunity to make her escape and seek her liberty.

For a moment she recalled the evening before—the undeniable desire that had raged between her and Ricardo, the indisputable, irrefutable need she'd experienced to be possessed by him. For a moment she closed her eyes and indulged in fantasy. Then she opened them, gave herself a shake and, boosting her resolve, headed onto the terrace for a cup of coffee.

She didn't trust herself with Ricardo. It was as if he held some kind of spell over her when he touched her. And that, she promised herself in the bright light of day, could not be allowed to happen again. She would never be subjected to any man, however much she might be attracted to him. And the truth was that was all it was: attraction. Not the basis for a solid marriage, of that she was certain. He was overbearing and dictatorial and she had no intention of obeying him—even if she had taken vows to that effect, she recalled uneasily.

One fruit salad and two more coffees later, Gabriella felt fortified enough to begin planning. Her head felt considerably better than it had on waking. Now she must think. This island was close to the Dominican Republic and not far from the US. She still had her credit card. From the Dominican Republic it was only a hop, skip and a jump to Miami, from where she could get a plane back to Brazil. The idea grew on her and she sat back, biting her lip, letting it develop. If she returned to Brazil then of course she would persuade her father's lawyer, Andrade, to go ahead with divorce proceedings. After all, she was a Brazilian subject.

It was brilliant.

Gabriella congratulated herself on her insight and set about implementing the scheme.

She began by seeking out Baron Alfredo and telling him she was planning a shopping trip to Miami the next day. She would pretend to Ricardo that she was bored. Frankly, he was probably too taken up with events in Maldoravia to bother about what she was up to anyway. She would simply pacify him and let him think everything was fine. And before he knew it she would have flown the coop.

As it turned out, she was right.

CHAPTER FIVE

GABRIELLA touched down at Miami International at ten in the morning. As the private jet that Baron Alfredo had chartered to take her there from the Dominican Republic landed, she wondered how she was going to shake off the two bodyguards and the chauffeur who had been ordered to accompany her. She glanced at her mobile phone. As soon as she was in the terminal she would phone the airline and book a flight to Rio tonight. But between now and then she would have to find a way of shedding her entourage.

Soon they were moving through the busy airport. Then she was in the back of a limo, driving down I-95 towards Miami Beach, satisfied that she'd managed to make a first-class reservation to Rio for that evening. The rest would just have to fall into place along the way, she decided optimistically. She was determined not to worry about it and to be positive. She always got her own way, didn't she? So why should that change?

As the car crossed the MacArthur Causeway and headed towards Ocean Drive, she sighed and, despite her determination to get away from him, wondered what Ricardo was doing right now. She quickly stopped herself from worrying whether he was safe, telling herself that it was nothing to her if he was or

63

not. She had no business caring what happened to him, did she?

After a brief look at the stores on Collins Avenue, Gabriella got back in the limo and continued towards Bal Harbour. It was fundamental that she gave the impression to her bodyguards and chauffeur that she wanted to shop until she dropped, so she wandered through the sophisticated shopping mall, in and out of several boutiques, and stopped in two exquisitely expensive designer stores where she bought a couple of handbags, a T-shirt and two pairs of shoes to justify her expedition, before sitting down at one of the outdoor restaurants and ordering some lunch. When the waitress proposed a glass of champagne she cringed inwardly. She would not be drinking champagne any time soon, she vowed, ordering a mineral water.

The offer of champagne reminded her of just how gentlemanly Ricardo had been, and how caring. She blushed at the thought of him removing her clothes and dressing her in his pyjamas. But she banished that thought quickly and focused instead on thinking up creative excuses for staying in town for the night. No way could she let herself be taken back to the island today, for that would put an end to all her schemes.

After some salad and some thinking, Gabriella decided to tell her bodyguards that she was too tired to return to the island that day and would check into the Ritz Carlton in Coconut Grove. She would tell them that they could have the evening off, since she planned to stay in her suite all evening. She just hoped they would all agree to go off duty—which she doubted, since they seemed to be a permanent fixture—in time for her to slip out, catch a cab and make it to the airport in time for her Rio flight.

By the time he reached Maldoravia it had already been established that the cause of the explosion was, as had been suspected, bad electrical wiring in an ancient building in the old town. Ricardo was glad that the cause of the incident was not terrorism, but that did not alter the dimension of the tragedy: the fact that seven were dead and three injured was distressing enough.

He had visited the bereaved families, and the injured at the hospital, and only now did he have time to think about his wife. Once he was back at the Palace in his office he began to pick up his voice messages. After that he would call her. But the first message on his machine was from Baron Alfredo, saying that Gabriella had gone to Miami for the day.

He frowned slightly and replayed it, then shrugged. Perhaps she was bored, being left on the island by herself. After all there was not much to do there. Probably better that she distract herself with shopping. But when he tried to reach her on her mobile phone he discovered it was turned off, and he experienced a stab of disappointment.

When next morning Alfredo rang to say that Gabriella had remained in Miami for the night and would be returning to the island later in the day, he really frowned. A niggling sensation of doubt assailed him, which he found difficult to shake off. He dragged his fingers through his thick dark hair and leaned back in the leather desk chair feeling uneasy, wishing he could leave at once. But that was impossible. He had been working most of the night, and today he had to attend the funerals. He glanced at his watch. He had no time now to worry about Gabriella, who would be back on the island in a few hours anyway. But something disturbed him.

It was only at the end of the day—once he'd returned exhausted from the burial processions and funerals, and with the press still awaiting his comments—that he received the news that Gabriella was nowhere to be found; her hotel suite was empty and her bags were gone. Somehow he was not surprised.

'Damn her,' he exclaimed, moving away from the crowd of journalists who were waiting to interview him. He glanced at his watch. The first thing he had to do was find out where she'd escaped to. Was she still in the US? Where was he to begin looking for his errant wife? Those incompetent bodyguards. He would have something to say to them.

But, in all fairness, if she had gone to her suite—as they'd assured him she had—and told them she would be staying there for the night, there was no way they could have avoided her escape. He had no doubt that she had found some creative manner of leaving the hotel. After all, he had sent them to protect her, not to spy.

Ricardo experienced a rush of anger. She had probably escaped in some unorthodox fashion. What the hell did she think she was doing? Didn't she realise that the games were over, that she was his wife now? Gabriella was a thorough pest, and right now he could throttle her for making such a nuisance of herself. Not to mention the underlying worry of not knowing where she was and the fear that something might have happened to her for which he would hold himself directly responsible.

It felt good to see the Corcovado, the Sugar Loaf Mountain, and Rio spreading out below her in the early-morning light. As the plane circled the city Gabriella let out a sigh of relief. The plan had worked. She was on her way home—where *she* called the shots. Soon this whole episode with Ricardo would be nothing but a nightmare.

Well, not quite a nightmare, she recognised uncomfortably. There had been wonderful moments—moments she would have difficulty in forgetting. But that was not something she planned to dwell on.

Soon she was outside the air terminal, feeling the familiar blast of damp heat. She had arranged for the hotel where she planned to stay in Rio to send a car to pick her up. Already at the terminal she'd felt good, knowing she was back on her own turf, hearing the reassuring buzz of people talking nineteen to the dozen and the sounds of samba music and laughter. She knew that she had finally come home. But now, instead of the rush of triumph she'd expected, she felt strangely empty, as if a large vacuum had suddenly popped into her life. But she banished that thought.

As soon as she arrived at the Copacabana Palace, Gabriella called Andrade, her father's chief lawyer and executor, and told him to send the jet to pick her up and take her back to the family estate. He promptly fulfilled her request, and a few hours later she was flying over

rainforest, huge stretches of farmland and varying countryside as the plane headed north. She had set up a meeting with the lawyer for the following day.

Gabriella still hadn't faced the fact that she would
have to talk to Ricardo and explain her actions. Or
maybe she wouldn't, she reflected, drinking a cola and
curling up in the big leather seat. Maybe she wouldn't
explain anything at all. After all, her actions spoke for
themselves, didn't they? After this he would probably
be happy to be rid of her.

Instead of making her happy, that last thought left
her somewhat gloomy. Of course it would be an international scandal, and she hated the thought of sub-
jecting him to that after he'd been really quite decent
to her. The idea was rather lowering, and for a moment
she felt a wave of sadness. But then she pulled herself
together and justified her behaviour. It was just one of
those things that couldn't be helped. Collateral damage. That was how she had to think of it. After all, it
was he who had been so determined to go ahead with
the wedding. So it was basically all his fault.

Still, even though she shrugged and picked up a
magazine to read, she found it impossible to concentrate. Somehow Ricardo's image, his deep dark eyes
and enigmatic smile, kept interfering.

'Damn him,' she mumbled, throwing the magazine
into the seat across the aisle and leaning back, closing
her eyes. She had finally rid herself of the man. That
was what she'd wanted, surely? Then why instead of
elation did she feel deflated? It made absolutely no sense.

No sense at all.

*   *   *

'You *what*?' Mae Isaura, Gabriella's old nanny exclaimed, her hands firmly planted on her wide hips, her girth framed in the doorway of Gabriella's room.

'I told you,' Gabriella muttered, pretending to unpack. 'I left him. I don't want to be married to him, Isaura. I don't want to be married to anyone. It was crazy of Father to force us. It just wasn't fair. To him or me.' She turned, lifted a blouse from her tote bag and glanced at it. 'This needs ironing.'

'Do not try and change the subject, Gabriella.'

'I'm not. I merely said that this blouse—'

'Oh, I wish you were small again. I tell you, if you were, you would have a very sore bottom by now, you naughty child. You have no business to behave in this manner. You will stop unpacking and return to your husband at once.'

'No, I won't,' Gabriella threw back. 'I refuse.' The two women confronted one another, eyes blazing, as they had so often over the years: Isaura, small and wide and dark, the only person to whom the girl had ever been known to give way; Gabriella, tall, beautiful and autocratic, her green eyes alive with determined zeal. 'I refuse to live with him, Isaura, to go back to that silly Principality with all its formal ways and protocol and stuffiness. Why, he barely talked to me when we were there. It's stifling, unbearable. I won't.' She whirled around to face the window with her arms crossed protectively over her breasts

'Gabriella, you are too old for tantrums. You are a married woman now, not a child. I'm actually surprised this man has allowed you to get away with this. He seemed a sensible sort to me. And very much a man. He won't take kindly to what you've done. You have humiliated him in front of the world. You should be ashamed of yourself.'

'He asked for it,' she mumbled, knowing she would have a hard time defending this position.

'Well, this time *you've* asked for it, *minha querida*,' Isaura said pithily. 'And I shall have no sympathy for you when you reap the results of this mischief. You'll deserve anything that comes to you.' With that dire warning she turned on her heel and closed the door smartly behind her, leaving Gabriella to brood on her own.

'What do you mean, she's gone?' The Contessa sat ramrod-straight in the high, tapestried Queen Anne chair, shocked, sending a horrified glance to Sara, who stood close by.

'Exactly what I said, Aunt,' Ricardo said, flinging himself down on the brocade sofa opposite. 'She simply upped and left—disappeared. She pretended she was going shopping in Miami, took a suite for the night in a hotel, told the staff she was staying in for the evening, then packed her bags and—away.' He snapped his fingers expressively.

'But where has she gone?' Sara asked, her expression worried.

'I'm not certain,' he replied, eyes narrowing, 'but I have a fairly good hunch that she's gone home to Brazil. After all, where else would she go? London?

Paris? She had some notion that she wanted to be a model. But I don't think she would risk exposing herself right now, when all the press will be at her heels.'

'Poor child,' the Contessa murmured, shaking her coiffed silver head. 'I think both of you have been placed in a most awkward situation.'

'Well, I didn't expect you to react like that,' Ricardo said haughtily. 'I just want to try and avoid an international scandal.' He passed a hand through his hair and sighed. 'She's been nothing but trouble from the moment I accepted Gonzalo's invitation.'

'Is that all that worries you, Ricardo?'

'Well, no. Of course I'm worried about her whereabouts. But I'll not let her make a fool out of me.' He nodded to Sara, who indicated discreetly that she would leave the two of them alone.

The Contessa raised her brows. Always that wretched Maldoravian pride, she reflected with an inner sigh. It might not, she reflected ruefully, do Ricardo any harm to be made to realise he was not the only fish in the sea. 'Well, I suppose if she's gone home that makes it much easier,' she said blandly. 'After all, if she's nothing but a nuisance to you, then you are well rid of her.'

'What?' He looked across at her, amazed.

'You just said that she has been nothing but trouble from day one,' the Contessa reasoned.

'That's all very well,' he muttered, rising and pacing the room. 'But she's my wife, and I'm damned if I'll have her leaving me in the middle of our honeymoon, making a fool of me to the world. How do you think that will look to the press?' he demanded.

'Ah, I see.' The Contessa raised her brows slightly. 'Appearances.'

'Yes, Aunt, appearances,' Ricardo muttered through gritted teeth. 'These are things that will have to be considered and carefully administered.'

'Mmm. I suppose you're right,' she replied, eyeing him with a touch of humour. 'But, you know, I really wonder if perhaps Gabriella isn't right, and if you should bring this marriage to an end despite the scandal.'

'What did you say?' Ricardo rose and stared at her, astonished. 'Of all people, I never thought I'd hear *you* express such a view, Aunt. Frankly, I am shocked to hear you say it.'

'I'm simply being reasonable. After all, there is no love lost between you, and it will be nothing but a seven-day wonder that's fast replaced by some other, juicier scandal.'

'Rubbish. I won't hear of it.'

'So you plan to go after her?'

'Of course I plan to go after her,' he answered in a withering tone. 'Despite this crazy notion of yours, she's still my wife, and she will be brought back here where she belongs and made to behave as befits her position.'

'I see. Well, it's entirely up to you.' The Contessa shrugged lightly, picked up her embroidery and remained annoyingly calm.

'I shall travel to Brazil and take any decisions there. At least we will be seen to be together. Perhaps we should not have allowed ourselves to be held hostage to Gonzalo's deathbed wishes,' he added thoughtfully.

'Still, there was little to be done. His will meant she would have lost all her money had I not insisted we go through with the ceremony.' He shook his head as his personal secretary appeared in the doorway.

'Your Royal Highness is expected,' the secretary said with a small bow.

'Of course.' With an automatic smile Ricardo said goodbye to his aunt and left the salon.

'I'm afraid what you ask is impossible,' Andrade, the white-haired lawyer, replied to Gabriella's request to begin divorce proceedings.

'But why?' she asked, spinning around and facing him full on.

'Because, *querida*, from the moment you married the Prince you became a Maldoravian citizen. You are now subject to the laws of the Principality,' he said, flipping through some papers. 'I took the liberty of doing some research on the subject before you married. Just out of general interest, you understand. For any court to grant you a divorce in Maldoravia, you would have to first prove that you have lived together for at least six months,' he said, checking the items with his index finger, 'secondly prove that the marriage has failed after a sufficient period of life in common to have given it a fair trial, and then have a period of separation in which you agree to counselling and are open to reconciliation. If after all that, and a two-year period of separation, both of you still feel that there are irreconcilable differences that cannot be surmounted, then the case can be heard in court. Even then it is not certain that a divorce will be granted.

The Constitution of Maldoravia is very ancient and old-fashioned, and its laws on the matter of divorce are very strict.'

'You're joking?' Gabriella sat down opposite him, deflated. 'But that's simply awful—what am I to do?' She threw up her hands in despair. 'I can't be stuck with him for the rest of my life. It's not fair.' Perhaps an annulment was the answer...

At that moment a servant appeared. 'Dona Gabriella, a visitor has arrived.'

'A visitor?' She looked up sharply.

'Yes, *senhora*. Your husband, the Prince, awaits you.'

'Goodness.' Gabriella paled. 'How has he got here so quickly?' She braced herself, tried to feel very brave and very grown-up. This was it. 'Please wait a moment, Andrade, while I receive my—the Prince.' Tossing her dark hair back, she marched through the door and prayed for the right words to be sent to her.

As he had on his first visit to the Guimaraes mansion, Ricardo heard the sound of fine heels on marble. He stiffened, turned towards the window and stood erect, hands clasped behind his back, staring out at the tropical landscape. When he heard her enter he waited a moment before turning around. When he did he caught his breath. She was perfectly lovely, her colour heightened, her eyes bright, her breasts heaving with anxiety. How he wished he could take two strides across the room and take her in his arms, teach her how to love and be loved. Instead he kept a cool, indifferent expression on his face and cleared his throat.

'Hello, Gabriella,' he said, as coldly as he could. The rush of desire was impossible to ignore.

'Hello, Ricardo.' She hesitated before advancing into the room, the silence broken only by the sound of the waves rolling in the distance. Their eyes met, held. Then she looked away and sat down, indicating the white sofa opposite her.

'I think we need to have a talk,' he said at last, remaining standing.

'What is there to talk about?' she asked, pretending to straighten her skirt. The shock of seeing him again was far greater than she'd expected. All at once scenes from the terrace on their Caribbean honeymoon island surfaced, and she swallowed. Why did he affect her in this way?

'Gabriella, we need to talk about the future. I cannot live with a wife who feels she is obliged to flee from me the minute my back is turned.'

'Then let's get divorced and be done with it.'

'Yes, let's.' He nodded. 'I think you're right. That is probably the best solution.'

She looked up, her eyes awash with amazement. 'But—you'd agree to a divorce?'

'If it is the only solution—why, yes. I certainly don't want to live with you under the present circumstances. It would make life impossible. And I really don't have time to come after you every time you run away or play the fool with this capricious behaviour.'

Gabriella's jaw dropped. She'd imagined everything: outrage, anger, anything but indifference. She clenched her fists. 'Well, good,' she muttered through gritted teeth. 'How convenient that my lawyer is already here.'

'Is he? That's great. Then why don't we get on with it?' Ricardo smiled politely. 'Just call him in and we can settle matters immediately. I would quite like to get out of here before dusk.' He glanced at the sky, then at his watch. 'It will get dark pretty soon now, I should think.'

Without a word, her lips tightly closed, Gabriella rose and rang the bell. A servant appeared immediately. 'Tell Dr Andrade to join us, please,' Gabriella said, her head in turmoil. This was not at all how things were meant to pan out. Not that she had any clear idea of what the correct script should be—simply that this wasn't it.

Andrade entered the room, all smiles.

'Your Highness—how nice to see you again so soon after your wedding.'

Ricardo smiled and shook hands with the man.

Gabriella's mind was working frantically.

'I hope you had a good trip?' the lawyer continued, accepting the chair being offered to him.

'Not as good as it could be, under the present circumstances,' Ricardo countered with a grave look. 'I believe you are already aware,' he said, with a brief mocking glance at Gabriella, 'that my wife and I find we do not suit and would like an immediate divorce?'

'Yes, that's right,' Gabriella agreed nervously, trying to pretend to herself that the words 'my wife' did not affect her in any shape or form. 'As I told you we—we want to get divorced. We—' She looked up and caught Ricardo's eyes.

'But that is impossible,' the lawyer repeated, shaking his head. 'Your Royal Highness, I just told Gabriella, before you arrived… Let me explain. Since you were not married in Brazil, the courts here have no jurisdiction over your marriage. Any divorce would have to follow Maldoravian law. As I mentioned to Gabriella, a minimum of six months in cohabitation followed by two years' physical separation would be necessary for you to even contemplate such an action. Plus, you would have to go through a reconciliation process and all manner of things. I'm afraid I really can't help you immediately.'

'I see.' Ricardo's expression gave little away.

'But that's so unfair,' Gabriella exclaimed once again. 'Ricardo, you're the Prince—surely you could change the law if you wanted to?'

'Changing the law at a whim is not within my rights,' he remarked dryly.

'Well, I'm sure you could do *something*. After all, it's clear that we can't do it that way. Isn't it?' Her voice was pleading now.

'It appears we have little choice, *cara*.'

'But that's ridiculous.'

'Maybe,' he said, eyeing her steadily, 'but by the look of it we will have to make the best of it.'

'Oh!' Gabriella got up, clenching her fists as she was prone to do in moments of utter frustration. 'Are you saying that I must return with you to that—that stuffy, mouldy, unbearable place, and wither away there for *six months*?'

'That, madam, would appear to be the case,' Ricardo said with a small nod of affirmation.

'But I'm a Brazilian. I'm not Maldo—whatever it is,' she cried, beseeching Andrade for help.

'From the moment you married you became a Maldoravian citizen, and you are now subject to that country's law,' Andrade replied apologetically. 'And by that law your husband can command you to return and live by his side, whether you like it or not. As I told you before, it is a principality that still holds on to old, time-worn traditions. Particularly where marriage is concerned.'

'Oh, I don't believe it,' Gabriella exclaimed, turning and peering at Ricardo through narrowed eyes. 'You knew all this,' she threw accusingly. 'You knew we couldn't get divorced quickly.'

'Actually, I wasn't aware of all the difficulties, having never contemplated the possibility,' Ricardo said calmly. 'But I think Dr Andrade is right. If we wish to proceed in this matter we shall have to follow Maldoravian law and take legal counsel there. In which case the sooner we get back there and get on with it the better—don't you agree?' He glanced once more at his watch. 'Could you be ready, say, in half an hour?'

'It's preposterous,' an exhausted Gabriella repeated to the patient Contessa, who was doing her embroidery while lending a sympathetic ear. 'Why can't we just get divorced and be done with it? After all, it's not as if either of us wants to stay married.' Gabriella whirled around to seek the older woman's agreement.

'Mmm. Of course, one must take into account that the customs here are not as modern as in other parts of the world,' the Contessa countered tactfully, snipping a thread. 'I think the general consensus is that people should try and give their marriage a chance before taking a decision to end it.' She glanced up, caught Gabriella's brooding expression and smothered a smile.

But she was worried about the two young people. It was obvious to anyone that a deep attraction lay between them. You only had to be in the same room to pick up the tense vibes that surrounded the couple. But she was too much of a diplomat to point this out to her errant new niece and her proud, aristocratic nephew. Unfortunately they were going to have to find things out for themselves, she thought with a sigh.

And, to make things worse, Ambrosia, Ricardo's ex-mistress, had arrived on the island that morning. Or so she'd heard from Constanza, who was here for the weekend. The bush telegraph in the Principality functioned at great speed. What could that young woman be up to? she wondered. Surely she would have lost interest in Ricardo now that he was married to another and there was no possibility of her becoming Princess.

Or would she?

The Contessa mused over the matter for several moments while Gabriella sulked by the window. Ambrosia was ambitious, ruthless, and a man-eater. Perhaps she planned to remain in Ricardo's life anyway? The Contessa had never understood what had drawn those two together in the first place. Sex, she supposed, was the answer.

Again the Contessa glanced at Gabriella: so young, so beautiful, so used to getting her own way, and so bewildered by a whole new set of circumstances. The Contessa was quite surprised that Ricardo, known for his prowess with women, had not managed better in this quarter.

'Have you seen Ricardo this morning?' she asked casually, rethreading her needle with a different-coloured silk.

'No, I haven't. He gets up before I get up and goes to sleep after I'm asleep,' Gabriella announced, unaware of how huffy she sounded and of how much that statement proclaimed.

'I see. Well, he must be very busy.'

'I suppose so. Aunt Elizabetta, what am I going to do?' Gabriella sat down on the velvet ottoman near the Contessa and turned her big flashing green eyes towards the older woman. 'I mean, we can't go on living like this,' she cried despairingly, waving her hands. 'It's perfectly ridiculous, don't you think?'

'Yes, I do. I think both of you should grow up and face your responsibilities,' the Contessa remarked calmly.

'What do you mean?' Gabriella sat up straighter, surprised at the response. She'd been looking for sympathy, not a lecture.

'Well, to put it in a nutshell, like it or not you're married—and will remain so for at least two and a half years. If it was me I would make the best of it. Right now you and Ricardo seem to spend the better part of your time avoiding one another. That is not much of a life for either you or him.'

'But what can I possibly do?'

'How about seducing him?'

'Sedu—' Gabriella stared at her, aghast. 'Aunt Elizabetta!' she exclaimed. 'I'm shocked.'

'Why? I wasn't always the age I am now, you know. I can very well remember what it was like to be attracted to a very seductive and handsome man.'

Gabriella jumped off the stool. She was wearing a pretty patterned peasant skirt and a blouse tied at her waist. With her long dark hair and flashing eyes she looked a little like a beautiful gipsy.

'How can I seduce a man that—well, a man who doesn't want me?' she blurted out woefully.

'Doesn't want you?' The Contessa frowned. 'Are you sure? I'm surprised to hear that. I had the impression—' She cut herself off, realising she was about to say too much. 'Well, of course you must know. After all, you are his wife.'

'Much good that does me,' Gabriella muttered. 'Why, after what happened on our honeymoon, he's never even— What I mean to say is, we sleep in the same bed and... Oh, this is too embarrassing—too ridiculous,' she exclaimed, letting out a deep breath.

'You mean to tell me that you are still a virgin?' the Contessa asked quietly.

A flush extended up Gabriella's long slim throat. 'I...yes.'

'Hmm.'

'Aunt, that is not helpful,' Gabriella cried in frustration. 'I don't know what to do.'

'I already told you what to do,' the Contessa said philosophically, a smile hovering about her lips. 'I'm sure that he'll at least be surprised.'

CHAPTER SIX

'RICARDO, darling.'

The husky voice reached him from across the terrace of the Royal Yacht Club and there was no mistaking its origin. Ambrosia stood tall and elegant, her long tanned legs showing below her short tennis skirt, her sleek blonde hair falling on her trim shoulders. She swung her racket casually as she approached. 'It's been an age, darling. I hear that you married?' She looked straight into Ricardo's eyes, a flash of anger quickly concealed as she smiled generously, then let her tongue flick her lips before reaching up to kiss him lightly on both cheeks.

Ricardo caught a whiff of her familiar perfume and experienced a moment's regret. He'd had good times with Ambrosia, even if she was a handful and could never have become his wife. He allowed his hand to slip to her waist. 'You look wonderful, Ambrosia. Tennis obviously suits you. A new lover, perhaps?' he murmured in a lower voice, aware that half the club was watching them.

'Oh, Ricky. We aren't all as faithless as you,' she said with a pout. 'Did you think I would bounce back that quickly?' She leaned back and looked up into his eyes.

'You've never lacked for male company.'

'And I could say the same to you about women,'

she snapped. 'As soon as my back was turned you went off and married. A nineteen-year-old virgin, I hear. How charming. How very quaint. You must be enjoying teaching her all your tricks.'

'Ambrosia, you sound positively jealous,' Ricardo remarked smoothly.

'What if I am?' She raised a suggestive brow and raised her mouth to his ear. 'If you get bored teaching your novice, you can always give me a call.'

'Well, they say that jealousy can provide a lot of spice,' he murmured, 'but we must remember that I'm a married man now.' He was breathing in her scent, seeing the sexy curve of her breast and taking note of the obvious offer she was making.

'I'm not difficult,' she responded in a low, husky voice that left him in no doubt as to her intentions. 'We're sophisticated people, Ricky, darling. What has marriage got to do with us? I like you in bed. You like me. Do your duty to your little brood mare; get her pregnant and get yourself an heir. I presume that this is what all this is about, right? Then we can get on with having fun.'

Ricardo looked down at her for a brief moment. Then he tweaked her cheek and laughed. 'You are always full of surprises, Ambrosia. A man could never become bored with you.'

'Perhaps you should have remembered that sooner,' she responded waspishly. Then, with a smile, she turned and raised her hand to her mouth. 'Oh, my goodness, isn't that your wife over there? She really does have a spectacular figure. Funny. She still looks awfully...untouched, if you know what I mean. I've heard half the men here at the club are taking bets.'

'Bets on what?' he frowned glancing in Gabriella's direction.

'Oh, nothing, really. There's just this rumour going about that says she's still a virgin. The odds on it are pretty high. I must say, it would be funny if she was. Though unlikely, I imagine?' Ambrosia raised her finely pencilled brows once more, then moved away before he could answer.

Ricardo watched as Gabriella and his sister Constanza entered the club, accompanied by Constanza's husband, the handsome blond Count Wilhelm of Wiesthun, and their children, to whom Gabriella seemed to have taken. He watched as she kneeled down in the most natural fashion to tie his niece's trainer lace, which had come undone. Then she raised her head and their eyes met across the large terrace, past the white wicker furniture with the blue and white striped cushions, past the tropical plants and the waiters weaving in and out among the tables with trays of cocktails.

So the whole club was betting on whether he'd bedded his wife or not? Well, damn them! He would not be made a public fool. So much for all the gentlemanliness he'd shown towards Gabriella. Now he was determined to make love to her—whatever the consequences!

Who was the woman Ricardo had been smiling at in such an intimate fashion? Gabriella sensed her pulse race and a rush of heat grip her. She'd never felt anything like this before. But seeing him so close, so intimate with another woman, had left her seething. She might not want him herself, she thought, taking little Anita's hand and leading her to their table, her head high, but she wouldn't be humiliated in front of the whole Principality. So that was why Ricardo hadn't tried to sleep with her again—hadn't attempted to make love to her. He had a mistress.

At the first opportunity, she leaned across to Constanza. 'Who is that woman over there?' she asked, pointing discreetly to the table where Ambrosia sat holding court, laughing expansively, throwing her head back and crossing her long slim legs provocatively.

'That? Oh, that's no one important,' Constanza lied, fussing over her daughter. 'Now where on earth is Nanny? Gabriella, have you seen her?'

'She was taking little Ricky to the loo. But, please, Constanza,' Gabriella insisted, 'don't pretend you don't know. Tell me who she is.'

'Who?' Constanza still acted as if she didn't understand.

'That blonde woman Ricardo was talking to so intimately only moments ago. I got the impression that perhaps—' Gabriella cut off, twisting her hands agitatedly in her lap, unable to continue. It was ridiculous to be nervous. Why should she care what he did? She wanted a divorce, didn't she? So what was she worried about? Who cared what Ricardo got up to?

Constanza glanced up, relieved at the sight of Ricardo crossing the club restaurant towards them.

'Ah, here he is. You can ask him yourself,' she said quickly.

'Hello,' he said standing next to the table. 'May I join you?'

'Why, of course! Ricky, darling!' Constanza exclaimed. 'Sit down here, next to your wife.' She smiled brightly as Ricardo allowed the waiter to draw up a chair. Then he sat down next to Gabriella and slipped his hand casually over hers.

'Everything okay, *cara*? You look a little pale.'

'I'm fine.' She swallowed and tried to ignore the electric shock that pulsated through her the minute his skin touched hers.

'I certainly hope so.' His thumb began to caress the inside of her palm and Gabriella had to muster every inch of self-control not to let out a ragged sigh. She breathed thankfully when the waiter appeared with shrimp cocktails and he was obliged to let her go. Why, oh, why did he have this effect on her? Surely it was madness?

But instead of remaining coolly aloof, as he normally did, the next thing Gabriella felt was Ricardo's hand gently caressing the inside of her thigh. She drew in her breath and sent a furious glance in his direction—to which he paid little attention. There was no room to move, no option but to pretend she wasn't dying of desire. When his fingers reached further, only masterly self-control made it possible for her to continue to maintain her poise, which was evaporating fast. How could he do this? How dared he? What right did he have to ignore her one minute, then seduce her almost publicly the next? It was outrageous, and she would have something to say to him once they were alone.

Only when he knew that she was thoroughly aroused did Ricardo remove his hand and continue with his lunch, content in the knowledge that although his wife might pretend to dislike him, her dislike did not extend to her sexual attraction for him. But enough for now. He had given her a taste of what was to come. Let her simmer for a while.

At least until tonight.

The state dinner with foreign dignitaries had taken longer than expected. Gabriella was glad to kick off her high heels and throw herself onto the bed.

During the meal she'd been seated next to a Portuguese minister who spoke no English. It was fast becoming clear that her knowledge of languages and her ease and gifts as a hostess were considered a great bonus by the government of Maldoravia, which made every use of her it could. She was spared no dinner or luncheon where it was thought that she could be an asset. And, to her surprise, Gabriella found that she had a talent for diplomacy and entertaining. Even the Prime Minister had hinted to her that she might like to broach certain subjects to her neighbour and see what answers she got.

Despite her desire to find everything she could that was wrong with Maldoravia, Gabriella had to admit that it was rather fun to be given important missions and see if by directing the conversation with apparent insouciance she could pick up on what needed to be known through veiled comments. She also had the advantage of being very young. This misled a lot of people, who believed her questions to be mere curiosity and often revealed far more than they might otherwise have intended. Why, only tonight she'd learned of plans for a new trade agreement Portugal wanted to get into with Maldoravia simply by fluttering her long lashes at the Portuguese minister and hanging on to his every word. She had learned early that men loved being the centre of a woman's attention, and played this card to the full. Tomorrow, first thing, she would tell the Prime Minister, who had a special affection for her.

Letting her head drop back on the armchair's cushions, she closed her eyes. There was no sign of Ricardo, who had become increasingly elusive since that day at the yacht club. In fact that night he had left on a state visit to Denmark and had only returned this morning. They had barely spoken. He seemed so distant and inaccessible, and all her plans to seduce him had come to nothing. She let out a sigh. It really didn't matter any more as he was probably making love to his mistress. And, actually, in view of her plans for the future it was probably better this way. What she must do was begin to map out her life after Ricardo. But that, for some inexplicable reason, seemed a difficult task to undertake. The future remained hazy.

Not that it was far off, she reminded herself severely. The time since their return from Brazil had sped by, and the remaining months of the obligatory six needed to complete the period of cohabitation would fast come to a close. She sighed, fiddled with the fringe of one of the cushions that adorned the bed, and tried to persuade herself that she was happy it was coming to an end. Soon they could separate, even if they couldn't get a divorce. So why did she feel so melancholy every time she glanced at a calendar or caught sight of the date of a newspaper? There really was no explaining it.

Laying her head back, Gabriella gave way to exhaustion. Not physical exhaustion, but something else that she'd never known before. As though all the joy of life had suddenly seeped out of her being and there was nothing left to look forward to any more.

After seeing off the last of his official guests, Ricardo made his way up the wide marble staircase and approached the apartments he shared with his wife. It had been a long day, and an even longer evening. The past few weeks had been fraught, with too much work and too little time to relax, he reflected wearily. And too little time to dedicate to trying to save his increasingly chilly relationship with his wife. Perhaps tomorrow he would simply tell Baron Alfredo that he was taking the day off and take Gabriella out on his yacht. If she would agree to come.

He sighed as he turned the door handle of the apartment, and hesitated a moment. This was not proving to be an easy relationship. Gabriella was polite, but cold. She made it abundantly clear that she wanted as little to do with him as possible. He silently entered the small salon but she was nowhere to be seen. Then, tugging at his bow tie, he moved towards the bedroom and stopped in the doorway at the sight of her lying on the bed, eyes closed, her hair splayed over the velvet cushions. Goodness, she was lovely: so young, so beautiful, so enchanting—not to mention sexy.

Ricardo moved across the room and gazed down at her for a long moment. Then he sat down carefully on the bed and allowed his fingers to trail gently through the thick long mass of her silky hair until he reached the contour of her face.

Gabriella opened her eyes, startled. 'Ricardo,' she exclaimed, trying to sit up.

But he kept his hand to her face, bringing the other one down on the other side of her, forcing her back among the cushions. 'My lovely wife,' he murmured. 'My beautiful, unattainable virgin wife.' Then, before she could do more than let out a tiny cry, his mouth came down on hers—not tenderly or caringly, but with a firm, hard movement of possession.

Her lips parted and against her will she felt his tongue seek hers, felt the charge of molten lava shoot from her breasts to her core. Despite every urge to resist, every part of her brain telling her this was not what she wanted, her breasts ached and her body arched. This couldn't be happening. She mustn't allow it to happen. Yet when she felt Ricardo's arm slip below her waist and he moved over her, his arms bracing on either side of her body, his eyes piercing into hers, there was little she could do—little she wanted to do.

'Ricardo, no. We mustn't—please,' she murmured, making a half-hearted attempt to move. Part of her brain was remembering that what she wanted was a divorce while the other half gave way to the desire for his fingers to caress her once more. What was it about this man that riveted her so? What was it that made it impossible for her to refuse him?

One hand glided over her soft silk dress while the other reached to slide down its side zipper. She should resist, make it quite clear that she had no intention of...

But the next thing she knew she was lying naked before him. How it had happened she didn't quite know, only that he was standing over her now, his hair windswept, still in his tux, his bow tie dangling about his neck, his shirt collar open, his expression completely different from that of the man she'd become used to in the past weeks.

'You're so lovely,' he exclaimed, reaching down and trailing his fingers from her neck, down past the taut tips of her breasts until he reached the soft mound between her thighs, where he stopped, letting his fingers slip deeper.

A sigh escaped her and her eyes closed. She wanted to resist, wanted to play the game—as she was sure people like that woman she'd seen at the yacht club did. But she couldn't, didn't know how, only knew that at this moment she could refuse him nothing.

After several minutes of expert caresses, when he felt that Gabriella was ready and longing for him, Ricardo removed his hand and undressed himself.

Gabriella opened her eyes. Part of her longed for him, longed to become a woman—his woman. The shock of this revelation hit home as she watched him slip out of his tux. This man, whom she had every reason to detest, who treated her with cold indifference, was the one she wanted to love her. It made no sense. That she should feel this torrid, uncontrollable attraction for him held no logic; it went against everything about which she'd convinced herself: that she wanted to be free of him. Yet now she could not stop herself. For the truth was, she knew he would stop immediately if she requested it; he was a gentleman, as she'd discovered that night on the island. But that, she knew, would be impossible for her—she wanted him, wanted him more than anything else in the world right now, however bad she might feel tomorrow morning. After this it would be far more difficult to escape him. Although, to her deep distress, he had shown no signs of wanting to persuade her to stay.

All these thoughts conflicted in her mind as Ricardo lay back down next to her on the bed and took her in his arms. Oh, how she wished that she were less confused, Gabriella cried inwardly. That she knew what she really wanted.

'Gabriella, my Gabriella,' he murmured, in a voice she'd never heard before, which left her heart aching. 'You may not want to be my wife,' he muttered huskily, 'but nevertheless I will teach you what it is to be a woman.' His thumb grazed the tip of her breast while his other hand investigated further.

There was nothing she could do, no resistance she could muster. All reason flew to the wind as his lips came down on her breast, his hands roamed her body and sought her core. She was experiencing love for the first time. Suddenly she felt a deep rising ache within her that she thought would never end, and she arched her body towards Ricardo. Then the spiral gave way, and she shuddered with joy as he brought her to some peak and she experienced her first orgasm.

Ricardo smiled down as she lay limp in his arms, satisfied that, whatever happened after this, he—her husband—had been the first to give her the experience. Then slowly he positioned himself over her and looked down into her eyes. And it was then that he knew he could not let her go. This woman whom he'd been landed with so unexpectedly had, he realised with something of a shock, become part of his life. And now he was about to possess her.

'I'll try not to hurt you,' he whispered, his voice turning gentle as he read the flash of fear in her eyes. This soft and pliant lovely creature was a very different woman from the Gabriella who had faced him every day with icy pride and from whom he had become so distant. This was the vibrant, feeling, sensitive creature whom he had been certain all along existed beneath her façade. Holding her now in his arms, he entered her in one quick movement, heard her tiny gasp of pain, and held her tighter, kissing her lips, her eyes, her hair while he thrust deep within her, unable to hold back from losing himself in her depths. Soon he felt her pain give way to pleasure, felt her body easing into the rhythm of his as naturally as if they had been making love for years. Now they were riding on the crest of a rolling wave, skimming the surf, roaring towards completion. Then, when he could bear it no longer, he felt her arch into him once more and gasp. Only then did he allow himself to let go, and the two of them rolled over the precipice and into oblivion…

CHAPTER SEVEN

THAT night they slept naked and entwined around one another. And when they awoke in the morning they smiled drowsily into each other's eyes.

'Good morning, *cara mia*,' Ricardo whispered, drawing her closer to him and enjoying the feel of her body against his.

'Good morning,' Gabriella murmured, letting her head rest on his bare chest, closing her eyes again and basking in the knowledge that this was the first time she had ever awoken in a man's arms. It felt good, wonderful. She wished it could go on for ever.

'I have an idea,' Ricardo said, propping himself against the pillows and drawing her up beside him. 'Why don't we take the day off and go out on the yacht?'

'But I told the Contessa I would go with her to visit the orphanage this afternoon,' Gabriella said doubtfully, still letting her head rest lazily against his broad shoulder, lost in the scent of him, the rumpled sheets, and the tiny ache deep down in her core that proved to her that this was not a dream but a reality.

Ricardo tipped her chin up and dropped a kiss on her full lips. 'My beautiful Gabriella. I shall rearrange the schedule and all will be fine. Let me ring Alfredo and tell him to deal with it all. Then we must have breakfast—I'm ravenous.'

But before he could implement any of these plans Gabriella held him back. Slowly her fingers caressed his chest, roamed down to his stomach as she began to do her own investigation. Ricardo drew in his breath when her fingers, hesitant at first, gained confidence. Her lips began kissing his torso and her hand sought further. When at last she found him, felt the hardness of his desire and gently began to caress him, he let his eyes close and submitted to the delight. She was in-experienced, but her natural womanly instinct guided her where her knowledge was lacking. Soon Ricardo could bear it no longer. Quickly he took her in his arms, and unlike the night before, when he'd taken the time to prepare her, he thrust into her, knowing that she needed him as much as he needed her.

Together they feasted on one another, Gabriella's legs curling about his waist as he moved deep inside her, knowing that never before had he experienced such intensity with any woman. How extraordinary it was for this to happen with someone who had been thrown involuntarily into his path.

Gabriella wondered how she had ever lived without knowing the myriad sensations she had been exposed to in the past few hours. It was as though a new world had opened up before her, a window onto a new and wonderful scene that she had not known existed. And now he was asking her to spend the day with him, to go away together, as in quiet moments she'd allowed herself to dream that he would.

Half an hour later they were in the shower together, laughing as the water sprayed their bodies. Ricardo lathered soap on her back and Gabriella dropped the shampoo, which bubbled up around them. Still laughing and kissing, they got out of the shower and dried each other in huge terry towels embroidered with the Maldoravian royal crest. Ricardo tied one around his waist while Gabriella donned a bathrobe and they headed back into the bedroom. Breakfast had been laid out for them on the balcony.

'This is simply divine,' Gabriella said, stretching and breathing in the fresh morning air as Ricardo came up behind her and slipped his arms about her waist.

'Yes, Madame Wife, it is. Now, sit down and drink your orange juice and have that croissant. You must be hungry after so much activity.'

'That goes for you too,' she said, laughing and allowing him to pull out a wrought-iron chair for her to sit on.

'I've ordered the yacht for eleven,' he said, glancing at the time. 'That gives us an hour and a half. I'm afraid I'll have to drop into the office for a few minutes before we go.'

'I know.' She rolled her eyes. 'I'm getting used to all the protocol, and to the fact that instead of being a regal parasite living on the blood of your people you're actually a very hard-working man.'

'Is that what you thought I was?' he asked curiously as she spread jam on her croissant and let her white teeth sink into it.

Gabriella shrugged. She had her mouth full so couldn't answer.

At that moment the telephone rang and automatically Ricardo picked up. 'Yes, Alfredo. No, not today,' she heard him answer in the clipped, businesslike tones she was used to.

Gabriella smiled when their eyes met across the table. Ricardo's rolled heavenwards as the Baron went through a long list of obligations, but he stood firm. 'I'll deal with all that tomorrow, Alfredo. But today you must count me out. I'm spending it with my wife and shall not be available except in the case of a dire emergency.'

Ambrosia walked to the edge of the terrace of the stupendous Mediterranean villa which she had received as part of her second divorce settlement. She wore a long flowered silk kimono and held a glass of orange juice in her well-manicured hand. She was frowning as she stared out over the rocks and down to the yacht which was at present sailing into the harbour. It was the royal yacht. Was Ricardo preparing to sail? she wondered, taking a long sip of her juice.

Things were not been working out quite as she had planned. Ever since the beginning of their relationship she'd known there was only a very slight chance of her ever marrying Ricardo. That was pretty well out of the question. A twice-divorced woman was hardly suitable material for producing heirs to the Principality. Plus, if the truth be told, she had no desire to become a mother. The last thing she wanted was a pack of squawking brats to look after, and bearing them might ruin her perfect figure. But still, his sudden wedding, taking place as it had out of the blue, had caught her by surprise. It had not only angered her, it had set her nose out of joint. And Ambrosia was not used to this.

She had seen Ricardo's new wife for the first time at the club that day. That had been another shock. She had seen pictures in the papers, but nothing had prepared for the simple raw beauty the young girl possessed. In fact, she was far more beautiful and poised than Ambrosia had expected. And apparently sure of herself. That was what had disturbed Ambrosia the most: she had naturally assumed that a nineteen-year-old would be easily dealt with, that Ricardo would tire of the girl fast once he'd got her pregnant, that he would return to his mistress and her life would go back to having its previous pleasures. But there was no sign of this occurring, and as the days went by Ambrosia was becoming increasingly worried. Her friends had begun to tease her, some to make sly remarks.

This would not do, Ambrosia realised, watching the yacht's progress slow as it reached the harbour entrance. She must either decide to cut with Ricardo completely and find someone else, or make a stand.

As she finished off the last of the orange juice she inspected the mimosa. The gardener was not up to scratch, and she would complain to her housekeeper later on. But right now she was determined to find out exactly where the royal yacht was headed—and who would be sailing on her.

Inside, she sat at her antique desk and picked up the phone. She had contacts connected to the Palace—people who had made it their business to ingratiate themselves with her, as she had with them. She had done a few favours. Now she needed a small one in return.

'Hello? Is that Gian Carlo? How are you, darling?' she cooed down the phone.

'Ambrosia, darling.' The high-pitched male voice came back down the receiver. 'How wonderful to hear from you. You haven't been in to have your hair done. But of course that is understandable.'

'Isn't it?' she answered the hairdresser sweetly, pretending not to understand the meaning behind his words. 'I suppose you're doing you-know-who's hair now?'

'Actually, you're right, darling. I am. Quite gorgeous hair, actually,' he added.

'I'm sure. In the meantime, maybe you can tell me what the royal yacht is doing in the harbour and who is going on a trip?'

'Well, sweetie, I don't know all the details…' Gian Carlo's voice became almost a conspiratorial whisper. 'But I heard that this morning they were having breakfast on their balcony. Very gooey-eyed, if you know what I mean.'

'I know exactly what you mean,' Ambrosia said through gritted teeth. 'Go on.'

'Well, I overheard the secretary commenting that the Prince had asked for the yacht to be prepared for eleven. Apparently they're going out for a little romantic sea jaunt *à deux*.' He giggled shrilly and Ambrosia closed her eyes, determined not to allow her irritation to show.

'Thank you, Gian Carlo, darling,' she said instead. 'I'll be in soon. I need a trim and a manicure.'

'Of course, *bella*. Any time. And anything else you need to know,' he added with a purr, 'you can always count on me.'

'Of course I can, you nasty little creep,' she muttered, after slamming down the receiver. Eleven. That left her only an hour to strategise. Time to get moving.

With a swift sweeping movement she rose and marched up the stairs to her bedroom, her mind working at full throttle. This was a chance she wouldn't miss. She would put him against the wall, whether he liked it or not.

And that cool little bitch of a wife of his with him.

Gabriella slipped on her bikini, a short pink cotton skirt with a matching top and pink ballerina shoes, and headed jauntily down the large staircase with her bag over her shoulder, happier than she had been since setting foot in the Palace. The whole place looked different this morning—brighter, jollier. Even the servants, who always seemed pretty stiff and formal, appeared more likeable. She said bright good mornings to everyone she passed before popping her head around the door of the Contessa's apartment to see if she was in.

'Hello, my love. You look very well and pretty this morning,' the Contessa remarked, tipping her gold-framed glasses down her nose and inspecting Gabriella closely.

'Yes,' she said, letting out a breath and smiling happily. 'I'm sorry that I had to cancel our trip to the orphanage. Ricardo and I are taking the day off. We're going to sail away all day, just the two of us.'

'How lovely,' the Contessa exclaimed, smiling benevolently, hoping that at last things were beginning to take on a new shape. Perhaps the couple had finally found common ground. She certainly hoped so, for not only did she like Gabriella very much, she could not have imagined a lovelier, more perfect wife for Ricardo—even if the girl was younger than she would have chosen.

'Well, I'd better be off. I just popped in to say hello.' Gabriella deposited a warm kiss on the older woman's cheek and left, skipping down the rest of the steps to where Ricardo's Ferrari stood parked, waiting for them. She looked up at the Palace, anxious for him to join her. Perhaps, she thought, taking a deep breath, they would make love again on the boat. Just the thought of spending all day lying in his arms soaking up the sun and the sea was delicious.

She didn't have to wait long before Ricardo appeared, casually dressed in white jeans and a navy T-shirt, a sweater flung over his shoulders.

'Ready?' he said, winking at her as they jumped into his car, and he took off down the gracious driveway and out onto the road.

Gabriella couldn't stop smiling as they drove down through the old town towards the harbour. Ricardo had dispensed with his security guards today, which he often did in Maldoravia. In fact, he was often to be found wandering about quite happily among the people—to the horror of his security team, who went crazy trying to keep track of him. It felt so good to feel the wind blowing her hair, see the people going about their business, the old men leading donkeys with baskets laden with flowers and fresh fruit, small children with their mothers in brightly clad clothes, some of whom waved at them, smiling.

Then they were entering the Royal Yacht Club marina, where the royal yacht lay out at anchor, for she was too big to dock.

They left the car with the club valet and went inside.

'I guess we might have time for a quick drink,' Ricardo remarked. 'It's only ten to eleven.'

'Okay.' Gabriella was on for anything right now. Just looking at him, knowing she'd spent the night in his arms, left her weak with longing for more, and as they sat next to each other on the terrace she had to hold back from extending her hand and taking his.

'Well, well—what a surprise.'

Suddenly a shadow extended over them and Gabriella looked up. She immediately recognised the woman she'd seen that day at this club a couple of months earlier. She saw the way the woman looked at Ricardo and a shiver ran through her.

'Ambrosia, hello.' Ricardo rose politely. 'May I introduce you to my wife? Gabriella, this is an old friend of mine—Ambrosia de la Fuente.'

'Delighted to meet you,' Ambrosia cooed, taking in every detail of Gabriella's outfit and making the latter feel as if somehow she'd got herself dirty.

'Hello.' Gabriella took her hand and experienced another shiver, as though she'd touched a snake. She hastily withdrew it.

'Won't you sit down?' Ricardo was saying.

To her horror, Gabriella watched as the woman accepted his invitation and slid sensually into the vacant

chair next to him. Her slinky tall figure seemed to
vibrate with sex appeal, and she made Gabriella feel
young and gauche and inexperienced, a sensation she
had rarely had before. Normally she was quite self-
confident, but for some reason this woman left her ill
at ease. She watched as Ambrosia ordered a cocktail
and Ricardo joined her, and felt stupid having ordered
a cola. Determined not to allow herself to be made to
feel inferior, Gabriella plastered on a bright smile and
tried to join in the conversation.

'Do you live here in Maldoravia?' she asked politely as the waiter served their drinks.

'Not too much salt in this margarita, I hope, Pepe?'
Ambrosia said, ignoring Gabriella's question and turning to the waiter, who bowed graciously and murmured that he hoped madam's drink would be to her
satisfaction. Ambrosia took a small sexy sip, then allowed her tongue to slide over her upper lip. 'It's perfect,' she said with a condescending smile at the young
man. Then she turned back to Gabriella.

'You were saying?' Her expression was as haughty
as when she had been dealing with the waiter.

'I was asking if you lived here,' Gabriella replied,
trying to control her temper. This woman was making
a conscious effort to make her feel bad.

'Actually, I used to spend quite a lot of time here,'
Ambrosia answered, casting a quick sidelong smile at
Ricardo. 'Whether I will or not in the future depends
on a number of things.'

'Ah.' There was really not much to say.

At that moment a group of sophisticated young people in their late twenties and early thirties entered the

club. Immediately they waved and came over to the table.

'Hello, Ricky! Ambrosia, darling, it's been an age,' one of the women said, kissing Ricardo and then leaning over to peck Ambrosia on the cheek. 'How wonderful to see both of you.'

Gabriella watched as they all chatted and laughed, feeling increasingly embarrassed and humiliated. Ricardo was turning towards her now, and introducing her to one of the men. She smiled automatically and watched as Ambrosia carried on an animated conversation, referring to people Gabriella had never met and places she had never heard of. It was with a sigh of relief that she saw the yacht's first mate approaching. Surely he must be coming to say that the vessel was ready for them to embark? At last they would leave behind this crowd of superficial socialites, who were fast getting on her nerves, and then the day would go back to being perfect.

'Ricky, are you going out for a sail?' asked one of the men—Peter something-or-other; she hadn't caught his last name.

'Actually, yes. I'm taking the day off.' Ricardo smiled over at Gabriella, who got ready to take her leave.

'But, Rick, you're not going out alone, are you? How dreadfully boring! Why, we can't let that happen—can we, gang?' protested one of the women, a small, lively brunette in large designer sunglasses, laughing.

'Absolutely not,' Ambrosia chipped in, tipping her shades and looking over the rim at Ricardo, her eyes alive with amusement and challenge. 'I can't think of anything more deadly than going out alone with one's husband. Poor Gabriella,' she said, turning and smiling triumphantly.

Gabriella was about to retort when, to her horror, she heard Ricardo inviting the group to join them. At that moment her eyes flew to his, but he had transformed into the perfect urbane host, offering the yacht and his hospitality. There was no sign of the smouldering embers that had been there only hours before.

Her heart sank and she had to stifle a sudden rush of tears. Only her pride held her together. But it was too unfair. The one day she had with him, the one time they could be alone, to consolidate all that had taken place last night, was being ripped from her by this dreadful woman whom she already detested. Her and her awful friends. She felt young and silly and out of it. And she hated Ricardo for giving in to them all so easily, for not preserving what he should have realised was so important.

Two hours later the *Blue Mermaid* approached the small ancient walled town of Travania. It was a charming, beautiful place that Gabriella had heard of but as yet had not visited. It was a historical gem, according to the guidebooks, a place that had known Roman settlers, Ottoman rule, a crossroads of cultures. How she would have loved to visit the place alone with Ricardo.

But that was out of the question. There were at least ten people on board. Drinks were being served, and as they anchored off the coast of Travania lunch was being prepared. Gabriella tried to keep up the best front she could—chatting brightly with several of the crowd, forcing herself not to judge them—while wishing them a million miles away. The worst was seeing her husband ensconced in a long conversation with Ambrosia up on the front deck. They were alone and talking intently. Gabriella watched them a moment—watched the intimate way in which they leaned towards one another—certain now that by some unknown means the woman had planned the whole thing. Reason told her that it was impossible, that it was just a coincidence—there was no way anybody could have known about their planned boating trip. But something about Ambrosia and the hard confidence she exuded told her otherwise.

Gabriella felt a shiver run through her. She must find out the truth, must know what her relationship with Ricardo was. And the only people who would tell her the truth were the Contessa or Constanza. After all, she barely knew any other women, had no girlfriends to speak of, and could hardly consult with Baron Alfredo on the matter.

With a sigh, Gabriella leaned on the yacht's railing and stared down into the deep.

'A penny for your thoughts?'

'Oh.' She looked up to see Peter, the handsome young Englishman who'd joined the party at the club, smiling down at her.

'Well?'

'Oh, nothing, really. Just looking at the water, that's all,' she lied.

'I don't think that's quite true,' Peter answered with a winning smile. 'You know, I imagine that suddenly becoming Princess and having to deal with a new life can't be altogether easy.' He spoke sympathetically.

'Uh, no, you're right. It's not. But one gets used to it.'

'In two months? That's pretty good. Particularly when your husband spends half his time working.'

Gabriella tensed and then stiffened. 'My husband does all he can to help me,' she said, her chin tilting upwards.

'That's very sweet and loyal,' Peter said in a soft voice. 'I like seeing a woman stick up for her man. Even when that man doesn't deserve it,' he added dryly, glancing towards the forward deck.

Gabriella's eyes followed his. She bit her lip. She could not ask this man for the truth. Would not subject herself to that humiliation. If it was true, and Ambrosia was Ricardo's mistress, then everyone on this boat knew and she must be a laughing stock.

Then suddenly Gabriella realised that if that was the case it really didn't matter what Peter thought of her, and that she might as well learn the truth.

'Ambrosia is Ricardo's mistress, isn't she?' she said, in a low voice that tried to sound off-hand, as if this sort of thing happened every day.

Peter hesitated. He was a nice man, who had not realised to what extent Ambrosia was prepared to push things and manipulate situations to get Ricardo back. As soon as he'd seen what was going on he'd felt ashamed at being a part of her dirty tricks and causing this lovely young girl problems.

'Please,' Gabriella said, gripping the railing, 'I know I must seem like the world's biggest idiot to you, but do me a favour and don't leave me in the dark. They sleep together, don't they?'

'Did,' he answered quickly. 'I don't believe that since your marriage they have been together. I think that is why Ambrosia staged this whole thing—to see if she could try and get Ricardo to go back to her.'

'Well,' Gabriella said, with a bright smile and a glance in the direction of the two, 'she seems to be doing a pretty good job, doesn't she?'

'I don't think so. You shouldn't worry about Ambrosia. She's history and she knows it. How could she be anything else when Ricardo's got you?'

'Ha!' Gabriella exclaimed with a bitter laugh. 'Do you think I'm so young and inexperienced that I don't know what links a man and a woman? You just have to look at them to know there is something more than just friendship—' The words caught in her throat and she turned and swallowed.

'Gabriella, don't,' Peter said, taking her hand impulsively. 'I hate to see you like this. It's not fair of either of them to put you through this. But don't worry. I'll see what I can do.'

'No, you won't do anything of the sort,' Gabriella remonstrated, whirling around, her eyes blazing. 'You will leave it well alone. This is my problem, not yours. Or rather it is Ricardo's problem, and my problem, and that woman's. If he wants to sleep with her, then he's welcome to her. I don't care.'

Turning, she pulled her hand from his grasp, hurried away and went downstairs to the stateroom, where she sat on the bed and took a deep breath. She should have known last night was nothing but an illusion—his way of securing her womanhood, his way of putting his stamp on her—and nothing more. She hoped the day would go by fast and that soon she could get back to Maldoravia. At least there she would be in the privacy of her own apartments and would not be made a public spectacle. From now on, she knew the truth and would not be made a fool of any longer.

He would never touch her again.

Not as long as he lived.

Not if she had anything to do with it.

CHAPTER EIGHT

'DID you have a nice day?' the Contessa asked next morning, as she and Gabriella sat in the back of the limousine on their way to visit the orphanage.

'It was all right, thank you,' she replied blankly.

The Contessa took a sidelong glance at the girl. Gone was the glow of yesterday. In its stead she saw tenseness, dark rings under her eyes and a deep sadness surrounding her. What on earth could have gone wrong in such a short time? she asked herself. She must try and get the girl to confide in her. Something was definitely not right.

Ricardo sat behind the large antique desk in his office and thought about the previous day. What a disaster. He should have known Ambrosia would set him up. At least he'd taken the opportunity to make it abundantly plain to her that their relationship was most definitely over and that there would be no more nocturnal visits to her house. He should have done that before he got married, he realised. But how could he have guessed that making love to Gabriella would be such a magical experience? He had never imagined that anything could turn into the night before last.

But he would rather not remember last night. Gone had been the loving, beautiful creature of the night before, the enchanting woman whom he'd breakfasted

with. In her stead had been an angry, capricious teen-
ager who had ranted at him for having his friends on
board. He had considered telling her the truth, but
thought better of it. If she didn't know about the past
and Ambrosia then there was no point in opening up
Pandora's box.

'I'm sorry about today,' he'd said as they returned
to the Palace last evening. 'I wanted to spend it alone
with you, but it would have been impossible to refuse
my friends a ride.'

'That has become abundantly clear,' Gabriella threw
at him angrily. 'Another time just tell me you prefer
their company to mine and I'll stay behind.'

'Gabriella, stop being childish.'

'Childish, am I? Okay, then, have it your way.
Maybe I am childish—or just plain stupid. You obviously had a good time.'

'What do you mean?' he asked guardedly as they
swung into the Palace driveway.

'Nothing. I didn't mean anything. And I really don't
want to talk to you any more.'

She had jumped out of the car and made her way
quickly up the stairs, and he hadn't seen her again all
evening. She'd sent a message saying she had a headache and would not be dining with him, and when he'd
come to bed only the nightlight had been on and she'd
either been fast asleep or pretended to be.

This morning he'd tried to raise the subject with her.
But instead of fury he'd encountered cold, icy indifference. And to his surprise it had hurt.

Now, as he fiddled with his pen and ignored the pile
of letters he needed to sign, he thought about her and

the night spent with her in his arms. And all at once he knew that he wanted to save this marriage that had taken them both so by surprise.

He would have to find a way of making her fall in love with him.

But the next few days gave no opportunities for his plan to develop. First he was called away to a state funeral in the Middle East, then on his way back he had to make a trip to Bahrain, followed by a few hectic days dealing with some business affairs in London and Paris. When he phoned the Palace he received the news that his wife had gone to join his sister at her *schloss* in Austria.

After some deliberation, he decided to go and pay his sister a surprise visit.

The towered Austrian *schloss* was like a building out of a Grimm's fairy tale—all towers and small mullioned windows and perfectly enchanting. But, although summer was lovely by the Wolfgang See, with small boats puttering on the mirror-like lake, children swimming and playing at the water's edge, Gabriella found little to be happy about. Her one joy was being with Constanza's children, whom she adored. The affection was reciprocated. They didn't want to go anywhere without her. Now, on the *schloss*'s private beach, she lay on a chaise longue and watched little Anita and Ricky splashing in the water. Their nanny stood close by, supervising, and Constanza drooped languidly, a large sunhat covering her face in the next chaise longue.

'What gorgeous weather. I'm so pleased it's held.

And I'm glad that you decided to come and stay, Gabriella. I wonder if Ricardo will think of joining us.'

'I doubt it,' she replied dryly. 'He's far too busy to spend any time relaxing.'

'Do you think so?' Constanza tipped up her hat and took a surreptitious look at her sister-in-law. The girl was tense, and looked positively haggard at times. What was her brother up to?

From the first moment she had set eyes on Gabriella, just before the wedding, she'd been convinced that this might just be the making of him. He might finally get rid of that dreadful Mexican woman, whom she loathed. Over the years Ricardo had had a number of girlfriends and mistresses, some of whom had been friends. Others, like Ambrosia, had been a real pain in the butt. Serve her right that Ricardo had gone off and suddenly married a girl fourteen years his junior, who was not only stunningly beautiful but struck her as intelligent to boot.

'You don't seem to spend much time with Ricardo,' she remarked, picking up her water bottle and taking a long sip.

'He is always very occupied.'

'Gabriella, I hate to interfere, and please tell me to stop if I'm being intrusive, but it strikes me that all is not well with you and Ricardo. And what's more,' she added perceptively, 'you have no one to talk to about it. I assure you that anything you say here will remain strictly confidential—even though I am his sister.'

Gabriella stiffened and she sat up straighter, tears knotted in her throat. 'I—I don't really know. I...'

Then to her horror she broke down, and tears poured down her cheeks.

Constanza jumped up and sat next to her, grabbing her hands. 'Oh, you poor darling. What has he done, the monster? I promise you he will regret it. You don't deserve to be unhappy.'

'It's not his f-fault,' she muttered through her tears. 'We only got married because my father insisted when he was dying. He made me promise. It was unfair to both of us, but there was no way out. If Ricardo hadn't married me I would have lost my entire fortune. So, you see, there was no love involved. He was just being a gentleman, I suppose. I hate the way things are between us, but the truth is he did his duty and I guess it's only normal that now he wants his old life back.'

'I don't believe it,' Constanza exclaimed, amazed. 'It is obvious that he cares for you, Gabriella. You just have to see the way he looks at you.'

'You think so?' Gabriella looked up, her eyes swimming. She sniffed loudly and searched for a hanky. 'There was one time when I—I thought that perhaps... But then—' She broke off, remembering the wonderful night followed by the awful day on the yacht.

'But then what?' Constanza prodded, frowning.

'Then Ambrosia appeared, with all her horrid friends, and it was simply awful. I thought we were going to spend the day together, but he preferred to spend it with her. They are obviously very intimate. That much was blatant,' she added, clenching her fists and gritting her teeth.

'Well? You're not going to let him get away with it, are you?'

'What do you mean?'

'Mean? Why, give as good as you get, of course,' the other woman exclaimed with a laugh. 'If he's encouraging that creature then you'd better let him know that there are lots of men after you.'

'Yes, well, that's all very well,' Gabriella responded dourly, 'but there aren't. And even if there were I would never encourage them. After all, I'm a married woman now. It wouldn't be right.'

'Big deal,' Constanza scoffed. 'Of course you wouldn't go as far as having an affair with anyone, but a little flirtation—just enough to make Ricardo jealous—would do him no harm at all, don't you think?'

'I don't know. Do you really think it would work?' Gabriella turned her face up to her sister-in-law, the idea taking root.

'I absolutely do.'

'But I don't know any men. Plus, surely it would be wrong and make me appear—well, vulgar, and...'

'Leave it to me,' Constanza said grandly. 'I shall organise the whole thing.'

'But—'

'Trust me. Just be prepared to look beautiful and be at your most charming,' she answered with a smug, mischievous smile. 'We'll see if it doesn't do the trick.'

The helicopter ride from Munich airport took barely twenty minutes, and as the chopper prepared to land Ricardo looked down at the lake, at the peaceful scene below, glad he'd decided to come. Maybe here he and

Gabriella could get off to a fresh start. They certainly needed to if anything was going to come of this marriage.

When the chopper landed he saw his sister coming out of the castle and stepping onto the lawn, waving. He'd called her earlier, to tell her he planned to arrive and not to tell Gabriella. When she hadn't sounded surprised at his visit, he'd smiled. Constanza knew him pretty well.

Brother and sister embraced and moved towards the house, Ricardo carrying a large tote bag which he laid down in the hall.

'How is Wilhelm?' he asked.

'Fine. He'll be back from Salzburg very shortly.'

'And where is Gabriella?' he asked.

'Oh, she's off somewhere,' Constanza replied with studied vagueness. 'Why don't you come onto the terrace and have a glass of lemonade? The heat is unbearable.'

'I'd love to. But where is my wife?'

'I told you—she went out.'

'Where?' he insisted.

'I have Ruddy Hofstetten and Jamie Reid-Harper staying. They all seem to be getting along rather well together. Ruddy asked Gabriella to go biking with them.'

'Ruddy Hofstetten? You must be kidding? What the hell is he doing here?' Ricardo frowned.

'He and Jamie asked if they could spend a few days here. As they're both good friends of Wilhelm's brother Franz, of course we agreed. Actually,' she said slyly, 'I think it's been rather nice for Gabriella to have some young people around her. She seems to spend so much time on her own. Ah, here's the lemonade,' Constanza added, glancing at Ricardo out of the corner of her eye to see how he'd reacted to the news that one of Europe's most notorious playboys happened to be staying.

Ricardo said nothing, merely sat down on the charming terrace and looked about him. 'You have done a lovely job on this place, Constanza. Very tasteful indeed.'

'Mmm.' Constanza had no desire to talk about her decorating skills. Instead, she hoped he would open up about his marriage. But she doubted that would happen. Ricardo and she had always got on well together but he always kept his private life exactly that: private.

Well, she'd done all she could, had primed the boys, and now she hoped that her plan would work. And, actually, Ricardo might really have to be careful. She had merely intended that the young men's visit be nothing but a ploy. But it had immediately been obvious that Gabriella's beauty and charm was not lost on either of them. Time would tell how Ricardo would react to seeing his wife being the centre of so much male attention, she figured, pouring lemonade from the crystal jug with a private smile.

'Oh, it's great fun,' Gabriella exclaimed as the two Harley Davidson bikes rolled up, stopping in front of the *schloss*. She alighted. 'Thanks, Ruddy. I enjoyed every minute of the trip. Can we go again tomorrow?'

'Your wish is my command, Princess,' the dashing young count replied, tossing his long blond hair back and loosening the leather jacket that he wore for biking.

'Oh, please, don't call me that. It makes me feel ancient.'

'Okay, Gabriella, then. It is a very pretty name, and it suits you rather well,' he said in his smooth sexy voice.

'We could take a picnic,' she murmured, unbuttoning her jacket.

'We could. On the other hand, I have a better idea.'

'Oh?' She looked up, smiling, her eyes sparkling. She hadn't had so much fun in a while.

'I have the perfect spot for us to lunch. Hey, Jamie,' Ruddy said, turning towards his friend, who was getting off his bike and coming to join them. 'Do you remember that delightful little *heurigen* we went to last year?'

'Yes. It wasn't far south of here. I'm sure we could find it again. Or maybe Constanza will remember. Well, Gabi,' he said, sending Gabriella a teasing smile, 'did you enjoy your first motorbike ride?'

'It wasn't my first ride,' she scoffed, tossing her head back with a mischievous smile. 'My father was a great motorcyclist. I went all over South America with him on the back of a bike.'

'Ah! A veteran, I see. That's great. Maybe we can persuade Constanza to join us tomorrow. Here—help me pull these gloves off, will you?' He held out his hands for Gabriella to tug.

Laughing, she pulled at the gloves, which were rather tight. Jamie pulled back and she fell into his arms.

'Oh, sorry,' she cried breathlessly.

'I can handle mistakes like these,' Jamie said smoothly, grinning down at her, a twinkle in his eye.

Gabriella flushed and, recovering her balance, turned away. Then she looked up. 'Oh, my God,' she whispered, a flush rushing to her cheeks.

'Hello, Gabriella,' Ricardo said, coming down the steps in a casual manner and nodding to her two companions. 'Hello, Ruddy. I haven't seen you about in a while—or you for that matter, Jamie. How is your father?'

'Better, thanks,' Jamie replied.

The three men took stock of each other while Gabriella tried to compose herself. What on earth was Ricardo doing here? He hadn't told her he was coming—hadn't even given her an inkling. Had he seen her fall into Jamie's arms? She knew Constanza wanted her to flirt with other men in his presence, but between flirting and being embraced there was a difference. She turned her flushed face towards him, a sudden shudder searing through her when slipped his arm around her and his lips met hers in a brief encounter.

'Hello, my dear. I thought I'd pay you all a surprise visit.'

'Yes. Well, it is a surprise. We weren't expecting you. I—' She stopped, smiled, and looked down.

'Apparently not,' he murmured.

Minutes later they were heading up the wide oak staircase and down a large corridor filled with empty suits of armour, its walls graced by portraits of

Wilhelm's ancestors, to the suite of rooms Constanza had allotted them.

'I had no idea you were coming to visit,' Gabriella said, to make conversation as they entered the room.

'No. I gathered that.'

'What do you mean?' she asked, posing her gloves on the chest of drawers and taking off the leather clothes she'd borrowed from Constanza for the bike trip.

'Merely that you seemed to be having a good time and probably weren't too concerned about my whereabouts.'

'Should I have been concerned?' she asked coolly.

'I don't know. That depends how much you care whether I'm near you or not.'

His eyes bored into hers and she looked away, unwilling to let him see just how much his presence affected her. She would not go through another humiliation, she reminded herself, remembering the incident at the yacht club and its aftermath.

'I think you're teasing,' she said at last, picking up her silk dressing gown and heading towards the bathroom.

'Wait, Gabriella. I want to speak to you.'

'Yes?' She turned and looked at him expectantly, trying not to show by her expression just how handsome she thought he looked in a pair of stonewashed jeans and a white T-shirt, so casual compared to how he was usually attired.

'Gabriella, I want to talk to you about the future.'

Her heart skipped a beat. 'This is hardly the right moment. I'm about to take a shower. I was out on a bike all day and I don't think that—' She broke off as he crossed the room and planted his hands on her shoulders.

'When is the right time, in your view?'

'I—I don't know. What I mean to say is—'

'That you would prefer not to have to talk to me at all? That you much prefer the company of young playboys like Ruddy and Jamie?' There was an edge to his voice and his grip on her shoulders tightened.

'I don't know what you mean,' she murmured, staring at his chest.

'I think you do. You look happier than I've seen you in a while. Do you plan to separate from me in a few months' time and begin a relationship with one of them?'

'How can you say such a thing?' she exclaimed, staring up at him, her eyes ablaze with righteous anger. Then she remembered Constanza's advice and, looking away, she countered. 'Of course if that is the way you would prefer things to be, then why not?' She shrugged, pretended to be indifferent, and had the pleasure of seeing his expression darken, his thick brows meet over the bridge of his patrician nose. His hands dropped from her shoulders and he looked down at her.

'I see. So I was right after all.'

'Right about what?'

'Right that you have forgotten this,' he said, his hands snaking to her waist and drawing her close against him. 'You may find Ruddy and his cohorts attractive, *cara mia*, but you are still my wife,' he said

bitingly. 'And I would appreciate it if you didn't forget it.'

His lips clamped down on hers before she could
move or do more than give a tiny muffled cry of protest that was silenced as his tongue worked its way
cleverly on hers. Heat soared to her core, leaving her
limp and wanting. What was it about this man that she
couldn't resist? In a hazy blur Gabriella allowed her
arms to entwine about his neck and obediently followed him as he pulled her over to the bed. She
dropped the dressing gown in a heap on the floor.
Soon the rest of their clothes followed and Ricardo
drew her into his arms, on top of him, so that she lay
draped over him. He held her tight, pressing her abdomen to his, making her feel the rush of desire consuming him.

Gabriella looked down into his eyes, her lips parted
and a new sense of her own sexuality suddenly taking
hold. All at once she felt powerful and in control.
Instead of embarrassment she felt triumph as slowly
she moved on top of him, easing herself until he thrust
inside her with a groan. Then slowly her hips began
to rotate. Ricardo gripped her waist. It was wonderful
to feel him deep inside her, to know that she was the
one controlling the situation, determining the rhythm
of their lovemaking, to know that he lay there at her
mercy.

Then, just as she was testing her skills, Ricardo
lifted her off him in one swift movement and, revers-
ing their positions, drove himself inside her, leaving
her panting and longing. Now he was the one calling
the shots, and she lay back with a little cry of ecstasy

as he loved her, easing in and out of her until she could bear it no longer, until she begged him to bring her to completion. When she thought she could stand it no longer he drove her further, until at last they climaxed together, falling among the rumpled sheets, exhausted.

Ricardo lay back, his head against the pillows, his eyes closed. Not in many years had he experienced the rush of sensuality that Gabriella caused. Lovemaking for him over the past few years had been an expert form of exercise—a pastime he'd indulged in with sophisticated, well-versed women like Ambrosia, who'd made sure they highlighted his preferences and pandered to his tastes. But with Gabriella all that had changed. This was raw, sensual lovemaking such as he had not known for ages—if ever, he recognised, shocked at how off balance she made him. The sight of her laughing up at Jamie had left him hot with a raw new sensation that he now recognised as jealousy. He had never felt jealous of any woman before. Had never needed to. Mostly women made sure they were exactly what he wanted them to be. And when things burned out, as they usually did after a while, it was all very civilised. Each of them moved on and they remained friends.

But this was different. He knew all at once that he could never remain simply friends with Gabriella. That would be impossible. Every time he looked at her he envisaged her as she was now, her beautiful sensual body lying naked among the sheets. His body; his woman. He would never let any other man touch her, he vowed, his fist clenching.

Then he turned and watched her, reaching down and dropping a kiss on the tip of her perfect young breast. When he sucked it she gasped.

'No, please, Ricardo. Not again. I don't think I could. I—'

'Mmm.' Ricardo paid no attention, simply continued to draw the soft nipple into his mouth, grazing it with his teeth, laving it until Gabriella thought she would die of sheer delight. Again the ache between her thighs mounted. She had thought only moments ago that she was saturated, could not move. Yet here she was, her hips arching, her hands seeking him, reaching out to him with all her being as once again they found one another.

Ricardo slid inside her, not hungrily or tempestuously as he had earlier, but softly and smoothly, as though completing something, sending her a message that said *I possess you in every way and you will not escape me.*

And the truth was that right then she didn't want to.

CHAPTER NINE

DINNER was served on the terrace. Champagne and delicious Austrian wines accompanied the meal. Conversation flowed and the ambience was delightful. For the first time since she'd known her husband Gabriella saw Ricardo really at ease. He laughed with them, told amusing stories, captivated his audience and was altogether different from the autocratic being she'd become so used to.

'So. What about tomorrow?' Ruddy asked, once they were all sitting in wicker chairs drinking coffee and partaking of after-dinner drinks. The moonlight reflected on the lake, sending a fine shimmering silver across the peaceful waters.

'What about tomorrow?' Ricardo rejoined.

'We are going on another bike trip. Want to come along?'

'Where to?'

'We thought we'd head south, maybe stop by one of the other lakes for lunch.'

'I really ought to be leaving tomorrow,' he replied. 'And you should be coming home too, Gabriella. There are several engagements that require your presence in Maldoravia.'

'But, Ricky, this is the summer vacation. Gabriella's having fun. Don't spoil it.'

'That wasn't my intention,' he said stiffly. 'Of course, if she wants to stay that is different.'

125

He looked across at Gabriella, sitting between Constanza and Jamie. 'Well?' His tone implied that he expected her to obey him.

A sudden flash of anger gripped her. Just because she succumbed to him in bed it did not mean she was going to let herself be treated like some nineteenth-century wife.

'I think I'll stay. I promised the children that I would take them fishing. I would hate to disappoint them.'

A look passed between Ruddy and Jamie. It was not lost on Ricardo. He was about to make a pithy comment, then pressed his lips shut. 'Very well. As you wish. I'm rather tired,' he added, getting up and altering the mood as he took his brandy snifter with him. 'If you'll excuse me, Constanza, I think I'll finish this upstairs and get ready for an early night. I'll order the chopper for seven-thirty.'

'I'm damned if I'm having that noise on the lawn so early,' his sister protested. 'Seven-thirty, indeed. How uncivilised, Ricky. No wonder Gabriella wants to stay, if you're being unbearable.'

She was caught in a web. On the one hand she would have loved to be with Ricardo. But his whole attitude was so domineering and arrogant. *Insupportable* was the word that came to mind. He really believed that because she was his for the taking in bed she would simply comply with his every wish. Well, she wasn't leaving and that was that, Gabriela decided, as she dressed to go on the excursion. There was no sign of Ricardo, who appeared to have left early. But she had heard nothing, and if a helicopter had landed then she'd slept through the noise.

At nine-thirty she descended to the large dining room, where breakfast was being served.

'Ah, there you are.' Constanza smiled and indicated to her to sit down. 'I didn't hear Ricardo leave, did you?'

'No, I didn't. Maybe he left by car.'

'I'll ask Hans the butler when he comes in. He must have seen him. So, are you off with the boys for the day?'

'Yes. Though it's a pity the weather doesn't look too great.'

'No,' Constanza agreed as Gabriella sat down. She passed her the toast. 'The forecast announced intermittent showers. You'd better take something to cover up, just in case.'

'I will. I'm really looking forward to it.'

'Good morning.'

Ruddy and Jamie entered the dining room, looking handsome and ready for the day's fun.

'We've got the bikes all set, and we thought we'd be off before eleven. Is that okay with you, Gabi?'

'Fine. Constanza says the weather may turn bad.'

'Think so?' Ruddy went to the window and peered out. 'It's a bit cloudy, but nothing to worry about. If it starts raining we can stop off somewhere and have a drink or something.'

'Sounds good,' Jamie said, joining the ladies at the table and tucking in to a large plate of ham and eggs.

At eleven sharp the three were ready to go. Gabriella mounted the back of Ruddy's bike and Jamie drove alone. Soon they were heading along the pretty lakeside road, and Gabriella clung tight to Ruddy's waist as the bike gained speed and they whizzed around corners, then slowed to go through picturesque villages, with little white houses, painted shutters and people walking around in traditional dress—the girls in dirndles and the men in traditional suede jackets and green feathered hats.

An hour later they were well into the Tyrol. The clouds that earlier had seemed light now hung low and dark in the sky, and a rumble of thunder could be heard in the distance.

'Let's stop for a bite of lunch. I think that place is only a little further on,' Jamie called as they rode side by side on the empty road.

'Right.'

Ten minutes later they drew up at a small hotel on the banks of a lake. Outside long tables were laid, and a big array of smoked meats, cheeses and delicacies was spread on a large wooden table adorned with a bright chequered red and white cloth.

'This is lovely,' Gabriella exclaimed, removing her helmet and shaking out the long black hair that poured over her shoulders. Then she took off her jacket and looked up at the sky. 'A bit risky to stay outside, don't you think?'

'Oh, I think we just might manage lunch,' Ruddy said, his eyes following hers. As she sat down he gave her a speculative glance, but said nothing.

Once installed at the *heurigen* they ordered cold meat, cheese and sausage and a bottle of Weltliner, the local wine. Ruddy kept filling her glass, letting his hand lie next to hers.

'Look, I want to go and visit a friend of mine who lives a few miles from here,' Jamie remarked, pouring them another glass. 'Would you mind if we split up and meet again in Graz?'

'No, that's fine,' Ruddy answered carelessly.

'Do you think that's wise?' Gabriella asked. The clouds were growing darker, and some people were beginning to head indoors. 'You might get caught in the rain.'

'Don't worry about me, gorgeous,' Jamie said, getting up and winking at her. 'I'll be fine. I'll see you in a while. Give me a buzz on the mobile when you're through,' he murmured to Ruddy.

Gabriella frowned. It sounded almost as if this were a planned thing between them. But she shrugged it off. 'I suppose we should get going too.'

'Oh, no, not yet. We've got lots of time. Anyway, it's rather fun biking in the rain. But first I want to show you this place properly. It's very old and charming. Dates back to the sixteenth century, actually.'

Gabriella experienced a moment's hesitation which she immediately banished. 'I'd love to.'

'Right. Well, why don't we finish this wine, then I'll give you a guided tour?'

A few minutes later Ruddy was leading Gabriella indoors. He spoke in German to the lady behind the desk, who beamed at him and handed him a key.

'What's that for?' Gabriella asked curiously.

'Oh, she thought you might like to see one of the suites. They're beautifully decorated. All in the original style of the region.'

'That would be very nice,' Gabriella said, smiling at the woman and following Ruddy up the creaking wooden staircase, delighted by the small crooked windows with their ruffled curtains, and the scent of pot pourri. The place was truly charming.

At the top of the stairs Ruddy stopped, then turned right. 'Here it is,' he said, unlocking a large hand-painted door at the end of the corridor. 'This is the

prettiest suite in the house. Come in and take a look.'
He opened the door for her and stood aside for her to
enter.

Gabriella stepped inside and was enchanted. The
small living room had been beautifully decorated with
wooden furniture piled with red and green cushions,
all in Austrian patterns. A fireplace stood in the centre
of the room, and through the windows at the far end
was a magnificent view over the Alps. 'It's perfectly
gorgeous,' she exclaimed, moving towards the window.

'And come and see this,' Ruddy urged, taking her
arm and leading her towards the bedroom, where a
huge antique four-poster graced the room 'Isn't that
delightful?'

'Yes, it is. Thanks for bringing me here and showing me all of this,' she answered, turning around and
smiling at him.

'No need to thank me, beautiful,' he responded, his
voice turning low and husky. 'I thought that we might
just spend a little time here together. I've been thinking of nothing else since the moment I met you,
Gabriella.' He reached out and to her shock pulled her
into his arms.

'Ruddy, no—this is ridiculous. I—'

'Shush,' he teased, stroking her hair, slipping his
hand to the back of her neck and tilting her head back.
'Just relax and enjoy it. It'll be a change from that
pokered-up husband of yours. He must be a royal pain
in the ass,' he muttered, laughing before bringing his
mouth down on hers.

Gabriella felt a moment's panic. Then she began to
struggle. 'Leave me alone,' she cried, pushing him as
best she could.

'Oh, so we like a tussle, do we?' Ruddy's eyes gleamed and he threw her onto the bed.

'Please, leave me alone. I never wanted anything like this to happen,' Gabriella remonstrated, trying to move out of his hold.

'Oh, come on, Gabriella. I know you're young, but don't let's play games, darling. You've been hot for this ever since I arrived. I've seen the way you and your husband behave with one another. I'll bet he rarely comes near you. Anyway, it's a known fact that Ricardo lays that Mexican tornado Ambrosia. He's not likely to give up a hot little number like that just because he married a schoolgirl. Now, come on, baby—let me teach you to enjoy yourself in bed. I'll bet he hasn't.'

Gabriella felt a rush of unprecedented anger grip her. And with it came a wave of unexpected strength. She raised her leg and gave Rudy a hard blow with her knee that sent him reeling back on the floor.

'You little bitch,' he muttered, grimacing. 'You're nothing but a tease.'

'I'm leaving,' Gabriella threw, getting up and hurrying into the living room.

'Oh, yes? And how exactly do you plan to do that?'

'I'll take a taxi back to the castle.'

'Really? Well, good luck to you. There's a festival on,' he said with satisfaction. 'All the taxis will be busy.' Gabriella felt a sudden rush of panic, but Ruddy shook his head ruefully. 'Look, don't worry. I'm sorry if I frightened you. Maybe I should have gone about this more tactfully. Let's forget about the whole thing and stay friends, okay? I'm sorry. Really.' He moved towards her, stretched out his hand and smiled disarmingly. 'I got it wrong. I'm sorry. I'll take you home now if you like, and we'll say no more about it.'

Gabriella hesitated again. She had no desire to go to the end of the street with this man, and wished she'd done as Ricardo had said and left with him to go back to Maldoravia. But it was too late for regrets. Now all she wanted was to return to the safety of the castle.

'All right,' she agreed reluctantly. 'Are you sure it's not dangerous to ride in this weather?' She glanced out of the window, to where heavy raindrops were beginning to fall.

'Oh, Lord, of course not. We're experienced riders. You're not scared, are you?' he teased, his eyes meeting hers in a daring challenge.

'Of course I'm not scared,' she scoffed, tossing her head back. She would not for a moment show any anxiety.

Back on the bike, they headed back on the road they'd travelled. To her horror, the bike picked up speed.

'Not so fast,' she shouted above the wind as a wave of nervousness overtook her.

But Ruddy just laughed, stepped on the gas and whizzed around the corners of the small country road at breakneck speed, forcing her to cling to him for dear life. In the back of her mind a niggling picture of Ricardo looking thoroughly disapproving haunted her. Oh, how she wished she had listened to him, and that he were here right now.

Another sharp turn had her screaming with fear. Then suddenly she heard the loud blare of a horn. The bike screeched, then swerved off the road, and she was flying through the air.

After that there was darkness.

*   *   *

Ricardo had not returned to Maldoravia, as he had led them to believe, but had merely driven to Salzburg for a morning of meetings. When he returned to the *schloss* at lunchtime he was met by his sister.

'So there you are. Hans told me you had decided to stay. Why did you go to Salzburg so early?'

'I had a meeting with a friend of mine from the music festival. I'm a patron. We had breakfast at the Sacher. Is my wife home yet?'

'No, of course not. They only left about an hour and a half ago. I think they are going to lunch at a *heurigen.*'

'I see.' Ricardo looked stern. 'I don't approve of her going off with the likes of Ruddy Hofstetten. I don't like him.'

'Why on earth not? He seems a perfectly nice young man to me. And Jamie's an absolute hoot. He tells such funny stories. I haven't laughed like this in years.'

'I've heard some rather disagreeable stories about Ruddy and his pals,' Ricardo continued as they stepped into the drawing room. 'I don't like the idea of my wife being alone with him.'

'Well, she's not alone with him,' Constanza pointed out in a matter-of-fact tone. 'Jamie is with them.'

'Hmm.' Somehow he could not rid himself of the uneasy feeling that had haunted him all morning that all was not right. 'Where did they go?' he enquired, accepting a glass of champagne from his sister.

'I don't know, exactly. But why are you so worried? Gabriella seems to be having fun.'

'That isn't the point.'

'Really, Ricardo, you're acting like a jealous husband, for goodness' sake.'

'That's ridiculous,' he retorted. 'I'm merely concerned about her being out in this weather with two reckless young men.'

'God, you sound like her father, not her husband.' Constanza gave him a look that spoke volumes but said nothing more. Perhaps he needed to come to the conclusion that he was far more taken with his young wife than he himself realised. If that was the case then she was happy. The more she knew Gabriella, the more she liked her. She just hoped that the two would work themselves out in the end.

It was four in the afternoon when a police car drove up to the Schloss and two solid-looking officers dressed in green marched up the steps. Hans opened the heavy front door. Moments later he was knocking anxiously on the door of the den, where Constanza, Wilhelm and Ricardo were watching a tennis match on TV.

'Your Highness, you are wanted in the hall,' he said, addressing Ricardo, his expression worried.

'What? Who on earth would want Ricardo?' Constanza exclaimed, her face tilting upwards in surprise.

'I'm afraid it is not good news,' Hans said, shaking his white head.

'Gabriella.' Ricardo was already out of his chair and marching into the hall, where he nodded to the two officers. 'What is going on?' he asked, in a voice that rang with authority.

'I'm afraid it is your wife, Your Highness.'

'What about her?'

'There has been an accident.'

'An accident?' Ricardo paled, clenched his fingers tight and forced himself to remain calm.

'Oh, my God!' Constanza exclaimed anxiously, following him out of the room with her husband.

'Where is she?' Wilhelm asked.

'The helicopter flew her to Salzburg, Herr Graf. We know no more than that.'

'What about the drivers of the bikes?' Wilhelm asked.

'There was only one, sir. He was not badly hurt. They kept him in the nearby village hospital to check him out. The more seriously injured was Her Royal Highness.'

'We must go at once,' Ricardo said, tight-lipped. 'Wilhelm, get a chopper.'

'In this weather? Forget it. I'll drive you. It'll be quicker.'

'Wait for me,' Constanza cried, grabbing a couple of old Loden jackets lying on one of the hall chairs. 'Thank you, Officer,' she said to the policeman, then rushed out of the front door to jump into the back of the Range Rover that Wilhelm was already revving up.

'You're all right now.' She heard a soft voice close by as she came to.

'Where am I?' Gabriella whispered, opening her eyes, a dizzy feeling making her close them again immediately.

'You are in hospital in Salzburg. You had a motorbike accident and suffered a mild concussion. You also broke your arm. It was thought preferable to bring you here.'

'Oh.' She closed her eyes again, the scenes of earlier that afternoon playing out before her. All at once a rush of tears burned her eyes and she wished, oh, how she wished that she had listened to Ricardo, and had not let her pride dictate her actions. But it was too late for that. Ricardo would be furious when he found out what had happened. Now, instead of getting better, things would probably get worse between them.

'Are you all right, my child?' The soft voice spoke again and she opened her eyes to see a smiling face under a wimple. 'I am Sister Perpetua,' the nun told her, pressing a gentle hand on hers. 'There is no need for you to be unhappy or frightened any longer. All is well, and you will be fine in a few days.'

'Does—does anyone know I'm here?' Gabriella asked in a small voice.

'Yes. A message has been sent to your sister-in-law, Grafin Wiesthun. Apparently the young man with whom you were riding provided the police with the address. I imagine your family will be here soon.'

Gabriella nodded and swallowed.

'The other good news,' the nun said, beaming, 'is that the baby is all right.'

'The baby?' Gabriela looked at her blankly.

'Yes, my dear. Your baby.'

'My baby? But—'

'You mean you didn't know that you were pregnant?' the English nun asked kindly.

'No! I... That is, I had no idea. How could this have

happened?' she whispered, trying to draw herself up in the bed, wondering if she was going mad.

'In the usual manner, I imagine,' the nun replied with a touch of wry humour. 'You are a married woman, I gather, so it is to be expected.'

'I didn't think that—I just thought my period was late,' Gabriella mumbled, almost to herself. 'It never occurred to me that... Oh, my God,' she whispered as the implications of what she had just been told sank in. 'Sister, please, do not tell anyone.' She turned in panic to the nun and clasped her hand with her good one.

'But why not? Surely your husband will want to know that the child is all right.'

'He doesn't know yet and I—well, there are reasons why I would rather tell him myself,' she said, a dull flush covering her cheeks.

'Well, of course, my child. It is for you to break the good news. I will tell Dr Braun not to mention it either.'

'Oh, please. This is such a surprise. It will be for him too, you see,' she added quickly.

'A happy one, I hope?' The nun looked straight into her eyes, read the confusion there and squeezed her hand.

'I—yes. That is, I don't really know.' Gabriella swallowed the growing knot in her throat.

'Are you not happily married?'

'Yes. No. That is... I must sound so stupid. But the truth is I don't know anything any more. Everything is so confused and mixed up.' Her hand trembled in Sister Perpetua's.

At that moment a knock on the door interrupted her confidences.

'Ah. This must be your sister-in-law now,' the nun said, rising from the chair and giving Gabriella's hand a last squeeze. 'We'll talk later. Now, don't get too tired,' she said, moving across the room to open the door.

But instead of Constanza it was Ricardo who stood in the doorway and then made his way quickly across the room.

'Gabriella,' he said, looking down at her and taking her hand in his.

'Ricardo. What are you doing here?'

'I could ask you the same thing,' he said, looking down at her, his expression stern.

'I...I'm so sorry. You were right. I shouldn't have gone.' Again a rush of tears surfaced that she could do nothing to stop.

But instead of showing anger, Ricardo's face changed immediately. He sat on the edge of the bed and stroked her hair gently, then dropped a kiss on her brow. 'Oh, Gabriella, darling, did you think I would be angry with you?' he murmured, a smile hovering about his lips. 'I'm just thrilled to know that you are all right and that nothing worse happened. I can't wait to get my hands on that little skunk Hofstetten. The police report says he was driving far too fast and that the fault of the accident was entirely his.'

He ground his teeth and Gabriella felt the pressure on her hand increase. It was wonderful to feel him so close, to feel the pressure of his fingers on hers. Even in her diminished state she could sense that same familiar tingle course through her, and she let out a sigh. God only knew what he would do if he knew what had happened at that inn, she reflected.

'Now, you must stay quietly here for a few days and rest,' Ricardo said, pinching her chin and smiling down at her.

'But can't I leave? Go back to the *schloss*?'

'Not for a couple of days.'

'Oh, but please, Ricardo, I don't want to stay here on my own. Please ask them if I can go back. I'm sure they'll let me.'

Gabriella tried to put the other thing out of her mind. She would think about it in a few days—once she was better. She would have to think what to do. On the one hand she experienced a sensation of wonder. On the other she realised in a quick moment of clarity that once he knew she was carrying his child Ricardo might insist she stay with him. It was all so complicated, so difficult. How she wished that he really loved her and that she could confide in him. But the way he was being now was just because of the accident. Soon he would be off again, to the arms of Ambrosia, or to some other sophisticated worldly woman's bed.

'Darling!' Constanza burst into the room, interrupting her inner thoughts, her arms overflowing with boxes of Mozart Kugelen—traditional Salzburg chocolates filled with marzipan—and flowers. 'I'm sorry you had an accident. I'm furious with Ruddy. I heard it was all his fault. Which just goes to prove that Ricardo was right about him after all.'

'What did you say about him?' Gabriella asked uneasily.

'That I think he's a bad character and that I've heard a few wild tales of his behaviour.'

'Ah.'

Ricardo looked at her closely, his brows meeting over the ridge of his nose as they were prone to do when he was concentrating. Had something happened? he wondered. Gabriella looked pale. But that was natural in her present condition. Or was there something more—something she didn't want to tell him?

For the moment he wouldn't press her, he decided, as Wilhelm joined them in the room and came over to talk to Gabriella.

In the end they let her leave the next day, under strict orders not to overdo it and to stay in bed for a few days.

'That's odd,' Constanza remarked, 'usually nowadays they try and get you up and about in no time.'

'Mmm.' Gabriella made a non-committal sound as the Range Rover, driven by Ricardo, entered the castle gates and they drove up to the front steps, where Wilhelm awaited them.

'Gabriella, how good to have you back among us,' Wilhelm exclaimed, helping her to alight.

Ricardo watched her. She still looked very pale, and it was obvious that the accident had affected her more deeply than he'd at first suspected. Was there anything else upsetting her? he wondered, remembering his pithy encounter with Ruddy Hofstetten the day before. Ruddy had returned to the castle sheepishly, to pick up his things, but had not escaped a lashing from Ricardo's tongue.

'If I ever find out that you molested my wife in any way you will have me to deal with,' he'd thrown bitingly. 'It's bad enough that you almost killed her. I advise you to keep away from her, or things will go badly for you.'

'Are you threatening me?' Ruddy had bristled.

'I'm warning you. I don't want to see your face anywhere near her.'

Ruddy had drawn himself up, about to retort, then thought better of it. Ricardo did not look like a man to mess with and, frankly, the idea of seducing Gabriella had grown old after the events of the past few days. Better to move on to pastures new, he'd figured with a shrug.

'You don't have to worry about me,' he'd said with a little laugh. 'You're welcome to your schoolgirl wife. I like them more sophisticated myself. A bit more bedroom knowledge needed for my taste.'

A few seconds later he had been nursing his jaw on the floor of Wilhelm's library. He had departed within the hour.

But now, as he observed his wife's pallor, Ricardo wished he'd done him more damage. Somehow he could not get it out of his head that Ruddy had in some manner upset her. Oh, well, it was too late to go over that territory again, and the sooner he got her home the better. But rest she must, and he would see to it that she did—despite her protests to the contrary.

*   *   *

Once she was installed in her large bed Gabriella was finally left alone and could think. For the past forty-eight hours she had done nothing but reflect upon her present situation and all its implications.

A baby. A baby that would grow up into a child. Ricardo's child.

She swallowed and fingered the edge of the sheet nervously. What was she to do? If she told him the truth then that would be it. He would expect her to remain married to him. She would be shackled for life. Or a good number of years anyway. If only things were different between them—if she knew that he loved her it would be different. But she was certain that although he was fond of her, enjoyed taking her to his bed, he was not in love with her. His sense of duty was what drove him to be so kind and nice to her. And every time she allowed herself to believe that perhaps his feelings were more engaged than she'd thought, she recalled that image of him and Ambrosia, side by side on the forward deck of the yacht, the intimacy between them so palpable, so impossible to deny.

She didn't want to be like other royal couples she could think of, with a third party in her marriage. If there was another woman in his life, then better that he live with her, not pretend that all was well with his marriage when all it would cause was unhappiness for everyone. Right now he was being charming—refusing to leave for Maldoravia until she was completely well, spending time with her while she rested. They had even played cards together and laughed at a TV programme. Then last night when he'd come to bed he had leaned over and kissed her so tenderly that she'd nearly collapsed with pain and wanting. He'd taken her into his arms and kissed her gently, prying her lips open and causing such new and deep sensations to ripple through her that she hadn't been able to help submitting to his caresses.

Now she closed her eyes and remembered the way he'd stroked her breasts, the way his lips had followed where his hands had left off, how she'd cried with unmitigated delight when he'd brought her to completion then entered her, delving deep inside her being, far deeper into her heart and soul than she could have imagined possible.

Gabriella let out a ragged sigh. She felt trapped. Trapped by her own feelings and the impossibility of her situation. She had to face the truth—that she was in love with her husband and that he, although he treated her with the utmost respect and kindness, was doing no more than his duty in the completion of a promise to a dying man.

She had to get away—had to leave him now before it was too late and they were both caught for ever in a web that was not of their making. She couldn't bear to live like this, to have him make love to her knowing that he was probably going to another woman. She would never know a moment's peace or respite. Her life would turn into a living hell where she saw potential threat in every other woman. No. That was no way to live. She'd seen that movie once too often—friends of her father's, whose wives had given them all they wanted but had maintained several mistresses in tow, some who even appeared socially and had to be tolerated. That was not how she planned to live her life. Whatever it cost her, and however much it hurt, she would make the break now.

But what about the baby?

Her hand slipped to her stomach and she closed her eyes. Was it really possible that from their few incidences of lovemaking this could happen? She had talked to the doctor and apparently there was no doubt about her pregnancy. That was why she had to rest longer than normally would have been required, must make sure nothing could harm the tiny speck of life growing within her. But what a responsibility it was to think of beginning a new life, just she and her child.

She would wait for a few days before taking her final decision. She would do nothing until she was entirely well again—until she felt stable and strong enough to make the right decision and stick with it.

It was only a day trip to London, with a business lunch at Harry's Bar, then back on the royal plane to Salzburg. But Ricardo worried that Gabriella didn't seem to be looking any better. In fact, since her return to Constanza's home she seemed more tired, and looked paler still. He thought she had lost weight.

As the plane flew over the Channel to London he thought about the night before last, when he'd held her in his arms and she'd opened to him, about how he was experiencing new and wonderful feelings that he had not experienced with any other woman. It was crazy that at his age and after all the women he'd bedded his wife should turn out to be so very special, should have that certain something he'd been looking for all these years.

When she was better he would take her away for that honeymoon they'd never had, he resolved, a smile hovering about his lips as they flew over Windsor Castle and headed for City Airport.

It was raining hard as he headed towards the entrance of the terminal, where his car awaited him, and he was walking quickly through the milling throng when he saw a face he recognised.

Ambrosia saw him, handsome and tanned in a light grey suit, taking purposeful strides towards the main entrance. She lifted a manicured hand and waved, calling his name. He stopped, turned, and, smiling, moved to where she stood.

'Hello, Ambro. How are you?'

'Oh, fine. All the better for seeing you,' she responded archly.

'Are you going into London? Can I give you a lift?'

Ambrosia took a snap decision to dismiss the vehicle that had been hired to meet her. 'Actually, that would be lovely,' she murmured, linking her arm in his. 'How long do you plan to be here?'

'Oh, not very long. I go back to Salzburg tonight unless this meeting prolongs itself. Then I may have to stay over.'

'Where's the meeting?'

'At the bank with Ludo. A loan Maldoravia wants approved for a new drain system throughout the country.'

'I didn't know Ludo was back in town,' Ambrosia said thoughtfully, her mind working furiously. If she could get Ricardo's meeting prolonged, then that would open up any number of possibilities. For Ambrosia was convinced that if she could get him alone for a single evening all would go back to the way it had been.

As she seated herself elegantly in the vehicle she smiled at him, a steely determination taking hold of her. She would not let this man escape—would not allow a child barely out of the schoolroom to displace her in this man's bed and affections. Ricardo had brought too much into her life for that. She had never hoped for marriage, knew that was impossible. But she was damned if anything as trivial as his nuptials would change their lives.

When he dropped her off in Chelsea, she smiled regretfully. 'If by any chance you do stay over, promise me that we can have dinner together. I miss you, Ricky. After all, we were good friends as well as lovers, weren't we?'

'Of course.'

'So we should see more of one another. You haven't been anywhere near me for the past couple of months, and that hurts.' She could be very convincing when she wanted. In a quick feminine gesture she leaned forward and straightened his already straight tie, then lifted her face and touched his lips with hers. It was fleeting and affectionate. Then she looped her large Hermès bag on her arm and exited the vehicle, leaving a lingering whiff of Calèche in her wake.

As soon as the car drove off, and before the door could be answered by the maid, she was on her cellphone. 'Ludo—is that you?'

'Oh, hello, Ambro. What can I do for you?'

'Something terribly important. I just drove in from the airport with Ricardo. He's on his way to his meeting with you at the bank right now.'

'Yes, and…?'

'And I want you to make things drag on long enough so that he has to spend the night here in town. Make some excuse. Invent something. Be creative.'

'Good Lord. Not up to your tricks again, are you, Ambro?'

'No, just consolidating my position—which has been a bit risky of late.'

'Well, I suppose I could do that for an old friend.'

'You're sure it'll work out?'

'Of course. Trust me, baby. Ricky's very keen on this new drainage system he wants installed in the Principality. I'll find a way of making him stay over.'

'Good. Just make sure you do, okay?'

'Fine. I'll give you the position later on in the day.'

'Thank you, Ludo. You're an absolute darling.'

'Any time, gorgeous, any time.'

CHAPTER TEN

'I REALLY don't understand why you have to have those other documents right away,' Ricardo said, frowning. It was five o'clock. Even though it was summer, he didn't want to fly out too late.

'Look, I'm sorry, old chap,' Ludo said apologetically. 'It's these damn new EU regulations. Why don't you stay the night? I'll have all the papers faxed in by tomorrow morning, and we can go over them and sign then.'

'I really wanted to get back to my wife,' Ricardo said reluctantly. 'But I suppose there's nothing for it but to do that.'

'Mmm.' Ludo, a good-looking chestnut-haired man in his mid-thirties, eyed him carefully. 'How about dinner tonight?'

'Why not? I've nothing else on the agenda. What shall we say? Eight-thirty at Mark's?'

'Sounds good to me,' Ludo replied, raising his palms and getting up. 'See you later, old chap.'

Ricardo followed suit. 'Yes. See you later.'

The Rolls drove him to Cadogan Square, where he owned a house fully staffed all year round. A secretary had phoned from Ludo's office, so he was expected. It was almost six o'clock. Ricardo went upstairs into a large suite of rooms and was preparing to take a shower when his cellphone rang.

'Hello?'

'Hello. It's me—Ambrosia. Are you on your way home?'

'Actually, no. I'm spending the night here in London.'

'Really? Well, then, you'd better stay true to your promise.'

'What was that?' He frowned abstractedly and pulled off his tie.

'We agreed that if you stayed in town you'd take me to dinner—remember?'

'Damn, *cara*, you're right. I forgot. It was an unexpected last-minute decision. I've made dinner arrangements with Ludo, but I suppose there is no reason why you shouldn't join us. We've dealt with business for the day.'

'I'd love to. Where and when?'

'I'll come round and pick you up a little before eight, if that suits you?'

'Fine. See you then.'

And it did suit her. Ambrosia hung up, rubbing her hands with glee. Finally chance had played into her hands. And she had Ludo to thank, she reminded herself. She owed him one. He had acted brilliantly. And now the evening was set up in such a way that she would recover her former lover with no problem.

What was keeping him? Gabriella wondered as she sat in the sitting room waiting for Constanza and Wilhelm to appear for drinks. It was after seven o'clock—six in England—and there was still no sign of Ricardo. Just as she was beginning to worry her cellphone rang.

'Hello?'

'Gabriella, *cara mia*.'

She swallowed at the endearment. 'Hello. How was your day?'

'Fine. Except we didn't finish all the business we had planned, and I'm going to have to stay the night and come home tomorrow afternoon, I'm afraid.'

'Oh.' She felt a wave of disappointment engulf her, but pulled herself together. 'Well, that's fine.'

'I'm sorry, but this is such an important project for Maldoravia—I can't let it flounder.'

'Of course not. Everything's fine here,' she lied, wishing she could forget the morning sickness that had overtaken her that day, and all that it signified.

'Good. Then I'll see you tomorrow afternoon. You are feeling better, aren't you?'

'Oh, yes, I'm doing much better.'

'Good. Then sleep well, *cara mia*, and see you tomorrow.'

'Goodnight,' she whispered, letting out a shaky sigh and wishing that she didn't have to lie to him the whole time, that everything could be easy and straightforward and simple.

Which it wasn't.

'I do adore this egg with caviar,' Ambrosia cooed as they sat at Mark's, ensconced together at their table. The head waiter had just told them that Ludo had sent a message saying he would be running rather late and to begin dinner without him.

'Typical,' Ricardo said, shaking his head and admiring Ambrosia's perfect profile and the ruby and

diamond earrings she was wearing. They were Cartier.
He knew. He'd given them to her not that long ago.

'So, tell me, Ricky darling, how is wedded life suiting you?' she said, turning slightly and smiling, all understanding and interest.

'Well, it's not as simple as I thought it would be. Gabriella is young and needs help finding her feet. Also she had an accident. She's recovering at my sister's in Austria.'

'Poor child,' she murmured. 'What happened?'

'Oh, nothing much. She fell off a motorbike.'

'A motorbike?' Ambrosia raised her perfectly plucked eyebrows in mock surprise. 'Why, I never thought you'd allow your wife to go out on a motorbike, Ricky darling. I'm most surprised.'

'Well, actually, I didn't. I wasn't there.'

'Then who was the driver?'

'Ruddy Hofstetten,' he said reluctantly.

'You don't say?' Ambrosia leaned back against the sofa and watched him thoughtfully. He was scowling. Something must definitely have been going on between Gabriella and young Hofstetten for him to look so glum. Wouldn't that be a perfect piece of gossip for the scandalmongers? she reflected, wondering how she could use it to her advantage. 'Is she all right after the fall?' she asked, assuming an expression of deep concern.

'Yes. Yes, she is. Though she seems to be taking longer to get well than I thought she would. She looks pale and is rather tired.'

'Poor girl,' she said in a sympathetic voice. 'It can't be much fun for you, I imagine?'

'No. I worry about her. It's weird. A few months ago I was free as a bird, and now I seem to have all these responsibilities.'

'Well, you chose them, darling,' she said, letting her fingers slip over his and squeezing his hand. 'But why don't you forget about all that for tonight and we can enjoy ourselves? Let's go to Annabel's afterwards and dance. I love dancing with you, Ricky. I miss it. In fact, I miss a lot of things that we used to do rather well together,' she purred, lifting her glass by the stem and raising it conspiratorially.

Ricardo smiled and his eyes twinkled. 'We did have good times together, Ambro, didn't we?'

'Did?' She arched a brow and smiled suggestively.

'Well, I'm a married man now.'

'What has that got to do with anything?' she insisted, meeting his eyes full on. 'You know I knew you'd never marry me, Ricky, that one day this would have to happen. After all, you need a son and heir. But I never thought it would affect our relationship in the bigger scheme of things.'

'That's very broad-minded of you, Ambro,' he said, twirling his glass and looking at his watch. 'I wonder where Ludo has got to?'

'Oh, he's probably been held up. But, darling— about us. We're not children. You and I have been around the block a few times. We know the name of the game. Now, why don't we stop pretending that you and I are *passé* and have a relaxing night to catch up? On second thoughts, I think I'd rather go straight home than out dancing.' She let her other hand slide under the table and onto his thigh, feeling the tension in his muscles. Surreptitiously she glanced at her watch. Jerry, the tabloid photographer she often gave tips to, and whom she'd phoned earlier in the evening, must be ready outside, waiting for their exit. 'I think we should just sign the bill and go,' she murmured.

'Okay. One drink at your place, then I must be off home.' He smiled at her and beckoned the waiter.

'Of course. I'll dash to the loo and meet you in the hall.'

'Fine.'

Several minutes later they were exiting the club. The Rolls drew up and Ambrosia took Ricky's arm. 'Look,' she said bringing her face close to his. 'Look how lovely the moon is tonight. It reminds me of that song—remember?—the one we always used to listen to in Sardinia?'

'I remember.' He turned and looked down at her. At that moment she raised her lips to his, planting a quick kiss there and praying that Jerry had got the shot. She hadn't seen any flashbulbs, but then she'd told him to be ultra-discreet.

Ten minutes later they were driving up to the Chelsea townhouse where Ambrosia lived. On the steps she took her key out and giggled. 'Just like old times, isn't it? What have you done with all your security? I didn't see them about.'

'They're here somewhere, I suppose. Just being discreet—thank God.'

'Well, don't let's dawdle here,' she said, pulling him inside. 'God, it's good to have you back here, Ricky. The place hasn't been the same without you.'

She slipped her arms around his neck and drew him towards her.

'Ambro, I said a drink, for old time's sake, and I meant it,' he said, disengaging himself.

'Oh, pooh—don't be so priggish. What man doesn't have a mistress, I ask you?'

'That's not the point. I feel responsible towards Gabriella. We're just beginning to get our relationship on its feet.'

'Well, she's hardly going to imagine you're here with me, is she?' she argued reasonably.

'No. But that doesn't make it any better.'

'You know, I never imagined you as a goody-goody,' she exclaimed, annoyed at his reluctance. 'What on earth can it matter that you're here and that we're going to make love?'

'We are not going to make love, Ambro. I thought I'd made that quite plain.'

'She's only your wife, for God's sake. Can't you get her pregnant? That way she'll be busy with her babies and won't bother us.'

'Life isn't quite as simple as that,' he murmured, distancing himself and moving towards the fireplace. 'There's more to marriage than I had imagined.'

Ambrosia watched him, taken aback. This wasn't going quite as she had planned.

'Well, forget it. Just for tonight. A goodbye send-off, if you will,' she purred, moving next to him and drawing his mouth down to hers. But Ricardo moved firmly away.

'I said no, Ambro, and I meant it. And now I really must be off.'

Red anger blinded her. It was too humiliating for words, too lowering for her to bear. He had come here, kissed her, and then, almost as if he were bored, had looked at his watch and said he had to go home. She would not forgive him lightly.

After he left Ambrosia stood with her back against the closed front door, nursing her fury. She hadn't had Jerry take pictures for any specific reason—more as a safeguard for the future. But now as her anger seethed she knew exactly what she would do. Marching to the telephone, she dialled.

'Jerry? Hi. Did you get the shots?'

'Beauts, darlin', real beauts. Got the kiss and the works. Boy, these will sell for a bloody fortune.'

'Well, I'm glad to hear you say that,' she replied, her voice laced with venom, 'because I'd like you to sell them with a story, to as many tabloids as you can get your busy little hands on.'

'Really, love? When?'

'How about right now? Come over and I'll write up the text for you. If we're quick we may just make tomorrow's papers.'

'You got it, babe. I'll be there in twenty.'

'Perfect, Jerry. I'll be waiting.'

The next morning dawned rainy again, and Gabriella glanced out of the window, wishing she could see a few palms, sun and sea. Then, as she was about to turn around and have another sleep, a sudden rush of nausea had her stumbling to the bathroom. Oh, God. How long would this last? It made her feel so terrible.

After half an hour she lay back in bed and decided

to ask for breakfast here in her room rather than go down. Constanza was going into town this morning early—had probably already left with the children—and Wilhelm was in Munich. The weird thing was, she realised, after calling downstairs and giving instructions, after the nausea passed she felt positively hungry.

Several minutes later a knock on the door announced the maid, carrying a large tray with the breakfast and the papers. The girl, Inge, smiled and said, *'Guten morgen.'* She spoke no English, so communication was limited.

Once the tray was safely installed on her knees and Inge had disappeared, Gabriella poured herself a cup of coffee before drinking her orange juice. There were several papers, and she placed them beside her on the bed. The family bought English papers—Constanza said she loved the gossip that came in many of them.

After eating a piece of toast and a boiled egg, Gabriella settled in for a comfortable morning relaxing and reading while sipping her coffee. She flipped over the papers and picked up the first one, then paled as she saw the picture splashed on the front page and the headlines.

'Oh, my God,' she whispered, her eyes filling with angry tears as she read, unbelieving, the words above a picture of a woman and a man whom she recognised only too well kissing in the moonlight.

Moonlight Escapade for Just-Wed Prince, the headline read. But worse was to come when she read the text, for in it were details—not all correct—of her biking accident. It even mentioned Ruddy, and implied that she was having an affair with him. How could this be? Who could have done this? And there was Ricardo, on the front page of the paper, kissing Ambrosia for all the world to see.

All her worst nightmares had become reality, Gabriella realised, her hands trembling as she discovered more pictures inside, and in another publication. All her fears were well-founded. Thank God she hadn't told him about the baby—hadn't risked her future with this man who was proving to be all she'd expected. The dream that one day they might have a real marriage had been nothing but that: a dream.

Pushing away the tray and pulling back the bedclothes, Gabriella got up. She ran into the bathroom, tears of anger pouring down her cheeks. But she was determined to be in control.

And out of here before he returned.

With this goal in mind she quickly entered the shower. Twenty minutes later she was dressed and packed. And ready to make a new life away from Prince Ricardo of Maldoravia, whom she hoped she'd never set eyes on again.

CHAPTER ELEVEN

'LEFT? You mean she's gone?' Ricardo exclaimed, staring at Hans the butler in shock. 'But when—and where to?'

'I'm afraid Her Royal Highness didn't say where she was going, sir. I heard the instructions to the hire chauffeur, of course, which were to take her to the airport in Munich.' Hans hesitated, then said in a softer tone, 'She seemed somewhat agitated, sir, if I may say so. I had the impression…'

'Go on,' Ricardo urged. 'What impression?'

'That all was not right,' he murmured, looking down.

'What gave you that impression?'

'Well, sir, without meaning to be indiscreet, the maid Inge found several newspapers strewn around the bedroom…' He paused.

'Yes? And?'

'Well, there was a picture of you, sir. With a lady.'

'Oh, my God. So that's what the press were trying to get in touch with me about this morning. I paid no attention—thought it was unimportant—had the secretary deal with… Hans, get me those papers immediately.'

'Very well, sir. I think the Grafin has them in the drawing room.'

158

'Then I shall go there at once. Thanks,' he added, moving towards the door and opening it.

Constanza sat by the window. She looked at him and shook her head. 'Really, Ricky, I can't believe that you're making such a muck of things. I tried to stop Gabriella leaving,' she continued, getting up in her agitation, 'but she refused to listen. And after I saw the front pages of those tabloids, frankly I'm not surprised—and I don't blame her one iota.'

'Show me.' His face was hard as granite.

'You mean you haven't seen them?'

'Constanza, I read the *Financial Times*, not the bloody tabloids,' he threw at her.

'Well, if this is how you plan to behave, then perhaps you should change your reading matter,' she responded tartly, thrusting a newspaper at him.

'Oh, Lord. I don't believe it,' he muttered, unfolding the paper and staring at himself kissing Ambrosia under a full moon. 'That bitch. I can't believe she would do this to me.'

'Well, you know what they say about a woman scorned. It was very foolish of you to go out with her at all. Unless…' Constanza paused and looked at him speculatively. 'Did you give her some bad news?'

'I suppose in a way I did. I told her that I was sticking to my decision, that it really was over between us and that I didn't like being set up and wouldn't be staying the night. You see, Con, although this marriage of mine has happened in such a strange manner, I have…deep feelings for Gabriella. I—' He cut himself off and looked out of the window, his features harsh in the afternoon light. 'I don't want to lose her, and she plans to separate from me in a couple of months.'

'What?'

'Yes.' He dropped the paper on the table and flopped into an armchair, dragging his fingers through his hair. 'It's a long story. But by Maldoravian law if we want a divorce we have to stay married for a minimum of six months. Then a separation of two years is necessary before we can petition for divorce.'

'A divorce?' Constanza cried, shaking her head. 'But what nonsense is this? Anyone can see that you are deeply attracted to one another.'

'I believe so,' he said with the ghost of a smile. 'Unfortunately, this is not the first time that Ambrosia has come between us. You see, she had no illusions about marrying me, but she believed that after my wedding things would simply continue as they always had done. Frankly, I thought so too. But then—'

'But then?' Constanza prodded more gently.

'But then I discovered that I really didn't want any other woman than Gabriella.'

'Well, why on earth didn't you tell her so?'

'I was going to. I just didn't feel the time was right. Perhaps I wasn't entirely certain myself,' he muttered, picking the paper off the coffee table again. 'The important thing now is to find her. I can't have her gallivanting all over the world by herself. Plus, she's not well. I suppose she managed to leave without security noticing?' he added bitterly. 'I really must do something about those agents. This is the second time she's slipped through my fingers.'

'What I'm most worried about,' Constanza said,

looking her brother in the eye, 'is that she still doesn't seem to have totally recovered from that accident. She looks pale and not herself. Oh, God, where can she have gone?'

'I don't know.' He dragged his fingers through his hair again and got up, starting to pace the room. 'Brazil, perhaps. Though something tells me that she wouldn't go home again so soon. I really can't think.' He threw up his hands, then dropped them. 'We'd better start by trying the airport.'

'Princess, how do you feel about seeing your husband kissing another woman on the front page of this morning's paper?'

As she made her way through the international departure terminal Gabriella was assailed by reporters. Who could have told them she would be here? she wondered, pulling on her shades angrily. This was all she needed. And where was she going? She didn't even know. She'd simply packed and left, planning to buy a ticket to somewhere here at the airport. But that was impossible now. The whole world would know where she was. For the first time she regretted not having the bodyguards who kept this kind of thing at bay.

Hastily she changed course and, waving to the chauffeur of the hire car, hurried back towards it and climbed quickly in before the press could catch her. But even as the car moved away from the kerb flash-bulbs popped and faces were plastered to the darkened windows of the large Mercedes.

Finally the vehicle left the airport and they were back on the highway.

'Where do you wish to go?' the driver asked, masking his curiosity behind a poker face.

'Go? I…' She hesitated a moment, then made a snap decision. She would go to Switzerland—go to Madame Delorme, her old headmistress. At least there she could hide without anyone knowing where she was.

'I need you to drive to Lausanne, in Switzerland,' she said at last.

'Very well, *madame*. It will take several hours.'

'I don't care,' she replied, sinking into the deep leather seat and closing her eyes.

Anywhere was better than here.

'There's no trace of her,' Ricardo exclaimed several hours later.

'Come and see the TV. Look.' Wilhelm pointed at the screen. 'There she is at Munich airport, but then she's getting back in the car.'

'We'd better trace it at once. God, this is awful,' Ricardo murmured, clenching his fists. 'I hate to think of what she must be going through—what she must be thinking.'

'The worst,' Wilhelm said unsympathetically.

'Yes. I should think the last person on the planet she wants to see right now is you,' Constanza added helpfully.

'I'm very well aware of that,' Ricardo responded through gritted teeth. 'I just want to know—number one, where she is, and number two, how to make her listen to me.'

'Both of which may be difficult under the circumstances,' Constanza murmured, eyeing her brother carefully. He looked determined and furious, with that same cold anger that she remembered in their father. But behind the angry front she read worry and concern.

'Have you tried her mobile?' she said at last.

'Only about fifty million times.'

'Right. Well, in the meantime we'd better have a drink,' Wilhelm said in a more practical tone, moving over to the drinks tray. He poured Ricardo a stiff whisky and handed it to him. 'Don't worry, old chap, we'll find her soon.'

It felt strange to be back at the school which she had left only months ago, graduating with honours. So much had occurred in her life since then—so many changes that it felt like a lifetime ago.

'It is wonderful to see you again,' said Madame Delorme, an elderly slim woman with grey hair swept back into a severe chignon, welcoming Gabriella warmly into her office. 'What *bon vent* brings you here? Are you staying a while, or merely passing through?'

'Uh, actually I thought I might stay a little.' Gabriella fiddled with her handbag, not knowing where to begin. It was all very difficult.

'Well, let's sit down and have a cup of tea,' Madame Delorme replied smoothly. Her eyes swept over her old pupil and she frowned inwardly. All was not well with Gabriella, that was clear as day. She looked pale, and too thin. And also she who had always shone among the crowd seemed tired and almost forlorn, as though all the spark had been punched out of her.

Tactfully Madame said nothing, but allowed Gabriella to relax. She told her of school doings, news she'd received from some of the old girls who had been classmates of Gabriella and who she might not be in touch with.

'In fact,' she said, glancing up and nodding to the maid as a tea tray was set down, 'I was quite surprised that you didn't invite Cynthia and Agnes to the wedding. They were your best friends. You are still in touch, I hope?'

'Uh, yes. We e-mail each other. But unfortunately my wedding was planned in such a rush that there was no time to invite anyone. If there had been you would have been on my guest list. You know that, Madame,' she said, with a ghost of her old mischievous smile dawning.

'I know I would,' the headmistress said, smiling at her warmly. 'But tell me now, what brings you here? I have the distinct sensation, Gabriella, that this is not just a social call.'

'Well, actually, you're right.' Gabriella looked up, tried to muster a smile, then gave up. Instead she raised her palms in the air and dropped them in her lap. 'It's all a disaster, Madame.'

'What is a disaster? Explain.'

'My marriage. You must have seen the papers?'

'Actually, no. What papers? I live here in

Switzerland and do not read all the foreign press, you know.'

'Of course not. I forgot. But it is all over the British and American press. On the front page.'

'What is?' Madame asked patiently.

'Him—with her.'

'"Him" being who, Gabriella? Please express yourself clearly,' she admonished, in the reprimanding tone Gabriella remembered well. 'I am failing to follow you.'

'My husband—the Prince. He was photographed kissing his mistress. It's on the front page of every tabloid. Oh, I won't go back, Madame. I refuse to,' she said, tears burning her eyes as she jumped up and paced the room.

'Now, calm down, *mon enfant*. You are telling me that your husband has been pictured kissing another woman and it is splattered all over the newspapers?'

'Exactly.' Gabriella whirled around. 'You do see why I couldn't stay, don't you, Madame? I thought of going back to Brazil but—well, there are reasons why I don't want to go on a long journey just now.'

'I see. So that is why you came back to school?'

'Yes. I loved it here. I was happy. I need time to think. Oh, would it be all right if I stayed a little? I have nowhere else to go, except to some hotel—and that would be awful right now.'

'But of course you can stay, *cherie*,' the headmistress said in soothing tones, rising and taking Gabriella's hands in hers. 'You can have Mademoiselle Choiseul's old room. Nobody is using it at the moment. But, Gabriella, tell me the whole truth. It is not like you to run from adversity. I would be less surprised if I'd heard that you'd had a terrible row about the incident with him.'

'Perhaps under other circumstances I would have,' she agreed with a little laugh. 'But you see, I've changed, Madame. Ricardo only married me because my father asked him to on his deathbed. He stays with me and is courteous and kind and—oh, so many things,' she said, gulping and turning away. 'But the truth is this marriage is nothing more than an obligation for him. He was with this woman long before he met me. In a way she has more right to him than I do.'

'I see,' Madame replied, reading between the lines far more than Gabriella was consciously saying. 'And what do you think the future will bring?'

'I think we shall separate, and then in two years we can ask for a divorce. Only…'

'Only what, *ma chère*? Please open up and tell me the whole truth. You will feel better, and together we will be able to seek a solution to the problem.'

'Well, I'm finding it hard to believe myself, because we only made—that is, we haven't been very close,' she said, blushing, 'but I'm expecting a baby.'

'Oh, *ma chère enfant*. Now I understand your affliction,' Madame responded sympathetically. 'Still, this is wonderful news, Gabriella.' She drew the girl back onto the high-backed Louis XV brocade chair and sat down opposite.

'I wish it were. I mean, part of me is thrilled to think that I have life inside me. But then I think of the future—a life without love, Ricardo coming and going, not knowing where he is or with whom, worrying the whole time, being made to look like a fool when everyone around us will know that he has a mistress or several other women. I don't think I could bear it,' she said, her throat strangled as she dropped her head. 'I don't think I could stand that kind of life. It's not what I dreamt of in a marriage.'

'No. I understand you very well, and I think you are absolutely right. That is no way to conduct matrimony. But are you sure he really loves this other woman?'

'Yes. I've seen them together. They're intimate. You can just tell.'

'I see. That, of course, is a problem. Have you told him about the child?'

'No.' Gabriella shook her head fiercely. 'I haven't said a word. Oh, I know he would be wonderfully kind and caring, and I would be surrounded by every comfort. But that's not what I want from him. I—' She turned away once more, stifling the tears, and Madame Delorme watched her carefully.

'Gabriella, do you mind if I ask you a personal question?'

'No,' she gulped. 'Go ahead.'

'Do you love your husband?'

Gabriella hesitated a moment, then her head came round and her eyes met the older woman's. 'Yes,' she answered truthfully, squashing the pain that the word caused her. 'Yes, I do. I know it seems crazy, when we were married in such a hurry and against our wills, but I do love him—which is why I have to leave him, or I'll make both our lives a living hell.'

'I see.' Madame Delorme sat thoughtfully for a moment. Then, briskly, she got up. *'Bien*, let's go and install you in your room now. After you're settled you'll feel better.' She smiled encouragingly and Gabriella got up.

Together they left the sitting room and headed up the stairs. The bell had just rung, and girls were pouring out of classrooms. Some of the younger ones recognised her and came up to chat. But even as she felt a wave of nostalgia at not being a part of this life any longer, Gabriella quickly realised that she had moved on. She was now in a different phase of her existence. One she had to deal with as an adult.

With a sigh, she followed Madame Delorme down the passage to the room that had used to belong to Mademoiselle Choiseul, the French teacher. At least here she could stop for a while and think. And make plans for what right now struck her as a bleak future.

Once back in her office Madame Delorme sat thoughtfully behind her elegant French antique desk. Gabriella was in a fix, and this situation could not be allowed to endure. It went against the grain, but, just as she often had to take decisions with her pupils, Madame knew it was her duty to take a decision now. Reluctantly she reached for her telephone book. She would ring her old friend the Contessa Elizabetta. Perhaps by putting their heads together they would come up with something.

'Hello—Elizabetta?'

'Yes. Is that you, Marianne?'

'Yes. How pleasing of you to recognise my voice.'

'Of course I do. How would I not recognise one of my oldest and dearest friends? Tell me, how are things?'

'Fine. But, actually, I'm calling about a slight problem that indirectly concerns you.'

'Oh?'

'Well, I have Gabriella here.'

'Oh, thank God for that!' the Contessa exclaimed. 'Ricardo will be so thankful. He's been looking for her everywhere. We knew she was headed for Switzerland. It should have occurred to me she might have gone to you. We've been going out of our minds, trying to think where she could have run to, poor child, after that awful display of vulgarity in the papers. It is unbelievable what the press will stoop to.'

'It is also unbelievable what a recently married man will stoop to,' Madame Delorme replied dryly.

'I know, I know,' the Contessa agreed with a sigh. 'But boys will be boys, you know. And unfortunately this marriage was not properly planned. Poor Gabriella. I feel so sorry for her, and wish she had come here if she felt she had to get away. We are trying to keep her absence quiet for the present— though of course the press are all over the place, trying to get more salacious titbits for their readers. But I am so worried about her. Is she all right?'

'Yes and no. I am worried about her. She looks far too thin and worn out, poor child. If I had the chance, I would haul your nephew over the coals for what he's done.'

'Oh, believe me, I already have. But, actually, I don't think things are quite as simple as they appear.'

'No?'

'No. I get the impression that this whole incident was a set-up—probably by the mistress. He assures me that he did not spend the night with her and that he had no intention of carrying on the relationship. That he told her so. She probably did this to take revenge. He did not spell it out in so many words, but I get the impression he is truly concerned and perhaps not a little in love with his wife—even if he doesn't know it himself yet.'

'Good. Well, we'll leave him to stew for a few days, *ma chère amie*, and then see what we can do to patch up this messy business.'

'I hate not telling him where she is, when he is obviously distraught with worry, but I do believe you may be right. Oh, Marianne, we are probably nothing but two old busybodies, but I would so like to see these two children happy. You know, I have an odd feeling that they really suit one another. Perhaps Gonzalo Guimaraes was right after all. He was a cunning old fox…and too handsome for his own good,' she said with a nostalgic sigh.

'Very well. Then I shall keep you informed.'

'Yes, my dear. But don't eke this out for too long. You know how bad I am at keeping secrets.'

Madame Delorme laughed heartily. Ever since they had been at boarding school themselves she'd known Elizabetta was a hopeless liar and could never keep a secret. 'I promise the suspense will not last too long. Just long enough for him to come to his senses. He's a man, after all, and if things are made too easy for men they don't appreciate it.'

CHAPTER TWELVE

THE phone rang and Ambrosia leaped on to it.

'Hello?'

'You saw yesterday's papers?' Ricardo's voice cut like a knife down the line.

'Yes, of course I did. It was awful. I can barely leave the flat. I can't think who did this. It's appalling.'

'Whoever it was, Ambrosia, I can assure you they will pay a high price for invading my privacy and trying to muck up my marriage.'

'Your marriage?' Ambrosia could not repress a smile of delight. 'You mean Gabriella saw the pictures? How awful. I'm so sorry, Ricky.'

There was a moment's hesitation. 'Thanks to this mischief my wife has left me. I have no idea where she is, and I am very worried about her. I hold you entirely to blame.'

'Me? But—'

'Don't play games, Ambrosia. I know how you operate when you want something. I've seen you in action before. I just never believed you'd stoop so low.' His voice rasped on her nerves, cold and unforgiving.

'But, Ricky, you have it all wrong. I was appalled. I tell you, I'm positively being invaded. I can't get the wretched press off my doorstep. I was thinking of coming to Maldoravia. After all, my villa there is very secluded and private. And at least that way we could see each other...'

'See each other? Are you completely mad? I forbid you to come anywhere near Maldoravia. As for seeing you, I sincerely hope that last night was the last time you'll ever cross my path.'

Ambrosia swallowed and her hands trembled. There was no disappointment in his voice, only icy fury. Her pulse raced. Had she played her cards wrong? she wondered, her heart sinking. But surely now that Gabriella was well out of the way—might even decide to leave him permanently—the coast would be clear, and after all this had died down he would change his mind. Yes, surely. This reaction was nothing but a natural passing phase.

'Okay, darling,' she said meekly. 'I'll do whatever you want.'

'Do not use that term of endearment ever again,' he hissed. 'Now, get the hell out of my life and stay out. You've done enough damage as it is, and I shall never forgive you.'

The phone went dead and she looked at it thoughtfully, wrinkling her nose. Strong words, of course, and the result of her handiwork was not great. But on the other hand it was to be expected that he would be angry. And serve him right, for leaving her on her own and running back to his little virgin wife. Once all the fuss died down she had no doubt that she would achieve her objective. Gabriella would probably make a scene, and that would annoy him. Little by little the couple would drift apart, and she would be there to pick up the pieces exactly as planned.

It sounded good, but Ambrosia was not quite as confident as she had been. She had a sinking feeling that she should not have allowed her temper to get the better of her.

For the first time she wondered if she would come out winning in the end.

'I've traced her,' Ricardo announced triumphantly, coming into the drawing room where Constanza and the Contessa were sitting having coffee.

'Really?' Constanza looked up, excited. 'Oh, I'm so glad, Ricky. I've been so worried. Where is she?'

'Apparently she's in Switzerland. My people tracked down the driver of the limo. She had the car drop her off at the Beau Rivage Hotel in Lausanne, but she's not registered there. I had the concierge check. And there is no one who matches her description in the hotel. Even under another name.'

'Very strange,' the Contessa murmured vaguely. 'Ricardo, have some coffee.'

'In a moment, Aunt,' he said, his eyes narrowing. 'Aunt Elizabetta, I don't suppose you would know anything about her whereabouts? If I recall correctly, you are very friendly with Gabriella's old headmistress, from her school in Switzerland. I remember you talking about her not that long ago. Perhaps you have an idea of where she might be?'

'Me? How would I know?' she spluttered, almost dropping the coffee pot. 'Now look what you've made me do, Ricky,' she exclaimed, placing the coffee pot back down on the tray and fussing over a spot on the cloth.

Constanza and Ricardo exchanged a look. They knew their aunt well.

'Aunt Elizabetta, if you know anything—anything at all—you must tell Ricky,' Constanza said, looking her aunt full in the eyes.

'Well, I…'

'Please, Aunt.' Ricardo came over quickly and, sitting down, took her hands in his. 'You have no idea how important this is. If she has confided in you, if you know anything at all, you must tell me at once. Our whole future could be at stake.'

'Well, after the way you've behaved I really don't see what future you have with Gabriella,' his aunt countered, regaining some of her composure.

'Look, I had nothing to do with that picture or those articles. It was some busybody reporter who happened to be spying on us. It was foolish of me to go out in public with Ambrosia, but the photo was just a piece of bad luck.'

'Are you sure?' Constanza got up and, turning her back to the window, leaned against the sill. 'Are you sure you weren't set up, Ricky?'

'By whom?'

'By Ambrosia herself.'

'It's possible,' he conceded slowly.

'It all strikes me as far too pat to be just a coincidence. I mean, who knew you were going to dine at Mark's? And all those details about Ruddy and Gabriella and the accident. You said you had no intention of having an amorous evening with the woman. Try and remember the circumstances. Did you kiss her out of the blue or did she conveniently kiss you?'

Ricardo dropped his aunt's hands and rose. He remained silent for a long moment, then turned and faced his sister.

'I've been a fool,' he said quietly. 'But I've already made it quite clear to Ambrosia that it's over between us. If she thinks otherwise, she's the fool.'

'I won't contradict you on either,' Constanza replied in a sisterly manner. 'I think she set the whole thing up to create a rift between you and Gabriella. Now, Aunt Elizabetta, spill the beans and tell us the truth. Gabriella's gone back to her school, hasn't she?'

'Yes. You are right. She went to seek out the one person she felt she could trust—my old friend Marianne Delorme, her headmistress.'

'And she's there at the school now?' Ricardo insisted.

'Apparently so. I believe Marianne is very upset with you. It seems Gabriella is unhappy and barely eats. You have a lot to answer for, Ricky. You had no right to marry that child and behave the way you have. I am positively ashamed of you.'

'That I am very well aware of,' he said bitterly. 'But this last episode was not of my making. Ambrosia will pay dearly for her tricks.'

'Right now, I wouldn't worry about her,' Constanza replied.

'I'm on my way to Lausanne,' Ricardo answered, with a smile in her direction. 'I'm so relieved that I've finally discovered Gabriella's whereabouts. How long did you plan to keep this a secret, Aunt? I can't believe you didn't tell me.'

'It serves you jolly well right,' Aunt Elizabetta replied firmly. 'You don't deserve her, the way you go on. And I'm not speaking just of this newspaper incident. You know very well what I mean.'

'I can assure you, *madame*, that from now on things will be different.'

'So I should hope,' she replied with a sniff as he left the room, leaving the door swinging behind him.

'So. Elizabetta let the cat out of the bag, did she?' Madame Delorme said as Ricardo entered the sitting room and the maid closed the door quietly behind him.

'No. Actually I traced her through the car company, then confronted my aunt. I remembered your close friendship and put two and two together, *madame*,' he said, raising her hand to his lips.

Madame Delorme eyed him askance. The man was more charming than she had imagined. No wonder Gabriella was in love. But still, she had no inclination to facilitate his task. 'And so you arrive here on my doorstep, without so much as a by-your-leave,' she said, in a tone that would have had her pupils quaking in their shoes, 'and expect your wife to be awaiting you?'

'Not at all. *Madame*, you must excuse the precipitous manner of my arrival. As soon as I knew of Gabriella's whereabouts I came at once. You must realise how worried I was about my wife.'

'Good. You deserve to be worried after the way you've behaved.'

Ricardo cleared his throat. He was not used to being treated like an errant schoolboy.

'I have come to relieve you of the responsibility for her,' he said in a grand manner.

'*Vraiment*, Your Royal Highness?' she replied, raising an amused and critical brow. 'Well, that is all very well. But who says that your Gabriella wants to see you?'

'*Madame*, I must insist. Gabriella is my wife. She has an obligation to see me.'

'You know, if I was you I would alter my approach,' Madame said in a pleasant tone, sitting down on the stiff-backed brocade sofa and crossing her legs. 'You may sit down. We need to talk this matter over sensibly.'

Ricardo sat opposite. It was the first time in many years that he had felt out of his element.

'I assure you, *madame*, that I want nothing more than to recover my wife and take her home, where she belongs.'

'Your Highness, Gabriella is not an object that you can bundle up and take with you. She is a very sensitive and hurt young woman who is suffering the deep humiliation of having been made a fool of in front of the world. Apart from anything else, she is not well.'

'Not well? What is wrong with her?'

'Among other things, unhappiness. It is an illness that can do much harm. And you, young man, are to blame for this state of affairs.'

'*Madame*, please,' he pleaded with a smile. 'I know I'm in the wrong, but I beg you to believe me when

I tell you that things are not at all as they appear. It seems that I was set up. I suppose that my friend—'

'You mean your mistress?'

'Uh, *ex*-mistress.' He regained his composure and continued smoothly, 'She perhaps thought that if she could separate me from Gabriella and create a rift I would return to her. I don't know. Suffice it to say that I have made it abundantly clear to her that whatever there was between us is definitively over.' He got up, raised his hands, then let them drop. 'All I know is I need to see my wife as soon as possible and explain to her what happened. I can't allow her to go on thinking that I…'

'That you?'

'That I betrayed her.'

'Well, I think you may find her a little difficult to convince. After all, the evidence is staring her in the face.'

'All I'm asking is a chance to talk to her.'

Madame eyed him, then she sighed. 'I suppose you're right. At some point you will both have to come to terms with the situation—face one another and clear this matter up. But I'm afraid right now that is impossible.'

'Why?' he asked, raising a haughty brow.

'Because Gabriella is not here. She is at the doctor's.'

'The doctor? Is she ill?' His expression changed immediately to one of concern and Madame felt relieved. Perhaps he did care far more for Gabriella than she had at first thought.

'Well, not exactly. She…'

'*Madame*, I demand that you tell me the truth about my wife's state of health.'

Madame Delorme hesitated. She hated interfering. On the other hand, she knew how stubborn Gabriella could be—and proud. At last she took a decision.

'This goes against the grain, and I would not normally betray a confidence.' She sighed. 'But I think it is for the well-being of you both. I do it on one condition, though.'

'Which is?'

'That you do not tell Gabriella that you know. Let her tell you herself.'

'Very well,' he said, mystified. 'But please, *madame*, whatever it is, I have to know.'

'I have your word?'

'Absolutely. My solemn promise that whatever you tell me I will keep to myself until she sees fit to tell me.'

'Do not be surprised if that takes a little time.'

'Fine,' he said impatiently. 'But what is it?'

'Gabriella is expecting a baby.'

'What?' Ricardo stopped dead in his tracks.

'Yes. There is nothing surprising in that, surely?'

'No. Yes. What I mean is… Oh, my God, what a mess.' He sat down abruptly. 'Is she okay? No, she isn't, is she? That's why she was so pale. Oh, God, what a mess I've made of things.'

'Well, it's too late to cry over spilt milk,' Madame pointed out in a matter-of-fact tone. 'The main thing is that you must be there for her from now on.'

'When will she be back?'

'In about half an hour. Now, I'm afraid I'm rather

busy,' she said, looking at her watch, 'but you're welcome to wait here.'

'Thank you, *madame*.'

'I shall tell my secretary to advise Gabriella to come to my sitting room the minute she gets in. And,' she added looking at him with a touch of humour, 'make sure you don't botch this up. It may be a one-time opportunity.'

With that she exited the room, leaving Ricardo to pace impatiently up and down, her words ringing in his ears.

'Gabriella, you're wanted in Madame Delorme's sitting room,' Katie the secretary said as Gabriella came into the hall.

'I'll go right away.'

Gabriella, her hair pulled back in a ponytail and wearing jeans and a white shirt, looked like any one of the students as she walked across the hall and knocked on the door of Madame Delorme's sitting room. To her surprise she heard a male voice answer. She frowned, but turned the door handle anyway, then stopped, rooted to the ground, when she saw Ricardo standing in the middle of the room, tall, serious and handsome in a light grey suit.

'Gabriella,' he said, moving towards her and taking her hands in his before she could react. 'I have been so worried about you, *cara mia*, you have no idea.'

'Oh, I think I do,' she said, regaining her balance and wrenching her hands from his grip. 'If the papers are anything to go by, I have an excellent perception of exactly how worried you are.'

'Please, you must let me explain.'

'Don't waste your time,' she said haughtily, taking a quick step back. 'There is nothing you can say to justify that. Frankly, I'm glad you've come. At least now we can talk and clear the air. Ever since we married you have been wishing you were with her,' she said, her head held high. 'Well, now there is nothing to stop you. She was what you wanted all along.'

'You're wrong. I—'

'I know our marriage was not fair on you,' Gabriella interrupted, determined to have her say, 'and that my father forced you into it. Also I know that you and Ambrosia are having a long-standing affair. I suppose you thought I would simply turn my eyes the other way while you carried on your relationship with her? Well, I won't. I won't be made a laughing stock. I won't go through the humiliation of my husband being unfaithful to me.'

'Is that all you care about? That people will laugh behind your back?' His eyes narrowed and he drew himself up to his full height.

'Of course. I refuse to be the victim of such humiliation.'

'Is that all you feel, Gabriella? Humiliation? Shame?'

'I don't know what you mean,' she said, turning away, her lip quivering.

'I mean, Gabriella, that you know as well as I do that when we made love it was not just a coming together of two married people. It was special. It was magical.'

She stopped dead at his words and swallowed. A shudder ran through her.

'Gabriella, I have made love to many women in my time. I believe I can honestly consider myself an experienced lover,' he said with a rueful touch of humour. 'But when you and I made love I felt something I had never felt before.'

'If that was the case,' she said in small voice, 'why were you kissing the woman you've been making love to for the past couple of years?'

'It was a set-up.'

'Yeah, right,' she muttered, clenching her fists. 'You know, I may look stupid, but actually I'm not. You were kissing her, and,' she added as a clincher, turning on him, her eyes flashing with emerald anger, 'you looked as if you were enjoying it. Did you have a pleasant night together, I wonder?' She stopped herself, swallowed once more, and shook her head. 'Oh, God. This is exactly what I wanted to avoid. Ricardo, you must understand…' she said, her anger fading as she sank onto a chair and unconsciously placed her hand on her tummy. 'I know you have had many women—I've read about you for years in the press. I can't expect you to give up your lifestyle; it wouldn't be fair when this is nothing but a marriage of convenience for you. But please understand that I could never live with you under those conditions. I couldn't bear it. I—'

'Why not?' he insisted, looking down at her, a new and intent gleam in his eye. 'Why couldn't you bear it? If for you our marriage is only an obligation, what do you care what I do?'

'Because I…'

'Because you have deeper feelings for me than you want to admit?' he challenged, drawing her up and into his arms, his hand snaking behind her head and forcing it back so that she was obliged to meet his eyes full-on.

'No! I—'

'Don't lie to me, Gabriella. I thought perhaps it was just I who felt those things when we made love, that for you it was just a first experience and you had let me teach you. But now I want the truth.'

'Why should I tell you of my feelings?' she whispered, her eyes holding his.

'Because I love you,' he said. 'And I want to know if you love me.'

She let out a little gasp and her heart leaped. 'How can you say that when—?'

'Oh, forget about that damn picture. It was all Ambrosia, playing her silly tricks. I've told her it is over—completely over. And, for the record, I did not spend the night with her.'

'Oh.' Gabriella swallowed, wanting to believe him.

'But I need to know the truth,' Ricardo insisted. 'Do you love me?'

'Yes,' she whispered at last, letting her head sink onto his chest. 'Yes, I love you, Ricardo. Which is why I can't stay with you. Because although you say now that you love me, I think you're just trying to make me feel better. There will be other women and—'

'Will you stop talking this damn nonsense, *cara*? Do you know that this is the first time I have ever said to any woman that I love her?' He gave her shoulders a little shake and smiled down into her eyes. 'Oh, my beautiful, wonderful girl. Gonzalo was a clever man. He realised far more than you or I ever could have, and I shall be eternally grateful to him for having forced our hands.'

He pulled her close and, sitting down, drew her onto his knee. 'Now, tell me, my love. Is it just *mal d'amour* that has been making you feel ill the past few days, or is there something else? I swear, I will never let you go through anything like this again as long as you live, my love.'

Gabriella let her head lean against his shoulder. She could hardly believe what was happening. She felt so wonderfully happy in his arms, so warm and secure, so filled with excitement and desire for him as they touched. But was it just an illusion? Had he really told Ambrosia that it was over for good? She looked up into his eyes. Could she trust him?

Then Ricardo turned her face up to his and his lips came down on hers. Her body tensed, her heart soared, and her whole being melted as his hands coursed over her.

After taking their leave of Madame Delorme, Gabriella and Ricardo drove to the Beau Rivage Hotel. They were shown to a sumptuous suite overlooking the lake.

'Come, my love, we have a lot to catch up on,' Ricardo said, once the bellboy and the manager had disappeared.

Gabriella hesitated. There was so much to tell him,

so much she needed to confide, but she needed to be completely sure first. Could not just take the leap.

'Ricardo, are you sure of everything you said to me earlier? Do you swear that you told Ambrosia it was over between you?' she questioned, looping her arms around his neck and feeling his hands caress her ribcage, feeling that same searing heat running through her, making logic fade and her feelings come alive.

'You don't believe me?'

'I want to believe you.'

'Good. Because I have many defects, but being a liar is not one of them,' he said, an edge to his voice. 'I have been very cruel with you, my darling, and I deserve any mistrust that you have of me. All I can tell you is that there is no cause for you to be upset or worried any longer. Ambrosia,' he added coldly, 'has cooked her goose.'

This last broke the tension, and Gabriella laughed heartily. 'What a wonderful expression,' she exclaimed.

'Well, it sums it up nicely. I never want to lay eyes on her again. If she had tried to hurt me, I would have understood. But I will never allow anyone to hurt you or our—'

'Or our what?'

'Or anything to do with you,' he countered.

Gabriella frowned. For a moment she'd thought he was going to say *our child*. She hesitated a moment, then looked once more into his eyes. All she read there was deep enduring love and sincerity. It was time, she realised, to tell him the truth.

'Ricardo, whatever happens between us, there is something you need to know,' she said at last.

'Then tell me.'

'I—I'm going to have your baby.'

'My darling.' He took her in his arms and gazed down into her eyes. 'I was wondering how long it would take you to trust me enough to tell me.'

'You knew?'

'I wangled it out of poor Madame Delorme.'

'You are something, aren't you?' she exclaimed, shaking her head.

'I'm yours, Gabriella, for now and ever more. Do you believe that, my darling?'

'I want to,' she responded, with a little smile curving her lips.

'Then let me prove it to you.'

Before she could protest Ricardo was slipping off her shirt, her jeans, her bra and panties, letting them fall in a pile on the oriental rug. Seconds later he was naked too, taking her into his arms, drawing her close against him, making her feel the intenseness of his desire. Then they were on the huge bed, Gabriella thrown back amongst the pillows, her hair tossed wildly, while Ricardo introduced her to new and wondrous sensations that she had not known existed. As his tongue traced a pattern down her throat, flicking her taut breasts then heading south until he reached her core, she thought she could bear it no longer. Her fingers dragged through his hair and she arched, feeling his tongue flick her in the most sensitive of spots. Then came a long shuddering release such as she had never known.

Just as she was coming to grips with the over-whelming experience, he moved above her. Pinning his arms on either side of her, he entered her, hard and fast. 'I will never let you go, my love, my beautiful wife. Not now or ever.'

She could not reply. Her eyes were riveted to his and her legs came up about his waist as together they fell into a fast, passionate rhythm. Gabriella thought it was impossible to come again after what she'd already experienced. But suddenly the rhythm changed, and all at once Ricardo threw back his head, let out a groan, and she a cry, and together they tumbled into a wave of delight among the rumpled sheets.

Later they sat on the terrace of the hotel's Rotonde restaurant, overlooking the gardens and Lake Geneva. Dusk was beginning to fall, but as they sipped champagne and held hands they could still see the pedalo boats on the water and the lights of Evian starting to glimmer on the French side of the lake.

'It is beautiful,' Gabriella said with a sigh.

'No more beautiful than knowing that at last we are one.'

Gabriella looked across at him. There was something new, something wonderful in his expression that hadn't been there before.

'I know, my darling,' she replied. 'I love you. And from now on I shall trust you from the bottom of my heart.'

'Thank God for that,' he responded, bringing his lips down on hers, 'because I have no intention of letting you go. Not now or ever.'

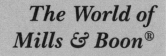